The Empty Flat

Elliot Lord

Published by Elliot Lord, 2024.

The Empty Flat
© 2024 Elliot Lord
All rights reserved

This is a work of fiction. Similarities to real people, places, or events are entirely coincidental.

THE EMPTY FLAT

First edition. June 7, 2024.

Copyright © 2024 Elliot Lord.

ISBN: 979-8227488510

Written by Elliot Lord.

All characters in this book are fictional.
Any resemblances to other people are coincidental.
The residence of the main character, however, is virtually the same as the one that the author lived in around the same time that this story is set.

Part 1

1.

As he slumped onto the chair, Andy gave his eyes a rub and yawned vocally. It was quite a nice day, mostly sunny with a few scattered clouds, but he hardly took any notice of it at this point. It was just after nine thirty in the morning and he waited at his table on the terrace of the first café he came across. He put his backpack on the chair next to him, eventually got his brain into first gear and began to notice that the world around him was still in operation.

After a couple of minutes, the waiter brought out his coffee, un cafe solo, to which Andy said "Thanks," forgetting that he should have said "Gracias." He wasn't feeling hungry yet and he didn't usually eat until about an hour after getting up. He put two sugars into the cup and stirred it, constantly trying to locate the cubes with the spoon to attack them. In his mind, this had to be the routine in case the sugar remained in their cube state while he started drinking it. It was at least one way that he could start to engage his actions with his brain.

It was the end of July 2002 and Andy Harper had recently got his degree result; a bog standard 2:2 in Sociology from De Montford University in Leicester. He'd ground his way through the last three years, not particularly enjoying the course or knowing what the hell he was going to do with it. It had been pretty early on when he realised that he wasn't actually that taken with the subject as he thought he might be. His attitude to uni was about the same as that which he'd had when he was at school – do what's necessary to satisfy the teachers, but make sure you never do anything that reaches beyond that. As long as he passed and the teachers weren't calling him to 'have a talk', then that was enough. He wasn't a bad student, but he would have got a solid first class honours if Apathy had been a subject.

Andy hadn't gone straight to uni after school because he didn't know what he wanted to do with his life. He'd been working in a supermarket part time while he was in the sixth form, which of course was useful to earn a bit of money and add towards the housekeeping while he lived with his parents, but while most of the others doing A levels had bright plans for their future, Andy was the only one to leave the sixth form and not be going to university.

He didn't feel that he was particularly interested in anything, so how could he know what he should study? He'd done English, History and Physics for his A levels; not really a coherent mix of subjects, but that just about summed up where his head was at the time of choosing them – nowhere that he could identify. Just some random place with no roads or distinguishing features where he would just wander round aimlessly.

He just about passed all of them, with two Ds and an E, which straight away diminished his possibilities of subjects to study and universities to apply to. So he didn't bother. He carried on working at Kwik Save for a couple of years, while his mates disappeared to London, Manchester and so on, leaving him stacking shelves and working on the till in Worcester. God, he hated that job. The same bloody thing every day, reducing his will to live as the customers complained that they didn't have the things they came in for. Even though it was true, due to having crap managers who never sorted things out, Andy didn't want to listen to them giving him shit for something he was neither responsible for, nor cared about.

He was still living with his parents after he finished school as he couldn't really afford to move out and things were okay there as they didn't give him a hard time or anything. Things were just ticking over. He'd never been that close to his parents, but there weren't really many dramas that took place so, as boring as life was for them all, they just got on with it in a mechanical way.

However, for Andy, he didn't know how much longer he could put up with that. He really couldn't see himself working in that dead-end job for the rest of his life; not even another five years. It was soulless, mind-numbing and something he consistently dreaded waking up to have to do.

In his second year after finishing school and trying desperately, yet lazily, thinking about how he was going to get himself out of this tedium, one of his friends, Sam, who was studying Sociology in Sheffield, managed to convince him to do the same, as he was enjoying the course and found it mentally stimulating. At that time, Andy kind of needed a kick up the arse and, after considering it for a couple of months and reading a couple of books from the library about it, it did sound interesting, so he thought "What the hell, it's got to be better than what I have right now."

He started studying at De Montford aged twenty, so wasn't that much older than most of the others. He made a few mates and hung out with them every now and then, but he never really had any close friends during his time there. However, much like school, he could cope with his studies and passed most of his modules to an adequate level, so knew that he was on course to get a 2:2 all the way through his studies.

Much like the point where he left school though, he had no clue as to what he was going to do afterwards. There were no jobs, sociology-related, that appealed to him, so by the time he graduated, he was at a similar point where he was feeling uninspired and had no idea what to do next.

It felt like life was just a boring, monotonous trip where nothing exciting ever happened, but he could see no light ahead of him. There was no way he was going to go back to working in a supermarket, nor in an off-licence, in which he'd done some part-time work while he was at uni. However, even though he had become accustomed to life trudging along in the same way, it also tore at his insides. He had to get out there and do something, but god knows what that would be.

So here Andy Harper was, sitting outside a cafe in Bilbao, lighting a cigarette from his new pack of Nobels, which he'd bought because they were cheap. He was slowly getting through his first coffee of the day, seeing the people go past him, but taking scant notice of them as he wondered what he was going to do with the rest of his day.

He'd arrived the day before, on a Eurolines coach from London, which took about twenty hours. The journey perfectly mirrored his life of the last few years, sitting in the same seat, surrounded by people he didn't know, watching the world go by that had no consequence to him, not really knowing where the road was going to lead to and when he got to his destination, he would not really know where he was or what he was going to do while he was there.

Andy had been on holiday with his parents in Spain when he was seventeen. They'd been right down in the south, near Malaga, and his memories of it were that it looked and felt better than being in Worcester or Leicester and, of course, the weather was a lot better. So, after finishing his course a couple of months ago, he'd had time, much more time than he would have liked, to consider what he was going to do. He was bored of being in England and felt that no matter where he might go to next, it would be just as repetitive as it had always been. He stretched his back, which was still aching from being on the coach; he must have got about two hours of sleep on the whole journey before arriving late afternoon in Bilbao, which, being about the shortest way to get into Spain, was the reason why he found himself here.

Over the last couple of weeks, since he'd forced himself to make his mind up about what he was going to do, he'd been learning Spanish from a self-study book. He felt that he was getting the hang of the basics. He'd done French at GCSE and got a C for it, but that didn't really help him much with switching to Spanish. He'd heard that the best way to learn a language was to live in a country that speaks it.

He finished his coffee and his second cigarette and, with the help of the sun, he felt awake enough to have a walk around. As he looked at various shop signs and posters on the walls, he didn't notice too many words that he had learnt so far. Even though he knew he was in the Basque Country, he had been oblivious that they had their own language here, Euskadi, that had absolutely no relation to Spanish.

He walked around the streets with no particular destination in mind, just wanting to get a feel for the place. He started taking notice of the people around him and he realised that they looked noticeably different from those he remembered from his family holiday. There were quite a few people with blonde or light brown hair and they looked closer to those in England. There were even a couple of auburn-haired people, which he didn't expect he would see in Spain, so he felt a bit confused as to what the deal was.

He caught the odd snippet of conversations and although he couldn't understand much Spanish yet, he didn't even hear any words that he had learnt thus far. Despite thinking he would be in something of a comfort zone from what he'd experienced before, he felt like he wasn't actually in Spain. This made him pay more attention to the language and he wondered what was going on.

He wanted to get something to eat, but had no idea how he was going to ask for it. He knew that sandwich was 'bocadillo' in Spanish, but in the cafes and bakeries he didn't see that word where the sandwiches were. He had to look at what the filling appeared to be and, being unsure of how to pronounce what was on the card in front of it, he just pointed and said "Esto, por favor." Fortunately the assistant just nodded, seeming to understand him, and handed it to him.

He went back out to find a bench where he could eat it and didn't know if this was the right place for him to be. It was as if the coach ticket he'd bought was for a different destination to that which he expected and he was in fact in a mystery country. He finished his ham and cheese sandwich and lit another Nobel.

Andy's suitcase was in his hostel, packed mostly with clothes and the usual items of necessity, and that was all he had with him. The plan was to find a job and somewhere to live and begin a new life that he would actually like to have. He intended to just find any old job: fruit-picking or working in a bar while he found his feet and got better at the language and, hopefully, after some time, he would get to know some people, maybe make some friends and finally discover what the fuck he wanted to do with his life.

He had no fixed plan as to how long he would stay in Bilbao. He just thought he would travel to a few places until he found one that seemed right for him. As he walked around some more, the less he felt that this was where he should be. There didn't seem much point in giving up learning Spanish and switching to Basque if he then felt that he wanted to go somewhere else and then had to ditch that and go back to Spanish. He pottered around for the rest of the day, not really bothered about seeing the sights, while he tried to come up with a plan of where to go tomorrow.

2.

Andy had thought about what to do that night as he hung out in his hostel room and decided he might as well just go to Madrid. He was sure that everyone would speak Spanish there and, being the capital, there were bound to be many tourists and maybe some English people living there that he could find and chat to, so he could find out more about how things worked for them and hopefully get some tips about what he could do to find work. After eating enough for breakfast that would see him through the train journey, he made his way to the station and bought a one way ticket that he was surprised to find out was so much cheaper than taking trains in the UK.

As he had no guide book with him, he didn't have much of an idea about where to go, so he didn't think about it and just listened to some CDs on his Discman to while away the hours.

He got into Madrid at half past one and managed to buy a map of the city from the station there. It seemed obvious to head into the centre, find a cheap hostel and start looking around. He managed to find one that only charged €20 a night. It was really basic with little more than a bed and a chair, and a shared bathroom, but that was all he needed. It wasn't too far from the main square, Plaza de la Puerta del Sol, so he made his way there.

The first thing he noticed about the city was how busy it was. Coming from a fairly small town and only having lived in Leicester otherwise, Madrid felt quite overwhelming. So many people walking about and so much traffic. The overall noise of the place was a shock to his senses. He'd been to London once and didn't like how chaotic it felt there, but here seemed even more intense.

He wanted to find out some English speakers, but wasn't sure how to go about it. He was not someone who found it that easy to go up to strangers and start a conversation. Every now and then he heard people speaking English as they went past him, but he didn't feel it was right to interrupt them. Maybe going to a pub would be the best solution.

Walking around the centre, he noticed that there were quite a few Irish pubs. He didn't go in one straight away as he thought they probably wouldn't be that busy at this time of the day, so he would just get something to eat and wander round the centre trying to find his bearings so that he could make a plan of a few places to try in the evening.

Andy found his way to the Plaza Mayor, which was a huge square with lots of stalls around the inside walls. He got another sandwich, this time pleased to find that everything was labelled in Spanish and he sat down to eat it, have his customary cigarette and try to take in what he saw around him.

Here, the people looked more like the Spanish people he expected to see. Plenty of very dark hair, varying shades of skin, but all of them darker than his. This time he felt like he would stand out more with his short blond hair, but they were probably so used to seeing tourists that he would hardly get any attention for it.

He went for another walk around the city, every now and then consulting his map and he made a few notes of where there were pubs that he might check out later on. As he was walking and smoking, a woman came up to him, signalling to him that she wanted a light for her cigarette. She was probably in her thirties and looked a bit worse for wear; certainly not attractive to him. He was able to oblige and she started talking to him in Spanish, which he didn't understand, but she gave him a grin and after she lit her cigarette, she put her hand between his legs. Naturally, he was taken aback by this and made his escape. "She's a bloody prostitute," he thought. She didn't follow him or shout after him, but he felt that was was going to have to be thick-skinned to get by here. It wasn't a great first impression for him, so he made a mental note to be on his guard when someone who looked a bit rough came up to him. He knew that "No entiendo" meant "I don't understand" and he hoped that would be his way to make a swift exit when need be.

He continued walking, but didn't want to stray off too far. Instead, he wanted to start remembering the streets, so he stuck to those that were close to Plaza del Sol and paid attention to the buildings that were there so that they would become familiar to him.

After doing this for two or three hours, he felt more comfortable. He was getting used to the place a bit more now and he walked some streets three or four times, remembering which way he'd turned before. However, it was a hot day, noticeably more so than in Bilbao and by five o'clock, he was starting to feel tired, so went back to the hostel for a nap.

He slept for about an hour and a quarter and when he woke up, he was hungry. He didn't want to eat in restaurants as he only came over to Spain with €460 and he didn't know how long that would last him, so he found a takeaway and got a cheap margarita pizza for €4.

It had just gone past seven o'clock and wondered if it would be a good time to try the pubs yet. The streets were just as busy and noisy as before. The only way he could find out was to go into one. There were a few near to each other just to the south east of Sol, so he went in one called O'Neill's. It was quite a big pub, but there weren't too many people in yet. He didn't want to get a drink and just be sitting on his own for an hour waiting for people, so after having a short look around it, he went back out to see if it was the same at another one. Dubliners was just around the corner, so he went in there, but it was pretty much the same. He heard a couple of guys sitting at the bar talking in English, so plucked up the courage to just ask them some basic questions.

"Hi, excuse me, guys. I'm new here and I just wondered, do people go out drinking later than this usually?"

"Yeah, mate," said one, who was probably around thirty five. He seemed friendly enough. "The Spanish go out much later, like around eleven or twelve."

"Oh, right!" Andy was shocked at this as this was what time the pubs closed in England. "Bloody hell," he thought.

"We don't though," said the other one, who had a distinctly Mancunian accent. "Us Brits will be out earlier than that."

"Okay, thanks." Andy replied, not knowing what else to say to them. "Well, enjoy your drinks. See you."

"See you, mate," they both said and Andy made his way back out.

He felt a bit gutted at hearing this as it meant he still had lots of time to kill. Half past seven. What was he going to do for the next few hours? He realised that he couldn't be bothered to just keep walking the streets as that hardly took up any time, but he couldn't think of anything else to do, so he might as well just do the rounds again. "Let's just see if anywhere looks any different yet," he thought.

He sat down on a wall near Sol metro station to have a fag and wished he'd brought a book with him. He only had one in his suitcase, Catch 22, which he wasn't really enjoying anyway as he found it too repetitive. He couldn't be bothered to go back to the hostel again, so he thought he'd just amble about for a bit. As he did so, a couple of young Spanish women walked past him, giving him a smile. He found one of them quite attractive, but he was caught off-guard and it just passed by him in an instant. "Oh well," he thought. "That's the first nice thing I've had here yet." It lifted his spirits a little and he had a wee smile to himself as he carried on his way.

THE EMPTY FLAT

He set himself a target to try the pubs again by half past nine. Hopefully some English speakers would be in them by then. He kept going over in his mind ways that he could introduce himself and what things he could talk about. As he wasn't someone who had had much more than just mates, he felt quite anxious about the prospect and, as he walked the same streets, he had imaginary conversations in his head, which made him feel even worse as he expected people to tell him to piss off and leave them alone. It really wasn't in his comfort zone to be doing things like that, but he knew he had to, otherwise he was going to get nowhere.

He was getting through his Nobels at a much faster rate than normal and already he'd smoked nearly a pack today, when he usually smoked half that. By twenty past nine, he was clock watching so much that every minute felt like ten, so he went back to O'Neill's to see how the situation was.

Fortunately, there were more people in this time. It was a large place with quite a dark interior – wooden surfaces in most places and bare brick walls that had examples of things that reflected Irish culture. He guessed there were about thirty people in by now, so he went to the bar and ordered a pint of lager. From speaking to the barman, he could pick up that he was a native speaker, so asked him the same question that he'd asked the two guys earlier.

"Around this kind of time is when people start coming in usually, earlier at the weekends."

"I've just arrived today so I'm trying to work out how things are here. I'm wanting to live in Spain and I want to get some ideas about what I could do."

"It's usually easy enough to get bar work," replied the barman, who looked like he was in his mid-twenties. Andy was trying to place his accent but could only ascertain that he was from the south somewhere. "People teach English fair bit."

As they'd got chatting, a group of guys, all of them much bigger than Andy came in and positioned themselves close to him at the bar to order their drinks. From their interactions with the barman, it seemed like they were regulars and they'd communicated with him before. Andy just observed what was going on, hoping to find a way to start chatting to this group. He looked at one who was facing in his direction and nodded his head as if to say "Alright?"

"How ya doing, mate?" said this one, who had a grade 1 haircut all over and was one of the shorter of the group, but still about four inches taller than Andy.

"Yeah, not bad, thanks. Just chatting to er.. him... as I'm now here and wanting to find out some things about living in Spain."

"Oh right," the man replied, his accent showing itself to be more of an Antipodean kind. "You just came over to check it out?"

"Well, yes, but I plan on staying here. I just don't know what I'm going to do yet. Do you guys live here?"

"Not really, we're a rugby squad, over from New Zealand and we're training some Spanish dudes for a few months."

Now it sunk in as to why they were all bigger than Andy. The other three guys were standing around chatting between themselves while they waited for their drinks, then one of them turned to find out what this conversation was about.

"Hi, mate," I'm Tom. He said, offering his hand to shake, presuming that the other guy had already introduced himself.

"Hi. I'm Andy. What was your name?" he said to cropped-haired man.

"I'm Phil. We're going to sit outside. You're welcome to join us if you want."

"Yeah, sure, thanks," Andy replied with some surprise. It hadn't been that difficult after all to get talking to some people. They all seemed friendly enough and they went outside to the terrace and found a free table easily enough.

The other two introduced themselves as Darren and Rob and they got talking about what they were doing here. It wasn't something that opened up as an option to Andy as they'd been contracted to come here and were being paid a lot of money. They were going to be here for the next three months and started a month ago.

"So what do you think of Madrid?" Andy asked.

"Yeah, it's pretty good, eh?" said Phil and the others nodded in agreement. "So what you got in mind, Andy?"

"I'm not sure," he said, filling them in on what he'd done since he arrived a couple of days ago. "Maybe teach English or work in a pub."

"Yeah, there's plenty of people doing that. We know a couple of English teachers, Kiwis as well. They got their jobs easily enough."

This made Andy interested and he hoped to dig out some more information about doing that.

"I don't know when they'll be coming out, we haven't heard from them, but maybe they'll show up later."

They carried on their conversation, but as the Kiwis all knew each other well, it moved away from Andy's investigation to normal chat that he couldn't really join in with. He stuck around with them anyway as he had no-one else to talk to. They were a lot more outgoing than he was, so he felt a bit out of his depth, but they were friendly and easy-going, so he didn't feel like he was unwelcome there.

The guys got through their drinks much quicker than Andy, and Rob was going to get the next round in. He asked Andy what he wanted.

"Oh, it's okay. I can't do rounds. I'm not working yet."

"Ah, don't worry, mate. I'll git you one."

Andy thanked him and asked for a pint of San Miguel. The remaining three of them got chatting about what Andy had been doing up till now and what brought him to Spain.

"Yeah, I don't blame you, mate," said Phil. "Us Kiwis are so far away from the rest of the world that there's loads of us in Europe."

"Yeah," added Tom. "You'll bump into Kiwis and Aussies all over here. Better to avoid the Aussies, of course!"

"Don't you guys get on?"

"Yeah, we do. I'm just having a laugh. There's friendly rivalry between us, ya know?"

Rob came back with the drinks and they carried on chatting and it was a much better introduction to Spain than his false start in Bilbao.

"So, do you guys always come here?" Andy asked.

"We go to a few different places. Been here a few times." Rob replied.

"So where you staying, Andy?" Phil asked. "In a hostel?"

"Yeah. I don't know how long I'll be here yet. I can't afford to keep travelling without doing any work, so I need to figure something out pretty quickly."

"Well, have you got a mobile? I can give you the numbers of those English teachers I told you about, so you can hook up with them."

"No, I haven't got one yet. It's a bit awkward as I've just got here and I'd need to pay for that and I don't have an address, et cetera."

"Yeah, fair enough. Well, you can still write them down and get in touch when you get a phone. Or just call them from a pay phone."

"Sure, go on then." Phil grabbed a beer mat and wrote down the numbers of the two women as well as his own, which Andy put safely into his backpack. It looked like he may be able to make more

THE EMPTY FLAT

progress than expected at this stage. He wondered if the women would be able to help him get on the ladder to teach English.

They stayed around for another drink. The Kiwis could handle their beer better than Andy, who was already feeling a bit drunk after three pints, so when they headed off to another pub, he had to leave them to it. He told them that he hoped they'd meet up again soon and he went back to the hostel.

When he woke up the next morning, with about half a hangover, he remembered what had happened last night and he felt pretty pleased about it. It hadn't taken at all long to make some connections here and it was comforting to not feel so much like he was on his own with no idea of what he was doing. That still kind of was the case, but if he could get in touch with those English teachers, he might be on his way to getting himself sorted.

The hostel didn't serve breakfast, so he had to go out and get something from a café again. This made him realise that he had to get on with things really quickly or he'd run out of money. As he had his coffee and cigarette, he went through possible outcomes and the order in which he should go about things.

The two priorities were finding a job and somewhere to live. It was hard to do one without doing the other, whichever way round he went. He'd need an address to get a job, but he'd need a job before he could afford to get a flat. He wondered if he could crash at someone's place for a while and use that as his address. The only problem here was that he didn't know anyone well enough. The rugby lads told him they lived right in the north in Alcobendas and were staying in posh houses that were allocated to them by the rugby team, so it didn't seem like he could ask them.

He needed to get to know more people, so his first port of call would be to try to ring the women. He fished the beermat out of his backpack and had a look at it. The numbers were legible, so he went to find a payphone. As he had no idea what hours they worked, he thought he might as well try them and if there was no answer, try again later. He tried Clare's number first, but straight away, a voice message came on. He understood "Este número..." but not the rest of it, but he guessed it meant that it wasn't available. Maybe she just wasn't awake yet, so he tried phoning Beth. The same thing. It was only quarter to ten, so he thought that was fair enough. From this, he deduced that they didn't work first thing in the morning, but then again, maybe they did and they had to switch off their phones when they taught. So much for his detective work. "Oh well," he thought. "I'll try them around lunchtime."

With too many things on his mind, Andy wasn't interested in sightseeing and he wondered if he could find some kind of easy work where he could be paid cash in hand. He first of all thought about the Irish pubs, but he wouldn't be able to get a bar job like that. Maybe washing up? Glass collecting? Cleaning? He wouldn't mind doing any of those in the short term. At least it would pay for his hostel and all the takeaway food he was living on.

It was now Thursday and Andy had been in Spain for four days. He thought about what he'd done so far: been in two cities, made some connections with a few decent guys. It wasn't too bad a start. His self-satisfied thoughts came to abrupt end when he heard a prolonged car horn being sounded right by where he was walking. He realised that these had been going off most of the time that he was on any busy street. He looked round and saw a man sat in his parked car with his hand on the horn. He was blocked in by another car double-parked right alongside him, so was obviously pissed off and wanted to alert the driver of the other car. As Andy carried on walking, he noticed that this kind of parking arrangement was commonplace. "Man," he thought. "They don't seem to care about anybody else much." He found Madrid to be a noisy city. He supposed this was to be expected from a capital, but it made him feel a bit on edge. Compared to Worcester, which was much more laid back, he felt like he might not be in the best place. When he pondered over this, he thought that he needed more time to get used to it, plus he had spent most of his time right in the centre. "Alright, don't let it get to you," he thought.

He got his mind back onto his to-do list. Look for work. It was probably too early for the pubs to be open, so he decided to investigate some streets he hadn't been on yet. The noise of the traffic and the whirlwind of general life followed Andy wherever he went. He wondered whether he would be accustomed to this and was not sure if he liked it; at least not yet. He wanted to locate some more Irish pubs and as he inspected other kinds of shops and offices, he couldn't really see where he could ask for the same kind of work. The disadvantage that he had was that he could barely speak Spanish still, so he made a mental note of using some of time to study it more. He really needed to start speaking to the locals, but that felt like such a daunting task at the present time.

He came across another Irish pub called Flanagan's which would be open at 11am, only half an hour away. He noted it down on his map and carried on walking. He didn't want to go too far from the centre because it seemed this was where the Irish pubs were concentrated and he found a couple more to add to his list. His hostel was near to the Anton Martin metro station and he realised he wasn't too far away right now, so thought he'd go and get his self-study book in the meantime, then start asking at some pubs. The more he walked, he started to notice that he was remembering the streets and his way more easily, so this helped him to feel more like he was getting to know the city. It was only his second day here, so he knew he couldn't expect to slot right in immediately.

He picked up his book and went back to ask at the pubs. It made sense to go to O'Neill's first as it has some familiarity to him and he'd already met one of the barmen. When he went in, he didn't see that particular one, but asked another if the manager was in. He was told that he wasn't in until 3pm, so Andy asked if he knew about any jobs going.

"I don't think so. I haven't heard it mentioned," the man, probably in his late thirties with a dark pony-tail replied.

"I'm just looking for something simple like cleaning or washing up."

"Ah, not sure, mate. I'd say just come back after 3 and ask for Tony."

Andy thanked him and went onto the next one, Dubliners. This time the manager was in so he asked him the same thing, but was told that he had nothing going at the moment. He looked at his map to find the best route to go to the others he knew and out of the four that he went to, he was told only that one needed a chef, which he couldn't do. He knew it wasn't going to be a case of finding something that easily, so he tried not to let it bother him. He had to keep trying so that he wouldn't run out of money and have to get a coach back to England in a week's time.

On his way out, he thought he'd just ask if the manager could tell him where some other Irish pubs were. He obliged and told him where another four were, but told him there were around twenty of them in the centre, which made Andy feel more hopeful.

He continued his trek and managed to find three of those that he was told about, but it was the same issue; only one of them had a job going and it was contracted, so he wouldn't be able to apply for it without an address.

He had to keep telling himself that it was only his second day in Madrid, but he was worried that he'd eventually have asked at all of the pubs and found nothing. He took a break from searching and found a spot in the Plaza de la Cortes to study some Spanish. He got out his notebook as he thought it would be handy to know how to ask for these jobs in Spanish, if the Irish pubs bore no fruit. The problem was that he would only understand an answer of yes or no, but what else could he do? Maybe the person he spoke to would know some English anyway.

He spent an hour or so looking through the vocabulary and grammar to put some basic sentences together, but he was getting itchy feet and he wanted to get back to his job search. He didn't know where any more were at this point and walking further afield made it feel like like he was moving way from the pubs. He checked his map to try to remember where he hadn't been yet and did a U-turn to head in the direction of Plaza Mayor. After walking for another hour or so, he hadn't spotted any of them and was prepared to give up for the day. Then he remembered that he should be trying to call the teachers again, so looked for another payphone and called. This time, Clare's phone was ringing but she wasn't answering so after about fifteen rings he hung up. He tried Beth and he was actually surprised to hear her answer. He explained who he was and how he'd got her number and asked if there were any teaching jobs going where she worked. She told him there weren't and she didn't know of any places where they needed someone. He thanked her and ended the call. Soon after he put the phone down, he remembered that he should have asked if they could meet up. "Bollocks," he said under his breath. He felt awkward to call her again straight away just to ask that, so he left it. He stood in the street, unsure of what to do with himself and just looked up at the tall buildings, which were everywhere. They made him feel small and out of place there and he wondered if he had done the right thing coming all the way to Spain.

3.

Andy needed to ground himself and get things back into perspective. He felt choked as he stood in, what to him, was a chaotic environment. He looked at the map to find a park or some area that would be quiet so he could get his head together. He saw that the Royal Palace of Madrid was not far to the west, which appeared to have large grounds. He arrived there in ten minutes and it was just what he needed. A huge expanse of gardens and benches to find some solitude.

He wanted to reconnect with himself to find out what exactly was making him feel uncomfortable. He knew he was rushing to try and sort himself out; that was something he needed to do. He hadn't got any results from the pubs or from Beth, but he said to himself that it was early days. Madrid was a big city and lots of people would be trying to find jobs. It was only his second day here, so he shouldn't expect everything at the click of his fingers.

As he looked out across the gardens, he realised he felt alone. At twenty three years of age, to have just made the almost snap decision to make a new life for himself in another country was something he didn't realise would be such a big step. He thought that maybe he should have tried to find a job before coming out here, but he didn't know how he could do that. Jobs in Spain weren't really advertised in the newspapers much, unless they were some high-profile business job. The internet had been going for a few years, but Andy hadn't really got on board with it that much. He'd only really made use of it when he was at university and that was to do research for his degree.

He kept coming back to the thought that maybe he'd bitten off more than he could chew. He felt he needed help to get his foundations laid. He hadn't really spent that much time dealing with independent living in England yet. He'd been in student halls for the first year, then shared houses with other students for the other two, where no-one really took that much responsibility for anything.

He rubbed his hands over his face and tried to tell himself to get a grip. Maybe a walk would help to clear his mind. As he went through the park he started to feel more relaxed. He enjoyed the tranquillity of it here. He couldn't hear the traffic any more, only the birds and the wind. He stopped thinking so much about the issues he had to deal with and just waited until he was ready to get back on it. He sat down on the ground, thought about lighting a cigarette then decided against it as he preferred the feeling of nature around him.

He remembered the suffocating feeling of being surrounded by the busy life and didn't want to be amongst that for a while. He lay down and watched the few clouds drift by, trying to take advantage of what this brought to him.

After about ten minutes he sat up again then got to his feet and carried on walking. The peace was still with him and his mind felt cleared. He knew that whatever he had to get on with, he could retire to places like this every now and then to unwind and he should be okay.

When he finally felt that he had got enough of this experience and his batteries were recharged he felt it was time to go back to the search for more pubs and to not worry if he didn't find any or whether none of them had any work for him. "It'll all come with time," he told himself. "I will find an answer."

He made his way back into the city, knowing what to expect, and he didn't allow himself to feel troubled by the noise and the people. He went north east, in the direction of the Opera metro station to look around that area, which he hadn't been to yet. He gave himself no expectations of finding any Irish pubs, but just let himself go with the flow. Cruising the streets in a more peaceful manner, he didn't see any but treated it as though he was just out for a casual walk. The Plaza de España was nearby so he headed towards that. It was another busy area, but again, he didn't find what he wanted. "Okay, no problem," he said to himself and headed east to cover some more streets he hadn't discovered yet to do a circuit back towards his hostel.

It was now late afternoon and he thought it best to call off his search for the day and just take things easy from now on. He had a more relaxed evening and instead of overloading himself, chose to get back to the job search tomorrow.

He had an early night and got to sleep before midnight and when he woke up, he noticed that he still felt relaxed. He smiled to himself and pointed out that he was going about things better now. Even though he knew of no other pubs, there were more out there and he approached it like an adventure to uncover them.

His map was getting cluttered from all the notes he's made on it, so he decided to organise things better and make a list of the pubs and their addresses on a separate piece of paper. From this he could try going to a few of them again and asking if any staff knew of ones other than what he had on his list. Going through this process gave him some satisfaction and he felt ready to face the world again.

It was still too early for them to be open yet, so he made a point of just going out and seeing where his feet took him. He even found himself smiling at some people that he made eye contact with, though this wasn't always reciprocated. He didn't care and just felt better about himself in general. Instead of buying ready-made food he went to a supermarket to buy some bread and other ingredients to save some money. As he looked around him, being more conscious than before of the other people, he was aware that he wasn't getting swept away by the hustle and bustle like in the beginning.

As he was getting to know the streets more, he could remember some of those that he had inspected previously, so tried to find others that he hadn't seen yet. He went in the general direction of Plaza del Sol and before too long he found an Irish pub called The Emerald Inn. It felt like it was the first one he'd seen in weeks, but tried not to get his hopes up. It wasn't open yet but it would be in less than an hour, so he added it to his new, neat list and carried on to see if there was another one before he came back here. He didn't find any others, so calmly made his way back there.

It was empty when he entered. It was a fairly big place with some open areas and the expected décor of things relating to Ireland. Someone was pottering around behind the bar getting things ready for the day, so Andy headed over.

"Good morning," he said to the lady, who he guessed was around his age, with long brown hair tied back in a pony tail. He went through his script of what he was there for.

"Hmm, not sure. Our cleaner is going to be away for a few days. The manager has said we need to cover for him, so I don't know if he'd let you do it for a bit."

"Oh, right," he remarked with some hopefulness. "Is the manager here?"

"I think he's in at midday, so you can try then."

"Great, thanks a lot. I'll come back in a bit."

Andy walked out and as the sun hit his face again, he suddenly felt really lifted. He took a deep breath as he knew he shouldn't assume he had found a job, but this was the most promising news yet. Not even an hour to wait, but already that seemed like a lifetime to him. He looked from side to side and wasn't sure where to go to fill the time. He'd been all around this area now and he just needed something to distract him. He thought about looking round a shop, but nothing grabbed his attention. All he could think of to do was to walk back to Plaza del Sol, then to Gran Via and back.

He found it hard to stop clock-watching as he walked and tried to drag things out by looking in shop windows, but they provided no meaningful stimulus to him and it was about as useful as looking at blank walls. He thought he should return to the Emerald a bit after twelve in case the manager had to do some things first, so he gave him a window of ten minutes. When Andy got there, the manager still hadn't turned up but the woman he'd spoken to before said he could wait inside.

"So how long have you worked here?" he asked.

"I've been here for just over a year."

"How do you find living in Madrid?"

"It's good. I've got a fair few friends here and yeah, I quite like it."

They carried on chatting for a few minutes, with Andy telling Alice of his situation. She didn't offer much in term of advice, just letting him talk as she went about her work and shortly after, the manager arrived.

"Here he is," she said. "Sean, this is Andy. He wanted to ask you about work."

"Hi Andy," Sean said with a smile. "How can I help?"

"Alice said that your cleaner is going away for a few days. I'm new here and was just wondering if I could cover the cleaning for a bit. I'm staying in a hostel at the moment so I can only, like..."

"You're looking for a cash in hand job."

"Yeah, exactly."

Sean wanted to get an idea of what Andy was like first, so he asked him about his circumstances, which Andy was more than willing to say once again. After they had talked some more, Sean, who been through some difficult times himself in the past, was willing to give him a chance.

"So, our cleaner is going to be off next week from Monday to Saturday. That's all I have available if you want it. It's a couple of hours each morning from eight till ten."

"Wow, that would help a lot."

"I can give you €15 for each shift. Have you done any cleaning before?"

"Yes, when I worked in a supermarket, we used to have to do the cleaning at the end of the day."

"Alright, that sounds good. I'll tell you what then, I'll let Pablo know about this, he'll be here at eight tomorrow and if you turn up after that, he can show you what needs doing and where things are kept. You can help him out a bit and we can take it from there."

"Thanks so much. It really means a lot to me right now."

Sean could see that from the excitement in Andy's eyes. He seemed like a good kid, so he'd just wait to see what Pablo said about him tomorrow.

Andy went back out, clenched his fists, screwed up his face and said "Yes!" to himself. It might only be a week's work, but it was something and he could keep looking for other things during the rest of the days.

He couldn't believe that he'd actually got some work sorted out. Yes, it was only for a few days, but he felt like he'd really achieved something. He could now relax for the rest of the day and not need to ask anywhere else. He wasn't sure what to do with himself, but he thought he deserved to sit outside a café and have a smoke. He went to the first one he came across, sat down and with a smile asked the waiter for a black coffee. He felt quite proud of himself for finding his first work abroad and thought he should phone his parents to tell them the news. The only time he'd phoned them was just after he'd got a hostel room in Bilbao, to tell them he'd arrived safely. He didn't speak to his parents much on the phone generally but was sure they'd like to know what he'd achieved.

He sat back, unable to stop smiling to himself, as he simply let the rest of Madrid go about their business before his eyes.

He thought about what finding the work meant to him. €15 a day wasn't enough to live on, his hostel was €20 a night, but at least it meant the money he'd come over with wouldn't be going down quite so fast. Six days of work added up to €90 – not that much, he thought, but it was better than not having it. He said to himself that he wasn't going to mess it up and he actually felt more enthusiastic about doing the job than anything he could remember doing before. Who would have thought that securing a few days' cleaning work would make him feel so content?

After he'd finished his coffee, he went to call his parents. Only his mum would be at home as his dad would be at work, but he didn't speak to him that much on the phone anyway.

"Hi, mum," he said with some elation in his voice.

"Oh, hi, Andy," she replied. "How are you? I've been waiting to hear from you."

"I'm doing pretty well, actually. I'm in Madrid now and I've just found my first bit of work."

He proceeded to tell her the story and she was relieved to hear he'd done this, knowing herself how lazy he tended to be. She asked him all sorts of motherly questions like whether he was eating properly and if he was able to get his clothes washed (which he hadn't looked into yet, but he said he could use the washing machine in the hostel). She finished off by saying she was pleased for him and that she wanted him to keep in touch more regularly as she was worried about him, but she was relieved to hear his news.

As it was Friday, he felt like he wanted to celebrate and go for a drink this evening. He would try calling Phil later to meet up with the guys again. He didn't know when he'd be free, but guessed it should be early evening. He wasn't going to overdo it as he had to get up early, but one or two drinks would be good.

He was getting bored of walking round the streets so much, but he had nothing else to really do. He looked at the map and thought he should check out the other big park to the east, the Retiro, so made the short journey there.

When he found the lake there, he was impressed with its scale and how beautiful it looked on this sunny day. He took his time walking around it and sitting at its edge and he got the feeling that he was starting to belong here. After taking in the sun and nature, he went back into the city as he wanted to phone Phil and also work out how long it would take him to walk to The Emerald from the hostel. Stepping back into the streets now felt as normal as anything and he didn't pay any attention to the car horns. He worked out it was only a fifteen minute walk to get to the pub, so that was another thing sorted and he went back to get changed.

At six o'clock he called Phil, who actually answered, much to his relief and they arranged to meet at O'Neill's again at nine.

When Andy got there, the guys weren't there yet, but he got a drink and they showed up twenty minutes later. He told them his news and they were pleased for him. Shortly after, some other people that they knew showed up and joined them at their table outside. There were two women and one man, one of whom turned out to be Clare, who he'd tried to phone before. She was quite tall and also had blonde hair, of shoulder length and a friendly smile.

"Oh, you're the English teacher?"

"Yeah, hi."

"I wanted to ask you about that. Phil mentioned you the other day, and Beth. I spoke to her but she said she didn't know of any jobs going where she works."

"Yeah, same at my place, actually. Do you have a CELTA?"

"No, what's that?"

"The certificate for teaching English as a foreign language."

"Oh, right. Is that what you need?"

"Usually, yes. You have to do a month's course in order to get it."

"Oh, I see. I haven't looked into it actually. I thought I might be able to teach it because of being a native, you know."

"There are some places where you could do that, but they're pretty shady joints. They probably wouldn't give you a contract and would pay less. It depends what you're willing to do, really."

"Hmm, right. How much does it cost to get the certificate?"

"I did mine in England and it was £800."

"Shit, I haven't got that much money."

"Yeah, it's quite an investment and to be honest, you'd be lucky to get a job, at least a decent job, without it."

"Shit, I might have to cross that option off my list then. Have you got any other ideas about the kind of job I could get here?"

"You could always work in an Irish pub. A lot of people do that."

"Yeah, I've already been asking, but it's that thing of not having an address that gets in the way."

"Sure. It's tricky. The best thing is to find a job before you come over, or you could try to find someone who's got a spare room and see if you can stay with them for a while."

"Yeah, I've thought about that, but I hardly know anyone yet. Do you know of anyone?"

"Hmm, not that I can think of. Hey guys," she said to the others. "Do you know anyone who's looking for a flatmate?"

No-one else could think of anyone, but said they'd ask around for him and the conversation moved away from Andy's circumstances. He was at least glad that he was getting to know more people, and he hoped that, bit by bit, things would eventually fall into place for him.

4.

He woke up at half past seven with the aid of the alarm clock that was in the hostel. He'd tested it the night before, but was still worried that it wouldn't go off. However, apart from waking up a couple of times during the night, he was fine with getting to The Emerald in time.

He knocked on the door at twenty past eight and Pablo opened it and let him him. Pablo, who must have been in his forties, with receding hair and stubble, didn't speak much English, but at least it gave Andy a chance to finally practise his Spanish. They managed to get by enough and it was easy enough to just show Andy where things were kept, what was used for what and the order that things should be cleaned in. They got to work with cleaning the tables, bar and chairs, vacuuming the floor and mopping it and between them, they were done by a quarter past nine. Andy made sure that he did whatever Pablo showed him and it was useful to have things explained to him. Pablo gave him the thumbs up and Andy would go back in later in the day to check with Sean if he still had the job.

When he went back at one, Sean seemed happy enough with what he'd heard.

"So Pablo's shown you everything and you know what you need to clean. Do you have any questions?"

Andy couldn't think of anything.

"I'll need to show you how the alarm works and I'll give you the keys."

He proceeded to do this and wrote down the code for Andy. Sean told him that he didn't need to be there at exactly eight o'clock, just close enough to so that he'd get the work done in time. This made Andy feel calm that he wasn't going to be spoken to if he was a few minutes late.

"I'll give you the €15 in cash each day, so you'll have to pop back when we're open of course."

"Sure, that's fine. I'll be free for the rest of the day anyway."

"Nice one. Now, I just have to say this because I don't know you very well, but there's no money kept in the tills overnight and we have CCTV." Andy nodded in a way that was as stony-faced as he could. "I'm sure you're a good guy, but I just have to inform you of that, you get me?"

"Totally. Look, you're doing me a big favour here and I really appreciate it. I'm not going to screw things up."

"I'm sure you won't, but this is my business and I have to be careful with things, of course."

"Don't worry. I need the money and I'll do everything by the book."

Okay, I believe you, Andy," he said as he looked deep into his eyes to give an air of authority, which Andy fully understood. He took the keys, thanked him again and left the pub.

He spent most of the rest of the day back in the Retiro, studying Spanish and taking things easy. He thought about arranging to meet up with the others again that night, but as he needed to watch his money, he decided not to and just wander the streets some more without buying anything other than food. Sunday was spent in much the same way as he felt a new chapter was about to start in his life, albeit a brief one, but he didn't want to make any mistakes at work, and he felt he had an objective to complete.

He got to the pub at bang on eight o'clock and managed to turn off the alarm without any issues. He got started on cleaning the tables and other surfaces, making sure he put all his effort into doing so. As he worked meticulously, he found that it was harder work than he expected. He actually broke into a sweat by the time he was mopping the floors and was surprised at how much it took out of him. He put it down to the fact that he wasn't used to doing anything more than what was actually necessary and it felt like a bit of a wake-up call to him.

He finished just before ten o'clock and was glad to put everything away. Just as he closed the cleaning cupboard, he heard the doors open, which he wasn't expecting and went out to see who it was. Sean had come in early just to be sure and he told Andy that he had to do some paperwork. As Andy hadn't done anything untoward, he didn't have to worry and Sean took him around to check his work, while he subtly checked that nothing looked like it had been taken.

"It looks like you've done a good job," Sean said, much to Andy's relief and he handed him his €15. "Cheers, same thing tomorrow, then."

Andy smiled, feeling a little nervous and he went on his way. As he walked back to the hostel he mulled over this and thought that it made sense if Sean wanted to check up on him on the first day, but he knew he hadn't taken anything and had just got on with what he was supposed to do. Before too long, any worries left him and he knew he would behave himself all week.

He had a shower at the hostel and thought about what to do for the rest of the day. He didn't want to just do the same things again, but couldn't think what else to do. He sat on his bed and thought about going to look for more work again, but couldn't think of where to ask. Even though he was making some money, he knew that it was only for a week and his current situation wouldn't be enough to sustain him. He was getting a bit fed up of staying in the hostel. He wished he could at least cook his own food and spend less money on it, but he had no other option. He remembered what Clare said about maybe being able to find a job at some cowboy English school and wondered if he should look into this.

"A *Yellow Pages* is what I could do with," he thought, then he remembered noticing one in the hostel reception. He went downstairs and found it, then after a bit of searching to find the section, he located where the schools were listed. There were a lot in there, which on one hand looked positive, but he also found it daunting that he'd have to traipse across the city again probably to be told that there was nothing going. "Well, I've got nothing to lose," he thought and he copied down the names and addresses of about twenty.

He had no idea which ones would ask him for a certificate, so he just found the ones that were nearest to him and set off to ask.

The first one he came to didn't have a big sign outside and was on the second floor of an office building. He was let in and went up to the reception.

"Hello, I was wondering if you needed an English teacher."

The evidently Spanish woman, with dark skin and black hair, just gave him a direct "No." She didn't give the impression that she wanted to say anything more than that, so after looking at her for three seconds, expectantly, he thanked her and left. "What a helpful woman," he thought as he went down the stairs.

The next academy he found was a larger one and looked more professional. Instantly, he thought that this one would probably require the certificate, but he thought he'd ask anyway. He got a friendlier response from the receptionist this time, but she told him that they were already doing their summer courses and didn't need any teachers. He asked when the next courses started and she replied that they would be in September. This was a month away and he wouldn't be able to survive that long unless he found some other temporary work in the meantime. This was turning out to be more complicated than he would have liked.

The next one, somewhere between the sizes of the first two weren't running any summer courses and would also not start till

September, but they already had their teachers lined up. Andy was starting to get downbeat about this situation, but made himself think about what he went through with searching the pubs and he'd found something in the end. He kept marching on, but was either told they didn't need anyone or that he would need the certificate to work there.

By late afternoon he had visited twelve places and had no success. He decided to give up his search for the day. "At least I'm trying," he thought to himself. "I haven't put this much effort into anything before." He told himself to keep in mind that he would find something in the end, but he also felt that it was hard work establishing himself in the capital.

He went for a coffee to think about things. "So my options are to keep asking at the rest of the schools, look up where others are and keep asking at the pubs to see if I can get some kind of work without needing an address."

He wanted to explore more options. Learning more Spanish would improve his chances, but that would take a long time to be able to do something where he had to interact with other people. He might have to go back to England, get some work there to save up to pay for the course to get his English certificate. That would probably mean staying with his parents, but he didn't know if he could do the course in Worcester. After feeling more relaxed over the weekend and pleased that he'd done some work this morning, his high spirits were starting to drain away.

He went back to the Retiro in the hope that it would help to clear his mind again. However, this time it didn't seem to be doing the trick. He tried to take notice of the birds and the peacefulness of the lake, but it wasn't really having an effect. He didn't stay there long, but couldn't conjure up enough motivation to study Spanish or do anything of any worth.

He went back to his room and listened to music for a couple of hours. At least that helped take his mind of things for a while. "I've still got work in the morning and the rest of the week," he thought. "Try to stay positive."

The next morning, he arrived at eight again and felt a bit better than last night. As he knew how to go about his work, he was able to do things without working himself to the bone. As he was mopping behind the bar, he noticed something on the floor. It looked like a bottle top and he bent down to pick it up, finding that it was actually a one Euro coin. Instead of the feeling of happiness at finding money, he looked at it pensively. "Is this a test?" he thought. "Did Sean put it there on purpose?" It could have been that one of the staff just dropped it and no-one knew about it. He thought about it for a few seconds. He knew there was CCTV behind the bar, so his actions would be on tape somewhere. In the end he thought that it was only one Euro and wouldn't change a great deal for him, so he put it to the side of the till.

He carried on his cleaning, set the alarm and went on his way without anyone coming in like yesterday.

While he hung around the city, waiting to go back and collect his wages, he wondered whether he should tell Sean that he'd found it and put it on the side. Even if it was there by accident, it should be in Andy's favour to point it out. He went back in when they opened and first waited to see if Sean said anything about it. He didn't, so pretending he just remembered it at the last minute, he told Sean, who seemed to not know anything about it.

"Oh, thanks," he replied and gave him a smile. Andy departed with his money and felt better about his deed. "Hopefully that will make him know I'm trustworthy," he thought.

As he walked back to the hostel, mulling over this little incident, Andy felt better about himself. It might have only been

THE EMPTY FLAT

a small thing, but it was enough to give him the lift he needed to keep asking at the language schools.

He looked in the *Páginas Amarillas* again and added another six schools to his list. He had a harder job of finding them this time as he couldn't find all of them on his map and they were further out of the centre. He still hadn't been on the Metro yet, but that would cost him. He also wanted a way to fill up his time more, so went off to keep asking. It was the same story as yesterday and after going to the six places he could find, he was no better off. At one of them, they needed someone for September, but as he hadn't taught before, they had to turn him away.

Andy decided that it wasn't worth the effort to keep looking for this kind of work. No training and no experience meant he wouldn't have a chance. It surely would have been better pay than working as a cleaner or a barman but it seemed like it was out of his league.

Wednesday went fine for him at the pub again. He got on with the work almost in auto-pilot mode now and there were no tests, or what he perceived to be tests, and he went back to get his money.

"So how's it going with the job search?" Sean asked him.

"Not great," he said and told him about what had been going on the last couple of days.

"You might find it's difficult here, being the capital. There's more competition in big cities like this. My advice would be to maybe try somewhere a bit smaller, where not so many people go. I get asked a lot about whether I have any jobs going. I must have turned away about thirty people this year."

This was not something that had really crossed Andy's mind. As he hadn't felt like Bilbao was the right place for him and he'd become focused on Madrid, maybe Sean was right.

"It's more expensive here, too," Sean added. "And it's harder to find somewhere to live."

Andy thanked him for his advice and this gave him plenty more to consider, which, even though he didn't want his thoughts and plans to become more complicated, was actually a useful piece of advice to try somewhere smaller.

He had a map of Spain that he'd photocopied out of an atlas, which was in his suitcase, so he went back to get that and made some sandwiches to put in his backpack, then went to a café. He lit a cigarette and began looking at the map. Barcelona was also big, he knew, so he ruled that out straight away. There were still plenty to choose from and he had no idea what would be the right choice. There was Seville, which was not too far from where he'd been on holiday. Valencia... La Coruña... Zaragoza. Out of those that appeared to be decent sized cities, Valencia kept drawing his eye back as it was on the Mediterranean coast. He looked at his surroundings to see how he felt about being in Madrid. He remembered feeling overwhelmed by the size of it as well as the noise. "Maybe a smaller city would suit me better," he thought. Just then, a middle-aged man came over to his table to ask for a light for his cigarette. The lighter was on the table and Andy handed it to him. The man lit his cigarette and started pointing at the map, but Andy couldn't understand him. "Perdona. No entiendo bien español." The man continued talking for a few seconds then just walked away.

Andy returned to looking at his map. He thought about whether being in a smaller city would make it easier to find a job. With Valencia being on the coast, maybe that meant more people would go there as well. He could do with asking Phil or the others if they had any recommendations of places to try. He went to put the map back in his bag but when he turned to get it off the floor, it was gone. He looked to the other side of the chair, but it wasn't there, either. He frantically searched everywhere around him but it was nowhere to be seen. Then he remembered the man who asked for a light. It was then that he realised that that must have been a distraction technique and his accomplice had snatched it. He checked his back pocket, where he always kept his wallet and it was still there. "Bastards," he said out loud. He thought about what he'd put in the bag. There was his food, a bottle of water, his list of the schools, his street map and...fuck... his Discman. That was the only thing of any value, which wasn't that much, but he was especially gutted to have lost that and his Folk Implosion CD. He looked around in case he could see anyone, but it was far too late and he hadn't seen the person who would have taken it.

After he'd given himself time to let it sink in, the first thought that came to his mind was "I need to leave here." He looked down at the map, pretty much all he'd got left apart from his lighter and five cigarettes. It then dawned on him that he'd also lost the phone numbers on the beermat. "Bollocks."

5.

It felt like everything had been torn away from him. It wasn't the monetary value of what had been stolen that mattered, but to lose his only contacts in Madrid was as bad as everyone he'd met saying they didn't want Andy to be their friend any more. Deep down he knew this wasn't the case; he could probably still find them at the pub, but he knew they didn't always go there on the same days. Besides, he was now thinking of leaving Madrid, so did it matter? He couldn't work out how to feel, except for one thing: alone. He lit another cigarette, it was the only thing that could give him any comfort right now. He went through the things he'd lost again. The food wasn't important. He'd walked around here so much already that he didn't rely on the map as much now. It was really annoying to lose his backpack as that would cost some money to replace, but his Discman felt like a big loss. That was the only way he could listen to what he wanted to. He still had his other CDs in the hostel and he could probably find the lost one again, although Folk Implosion wasn't that well known a band. But he still needed something to play his CDs on. It was a real setback for Andy after he felt he'd been trying so hard to get himself sorted out. For the first time ever. As he reflected on what had happened over the last week, it was like he'd finally become a proper grown up and was looking after himself, but then to have his things stolen was like a kick in the face.

"Why, man?" he thought. "Why the fuck did this have to happen? I start making the effort then someone brings me crashing back down. I don't deserve this."

He did not know what to do with himself. He hadn't decided for definite that he was going to try Valencia instead, but right now he hated being here. Was it even worth carrying on with the cleaning work? It wasn't even covering the cost of his hostel.

"What's the point? I might as well just go right now." He then thought that he didn't want to let Sean down though. This was the only contact he had left in Madrid. He was helpful when they last spoke. Andy was feeling really confused and thought about going to talk to Sean, but he might be busy. "Maybe I need to take some time out to try and get my head around things."

He was nearer to the Royal Park, so he went there to calm himself down. He found a spot far away enough from other people so that nothing else would distract him. He was a bit more relaxed, but still fuming deep inside. He weighed up his options.

"First of all, what could happen if I stay here? I could probably find the guys again, but if I couldn't find them this weekend, I'd probably feel lonely for another week. Plus, I have no work after Saturday. No English jobs are going to be happening for me. As Sean said, it's too competitive here and too expensive. I'll run out of money if I don't find something quickly. But if I go to Valencia, I'll be back at square one. I won't know the place, won't know any people and I won't have a job. Jesus, nothing seems like a good option right now. Should I give in and go back to England? What have I got to do there? It's easier to find a job, but I left there because I'm fed up with it. Fuck it, I'm going to Valencia. What's the worst that could happen?" As soon as he thought this, he frowned and wished he hadn't used those words after what had happened today. He sat quietly with no coherent thoughts going through his head for a while. He just wanted to shut it all out and have a break. He still had about €200 in his suitcase. He would go into work tomorrow, but head off straight after that as he'd just be losing money anyway. But he'd better tell Sean his plans today.

As he walked back across the city, the familiarity of the place wasn't making him feel at home in any way. He took practically no notice of any street, building or person as he went over things in his mind again and again. God knows what he would do in Valencia, but the more he thought about things, the more he was sure that he needed to get out of here.

He got to the pub and Sean was behind the bar. He was surprised to see Andy again today.

"Did you forget something?" he asked.

"No. Do you mind if we have a chat for a couple of minutes? I've had my bag stolen today and I'm not sure what to do."

"Oh, shit, mate. Did you lose much?"

Andy told him what he'd lost and how it had affected him.

"That's bad news, but I'm afraid it's another thing you have to get used to here. They probably picked you out because you have blond hair. Obviously not Spanish, looking at a map, out of your comfort zone."

"Yeah, probably. But because I'm not getting anywhere with finding any work, I think I'm going to head off."

"Going back to the UK?"

"No, I think I'm going to try Valencia."

"Okay. Why there? I mean, it's a nice place."

"Like you said about Madrid, I don't feel it's the right place for me. It's too big and too hard to get by. I need somewhere a bit quieter. I've no idea what I'm going to do when I get there, but I might as well give it a go."

"Fair enough. I've been there a few times. It is a nice place. A bit more chilled than here, but there's still a lot going on. So when are you going to go?"

"That's partly why I came in. I think I'll do the cleaning tomorrow and then head off after that, if that's okay with you."

"Mate, don't you worry about me. I was going to get the staff to cover for Pablo anyway and it's only a couple more days."

"Thanks, Sean."

"I'll come in at ten to get the keys off you and give you your money."

Andy felt better to have at least got something done. He was glad that Sean wasn't pissed off with him and it meant he had the freedom to leave tomorrow and get to Valencia with plenty of daytime left. He had no reason to do anything in particular for the rest of the day, but thought he might as well go to the station and find out about train times to Valencia. He wondered if it was cheaper to get a coach and thought it probably was, so he went to the bus station instead and booked a coach to leave at midday.

The next morning, he did his work properly again while all the time trying to think what to do in Valencia. Should he try a different approach? He had no clue as to what that might be. Nothing concrete came to mind, so he just thought he'd see when he got there. Sean came in at about a quarter to ten and Andy was nearly finished.

"How are you feeling?" Sean asked.

"Alright. I've got a coach booked for twelve."

"Good stuff. It's better to make a change than just hang around when you don't know what's going on." Andy nodded without conviction. "Well, listen. You had your backpack nicked yesterday. Did you get another one?"

"No, I can get by without one for a bit. It's not worth spending money on right now."

"Well, I've got you one." Andy eyebrows raised in surprise as Sean handed him the bag.

"It's just a spare one I had at home. I've barely used it," he explained even though this wasn't true. He'd just bought it for him before he arrived.

"Are you sure?"

"Yeah, it was just sitting there. No need for it."

"That's really nice. Thanks, Sean."

Sean wanted to play it down. He could see Andy was having a hard time and it was the least he could do to help him out.

"Here's your money, too." He handed him some folded up notes in the hope that Andy wouldn't even bother checking them, but he unfolded them to put in his wallet and noticed that there was an extra €10 note in there. Andy looked up at Sean, wondering if he'd made a mistake. Sean didn't say anything, but just fluttered his hand as if to say "Keep it."

Andy felt emotional. This was not something he was used to experiencing. Someone being kind to him. It was what he needed right now and he had to try to stop himself crying as he shook Sean's hand and said goodbye.

6.

The coach journey to Valencia was of little interest to Andy. It passed through hardly any habitable regions and he just watched passively as the stretches of farmland and desert came and went. He rued not having his Discman to keep him company, so instead just sang songs in his head to pass the time. He arrived shortly after three in the afternoon and the weather was as in full force as in Madrid. Not a cloud in the sky and the power of the sun made him sweat as he dragged his suitcase into the centre. He'd bought a street map from the station and it only took him a few minutes to get there. He crossed over an unusual long park that was below the level of the streets, and was straight in the old town. His first task was to find a hostel before he tried to get an idea of what the place was like. He noticed straight away that it had a very different feel to it than Madrid. It was much less congested, at least so far, and he liked the peacefulness of the old streets. He headed south on the Calle de Dalt, which was mostly residential, followed it for ten minutes until he came to a square called Plaça del Tossal. The first thing that struck about this was how the spelling was not Plaza, but Plaça. Did they speak another language here, like in Bilbao? He made a sarcastic smile as he wondered if he'd screwed things up again.

The square itself was nothing special. It was concrete with a café terrace on it and no grass. To the left was a busy looking street, so he went along Calle de Caballeros as it said on the map, but Carrer dels Cavallers on the street sign. "Hmm, not too far off actually," he thought. "It must be a regional dialect that's not too different."

This was where the city seemed to come to life. There were plenty of shops, bars and clubs along the way and Andy liked the overall feel of the place. It was a narrow street with very little traffic on it; the odd motorbike or van parked somewhere along it. He wasn't sure where to go to find a hostel though. He waited around for a couple of minutes to see if he could hear anyone speaking English. There was a small group of people, who judging by their lighter skin tone and lighter hair, at least on some of them, were probably foreigners. They were just across the way and he went over to work out what language they were speaking. It was actually English, so he thought he should ask them.

"Hi, excuse me. Do you know any hostels nearby?"

The group of four turned to look at him. They were of around his age, two men and two women. One of the women said "Yeah, there's one further down there." She pointed in the direction that he had been walking. "Go to the end then turn right onto Calatrava. Follow the street to the end then turn right again. It's called Home. It's really good."

Andy thanked her and he carried on his way. He found Calle de Calatrava and turned down there. The street went on for quite a way and wondered if he'd missed it. He looked down the next street on the right and saw the sign. He pressed the buzzer and was allowed in. When he went upstairs, he was taken aback at how well it had been designed. There were walls with bright colours and a common room that greeted him. He asked the man at the desk if he had any rooms free.

"We have some beds free. They are shared rooms. I'll show you."

The man took him to a room, which Andy thought was going to be a dormitory with bunk beds. "Probably cheaper," he thought. "That could be useful."

They went into a room and again, the walls were painted bright red with some really cool artistic designs. In it were three beds and the man told him there was one free. Andy was already impressed with it, so he asked how much it was. Only €17 a night. It was cheaper and a lot nicer than where he'd been in Madrid, so he took it straight away. He would be sharing with two other men. There were lockers in the room, so after he was booked in, he put what he could in his locker, not that he had much of any value, but after being robbed, he wanted to get as much as he could in it.

Andy felt a lot better already. He went back to the common room to have a look around and found there was also a shared kitchen, where he'd finally be able to cook for himself. "What a cool place. I won't have to get takeaways any more." A couple of other guests came into the kitchen and they all said hello. They were from Italy and just meeting other people made the whole experience much better. He'd barely said a word to anyone else he'd seen in the Madrid hostel, but here it felt like it was more like a community. He was amazed at how different things felt here.

He asked where the nearest supermarket was and the Italian guys explained to him, so he went there to stock up on a few basics and made himself a snack. A few more people came and went and also said hello to him, which made him feel more welcome and he thought he was going to enjoy it here.

Andy went out for a walk to see if the other streets in the area were like the ones he'd seen so far. He was pleased to see that many were. The old city with its many pedestrian parts seemed a world away from Madrid. Even though the capital was more spacious, the scale of everything felt claustrophobic by comparison. There was a more relaxed ethos to Valencia and, given what he'd been through just the day before, Andy's head was clearer again. He thought back to yesterday and how fed up he was, but it was like this new city has washed all that off him. He took a deep breath and reminded himself not to get swept away by this; he still had a long way to go to sort his life out here, if he could manage that at all, but he really wanted to make it work this time.

His plans were still the same as when he was in Madrid and there was no way he could know if he could make them work, but in a strange way he felt like he was more experienced at going through the process now. He knew what kind of places he was going to look for and what he was going to ask them and it seemed less daunting this time.

He had no particular plan as to where he was going, but he was aware that it wasn't going to take as long to get around here. He found his way to the main square, the Plaza de la Reina, and even though this was busier, it was a well designed open space that still managed to retain its calm. He walked all around the perimeter of it and noticed the first Irish pub, Finnegan's, which he made a mental note of. He didn't want to start looking today as he felt he needed a break from this for a day, but he would crack on with it tomorrow.

He then went past the cathedral, a domineering piece of architecture, which led onto another main square called Plaza de la Verge, which was a huge open square of concrete and no vehicles. He thought it was a shame that there was no grass here, but he still liked the feeling he was getting.

The square brought him back to Caballeros, which he'd been down earlier, and this time he took more notice of what was there. Balconies on both sides watched over him as he cruised the old street with plenty of people milling about, going into shops and sitting outside cafés. He veered off down some side streets and noticed that the atmosphere remained the same wherever he went. Already he was getting a good impression of the city and he just hoped he could get things working this time.

By around six o'clock he was starting to feel hungry and remembered that he could cook at the hostel, so he went back. There were a few people around now and he saw the woman who'd told him about it when he first got here. He introduced himself and she told him her name was Liz. She was around the same age as Andy and had light brown hair, tied back, but not that long.

"So what do you think of this place?" she asked him.

"It's great, isn't it? It's good just to be able to meet people more easily."

"Yeah, we've all been getting to know each other here. So are you on holiday?"

He gave her a brief account of what he'd been up to, omitting some of the less favourable details. She, in turn, told him that she was doing a tour of Spain with her friend Hannah, who he would have seen in the street earlier as well.

"A few of us are going to cook dinner together this evening if you want to join us," she said.

"Yeah, cool, thanks. I was thinking of making some food."

Just then, one of the guys who was with them earlier came through and Liz introduced him. Joe was in his late twenties, with dark, curly hair. He was from York and was another friendly person. Andy got to know him a bit and found out that he had been to Seville before her and then would go to Barcelona for a few days. People started congregating and the atmosphere was very lively and friendly. It was just what Andy needed right now. He didn't have to think about finding work or be stuck with his own thoughts and the group had a pleasant evening together.

They all went out for a drink afterwards in a small square not far from the hostel. There were three bars around the three edges of Plaça del Negret, with the street forming the other side. It was full of tables and people and it was still really warm at eleven o'clock when they got there. Andy felt that he was welcome in their company and he had his most enjoyable day in Spain so far. All around them was merriment, laughter and a warm night. Spanish people mixed with different nationalities and there was an overall feeling of friendliness. Andy hadn't experienced a social life quite at this level before.

When they got back to the hostel it was late, so people didn't stay up much longer and retired to their rooms. Andy hadn't met his room mates yet, but they were already in bed, so he quietly got undressed and got off to sleep quickly.

Being in a shared room meant that when one person got up, the others woke up too. They all introduced themselves. One was Rob, who didn't seem that interested in chatting. Maybe he just wasn't a morning person or maybe he was as grumpy as he first appeared. The other one was more receptive and was called Paul. With short hair and glasses, he was a fair bit taller than Andy. He was twenty five years old. He was already working in Valencia and Andy especially became interested when he told him what he did.

"So I teach in a British school and I'm carrying on there, but I've been back in England over the summer. I'm just staying here for a week before I move into my new flat. I just fancied a bit of a holiday here before I went back to work."

"So you teach English?" Andy asked him, inquisitively, hoping to get some inside information.

"No, it's not a TEFL school. It's like a normal school, but everything is taught in English. I teach Maths in secondary."

"Oh right." Andy hadn't been aware of this kind of set up before, but maybe it would give himself another option to explore. "I've been trying to find jobs in English schools in Madrid, but couldn't get anything."

They talked about the various ways that people could teach abroad. Paul had done a year's teacher training, called a PGCE, which meant he was a qualified teacher, so it was even more advanced than teaching English. Andy's heart dropped when he found this out, but Paul said he might still be able to find a job teaching English as a foreign language.

He found Paul to be helpful with explaining how things worked in teaching and it looked like they might get on well, too.

They all got up and went to the kitchen to have breakfast. Paul made them both a cup of coffee, but Andy didn't want to eat yet.

He wanted to ask Paul some more about TEFL as he'd been here for a year already and knew some people who did that.

"I can give you a few pointers about EFL academies here, but I'll have to introduce you to some people I know who work at them and they'll know more about it than me. I don't think it's that hard to get a job somewhere."

"I was told that there a some dodgier places where you don't need a certificate."

"Exactly. There's always a way in somehow. It might be crap money, but at least it's a start."

"The only problem is my timing. I'm too late for summer schools and too early for September.

"Yes, that's true, but maybe you can just find some more cleaning in the meantime."

"Do you think I should just ask around at any place?"

"Not really. Just keep your eye open for adverts for *limpiadores*. The other thing you can do is sign up with an agency."

"Of course! I didn't even think of that. Do you think that'd be easy enough for me, like not speaking much Spanish?"

"I don't see why not. All you're doing is cleaning, right?"

"True. I didn't have to deal with anyone in the pub. No-one else was there."

"There you go then. I can give you a hand with signing up with one. My Spanish isn't great, but it's good enough."

"Thanks, Paul. I can't believe I didn't think about agencies."

"No problem. Then you'll be able to start looking for a place to live as well."

"That's the other thing. How can I sign up to an agency without an address first?"

"I don't think they'll mind that much. Things are generally more easy-going in Spain than in the UK. You can just tell them my new address and that'll be enough. I doubt that you'll need to show a contract."

Andy pondered over this and thought it sounded like a much better way of going about things. Paul could see the cogs were turning and he left him to it, while he went for a shower. The very idea of using Paul's address made him think about something else. "Would he let me move into his? No, he probably would have said if there was a room free. I can't ask too many favours. We hardly know each other." But still, it was really tempting to ask if he could crash at his until whoever he was going to share with arrived. "It would really help to save money, even if I could only stay there for a week." He had to let this thought go. Maybe Paul would suggest it himself later on. His mind went back to the agencies and he asked for the *Páginas Amarillas* to find out where they were. Diego, the guy who worked there and who'd booked him in, was Argentinian and could help him find the section with cleaning agencies. There were a few not too far from the centre, so Andy made a list.

Paul came back from the shower and could see what he was doing.

"You don't waste time!" he said.

"I can't. I need to start making money soon before what I've got runs out."

"Do you want to go to them today?"

"I would, but don't worry if you've got other plans."

"Not really. I'm just taking it easy over this week. It won't take more than about an hour, I'm sure."

"Thanks a lot. It would really help me."

They agreed to get themselves ready and just head off to make a start. As Paul knew his way around Valencia, this also sped things up for Andy. They arrived at the first agency and Paul did the talking for him.

"She's asking what kind of cleaning you're looking to do," he translated back to him.

"I don't know. What are the options?"

"They do commercial buildings, like offices and also house cleaning."

"I don't mind. I can do anything."

"She said there's more hours with house cleaning. You'd go to one once a week and clean for maybe four hours then clean at another house the next day." He listened to her explain some more. "With offices, it's usually after they close then you might clean for an hour or two in the evening."

"Right," said Andy. "I'm happy to do anything right now, whatever it is."

"Puede ser cualquier tipo de limpiar," he relayed back to the woman.

Paul helped him to fill in the form and there was no issue with writing down the address. He just had to show his passport and there he was, registered with the agency. As he didn't have a phone, they had to think of another way of communicating.

"I can come in here every day to see if they've got anything."

The woman was fine with that and she said she would start looking for things for him.

They left and Andy was really happy that he'd made some kind of progress. It meant that he wouldn't have to do the searching, but just be told what they had and he could take it if he wanted. Paul suggested that they got him signed up at a couple more places, just to increase his chances of finding what would work for him. As Andy didn't know the city at all yet and was staying in the centre, he'd have to restrict his options to walking distance or he could easily get lost.

They went to two others and everything went according to plan. The second agency also offered him cleaning in a small jewellery shop on Sundays. It was just two hours, but he could go in to work any time as the shop would be closed. Andy thought it would be foolish not to take it, so he said yes. He couldn't believe how easily things were falling into place now. He and Paul went for a beer afterwards to celebrate. It had gone through Paul's mind about letting Andy crash at his, but wanted to get to know him better first before asking him. Andy had less urgency about it as he'd already got his first bit of work and hopefully more would come to him in the next few days.

They had a drink in the Plaza de la Verge and got talking about their pasts. They were getting on well and didn't end up with any awkward silences. When a topic of conversation did come to an end, they would just sit back and look at what Paul referred to as "television square", where people just watched everyone else go by. It was a relaxing way to spend the afternoon and Andy hoped that he would stay in touch with Paul.

"I'll need to get a mobile phone at some point," Andy remarked.

"Do you need some help with that?"

"Maybe. I can't get one till I've started earning money though."

"Yeah, sure. Well just let me know when you want to do it."

That comment gave Andy the sign that Paul wanted to stay in touch. It felt natural for them to be chatting, although being in this kind of situation was not that familiar for him. Maybe it was just being in a different country that meant that things would be different. He'd been on a bit of a roller coaster journey so far over here, but with a bit of luck, he would soon be able to get off it.

7.

That evening, Andy was still in a good mood after what he'd got done that day. He couldn't remember feeling this sociable before, but he liked it. He had a communal meal with the others again and played more of a part with helping to prepare the food. He wasn't the greatest of cooks, but he was happy to take orders from others and chop vegetables and get rid of unwanted bits and so on. Liz noticed how different he was today and she seemed to be taking a like towards Andy. She didn't let him know, but she was watching him more now as he went to and fro about the kitchen.

They went out afterwards to El Negrito in the square where they were last night and Liz continued to cast glances at Andy. He was quite unaware of this. He had never been a ladies' man and wasn't very good at picking up cues. He'd had so much on his mind that he simply didn't have the mental space to think about women. The last time he'd been with anyone was in his second year at university when he'd had a fling with another student for a few weeks, but to him it was more like having to go through the motions because she wanted to hang out with him. He couldn't be bothered, but it was far too much effort to call it off. Eventually, Fiona got the message and was not getting many signs of life from him, so they just suddenly didn't get in touch again.

Andy had been looked at by a few women and girls since he'd been in Spain, but the only ones he could remember were in Madrid when he was in a good mood. Having blond hair did stand out for him in this country. He wasn't especially good-looking, but blond hair automatically got people's attention in a country where almost everyone had very dark hair.

After Andy had stopped talking to Joe, which had been going on for about half an hour, Liz seized the chance to talk to him.

"You look in good spirits tonight," she said with a wry smile.

"Yeah, I've got my first proper work here and should get more soon," he said, taking no notice of anything more than the content of the conversation. "Paul's a good guy, isn't he? I hope we stay mates after the summer."

"I wish I could stay longer, but we're off in a couple of days," she said with a lingering look in his eyes as he immediately looked around him at the square.

"Yeah, it's great here. I like it a lot."

He really wasn't picking up Liz's signs. There had been talk of going dancing later at one of the clubs on Caballeros. She planned to take his hand and drag him onto the dance floor with her.

The group stayed around the square for another hour before heading to Fox Congo on the main strip. It was a modestly-sized club and there were people of all ages in there. They got a drink and checked out the venue and the Latino dance music which really wasn't Andy's thing, but he wasn't that bothered as he was having a good night regardless.

"It's interesting," he said to Liz as he leaned in closer. "You don't see this so much in England in clubs. There's people in their sixties and teenagers and it just feels totally normal."

"Yeah, it's good. Everyone just dances together," she replied. "Shall we join them?"

"Nah, not yet," he said, looking round. There were only about ten people dancing on a floor that would hold about fifty. "Maybe later."

Liz nodded in disappointed agreement. "He's really not getting it," she thought as he walked over to talk to Joe.

Gradually, the dance floor filled up and Liz decided to waste no time. If she left it to him to realise she liked him, she'd already be back in England and would have probably forgotten about him by then. She basically ordered him to come and dance with her, so he gave in and Hannah and Joe followed them.

Andy didn't like dancing much. He was more into indie rock and didn't listen to any of this cheesy stuff. Liz took his hand and tried to show him how to do it, smiling at him and making lots of eye contact. Andy felt like someone had put his limbs on the wrong way round and was feeling very uncomfortable dancing to this music that he'd never heard before. He tried to make the effort to join in, but really wasn't feeling it and signalled that he was going for a cigarette after about five minutes. Liz let out a sigh and thought she might as well give up. She carried on dancing with the other two and was soon joined by a couple of Spanish guys. "At least they know how to dance to this," she thought and allowed herself to forget Andy and flirt with the one that she found more attractive. He put his hand on her waist and took her other hand in his. He was quite a good dancer and his friend attempted to do the same with Hannah, but she wasn't interested. Andy stood by the wall just looking around, not bothered that Liz had been swept away by someone else. He had no idea that he'd been in the game to begin with.

As the night went on, Andy was approached by a couple of young Spanish women, but they didn't speak English and he couldn't understand them with the music blasting out. They too had the intention of pulling him, but he was blissfully unaware of that, as well. Liz had had enough of her dance partner well before the club closed and the four made their way back to the hostel.

They went into the kitchen to get a glass of water and Liz had already told Hannah that she wanted to try to get with Andy, so Hannah made a quick exit and winked to Joe to do the same.

Andy was standing with his back to the counter, leaning against it and Liz came up right in front of him. "So, just you and me then," she said, raising her eyebrows suggestively.

"It looks like it." He could see how she was looking at him now and the telegraph had finally reached its destination. She put her hand on his chest and leaned forwards. Andy felt a bit unsure of himself, but after having drunk a few beers, could tell what she wanted and he kissed her. She was more passionate than he was and he couldn't fully relax, but they kissed for a few minutes, though Liz couldn't get anything more out of him than that. Because of them staying in shared rooms, there was nowhere for them to go, then another couple came in from their night out and also got some water, inadvertently putting out Liz's fire. The moment had gone and Andy just said he'd better go to sleep. Liz shrugged it off once again and they went their separate ways.

On Saturday, Andy was due to go to the shop that he would be cleaning tomorrow. The owner was a man in what Andy guessed was his sixties. He didn't speak any English, so Andy made an effort to use his Spanish. He needed to make headway with that as he'd been hanging around with English speakers for most of his time here. The shop, which was just off Caballeros, near the Plaza del Tossal, was quite small and it looked like it probably hadn't changed for over forty years. All the jewellery was locked in cabinets and Andy would have to do the dusting and polishing of the glass, as well as mopping the wooden floor. Señor Hernandez showed him around and gestured to Andy what he would need to do, which was understood easily enough. It was all very matter of fact and the owner didn't show any humour or that he was grumpy. He just seemed like an average elderly gentleman who had been doing the same thing all his life.

"No es importante a que hora vengo aqui, verdad?" Andy had been practising this line of how to ask if it mattered what time he came. Señor Hernandez confirmed that "No, no importa. Puede trabajar cuando quiere." Andy understood his reply and could come when he wanted. He showed Andy how to use the alarm and gave him a spare set of keys.

As he left the shop, Andy actually felt quite good about himself just for managing to use some Spanish and understand the owner. "Yeah, I'm going to start working just three days after getting here."

He spent the day with some of the people from the hostel again. It was Liz's last day and she spent some time with Andy. Despite the potential awkwardness of them kissing last night, everything seemed quite relaxed. She was getting to like him more, especially from how proud he came across when telling her about going to the shop. She could tell that he was a good guy; no fuss, no messing around, just someone who wanted to get his life together. They went for a walk around the centre. She wanted to tell him how she felt about him, but as they wouldn't see each other again after she left in the morning, she thought it best not to go too far.

When they got back to the hostel, Paul was in their room and Andy recounted what he'd been up to. Paul was pleased for him and took special note of his demeanour. He felt that Andy was genuine.

"I've been thinking," Paul began. "I'm moving into my flat on Monday and if you want, you can stay with me for a couple of weeks before the other two get back here."

Andy was shocked. He'd barely thought about this recently due to being focused on work and Liz. "Seriously?"

"Yeah, you seem like a good guy to me. Hopefully it'll give you time to find more work and then start looking for a room for yourself."

"Oh, wow. That would be amazing. Thank you so much!" He couldn't help himself but to give Paul a hug, which was totally out of character for him. "Mate, I won't cause any trouble. I won't make a mess or anything."

"I'm sure you won't. I just wanted to get to know you a bit more before I asked, but you're welcome to stay."

"That means a lot. It really does."

Paul's new place wasn't too far out of the old town. It was a few minutes west of the ring road and Andy could quickly get back into the centre for any other work he might get. They went over there so Andy could get his bearings and Andy could barely stop smiling. "You've made my day, man!" he told him. "Let me buy you a drink tonight."

"Ha, yeah, okay." Paul didn't care about that, but it was a nice gesture and he would let him.

That evening, after having something of a celebratory dinner for Andy, the group of four went out again for drinks, but as Liz and Hannah were getting the train to Barcelona, where they were flying from, they had a quieter night. Andy, even though he could go into work at any time, still wanted to treat it seriously and not mess anything up, was fine with this plan. He and Liz were quite close all evening, but Andy had no intention of trying it on with her and they just had another kiss or two before they went off to their separate rooms by half past twelve.

Andy wanted to say goodbye to Liz in the morning and as soon as he heard someone going past his door it woke him up and he went out. Liz and Hannah were finishing getting their things together and chatting with Joe, who had been up for a while. They all went into the kitchen. The women were heading off quite soon, so they didn't have too much time to spend together. Even though they'd only spent a few days together, they had got to know each other quite well, but Andy, being reserved in general, could prevent himself from getting emotional.

"I really hope things work out for you," Liz said. "I'm sure they will, you're making a good start."

"Thanks. It's been nice to know you and I hope you enjoy being back in England."

"Ugh, don't remind me, I have to be back at work in Monday. I won't even have chance to rest from travelling back."

They looked at each other in silence for a few seconds, before Hannah interrupted to remind Liz that they'd better get going.

"Okay," Liz said reluctantly. "Come here and give me a hug," she said to Andy. She gave him a long hug and he couldn't remember having such a loving, meaningful hug from anyone before. He was quite taken aback by it, but she gave him a quick kiss on the lips and the women made their way downstairs.

Joe and Andy were left in the kitchen and Joe poured him a cup of coffee. "It looks like you two would have got on well," he said as Andy stared into the distance.

"Hmm? Yeah, she's nice."

"Did you manage to... you know...?" Andy was stirred from his reverie.

"Huh? No, there's nowhere we could go here."

"True. Oh well. You must have had a nice little holiday romance anyway."

Andy wasn't really paying attention to him. He knew very well she wouldn't be here for long, but he was distracted by his own thoughts about her. Maybe he should have tried to make the sex happen. They probably could have found somewhere to go. Joe could see he was lost in his own thoughts, so wandered off back to his room.

Andy stared out of the window as he slowly got through his coffee. He thought he'd never had a proper relationship before, just a couple of times where he'd been seeing someone, but they hadn't stimulated many emotions in him. He thought about Liz and what it might have been like if they were a couple. He imagined them going for walks through the city, even lying in bed together talking with his arm around her. He was lost in his own world until the other guests starting emerging from their lairs and background noise started to interrupt his thoughts.

Once he'd re-entered the real world, he remembered that he had his first day at work today. He wasn't hungover as he'd only drunk a couple of beers last night, so he thought he might as well get ready and head on over to the shop.

He managed to negotiate the alarm system and made his way to where the cleaning stuff was kept. From his brief stint in the pub, he already had an idea of which order to clean things in. It was relatively easy other than trying to make sure that streaks weren't left on the glass cabinets and he got through the work without any incidents. He paid little attention to the products under the glass, but found himself thinking of Liz at regular intervals. He wondered where she would be right now, "She's probably at the airport and has forgotten about me by now." He often managed to see the negative side of things as that was how he'd always been. He tidied the equipment away, locked up and headed back out.

He chose to go for a walk rather than just go back to the hostel. It was yet another hot and sunny day in Valencia. He wasn't sure if he'd even seen a cloud yet. It was already hotter than 30ºC so he opted to go down the streets that were in shade. Trying not to think of Liz now, as it was starting to get him down that she wouldn't be around any more, he remembered that he was going to move into Paul's flat for a while. Paul had said he could go as soon as he'd got the keys and the landlady had gone tomorrow. He was meeting her at one o'clock, so Andy would head over about two. They hadn't talked about whether Andy should pay him any rent. Paul had no intention of charging him as he knew how much Andy needed his money. He just had to buy his own food and that was it.

This lifted his mood again and he thought he'd go and see if Paul was around. He wasn't there as he didn't know where Andy was so they didn't see each other till later. When they did meet up, they discussed Andy not having to pay and just to take care of the bedroom that he'd be using for a while. They talked about how

THE EMPTY FLAT

Andy could go about finding his own place to live. Flat-sharing was probably the best option as it would be cheaper than going through an agent as they'd charge a month's rent just to use their services. Money, of course, that Andy didn't have.

Andy went back into the cleaning agency the next day to see if they'd got any more work for him. The woman, Belén, had spoken to Señor Hernandez that morning and she reported that he'd been happy with the work. He would get paid every two weeks which was really handy for him as he would run out of money if he had to wait till the end of the month.

"Hay más trabajo?" He wanted to know if anything else was available.

"Si," she replied, satisfied that he'd started off well. "There's a job in an office for three evenings a week on the Plaza de la Reina." He remembered that was the main square. "Two hours a day from seven until nine."

"Si, gracias." He was only too happy to take it. She explained that she'd phone them and he could go along and start this evening. "They will show you everything when you go."

"Perfecto, gracias!" He couldn't believe his luck. He was going to move into Paul's today and soon after, start his second job. "Why couldn't things have been like this before?" he asked himself, knowing full well that it was just how things went sometimes. He would need to open a bank account before his payday as well so would ask Paul to assist him with that.

So once again, he'd had a couple of days where his emotions had been up and down, but he had plenty to see the positive in right now. He met up with Paul just before he left the hostel and they would meet again in about an hour.

He packed his suitcase again, said goodbye to Joe, who was off in a couple of days, and went to the address just after two. Paul let him in and showed him the room he'd be staying in. It was sufficient. One of the smaller rooms, but Andy was fine with it. It was only for a few weeks. The flat was nothing special. Just about big enough for three people with a smallish kitchen. It was fairly tidy and had been painted over the summer. Paul wanted to get some more furniture, but was in no rush. They had enough to get by with for now.

"Honestly," Andy said with a sigh. "I can't believe how quickly things are moving for me right now. Oh, I've got some more cleaning in an office in the main square."

"Oh, really? Well done!" Paul was pleased to hear this as well as get the confirmation that Andy was true to his word. "When do you start?"

"Tonight! It's three days a week, two hours a time, so I've now got eight hours under my belt."

"That's brilliant. You're well on the way, then." He patted Andy on the shoulder. "Right, I'm going to sort out some more of my things, I guess you'll want to unpack, too, so see you in a bit."

Andy was glad to be able to hang up his clothes and be in a room that at least resembled a home for him. It was such a relief not to have to pay for a hostel any more. He was down to €120, which would last him till the end of next week easily, but he would still spend as little as he could because of having to save it for a room that he could rent. He didn't want to think about that, but just enjoy the freedom and security he had for the time being.

Later on, Andy made his way to the office and was shown around by one of the staff, Jorge, who went through the usual things. Everyone would finish work by seven, then he could get on with it as he was already accustomed to. The office was already quite clean and he didn't have to do a great deal of work. After an hour, he was done and just went to see if he'd missed anything, but couldn't find much else to fill his time with. "I wonder if I'll get in trouble for leaving early," he thought. "I don't see how anyone will know." He wasn't sure what to do, so sat around for ten minutes until he became bored and couldn't see how anyone would find out if he left now, so he locked up and went.

"I suppose all that matters is that I get the work done," he thought as he went back to the flat. He was trying to understand his feelings. He felt strange, almost like he didn't have a care in the world. This was not something he was used to. He tried to figure it out and concluded that it was indeed that he was feeling quite stable right now. "I can take this," he said to himself, not quite believing what was happening.

8.

That evening, Andy and Paul had a celebratory beer in the flat and got to know each other some more.

"So how long do you think you'll stay over here?" Andy asked.

"I don't know. It's hard to say. I quite like it at my school. It's one of the better ones."

"How do you mean?"

"Well you get two types of British schools in Spain. Those that care about the education and those that just care about the money. I know some people who work at one of those types here. They never ask you for your plans or give you any support. They just have to make sure they give the kids a good report so their parents won't raise any issues and the owner just rakes the money in."

"That's shit. Are there a lot of ones like that then?"

"I've heard about a few around the country. It's not my thing. I actually care about whether my students learn."

"Fair enough. Is it hard being a teacher?"

"People say it's better working in a school abroad because you have less paperwork. You still have to mark everything and do a lot of preparation, but it's doable, so maybe I'll stay here for a few years, then try somewhere else."

"Have you got anywhere in mind?"

"Nothing concrete, but I might try somewhere like France or Germany."

"What about Thailand or something?"

"It's not really my thing. There's probably a lot of shitty schools over there, plus the culture is just too different. I don't know if I'd like such a massive change."

"It sounds like you've got something of a plan, though."

"I guess, for now. So what about you? You've mentioned teaching English. Do you still want to go into that?"

"Maybe. The cleaning has started off well so far, so I might just stick with that for a bit, then see how I feel. I can imagine I'll get bored of it before too long."

"I see what you mean. You've got to get yourself a bit more sorted first."

"Yeah. Anyway, cheers to the first night in your flat and thanks again for letting me stay here."

Over the next two days, Andy helped Paul with getting his new place in order. They went out to buy some cheap chairs for the dining room, which had a table already. Paul bought some basic things like bin liners, a mop and a shower curtain. Even though Andy was more than happy to help with anything Paul wanted doing, it was on his mind that he only had a short amount of time to find somewhere for himself. He would prefer to share with some English speakers, but, like Paul's friends and colleagues, not everyone was here right now. He knew had to look for the sign "Se Alquila" to see what was available for rent, so he spent Wednesday looking around the city centre.

There weren't that many that he found and as he didn't have a mobile yet, it hindered his progress with contacting the numbers. He noted down where some of them were and planned to contact a few of them from a payphone. With Paul's help, he wrote down his lines to explain what he was looking for and practised those, as well as questions to ask about the price and if it was sharing. The first two he called were to rent the whole flat and they were far too expensive for him. When calling about the third one, he couldn't understand the man on the other end of the line so he got nowhere with that.

Over the course of the week he kept looking and phoned some more numbers which were a mixture of being too expensive or they were through agencies, so he felt a bit deflated from his efforts. He still had another couple of weeks at Paul's so he wasn't too desperate, but he couldn't leave it too late. He could always go back to the hostel, but he'd prefer not to.

Work was going fine for him, but he couldn't wait to get paid next week. He opened a bank account and found it quite amusing if a little weird that his bank assistant was called Jesus. Apparently it was a fairly common name in Spain, but he wondered if Jesus would have followed a career in banking way back when.

Andy had been spending as little as possible and by the middle of the next week, he decided to buy a cheap mobile phone. He'd had a 'pay as you go' one in England and opted for the same here as he didn't need to use it that much, but it would be more useful for his flat search.

He was walking around the centre on the Wednesday to try to uncover more flats for rent, when he saw one that was not far from the old market, the Mercat Central. He'd not explored this part of the town yet, El Pilar, and it was quite grotty, but there was a sign on the balcony of a flat on Carrer del Bany. He thought that it might be cheap, so he called the number. A Spanish woman answered and he read through his script. She told him that it was a two bedroom flat, which was empty and cost €160 a month. He repeated the price back to her to make sure he understood correctly, and she confirmed it. Paul was paying €180 just for his room along with the two others, so this was really cheap. He asked when he could see it and the woman told him he could go there tomorrow at 10am.

With the work he had so far, he would be making just over €300 a month, which was just about doable, but hopefully he could get another work location added soon.

Paul was equally amazed when he told him later, but warned him that it was probably in very bad condition.

The next morning he went over and met the landlady, Maria, who took him up to the first floor flat. The door led directly into the living room. The walls were filthy with brown stains over most of them, but he could see they could be cleaned. To the left was a balcony. This was something he'd never had before and it really caught his eye, even though it was small, and it also needed some care and attention. There was some furniture in the room, that being a long cabinet, a smaller one, a large folding table, a smaller dining table and not much else, but he could see its potential. They went through the doorway which had no door into the kitchen. It was small and basic but had the essentials: a sink, cupboards and an oven. Off this was the bathroom, again with no door to separate it, but he could see to that. There was a bath with a shower head, a toilet and small sink.

One bedroom was at the back and it had a bed frame, but no mattress, a bedside table and a wardrobe. There was very little else to report other than it had a window which looked out to the rear of the block. "It should be quiet anyway," he thought. The other bedroom, which was between the living room and the kitchen had a single bed and the typical furniture but no window. He could use it as a spare room, not that he had much to put in it as yet.

Despite it being a run-down place that needed a lot of work, it was affordable to him and right in the centre. He looked around it again as he thought of what he could do with it and looking out of the balcony did it for him. He asked if he could paint the walls and Maria said "Si" without any questions. Did she want a deposit? "€100" "Blimey," he thought. "Is that all?" He accepted her deal and agreed to move in after next week. She had a contract with her and he did his best to read it, understanding about half of it, but it seemed like he had to take it in case someone else did the next day. Maria, a short, middle-aged woman, offered very little in terms of how she was, but Andy didn't care. He would meet her the next Friday with the money and sign, and it was as straightforward as that.

He couldn't believe his luck as he walked around the area a little. It didn't seem like it was in too bad a state and he was already thinking of scrubbing and painting the walls. He checked the time and it was a quarter to five. "I think I'd better tell Paul the news," he thought. "He's really not going to believe this."

"Well, you've got another bit of luck, mate," Andy said. "Are you sure you've got enough money to move in?"

"I get paid this Friday, so will have a bit. I was thinking about asking for an advance from the agency."

"I doubt they'll do that. You could easily do a runner with it."

"Yeah, I suppose so."

"I can lend you some. You wouldn't let me down, would you?"

"God, of course not. That's be great. Thanks."

"I can't kick you onto the streets and you're really close to getting yourself sorted. I haven't got much, but work out how much you need and I should be able to help you out."

"Thanks so much. I'll see what I get paid tomorrow and we'll take it from there."

Paul did trust Andy. He hadn't had any issues with him staying there and didn't doubt him for any reason. They were becoming good friends and there was no way he could watch him fall down again.

On Friday, Andy checked his bank balance and was pleased to see he'd received the full €45 he was due. It wasn't much when added to the €93 he'd still got left, but it was only just over €100 short of what he needed. He'd have to ask Paul to give him a bit more so he could at least buy food and when consulted, Paul was fine with that.

Andy called his mum to tell her his news.

"That's great, but I wish you'd called me sooner. We are worrying about you, you know."

"Sorry, but I just wanted to wait till I knew something definite."

"Make sure you call me once a week please, at least. We want to know if that flat is actually okay. It sounds horrible, to be honest."

"Look, I'm going to clean it up nicely. It's going to be my home, so I want it to be the best I can get it."

"Just let me know, alright?"

"Yes, of course."

From having walked around many streets in Valencia, Andy had noticed that people very frequently threw out all kinds of furniture, often with hardly anything wrong with it. "It seems that Spanish people either don't know how to fix anything or have plenty of money to keep replacing stuff," he thought. In his position, it seemed like an easy way to furnish the flat better. He would be able to store it at Paul's place in the meantime. He found an old wooden box that he liked the look of. It reminded him of a treasure chest, painted a dark green and with old metal handles. There was a wooden bench that looked like it was used as a workbench or something, but was the right height to sit on. He would sand it down and get some cushions to put on it. The more he looked, the more excited he became about turning this dungeon into somewhere liveable. He wondered why it was in such a state currently. The people who lived there before must have been poor, he thought, maybe drug addicts. How could they live in such filth and make the walls that grimy? He looked forward to using his free time, which he would have plenty of, at least for now, to do it up well. It would definitely need painting, but he could probably buy that cheaply enough.

Paul went with him on a couple of journeys to help him carry some things back. One of his best finds was a kind of office chair with a metal frame and padded green seat. The only thing wrong with it was that one of the wheels was missing and cost €1 to put right. He managed to get a foam mattress cheaply from a shop not too far away. It wasn't a standard bed size and was a little narrower, so managed to get it for €20. Over the following week, he'd amassed a good number of items and couldn't wait to finally move in on Friday.

"I can't wait to see it, too," said Paul. "It sounds like it's going to be an exciting project."

"I hope so. There'd better not be anything wrong that makes it unliveable, like a leak or something."

"For that price, I wouldn't be surprised if you find something, but hopefully when you've got some more money together, you'll be able to sort it out."

Paul was going to lend him €150 and they agreed that Andy would pay him back €30 each fortnight. Paul said that if he needed the money, it could wait a bit, but Andy insisted that he'd pay what they agreed. That way, he'd have his debts cleared earlier and be more relaxed about his money after that. He hadn't got any more work just yet, but Belén told him that she was in talks with some people about getting more work and would let him know.

Finally, the big day came around and Paul went with him in case he needed any help with understanding. He also wanted to get a look at the place before Andy signed, in case he saw anything that looked dodgy. He was less than impressed with it, but could also see the potential and there didn't seem to be anything that looked serious. Andy signed the contract and paid Maria the money. He now officially lived at Carrer del Bany, 35, 2nd floor.

Part 2

9.

Straight afterwards, the two men gradually brought Andy's new things over and got them into the preliminary places to make it look like home. The state of the walls offset everything, of course, but Andy had found half a pot of light blue paint a couple of days ago and he thought it would be nice to use in the living room. He'd also found various rags and old clothes and they both set to work with trying to scrub what dirt they could get off the walls. It wasn't perfect, but they made a noticeable improvement and were satisfied after a couple of hours work.

As they looked around the room, Paul was looking at the doors to the balcony. They had wooden shutters on them and he opened them to check them out.

"These haven't even got glass in them," he remarked to Andy who was looking in the cupboards.

He went over and it was true. Where there should have been windows, there was nothing.

"Hmm, that's not good," said Andy. "Oh well, it's always hot here, so I probably won't need them."

"It's not always like this, you know. We do get rain in the winter and it's sometimes chilly."

"It doesn't matter now. I can come to that another time."

With the office chair and the one metal chair that was already there, they sat down to have a rest.

"Yeah, I reckon this is going to turn out alright in the end," Paul said.

"It's not too bad, is it? It's a shame it's so dark in this room, though. I don't see what I can do about that." The front window was north facing and there was a three storey building across the road. Being a pedestrian road, it meant it was also quite near and it blocked out a lot of the light.

THE EMPTY FLAT

"Yeah, not great, but I'm sure you'll get used to it."

After arranging a few more things, Paul went back to his place. One of his flatmates was arriving tomorrow and the other one on Tuesday, so he left Andy to start getting acclimatised to his new home.

Andy walked around the flat, finding the odd plate and cup in cupboards that would save him a bit more money. He saw it as something of an adventure to see how much he could acquire for free. He'd bought some bed sheets from a cheap shop. Whereas in the UK they'd be referred to as a pound shop, the one he'd been to had an interesting sign that said "Todo por 25c, 50c, €1, €2, €5." So everything for a range of prices then.

One thing that he hadn't taken in was that there was no curtain on his bedroom window. That first night he'd have to sleep with it uncovered, which he really didn't like the idea of, but he could look into that tomorrow.

After doing some cleaning then going to work and doing more cleaning, he got back home and after switching the light on, he noticed how quiet it was. Almost eerily quiet. There was no-one outside and nothing but the sound of his own footsteps inside. He didn't have anything to break this silence, so added a stereo of some kind of his mental list of things to buy. Eventually.

The peace of his new flat meant that he slept soundly on his first night. He was woken just before seven due to the light, but at least the window was south facing, so he managed to doze off some more without being blinded by the sun. He got up around eight as he'd started going through all the things he wanted to do that day. He went to the toilet and thought "I've got to get a door or something there. That won't be good when I have people round."

He made himself a coffee and and noticed something moving on the floor. It was a cockroach. He'd seen a few around here already in the street, but in his flat? "Oh, fucking hell," he thought.

"What a start to the day." It scurried under the sink cupboard and sorting that out instantly became a high priority. It was about 3cm long and he had never seen them before coming to Spain. The idea of them living here freaked him out and he would have to find some traps of some kind.

He went into the living room and sat on his comfy chair by the dining table that he'd put in the middle of them room. Even though it was morning, it was really dark inside. Having the balcony doors wide open barely did anything, but at least he could stand on his balcony and have a cigarette. It was so narrow that all he could do was stand on it. He inspected it for safety as the paint on the outside had probably been peeling off for a number of decades. It was even worse further down. The red-painted wall was in a horrible state, but that wasn't really something that was up to him to improve.

He looked across at the neighbouring flats. He hadn't seen or heard anyone else around him yet. Was he the only one here? He knew there was a flat above him, but didn't know if it was occupied and the flats to the right seemed like they'd been abandoned long ago. "Oh well, hopefully no disturbance from any neighbours then."

He got dressed and looked again at the cockroach situation. That would be the first thing on his agenda and he went out to buy some traps. On his way up the road, there was still hardly anyone about until he came to the end. There was a fairly old woman sitting on a chair outside and a couple of young, black women standing on the opposite side to her. The old woman smiled and said something to him, which he didn't understand, but he just said "Hola" and carried on. He quickly came to the conclusion that the younger women were prostitutes. "Oh, God," he thought. "No wonder it's so cheap around here." He went into Mercat Central and found some cockroach traps and a few other bits and pieces, then walked around some more to see if there was any other free stuff he could make use of. At the side of a shop was a paint tin and he picked it up. It was brown paint and was probably about a quarter full. Two brushes congealed in paint lay next to it and he took them all. He didn't find anything else, but remembered he wanted something to make a curtain out of. He went back to the cheapo shop and bought a piece of brown, patterned fabric that was about twice the size of the window. He wondered how he could fix it on the wall and went for the easy method of using drawing pins. When he got back, he put the traps on the kitchen floor and proceeded to affix his new curtain. It did the job well enough as he could fold it in half and it just about did the job.

After doing all that he could so far, he got a text from Paul in the evening. It just said "Hi. Negrito 10pm?" He replied with a simple "OK" as texting on his Motorola took far too much effort and went out to meet him.

"This is Steve," Paul said and introduced his flatmate to Andy. Steve was a teacher at the same school and taught Biology. He'd been here for two years already and wasn't as outgoing as Paul, but seemed like a decent guy. About thirty years old with side-parted brown hair and a beard. They had a couple of drinks in the square and discussed how Andy was getting on in his new place.

"Yeah, it's good," he said. "I woke up to find a cockroach in the kitchen, which was a pain, but I've put traps down. I'll have to work out where they're coming in and block it with something, but otherwise, things are fine."

"Yeah, they're an eternal problem here. You'll just have to get used to them."

Andy didn't like the sound of that, but vowed to find a solution somehow. They had a relatively quiet night and went back to their respective homes.

Andy went into work on Sunday, again getting it out of the way earlier and inspected the issue with the unwanted flatmates. He pulled the few things from out of the sink cupboard and saw a couple of them run for cover. The back wall was in a bad state and he didn't know how he could block it. It would need plastering to have any effect, which was out of his budget at the moment.

He looked at the cooker. A simple little affair, but it wasn't connected to any gas mains. He found that it contained a gas cylinder, which immediately became another problem for him. "How the hell am I going to do this?" he thought. He would have to buy bottles every time and didn't know how that worked. It would be heavy to carry these back from a shop and god knows where he would get it from, not to mention not knowing when it was about to run out. It became another thing that he would have to look into.

The silence of his place was already starting to do his head in. He really wanted to get some sort of entertainment system in place. All he had for his free time was his book, *Catch 22*. He hadn't read any of it for a while, so decided to get back to it. As he read, he remembered why he didn't like it. "I've got flies in my eyes. All the bloody time," he thought as that was a line that cropped up in practically every chapter. "God, this is boring" and he put it down after little more than five minutes.

"I know," he thought. "I'll phone mum and dad." He went out to a payphone and got them up to date with his news. His mum was pleased to hear from him after just a few days and they were both happy to know that he was getting on well in the flat. He chose to omit the detail about the cockroaches as he knew his mum would shout "Oh, my God!" but he didn't have to fabricate much of what he said.

One thing that the flat lacked was a kettle. He would just boil water in a small pan, so added that to his wish list. There was not so much to do at the moment, so he just had a walk around town, feeling quite happy about where he'd got to so far.

10.

He really wanted to get on with painting the walls, but if he couldn't find any more paint, he'd have to buy some when he got paid next Friday. He had nothing else to do so he went on a longer walk in areas he hadn't searched in yet. There were more bits of furniture and junk but nothing that he really needed. He found a few planks of wood and thought he'd take them back in case he got an idea to build something that would be useful. He got back early evening and remembered that he should wash his clothes somehow. He couldn't afford to go to a launderette, so just filled the bath with water, squirted in some washing up liquid and scrubbed them in there. It was hard work on the hands, but at least it was a way of getting them more or less clean. But where could he dry them? He left them in to soak while he looked around to work out some options. The obvious one was to buy a clothes rack to hang them on, but again he needed money for this. His balcony would be of some use, but he couldn't fit everything on it all at once. He'd seen some clothes pegs lying around somewhere, so he pegged his clothes so they were all hanging down off the balcony. Finding another easy solution gave him more inspiration and he was more energised than he had been before in his life. He felt he was properly being an adult now, taking control of things for himself and not having to pay other people to do things for him.

There was still the issue of silence and boredom to sort out though. He was still surprised to see how quiet it was in his area, despite it being in the old centre. He stood out on the balcony and smoked a cigarette. He noticed someone walking further down the street, going away from him and that was about as busy as it got. He looked to the left and saw a cat sniffing around. This provided a tiny scrap of visual stimulus for a few minutes and he tried to get its attention. The cat looked up and meowed at him. It was a

THE EMPTY FLAT

beautiful Siamese cat with a light and dark brown body and almost black ears. He'd had a cat when he was younger, called Timmy, a black and white one. The family had only had it for a couple of years until it vanished and they never found out what happened to it. His parents told him that it had probably gone to live with some other people, but for all he knew it became the victim of road kill.

He wished he had some food to give to this cat as he guessed it was looking for food. This would be nice if he had a companion of some kind and he made a mental note to buy some biscuits for it tomorrow, as long as they were cheap enough.

He went back on the discovery trail the next day, bought some cat biscuits for less than a Euro and he found a second hand shop near the train station called Segundamano. This was something of a revelation as they had electrical items, including kettles, that looked unused. They were on sale for only €10 and hoped they'd still have some when he had the money. They also had stereos and things like lamps, which would be nice to get for the bedroom. It made him realise just how much he still lacked. Even though he had plenty of targets to reach, the fact that he couldn't cross them off the list yet was frustrating. His life was going in slow motion, but he had to keep telling himself that it would all come with time. He walked round some more streets that were new to him and he was thrilled to find some more paint. There was one five litre pot that was about half full. It was red, which wasn't really what he was looking for, but it would be better to take it just in case. He'd got three different colours so far, which made him think about doing some kind of design on the inside walls that would look cool. He thought back to the Home hostel and how he'd liked how they'd painted their rooms.

He went back to the agency to see if they had any more work, but nothing else was available at the moment. He could do with getting something else so he could speed up his renovation project and wondered if he should look into doing some other kind of work. As he had an address now, that should open up his possibilities. Maybe get some bar work or think about teaching English again. As he reflected on this, he knew that he was quite content with his cleaning work. He seemed to be getting away with being able to leave the office early and still get paid for two hours. The only downside of it was that he still had to fill his time with something else. He hung out with Paul and Steve every now and then, but didn't want to turn up on their doorstep every day. He could invite them round, but without having any way to entertain them seemed a bit pointless.

On Friday he got paid for two full weeks of work and to Andy it was like winning the lottery. Ninety whole Euros. After what he owed to Paul, he'd have €60 for the next two weeks. He could get by with spending less than ten for his weekly food, so would have about €40 to spend on everything else. He considered getting a stereo first and the cheapest little one was €20. He wouldn't be able to afford to go out if he got that, but the lack of things to do in the evening were now driving him mad. He thought it best not to rush into getting the stereo yet, but to plan his budget carefully and work out his priorities.

Andy had put some cat biscuits out for his new friend. Downstairs, there was a storage area under the flat next door that had a gate where he could put them in a more hidden spot. Every now and then he'd look outside to see if he or she was there and when he saw it he would get the biscuits to show that it was him who was feeding it. He went down and at first the cat was quite wary. He put some biscuits down in front of him and stepped back. The cat came over to eat them and meowed for more. Andy smiled as he thought he'd got the cat's trust. He put some more biscuits on the saucer he'd taken from his flat, which the cat ate, but he didn't want to push his luck with getting too close yet. However, after finishing its food, it ventured over to him, meowing as if to say "Thanks, you are now allowed to stroke me." Andy thought the cat was so beautiful, with blue eyes and clean fur. "Hello, Precious," he said, which he decided would be his name for it.

He'd been thinking of many options as to how he would paint the walls. The walls were textured, which would be a pain to paint over fully, so he thought about using the texture for an effect. He would try to create a scene that looked like it was outside. The red would be used to form a kind of sandy part for the lowest metre or so, the blue, at least when he had some more, would cover the rest of it to represent the sky and in the corners he would paint what looked like brick columns in brown. He loved being able to do whatever he wanted and made a start with what he'd got as he was fed up of looking at these still grimy walls. He put some blue in the corners, over which he could complete the brick effect and could get a couple of walls done with the red.

He got a call from Belén at the agency the next day to see if he wanted some more work. It was only a couple of days, for an hour a shift in another shop just outside the centre. He gladly took it and now his weekly work was up to ten hours, which meant he would now get €150 every two weeks. It was still not ideal, but an improvement nevertheless. "I'm slowly getting there," he thought.

With still very little to do outside of work hours, Andy was interested in doing something to fill his time. He was smoking on the balcony and wondered about the building next door. Clearly abandoned, he was curious as to whether there was anything of any interest still in it. The shutters were closed and it looked like the wood was rotten. He'd seen on the ground that there was a padlock on the gate, which must have been the entrance. Next to the gate were two narrow doors that opened from the middle, that had twelve small windows each. He had no intention to break in as, even though it was quiet here, someone might still hear the glass breaking, so what was the point of breaking in and getting caught if there was probably nothing inside that was worth it?

He looked up at the balconies. They weren't too far apart and maybe he could make a ledge from some wood to get across. He smirked as he thought he had a new project to work on.

The next day he used a piece of string to measure how long he needed the wood to be. It was only around two metres, which should be doable, he thought. He went on the hunt again and finding such basic materials was easy enough to accomplish. He found a few planks, which he would fix together so they'd be strong enough to take his weight. He bought some nails and went back home.

He looked outside to see if anyone was around. Nobody, as usual. He took a plank to see if it would reach and it was just about long enough. He'd brought back five of them and doubled two of them up to increase their thickness. He realised that he needed to fix these together side by side and also nail some bits of wood to the ends of these so they would catch over the balconies and not slip off while he made his way across. He went back out and found some more wood that would do the trick. First, he joined the ends together by nailing a piece perpendicular to them. He looked outside to see if the coast was clear. Someone was walking down the street, so he silently waited, peering out to see when he had gone. He took his ledge and hooked the brace over the balcony next door and marked where he'd need to put one on the other end. Just to make sure he also nailed two more pieces along the length and tested it again. It was perfect. He would have to wait till it was night time to make his first crossing, but he wanted to make sure it would be strong enough to hold his weight, so he went downstairs, rested one end on the bottom step, one on the floor, and stood on the middle. It seemed fine and he didn't think there was anything else needed so he took it back up.

THE EMPTY FLAT

He went to work at the new shop, which sold shoes, and it was another easy job, all the time thinking about what his plan of action would be for that night.

11.

Andy couldn't wait for the day to finish. This time it wasn't because of his boredom, but the tension of waiting to take the risky crossing to the empty flat. He had plenty of time to think through what he needed to do. It would be dark inside. He had a candle that he'd found in a drawer in the spare bedroom, but how would he get in in the first place? The doors must be closed, hopefully not locked, but he knew the wood would be weak and he might be able to gently force them open. If there was a sliding catch it would prove more difficult to open. He'd got a screwdriver that might do the job. If it failed, he would come back and think about what other tools he might need to get.

He thought about going over around eleven o'clock, but wanted to wait till later to reduce the probability of there being anyone around. He imagined that it might only take him a minute to get inside, but he wanted to cover his tracks. There was a lamp between the two balconies, slightly lower than the tops of them. The lamp reached out further than them and was never lit, so it wouldn't get in the way or illuminate him as he went. He wondered if he should wedge something between the plank and the lamp to provide extra security. He'd seen that the plank didn't really bend, but he didn't want to take any chances. However, that would mean finding something that would take up the space exactly. He could just about reach over to the lamp, so put the ledge across and measured the distance of the gap. He took the ledge back and pressed down on the lamp arm to see how secure that was. It didn't budge, but he had no way of working out if the other balcony was safe. He looked around the flat, but couldn't find anything that he could nail the ledge to that would fit exactly. Should he go down and try to make a grapple hook to test it by pulling on it? What if someone walked by. He'd never get it off in time. He'd just have to trust that it would be strong enough. He thought about creating some sort of anchor rope that could tie around his waist if he did come off for some reason. He looked up but there was nothing to tie one to. He was getting nervous the more he thought about it. Half past eleven. Was there any point in waiting for midnight? Would that make any difference? He looked up and down the street. There was some sort of activity at the top end, where the prostitutes were, but no-one was coming down the road. "I'll be over there in seconds," he thought. He checked again both ways and it was quiet. He took his ledge and placed it across. It looked very professional. He put on his backpack equipped with the candle and the screwdriver. He took the metal-framed chair to use as a step to get up onto the ledge. He wished he could do the same on the other side but of course couldn't put anything there until he was over. "I'll just have to crawl back, maybe." He checked for any pedestrians. Someone was coming up from the bottom end of the road. It looked to be a man dressed in dark clothes, walking quite slowly and unsteadily. Should he take the ledge off again? This man might notice. He probably won't look up. Andy went back in a little to keep a subtle eye on him. The man didn't look up. Andy guessed he was drunk or on drugs. He wished he would hurry up. It took him about two minutes to be out of sight, but it felt like half an hour to Andy. He checked again. No-one. He took a deep breath and stood on the chair. He checked again. It was clear. He tentatively stepped onto the ledge with his hands against the wall. It seemed okay. "Two steps and you're there," he whispered. One step. A slight bend. Two steps. He was on the edge of the other balcony. He crouched and, as silently as he could, got down.

He'd made it without any problem. The relief was almost too much for him to bear. He stayed crouched down in case anyone else appeared. The night was almost too silent. He could hear every tiny little sound. A piece of rubbish blowing in the street. A creak somewhere in the distance. He gently pushed at the balcony doors. There was quite a lot of give in them. More than he expected. They were closed in some way but he could reach his finger into the gap he had made. He slid it up. In the middle something stopped him. A metal catch of some kind. He could barely see anything, but he gripped it and tried to move it. It popped up straight away. It was simply a pivoted hook resting down in a staple. He had made it, as easily as that. He gently pushed the doors in in case there was a squeak, but there was nothing loud enough to be heard by anyone but him.

He was inside, but couldn't see a thing. He closed the doors again, then remembered that the ledge was still across the balconies. He didn't want to raise any suspicion. He carefully went back out and gently lifted it over and put it on the balcony floor. He went back in and closed the doors. He reached in his bag for the candle and at this point suddenly became very nervous. What if there was a dead body on the floor? What if someone was actually living here? He stood completely still for a while, listening intently. He made sure that he was breathing silently. He couldn't detect any sign of life, or death. It did smell pretty grim, though, but not like rotting flesh probably would. It was the combination of mould and damp or something. Exactly what he would have expected. He held the candle in his left hand and his lighter in his right. Okay, now's the time. He took a deep breath and lit the candle. Slowly the room opened up to his eyes. It was about the same size as his front room. He waited till his eyes adjusted. He was still frozen to the spot and barely turned his head at first, relying on his searching eyes. There was a table to his right, an old cupboard, similar to the big one in his front room, against the end wall. Some indeterminate objects on the floor to his left. He finally took two steps forward. The floorboard creaked. He stopped to process this and it didn't concern him too much. He went to the doorway. The layout seemed the same as his flat, but mirrored. He went into the corridor and there was a door to his left, which was closed. Ahead was the kitchen, which was practically empty apart from a plate next to the sink and glass in it. A cupboard door above the sink hung precariously, due to a damaged hinge. He didn't want to touch anything until he had seen everything that was here. The bathroom to the side of the kitchen had a door. "For fuck's sake," he thought. "This one has a door, but I don't." He thought about seeing if he could take it to put in his place. The door was open and he peered round the corner. The bath looked filthy. He could make out that the base of it was covered in some black sludge or something. Nothing else of note in there. He expected to find the back bedroom, so turned round. Suddenly he heard a noise. It came from the front room. Something had moved. His eyes widened in fear. He waited, but it didn't happen again. He thought about what the noise could have been. It wasn't footsteps. It happened again. A slight knocking sound. No-one else could have followed him in. He had the only way of entry. Or did he? Of course there was the front door. "Shit..." He was as still as a statue for thirty seconds. Another knock. He crept forward and due to a relative amount of fluctuating light at the front, he realised it was just the balcony doors moving in the wind.

Right, the bedroom then. He felt calmer again and went towards it. The door was almost closed, but he couldn't see through it yet. He pushed it and it creaked. He grimaced. Now he was sure he was going to find a decomposing body on the bed and blood splattered over the walls. He opened it some more and the candlelight crept in before him. A bed frame, empty. A chest of drawers to the left of the door. That was all. He'd seen enough horror films to suspect that by now, someone was bound to be standing behind him wielding an axe above their head with an evil, toothy grin. He slowly turned around. There wasn't. He took stock of the situation and was now sure that this was just an ordinary abandoned flat with no monsters hiding in the corners.

He opened each drawer in the bedroom. There was virtually nothing in there except for a few bits and pieces like fragments of paper with nothing on them and a couple of paper clips. The candle wax kept dripping down and burning him, so he thought getting in was enough work for one night. He'd buy a cheap torch tomorrow and come back the next night to search some more, although it wasn't looking like he was going to find any expensive jewellery.

He went back out to the balcony doors and at this point he realised that he hadn't thought how he was going to close them again. It may raise suspicion if they blew open again during the next day, but after checking that the coast was clear, he knelt down on the balcony and just about managed to get the hook back in. Then he thought that he should have got a chair or something out so he could climb up onto the ledge again. That would mean something mysteriously appearing on the balcony, so he decided not to and got back up by putting his foot on the front part of the balcony and he got onto the ledge without too much trouble. He carefully made his way back over and put his ledge back in his flat.

It hadn't been the most exciting of investigations, but at least it was something different to do. After this anti-climactic episode he went to bed.

He thought about it as soon as he woke up and wondered how risky it would be to go in again during the daytime. He was sure he could find a time when no-one was about again. The building opposite also seemed to be abandoned. It used to be a furniture shop or factory, but he'd never seen or heard anything going on there. There was still a chance he would be spotted if he opened the balcony from the inside just as someone was around. He would wait again until night time.

It was Wednesday and he hadn't seen Paul since the weekend. He wondered if he should tell him what he'd been up to. Technically it was breaking and entering, so he thought he would keep it to himself for now. There was not much to report anyway. He went over to Paul's and they had dinner together with Steve. Paul was intrigued to know how Andy was getting on.

"It's slow progress, but I am getting there. I've got used to the idea that it'll take a few weeks, but it's okay."

"Have you got any more work yet?"

He told him about the shoe shop, which was as easy as the others.

"Do you think you'll stay working as a cleaner?" Steve asked.

"For the time being. It's easy work, but I really could do with more hours."

"You really should look at getting into teaching," Paul offered. "I'd be bored to death with cleaning."

"Yeah, maybe. I doubt that I'll do it for too long. It's certainly not going to be my career. Imagine that. Sociology graduate emigrates to Spain and cleans offices and shops for the rest of his life. Nah, I don't think so."

"You must be living hand to mouth right now though," Steve said.

"Yeah, it's pretty tight. I do need to get something better soon. If I could get a job cleaning a house for about five hours, that'd be an extra €37.50 a week."

"You'll have bills to pay, too," Paul reminded him.

"I know. I didn't ask about that. I'll just have to make sure I keep some money aside each week for when they arrive."

"At least your electricity won't be much. What have you got there, just lights?"

"Basically, yes! I want to get a stereo as soon as I can, and a kettle, but that won't amount to much, either."

"I don't think I could live like that," Steve said. "Every few weeks getting one more basic thing. It must be hell."

"Don't remind me, I'm bored to tears sometimes."

"Well, listen. You know you're always welcome here," Paul pointed out. "I'll buy you a beer every now and then, too, till you're earning more money."

"You don't have to do that, but thanks anyway."

"There's a second hand bookshop just off Caballeros. They have some books in English that you can get for pennies," said Paul.

"Oh right. I think I know the one you mean. Near to Fox Congo, isn't it?"

"That's the one."

"Cool. I'll go there tomorrow and see what I can find. Thanks."

Andy was secretly keeping an eye on the time as he wanted to go exploring and hopefully looting tonight. He left the guys just after eleven.

Back in his flat, like a trained criminal, he checked his new torch still worked. Click, click. That was the extent of his pre-break in preparations. He went through the same ritual as last night: check both ways to see if anyone is coming. Ledge secured, head over. He lifted the hook again, removed the ledge and went back in. This time he used the ledge to keep the doors closed from the inside. He took a few steps in and turned on the torch. He looked behind and hoped the light couldn't be seen from outside. He should be alright as long as he was careful where he pointed it.

As he'd checked the bedroom last night, he thought he'd start in the kitchen. There were no windows there to arouse suspicion. He thought about the cockroaches in his place, which he had started killing via the traps. He wished he'd put rubber gloves on before he came over, but braced himself for them as he opened the sink cupboard. He shone the torch in and there were a few that ran about to get out of the light. He felt pleased that they didn't bother him so much now. "I'm a veteran," he said out loud in his best American accent.

Under the sink was nothing but dirt. He was quite happy not to have to root around in it to pick up anything, so closed the door and checked the cupboard with the broken hinge. It almost came off in his hand, but he gripped it tightly so it wouldn't fall off. Inside he found two plates, which were slightly dirty and had a layer of dust on. There was a cork at the back of the shelf. It didn't give him many insights into the lives of the last tenants. He tried to close the door, but now it was less secure than before. If he left it, it would probably fall off of its own accord. The bottom hinge was now bent, so he had no choice but to keep bending it until it came off. "I don't think anyone's going to be home soon," he thought and he left in on the worktop as though it had come off with time.

For all the planning and excitement he'd had about breaking in here, he was not getting much of a reward. There was one other cupboard next to the sink. The door was fine on this one and the contents of this were more unexpected. On the middle shelf was an old set of scales, maybe made of brass. There were a few small weights of varying sizes. He looked at them closely. A normal thing to have in a kitchen, he supposed. Should he take them? Why not. They might come in useful for something. He wasn't much of a cook, but maybe, as he was feeling more like an adult now, he would learn some recipes. He took the scales and the six weights and put them in his backpack.

Bedroom cleared. Kitchen cleared. He had another quick look in the bathroom, but there was nothing other than that horrible stain in the bath. Cleared. He hadn't even seen the spare bedroom yet. His trepidation returned as he cautiously opened the door. He swung the torch around to locate any hiding suspects, but to his relief there were none. There was a single bed frame, the same as in his spare room. Odd, he thought, but not really that unusual. There was a wardrobe in here. Maybe this was where the secrets were kept. His imagination brought back the archetypal horror film scene where a severed head would be in a box along with the message "You're next." He pulled at the door, but it was locked. He found the keyhole, but there was no key in it. Now he felt like he was moving into detective mode. He took on the challenge of finding the key. It must be in here somewhere. He scanned the floor, but it was nowhere to be seen. The bedside table had a drawer in it. He pulled it out and lo and behold, there it was. "Okay, men," he said to himself. "The search is over." He took the key and put it into the wardrobe door. It wouldn't turn. "Oh, for God's sake," he said in a huff. He tried again but still nothing. He took it back out and wondered what it was for. It has to fit something. He put it in his pocket as he was sure he'd find the right lock somewhere else in the flat. He had another quick look around the room, but could see nothing. There was just one room left and that was the living room.

 He hadn't taken a look at the front door yet. He went over and it looked secure. Painted white but covered in dirty marks. He thought about whether he should risk opening it. There was no-one in the building. Or was there? He turned the knob and pulled. It wouldn't open. He looked down and saw there was another lock, which needed a key. "Aha," he thought and reached into his pocket. The key looked too small, but he tried it anyway. It was too loose and wouldn't turn. He sighed, thinking he had solved at least one puzzle, but put the key back into his pocket and scanned the room, keeping the torch light low. The only thing was that cupboard against the back wall. He walked over and caught his foot against something. He inspected it and found it was a floorboard that was slightly raised. Just old, he thought and went to the cupboard. It had a door on each end and three drawers in the middle. He tried the drawers first. The top one was empty. So was the second. In the bottom drawer he found two tiny plastic bags with sealable tops. They were empty, so he thought nothing of them and closed the drawer. He tried the door on the left. Locked. The keyhole was smaller here, so again reached into his pocket and put it in. Eureka! It actually worked! This was where he was bound to find the treasure. On the bottom shelf he saw a small box, made of card. It had no top, but when he picked it up he saw that it was empty. Another sigh emanated from his lungs. Okay, one last door. The key also unlocked this one and would you believe it, it was completely empty. He left the key in it and closed it again. He scanned the room once more, but could see nothing other than dust, cobwebs and grime. He had searched the whole place now, so called it a night and made his way back into his flat.

He opened his backpack and took out the scales and weights. He looked at them carefully. The weights were 1g, two 2g, 5g, 10g, 20g. He put them in his kitchen cupboard, unimpressed with his find and went to bed.

On Thursday morning, during his usual wake up routine, Andy thought about what he'd done last night. He was disappointed that he hadn't found anything exciting, but he supposed it was quite normal that once whoever had been there before had left, most things would have been taken out. Considering that there was more stuff here when he moved in, he guessed it would have been a similar situation. He remembered that he hadn't cracked the wardrobe and that still remained a target for him. He should be able to break it open somehow, especially because there was no-one around to hear him. This made him think about the flat above his. He'd noticed some letters in the letterbox downstairs, so there must be someone in there. He'd never seen them, but thought he had heard some kind of sound coming from there one or two times. Maybe it was an old person who didn't go out, but no-one seemed to visit them and they must have to get food and things at some time. He could always go up and knock the door to say hello. He would consider this during the day.

A short while later he went out to the bookshop that Paul mentioned. There were a few books in English, mostly tatty, old ones, but he might as well get some to pass the time. He bought four for €3 by authors he'd mostly never heard of. One of them was a a collection of Sherlock Holmes stories and because of his slight foray into the crime world, that was the first one he would read.

He walked around somewhat aimlessly again, keeping an eye open for any more stuff that had been thrown out but he saw nothing of real interest. He remembered that sort of underground park he had crossed when he first arrived and thought that would be good to check out.

He found out that it used to be a river, the Túria, that had been diverted due to the flooding that used to happen. Now it was massive, long park, about a hundred metres wide and had been designed beautifully. There was an athletics stadium and rugby pitch in there and he was amazed at this feat of engineering to divert what would have been a huge river. He thought it would be the perfect place for him to go and read and he felt pleased that he would be able to relieve some of the boredom of having nothing to do. He found a quiet spot and began reading the Sherlock Holmes book.

He found that he was really getting into them and he read five stories before he went back home. From all the plot twists and innovative techniques that the characters used, it got him thinking again about going into the empty flat. He didn't know how to pick locks, but he was sure that he could break the one on the wardrobe, even though he didn't expect to find anything inside it. Opening the one on the front door was probably beyond him and the landlord was likely to have the only key.

He wondered what else he could do with that flat. He could turn it into his secret base and do it up in the same way that he was doing his, although how he would get any furniture in was another matter. He needed to focus on his own place first anyway, which was still going along at a snail's pace.

It was going to be another week until he got paid next and he wanted to do something to his flat, even if it was just something small. As he walked back he found a long window blind made of wicker strips. He didn't like that people could see up through his balcony into his flat and this could be a good thing to fix sideways to it to give more privacy. At is was still very hot, he often walked around in just his boxer shorts, so he rolled up the blind and found a few more pieces of wood that he'd figure out what to do with once he was back.

The window blind fitted almost perfectly. It was just a tiny bit short but covered most of it, so now he could get on with his criminal plans without anyone seeing him. He didn't actually have any real plans other than to break into the wardrobe, so read another Sherlock Homes story to get some inspiration. *The Adventure of the Speckled Band* was the next one and in it, it described a bed that was clamped to the floor. He thought back to the bed frames he'd seen. He hadn't touched them but doubted this would be the case with them, but he also remembered when he stumbled over the raised floorboard. He would have a go at lifting it up with his claw hammer to see if anything was hidden underneath.

He couldn't afford to go out for a drink, but would meet up with Paul on Saturday. This gave him another two nights to see what else he could achieve next door. "Why can't real life be as exciting as those stories?" he thought. Finding a set of scales and a couple of empty plastic bags was nothing to tell anyone about.

For this night's adventure, he remembered to take his rubber gloves in case he could get the floorboard up. He didn't want to come into contact with a dead rat with his bare hands.

He headed back over in what was now a routine operation. He located the proud floorboard and with not too much effort, prised it up. He used the torch to look under it, but he could see nothing other than the beams and dust. He levered it up some more and reached in anyway. Nothing. Oh well. Having thought about the bed frames, he thought he'd take a look at them just in case. In the side bedroom, he could move it easily. He turned it onto its side and found that the bottoms of the legs were hollow metal tubes. He shone the torch in each of them but could see nothing, put the bed back as it was and went to the back bedroom. He inspected it in the same way and to his surprise a paper clip fell out of one of them. "How did that end up in there?" he thought. He checked the top to see if it could have been dropped in through there but they were closed off by round knobs that didn't unscrew. Could it have just got in there from being on the floor? Even though it didn't seem like a big deal, it was, as Sir Arthur Conan Doyle often wrote, a most singular incident.

Now he was curious. Had this paper clip been attached to something that was hidden in there? He looked in again with the torch but couldn't make out anything. He rooted around with the screwdriver, but nothing else fell out. He put the bed back down and looked at the floor. He wondered how easy it would be to get some of these floorboards up. He found one with something of a gap between the end of the next one and got his claw hammer back to work. It was more difficult to get up than the one in the living room. He went through the same procedure, but found nothing. He looked around at the floor pensively. "I've got nothing else to do," he thought and tried another one. The same result. If anything had been hidden under one, it should come up more easily. He went around the room lifting about ten or twelve, not really finding any that were like that until one near the door seemed a bit loose. Probably only because of age or a substandard job of laying it, but he was able to get it up without too much effort. He reached in and it seemed that he had found something.

12.

With his fingertips he could feel some kind of package. It was hard to pull it back, so he lifted the floorboard some more and could just about get his fingers on top if it. It didn't seem like it was a box as it felt softer. Gradually he edged it towards him and lifted it out. It was a packet of something about half the size of a bag of sugar, wrapped in cellophane and with what appeared to be brown paper under that. His mind raced to guess what it contained: maybe gold jewellery, maybe a stack of bank notes, maybe drugs. In case it was that he thought he'd better take it back to his first, so he put it in his bag, put the floorboard back down, collected his things and headed back.

He put it on his dining table and sat down. He carefully peeled the cellophane back and pressed it. It was definitely soft. He found the edge of the paper and lifted it. It revealed that it was powder of some sort, white and very fine. He touched it and rubbed it between his fingers. He had never done drugs apart from smoking some weed at university, so wasn't sure what it was, but it could be cocaine or heroin maybe. He didn't want to taste it in case it was poison. It didn't really have much of a smell and he was stumped. "What if it is cocaine?" he thought. Nobody would hide something that wasn't of any value under the floorboards, so it must be something like that. He looked at it, unsure of how to proceed from here. Whatever it was, he thought that he might be able to make some money out of this. He remembered the scales and the plastic bags. "It's got to be drugs. Fucking hell."

He tried to imagine what the scenario could have been with the flat. A drug dealer who got caught, the landlord emptied the place and didn't bother renting it out again because people would know about its history. It made sense to him.

THE EMPTY FLAT

When he went to bed, Andy had a million questions going through his mind. Should he turn it in to the police? Should he try to sell it? He didn't know how drug dealing worked, but he was sure it was a dangerous business. How much could he make from it? Should he confide in Paul and Steve? He didn't sleep well as you can imagine and in the morning he found himself back at the dining table, staring at this package.

The main question that he had on his mind was talking to Paul about it. He was his closest friend here, but they'd never spoken about drugs and he didn't know if Paul would turn him in to the police. He probably wouldn't, but it was still something he didn't know. How could he work out if it was cocaine or some other drug? He toyed with the idea of just trying a bit, but again, if it was poison... It was the same problem with selling to someone. What if that person died from it? He wouldn't be able to live with that at all. He needed to get some advice from someone who knew about drugs, but who? Then, he had a brainwave.

He remembered the small plastic bags. That was what it was sold in, he at least knew that. He would go back to the empty flat and take them, put a bit in one then tell Paul that he'd found it in the street and ask him if he knew what it was.

Even though he wanted some answers right now, he couldn't risk going back over in the daytime. If he got caught then, and the police found all these drugs in his possession, he would be sent to prison. He could just go to the shops and find some bags instead, so he got his trainers on and set off.

He didn't take notice of anything on his way and thought the best place was the Mercat Central. Surely someone would sell things like that. He wandered around, not seeing anything of the kind and after a few minutes heard someone call his name from behind. He was initially shocked and thought someone had caught him already, but it turned out to be Paul and Steve.

"Hey, I thought it was you," Paul said. "What are you up to?"

"Oh, er, nothing. Just browsing. You?" He wasn't ready yet to face them and hoped they would go away soon.

"Just getting some veggies. We were going to grab a coffee. Do you fancy joining us?"

He tried to think of an excuse quickly, but nothing came to mind. All that went through his head was 'drugs, cocaine, danger.'

"Er, yeah, sure," he said, regretting it the moment he'd answered.

So off they went without Andy fulfilling his task. He'd have time to look for some bags later, but he didn't want any company right now. They went to a café on Caballeros and Paul bought Andy a coffee.

"We were thinking of going for a picnic later," Paul said. "Do you want to join us?"

"Thanks, but I'm not really in the mood," Andy replied.

"Not in the mood? What's up?"

"Nothing, I just fancied spending the day on my own."

"Okay, it's up to you. What have you got planned?"

"Not much, I just thought I'd take my book and go and read in the Parque del Túria."

"That's where we're going." Shit, why the hell did he say that? He could have left them in the dark about his fictional destination. "Come on, join us. It's a nice day."

He felt he had no choice but to accept the offer, so he agreed to. As they sat and had their coffees, Andy didn't offer much to the conversation and Paul noticed he had something on his mind. He asked him if there was anything wrong.

"What? No, I'm fine. Just thinking about work."

"Really? I thought you said it was easy. What's the problem?"

Andy didn't like being put on the spot. He was hopeless at lying, but had to conjure up something.

"Oh, I just had a run in with someone at the office." What the fuck was he talking about? What was the point of saying that? Now he had to invent a whole story.

"What happened?"

"The boss just had a go at me for, erm, for not..." He couldn't think of what to say. Paul and Steve looked at each other. Something was not right here. "For not putting the cleaning stuff away properly." He was watching himself dig a stupidly deep hole.

"How the hell are you supposed to put it away?"

"I just put the bleach in the wrong cupboard and he got angry with me."

"Are you serious?" Paul really doubted what he was talking about.

"Look, it's nothing. He just had a go at me, but it's okay now. Don't worry about it."

Paul was very suspicious and they sat in silence for a few moments, Steve and Paul subtly glancing at each other while Andy looked down at his cup. Paul guessed that he was hiding something, but it may be personal and Andy didn't want to talk about it.

"If you want to spend the day on your own, that's fine. Don't worry about coming with us," Steve said. Andy wasn't listening, he was beating himself up for trying to invent a story when he had no idea where he was going with it.

"Andy," Paul said. He looked up at him. "Don't worry about coming with us. If you need some time alone, that's cool. We're going to head off."

"Okay, thanks." He offered. The other two said goodbye and walked off. Andy closed his eyes and thought how stupid he had been. "You absolute dick," he said under his breath.

He lit a cigarette to try to calm himself down, but kept thinking about how he was going to get around this when he next saw the guys. He'd have to come up with some other lie, but at least he had time to think about it first. "Don't make it so dramatic this time," he ordered himself.

He was not in the mood to go looking for the plastic bags, so just went back home to think about things. What was he going to say to Paul? He could just say that he was feeling down about not making enough money, but no, Paul knew he could talk about things like that. Should he show him the little bag of drugs and say that that was on his mind? He didn't want to address that issue just yet. In the end, he thought he should just say it was some issue with his parents that he didn't want to talk about. People usually don't press you when you say it's something personal. Yeah, that would do it. He texted Paul with a simple "Sorry, it's family stuff." A minute later he got a reply: "No worries, mate. See you soon."

Andy breathed a sigh of relief and thought that he'd drawn a line under it. He had a smoke and went back out to the cheapo shop and bought a pack of ten little bags.

13.

"What do you think about Andy?" Paul asked Steve when they were in the park.

"He seems like a nice guy, but there's something mysterious about him. I mean, you know him more than I do, but that was a weird episode at the café today."

"Yeah, if it was family issues, then why didn't he just say that? He knows I wouldn't have had a problem with him not wanting to talk about them."

"On the other hand," said Steve "Maybe it's something else. I mean, that shit he was saying was ridiculous. Would anyone really make that up if they could have just said it was a problem with his family?"

This made Paul think for a minute. It sounded logical to him. "Well, I doubt it's anything that bad. I know he's struggling with money, *maybe* his parents are giving him grief about that and telling him to go back to England. I can't think of anything else, but then, who knows what secrets he's got hidden?"

"If I was in his position, there would be only so long that I would put up with it," Steve said. "I mean, if he doesn't get any better work, do you really think he'll be here in a year's time? Cleaning a few places?"

"Who knows? He's not you, is he? And lots of things can change over a year. I'm sure he'll figure things out."

Back at Andy's flat, things were already changing, but he didn't know how yet. He got the scales out of the kitchen and methodically arranged everything on his dining room table. He looked over towards the balcony. Was he sure that no-one could see in? He couldn't see the street. Was he absolutely sure that there was no-one in the old furniture shop across from him? There was a window that he could see that almost faced his. He closed one balcony door just in case. What if the police used it as a secret watchtower? No, they wouldn't. Would they? It was a pretty rough area. Every now and then he would see people who looked like they were junkies sitting or staggering around. The prostitutes at the end of the street. Andy was on fairly polite terms with them these days as he often walked by them on his way to the shops. The old woman was never nasty and he'd just ask her how she was. She tried to entice him for business, but he just carried on going. However, he'd never seen a police officer in the area. Maybe the problem wasn't out of control and they just left everyone to get on with their lives. Maybe the police didn't care. Either way, it gave him some comfort to realise that this area wasn't being patrolled.

He got a teaspoon and put the 1g weight on the scales. He carefully got some of this still as yet unknown powder and weighed out a gram. Then, he realised it would be hard to get it into the bag, being such a small amount. "Schoolboy error," he said. He scooped up as much as he could, got it in the bag and wiped off the residue. As it was on his finger, he was tempted to put it in his mouth. He needed to know what it was. He stared at it and licked a tiny bit off. It didn't taste very nice and he had to get a glass of water to get rid of the taste, but he tried to notice if it was doing anything to him. He couldn't feel any difference, but thought it best to leave it for now to see if he felt ill later.

He went back to the table. He'd got his first gram of something bagged. Should he do the same with the other bags? He wasn't going to try to sell them, but he thought it would be cool just to see them all lined up. He put the powder into the bags and weighed them, making sure that with the bag added, he needed to go just past the balance line. After doing each one, he put them in a neat line on the table. He stood up so he could see his whole operation and he felt like he was in charge. The package was still essentially full and he couldn't believe how much he'd got. "Why was this left there?" he thought. "Surely you wouldn't move out and forget that you'd got all this stuff under the floorboards. It's got to be worth hundreds, maybe thousands. God, what if it's worth thousands?" He was itching to find out what it was and how much he could make from it.

How was he going to go about that now? He felt like it was an awkward time to see Paul again after the dick he'd made of himself a couple of hours ago. He didn't want to wait that long as his thoughts would be gnawing away at him. He sat back down and thought of the best way to go about it.

Today wouldn't be the right time, but he thought that he'd ask to meet Paul on his own tomorrow and say that he'd found a 1g bag in the street. That was believable considering the area he lived in. Hopefully Paul would know more than him and if he could confirm what it was, then he'd be off and running. Well, in a way. He still had to work out what his plan would be to move into drug dealing. It wasn't something he really wanted to get into, but surely he would learn along the way. Start off small. Maybe the prostitute madam would buy some off him and the other prostitutes. At least he wouldn't have to go out of his comfort zone, but they would know where he lived. He didn't want a succession of junkies knocking on his door at all times. He was bound to get caught eventually like that. Man, he had a lot of research to do.

He could do with trying to find out someone else who sold drugs and getting some information that way, like how much they sold a gram for and how they went about it. He didn't know of any places where this would happen. He put the scales away and thought that he'd need to work out a good place to stash the powder. Obviously under the floorboards would be an option. He looked around his flat, but couldn't see where any would come up easily. He considered different ideas, like making a box with a false bottom, hiding it under the bath, behind the wardrobe. If the police came round they would know all the tricks and would find it easily. But if a drug dealer was caught next door, they hadn't found this package under the floorboards. Maybe he should keep it there. It would be a hassle to keep going over there every time he needed to get more, but it would mean that it wasn't stored in his place and this could be the way to avoid punishment. He could keep a few little bags with him and go over every now and then to get some more. Brilliant. That was the plan.

Over the rest of the day, he couldn't stop thinking about every little detail of what he was going to do. While he thought about the point where he found the stash, he wondered if there were any more under the floorboards. He had only lifted a few of them, but it was possible and he would have all the time in the world to go through the whole place. He didn't relish the thought of lifting the entire floor bit by bit, but maybe. He stopped himself and couldn't believe he was actually wanting to find more drugs. This really was a dangerous game he was getting into. What if he couldn't control himself? If he made a load of money from selling what he had, would he use it to buy another batch? "Take it slowly," he told himself. "And carefully."

The cat, Precious, would turn up regularly now as he always tried to leave some biscuits out for it. These visits gave Andy some respite from his current dilemma. He would either go down and stroke it (he still didn't know if it was a boy or a girl) and Precious would enjoy his company equally, or he would play with it from the balcony using a long piece of string with a piece of plastic tied to the end that Andy would dangle over so Precious could play with it. He would love to be able to keep the cat as his pet, but thought that it was more used to an outside life.

He decided to use Saturday night to try to scout out some clubs and see if he could find anyone who sold cocaine and ask them how much they charged. He'd only been to Fox Congo so far and that didn't seem like the right place. He found another club called Mosquito a little bit off the beaten track and got a small beer. Looking around, he couldn't tell if anyone had taken any and he wanted to tread carefully. He went outside for a smoke and casually looked around. He saw a couple of guys who might be the kind to use it. They had leather jackets and one had long hair. He asked in Spanish if they had any, but they said no. Then he asked if they knew anyone who sold it, but again it was a no. He hung around there for a bit and he saw another guy go up to someone who he guessed he didn't know. They chatted for a few seconds then walked off together. They came back shortly and this gave Andy the sign that the second guy was a dealer. He waited a bit then went up to ask this guy if he had any. The guy could tell he wasn't Spanish from his accent, said yes and it was €80 a gram. Andy pretended he was thinking about it, then said "No, gracias." The guy asked him how much he had and Andy said that it didn't matter. The guy looked at him suspiciously and asked if he was the police. He replied that he wasn't and went back inside. He'd found out the main thing he wanted to know and just stayed until he'd finished his beer and left. The guy was still outside and they made eye contact briefly, then Andy walked off. He hoped he wasn't going to be followed and as he got to the end of the road, he looked back, but the guy wasn't coming. He made his way back home.

"€80 a gram," he thought. "That's more than I expected." He wasn't sure how much he had found but guessed it was half a kilo. He did the maths and worked out that he could make €40,000. "Jesus Christ!" He only made €80 a week and could get that by selling just one gram. He couldn't believe that he could get really rich from this. He thought about what that could mean to him. "I could pay my rent from just two grams! If I sold ten a week, that's €800! Oh my god." All the things he could buy with that. The first thing that came into his head was the kettle and he laughed. "I can get a bit more than that!" He stayed up for a hour or so making a list in his head of things like a TV, a computer, maybe even a car. This couldn't be real.

When he finally woke up at ten, he thought he should go to work, then get in touch with Paul. He went through the conversation he would have, to try and put yesterday's issue to rest. His parents were telling him he should leave Spain and go back to stay with them. Yes, that was easy enough. He knew the kind of things they would say, but he didn't want to go into details again in case he screwed things up. "Leave it at that then tell him that I found this bag."

He went into work and it was as easy as it always was, but his mind was racing with thinking about how rich he would be. By half past twelve he was finished and he would text Paul when he got back home. He asked him to come to his place and made sure that there wasn't anything left around that gave it away that he had all these drugs. He put the package in his wardrobe under his t-shirts. Paul came round at two.

"How's things?" Paul asked.

"I'm fine. Sorry about the other day. I just had things on my mind."

"It's okay. I know family can get in the way sometimes. Do you want to talk about it?"

"Not really," Andy replied. He'd gone through what he was going to say a few times before Paul arrived and stuck to the script.

"Yeah, it's normal. Parents worry. Mine were like that in the beginning, but as soon as they knew I was doing well, they stopped going on about it."

"Yeah. I'll be alright before too long." Andy wanted to leave it there as he had nothing else on his mental script. He thought it best to address the little bag of powder before he left it too late.

"Anyway, the main reason I asked you to come round was because I found this last night." He took the bag out of his pocket and put in on the table. Paul raised his eyebrows as he saw it.

"Cocaine," he said upon lifting it up.

"Are you sure?"

"Yeah, I don't do the stuff myself but have done before."

"How do you know it is?"

"Well, it's not crystallised, which some drugs go like and it's pure white. Where did you find it?"

"I went out for a walk last night and I just saw this on a side street."

"So I guess that you've never done it before then."

"No, that's why I wanted to ask."

"Are you going to take it?"

"I don't know. I just wanted to find out what it was first."

"It's a dangerous drug. I've had friends who were addicted to it. It fucked them up. Be careful, man."

"Yeah, I'm not into drugs, but I might try and sell it. I could do with the money."

"Steve does a bit of coke. You could ask him."

"Oh right." Steve could be a useful person to get information from about how he gets it and how the dealers operate. This was something that he already felt anxious about doing, so he wanted to know as much as he could before embarking on this dark path.

"I'll let him know if you want. He'll probably buy it off you."

"Sure, thanks."

They just chatted a bit more and Paul was no longer suspicious of Andy. He was satisfied with his story about his parents and it was possible that the cocaine could be found on the street. Andy was feeling that he wanted Paul to go and didn't want to prolong the conversation. He stayed for about half an hour and went.

Paul told Steve about the coke when he got back. "Lucky bugger!" was his response and he told Paul that he probably would buy it off him.

"Yeah, he could do with the pocket money," Paul said.

By now, Andy was feeling quite fired up after finding that it was what he hoped it to be. He still needed to work out his strategy, but in his mind he was going to be rich. Looking at the bag, he was more tempted to try it. He at least knew that people snorted it through rolled up bank notes. He wouldn't do it right now in case Steve got in touch and wanted to come round. He needed some safe space to see what the effects were first.

He didn't hear from Steve for the rest of the day, so by nine o'clock he thought it was time to go for it. He got his €5 note rolled up and put a small amount on the table. He didn't know how much was in a line of coke, so he just made one that was about two centimetres long. He wondered how he should snort it, hard or softly? He thought about when he'd seen it in films and he remembered that people snorted hard, so he did that. He could feel it in the back of his throat and it wasn't very nice. He kept sniffing to try to dislodge it from his sinuses and drank some water. He expected something to happen straight away, but as he sat there, he felt nothing. Maybe it takes time then… After about half an hour he thought he could feel it working. He was feeling energised, but not that much. He waited some more and felt he needed to stand up as he was getting fidgety. Over the next hour he couldn't stop himself from walking around the flat and gesticulating with his arms. He felt happy and wished he had some music to dance to. "This is pretty good!" he said out loud, not realising that his eyes were more open than usual. The sensation continued and after another hour it started to wear off.

By midnight he felt back to normal except he was still quite awake. "I can see why people use this so much, it's good stuff," he thought. He was pleased that he hadn't lost control of his mind but just felt really active. He wondered what would happen if he snorted more than what he had. Would the feeling be even better? He guessed it would, but with him not being such a wild child, he wasn't going to do any more tonight.

He didn't feel like he could sleep yet and tried to read his book in bed to help him fall asleep. He found it hard to concentrate, partly because of the effect of cocaine and partly because he couldn't stop himself thinking about how this could change his life. It was after three o'clock when he finally nodded off, but he still woke up at nine and couldn't get back to sleep.

He had a lot to reflect on that day. He'd learned quite a few things from this whole experience, but wanted to get selling the cocaine as soon as he could. Payday was this Friday and it seemed ridiculous that he had about €40,000 worth in his wardrobe but couldn't even buy his kettle yet. This week was going to be gruelling to get through.

On Tuesday, he got a text from Steve, asking if he could come round. Andy smiled and immediately thought that he was going to be able to sell the bag to him. He came round soon after.

"So I hear you found some coke," Steve said.

"Yeah. I don't do it, so I'm happy to sell it. Do you do it?" He already knew the answer to this but tried to play dumb for his own sake.

"Yeah, a bit. Well, to be honest, I do it quite often, but only when I go out clubbing." Andy was using Steve's words to work out if he could get him to be his first regular buyer.

"How much do you take each time?"

"Just a couple of lines. Haven't you ever done it?"

"No, never."

"Maybe we should go out this weekend and do a bit. I'll look after you." This sounded enticing to Andy, remembering that he felt like dancing last night. "So how much do you want for it?"

"€80?"

Steve was surprised that Andy knew how much it sold for despite never doing it before. "Let me just have a taste." He licked his finger and put a small amount if then rubbed it across his gums. "Yeah, it seems legit." He looked at the bag to ascertain if there was a gram in it. "Why did you say €80?"

Andy was caught off guard here and realised that as a novice he shouldn't have known the street value of it. "Erm, I dunno. I guessed it was worth that much."

"It is actually. That's how much you generally get it for here." He took out his wallet and handed him the money.

Andy didn't want to risk asking him anything else yet. He wasn't sure if Steve was a safe person to declare his findings to just yet, but he liked the sound of the plan to go out clubbing this weekend.

"Alright, I've got to get off now," Steve said. "Cheers. I'll text you this weekend. Probably Saturday as that's when Jessica will be here. We can all go out together."

Jessica was the third person who would be living with the guys. Their school year would be starting soon.

"Nice one. Thanks, mate."

After he shut the door, Andy grinned to himself. "First gram sold. Here we go!" With €80 in his wallet, he could now buy that holy kettle and a stereo at the same time, It seemed very much like things were starting to get a lot better for him.

14.

He went along to Segundamano and bought his kettle, a bright yellow one. It had dust on it, so must have been there for some time. It was actually brand new, so he didn't understand why it was in a second hand shop. He wasn't aware that it is not common for Spaniards to own kettles, not being big tea drinkers and drinking filter coffee as a norm. Looking through the stereos, he chose to get one that was not the cheapest, but bought an Aiwa CD player for €30. Even though he still had money left over, thought he would wait until he was sure the money would start coming in before throwing it all away.

The first thing he did when he got back was make a cup of tea the normal way. Such a little difference meant the world to Andy and he put one of his few CDs in his new player: Blur's *13*. He stood on the balcony smoking and singing along to *Coffee & TV*, despite neither of those things being present with him at the time. It felt like he was really living in a home now and planned to get plenty more CDs soon.

Andy was in a good mood for the rest of the week, enjoying listening to music and not having to worry about the volume he played it at. He'd searched for somewhere that sold cheap CDs and it dawned on him that Spain didn't seem to have charity shops, which seemed odd, so he would wait a bit until he could afford them. Of course, his thoughts were still focused on selling his cocaine. After seeing the guy at Mosquito selling it outside, he didn't want to do it that way as he felt it would be risky to get caught. He still had to think of a way to sell more to Steve without him knowing that he'd found half a kilo. If he said he'd just got a few grams, it would mean he would have had to buy it in the first place, which wouldn't be realistic considering he was living on the breadline at the moment. He couldn't think of any other way to do it, so thought it would be good to get to know Steve better until he felt he could trust him. He trusted Paul, but when he told Andy that he was not into cocaine and seemed against it, maybe he wouldn't like to know that Andy was about to deal on a large scale.

When it came to Saturday, Paul, Steve and Jessica would be meeting Andy at Negrito, which was already their local bar. Andy thought about whether he should take another gram or two to sell it wherever they would end up at. Nobody would be aware of him as a dealer and he didn't want to ask anyone if they wanted to buy it. They might grass him up to the staff and he would be screwed right from the start. In the end he decided to compromise it and took one gram out with him.

Jessica was another teacher, but she worked at one of the other British schools a bit further out of the city. She was twenty six and black. It dawned on Andy that he hadn't seen many black people since he'd been here. Some tourists, but in terms of people who lived there, he'd seen the odd African immigrant, but Spain wasn't as culturally mixed as the UK. Jess, as she was generally known, was more outgoing than her flatmates. More animated and smiley than the rest of the group. They had three drinks before deciding to go to a club called Salamander, which was in the north of the old town. It was a fairly small club with the dance floor underground. It was pumping out house music that had a Latino flavour to it, which wasn't the kind of music that Andy looked for, but he was looking forward to taking the coke with Steve. Jessica didn't want any, but wasn't as much against it as Paul. Steve instructed Andy how he should go about it. "Just go into a toilet cubicle, make a line about this long and this thin, then just snort it hard." They took it in turns to go about it and it seemed quite relaxed in terms of security. There was a doorman, but he paid little attention to anyone going in and didn't monitor the inside. Andy was trying to work out if any of the other customers were high, but after he'd seen how lively the Spanish tended to be when dancing, he couldn't tell. The group hung around and danced to try to get in the mood, which felt like a trial for Andy, but after about half an hour he was starting to loosen up.

"I think it's working," he said to Steve.

"Yeah, me too. You found some good stuff there."

Andy was feeling more relaxed about dancing than he had ever felt before. The music was taking him over and he just wanted to smile at everyone. He was starting to understand why cocaine was used so much and it seemed like just the right thing to compliment this kind of music. Paul and Jessica danced with them and Paul was keeping his eye on Andy to see how he was doing. He was worried that he'd lose control, but he seemed to be having the time of his life, so he dropped his guard after a while. An hour and a half after they'd done a line each, Steve said he was going to do some more.

"Do you want some more?" he asked Andy. Andy felt like he had no inhibitions at this point and said yes. They both took some and went back to the dancing.

By now, Andy was talking endlessly to the other three. He was on the same level as Steve. Jessica was naturally talkative anyway, but Paul felt like Andy was going too far now.

"Mate, be careful with this stuff. It's addictive."

"I love it, man. I just feel so happy."

"I can see that, but don't take any more, will you? Things will go messy if you do too much."

"Ha! Don't worry, mate. I'm fine!" He went back to his dancing and Paul wasn't that comfortable with seeing him so off his head.

They stayed at the club till it closed at three, after which, Steve said they should go onto the next place.

"There's another one open?" Andy asked.

"Yeah, didn't you know? There are late night places here, so it's like the early ones and late ones."

"Oh, right." He was still feeling high and wanted to carry on. Paul had had enough and Jessica was tired after travelling over that day so they both went home. Paul wanted to have a word with the other two first.

"Steve, keep an eye on Andy. You're used to it, but he isn't."

"Don't worry, my man. I'll take care of him." Paul wasn't so sure about that, but there was nothing else that he could do.

They headed off and Steve took Andy to another place not far away called Casa Blanca. He put his arm around Andy's shoulder and and asked him, "Are you having a good night, then?"

"Yeah, brilliant! I can't believe I've never had coke before."

"I wish we had some more. We'll be able to find some when we get there, though."

"Oh, I've got another gram." He spoke before he thought about the consequences of saying that.

"You've got more? How?"

"What?" It still hadn't dawned on him. "I've brought some more with me, look." He pulled the bag out of his pocket and waggled it in Steve's face.

"Don't do that!" he warned. "I thought you'd only found a gram."

Andy was starting to become aware that he'd let too much slip, but he was too high to be able to care. "I've got loads of it at home."

"What the fuck?"

They arrived at Casa Blanca and could hear the music. Andy wanted to go straight in. At this interruption, he just said "I'll tell you later. Let's go in and take some more."

Steve wasn't sure what to think, but was also less able to care that much, so they did another line and stayed out for a couple more hours. By the end of it, both of them were coming down. Physically drained, but still mentally alert, they didn't say much afterwards and they went their separate ways.

Andy collapsed on his bed and lay awake for another hour, getting annoyed that he couldn't go to sleep. He woke up after about five hours.

"Christ, I feel like shit," he said as he sat up in bed. He tried to think about what had gone on last night and knew he'd had a good time, but had no idea what he'd been talking about. He dragged himself out of bed and made a cup of instant coffee. He flopped down into his office chair and small details of last night popped into his head. He remembered talking incessantly, but about what he had no idea. He'd gone to another club with Steve, but the other two went home. How much coke had he done? It was then that he remembered the extra bag he'd taken with him. "Did we do that?" He went to find his trousers and check his pockets. He couldn't find the bag and tried to think back. He remembered doing another line in the second place and giving some to Steve. "Did I tell him I had some more?" This memory wouldn't establish itself in his mind. "I must have done. What the fuck did I say?" He had no idea. He remembered that Steve didn't think he had any more. Maybe Steve didn't remember what happened, either. He hoped so.

Andy felt exhausted for the rest of the day. He had a nap early afternoon and went into work later than usual. He kept trying to work out if he'd told Steve about the stash he had, but his mind was a blur. His shift was more of a grind than usual and he slowly made his way around the jewellery shop.

Steve had been having a similar day, spending most of it in bed. Paul had asked him if Andy had been alright, to which Steve gave an unconvincing reply of "Yeah, he was fine" as he lay on his side. "Did he get home okay?"

"Mate, leave him alone. You're not his dad."

Paul then thought that he probably was being too protective. As Andy didn't earn much, he probably wouldn't do coke much. Maybe never again if he was suffering like Steve.

By Monday, Andy had recovered. It was still on his mind about what he had told Steve. As he hadn't heard anything from him, maybe he hadn't said anything or Steve had just forgotten. He hung around his flat and had a visit from Precious, which, as always, helped him to switch off for a few minutes. As soon as the cat had ambled off, Andy's thoughts were back to the question of what to do. He reluctantly accepted that he was probably going to have to peddle cocaine at clubs, at least for a while, then hope to get regular clients, whom he could sell to on demand. He remembered that he was going to see if there were any more drugs buried under the floor next door. On one hand, he didn't want to go through all the hassle of lifting all the floorboards, but if there was anything, he could double his money or even more. That was too tempting to let go. And there was the wardrobe. He doubted that anything would be in there, but he might as well try to break into it. This would be the easiest thing to do, so just after midnight, he went back over to break the lock off using his screwdriver as a chisel. It proved to be harder than he expected, so instead used it to lever open the doors. After a few minutes, trying to be as quiet as he could, he did it. All that it contained were a few coat hangers on the rail and nothing else. It would have been too obvious a hiding place for anything valuable and the landlord had probably locked it and taken the key with him.

So, the floorboards then... The back bedroom seemed like the place to start with. He'd already pulled up a few of them, but there must have been something like fifty or sixty to get through. Was it really worth it? He started in the corner of the room on the window side and got to work. Within half an hour he had lifted about twenty, but found nothing. The more he went on, the less hopeful he became. He didn't notice any that gave him the impression that they had been regularly lifted, so after working through half of the floor he called it a day and went back.

When he thought about it some more, he decided he should focus on the load that he already had. That was enough of a task in itself, so he made a decision not to go next door again.

On Tuesday, Andy got a text from Steve to ask if he wanted to go for a drink. He thought about it for a couple of minutes, wondering if Steve was going to interrogate him or if it was just to hang out. He had to face it. He didn't have to tell him the whole truth.

They met up at the usual place and chatted about Saturday night in a normal kind of way, just to see what each other thought about it and if Andy liked the effects of the cocaine.

"Yeah, it was great for dancing, but I can't remember anything that I talked about. I know I was talking a lot, but..."

"Yeah, that's one of the effects of it! It was good stuff though, it didn't seem like it was cut with anything too bad."

"What does that mean?" This was a new aspect to Andy.

"Coke always gets mixed with different things to dilute it. Easier to make more money if there's not just pure coke in it. It could be paracetamol, rat poison, all kinds of shit. I've had some coke that made my throat close up. I could barely swallow. Nasty stuff."

"Shit, that sounds bad."

"Yeah. Anyway, you had another bag with you. Where did you get that?"

This was not the question that Andy wanted to hear. Steve wouldn't believe him if he said he just happened to find another bag in the street, not that he could afford to buy another, so it was time to give him the full story.

"Right, I'm going to let you know something, but I really need you to keep this secret." Steve looked into his eyes with total focus. "You know I've been finding some furniture and stuff in the streets." Steve nodded. "Well, I saw a cigarette packet and I just looked in it in case there were any fags left in and it was full of bags of coke."

"Shit. Seriously?" How many?"

"Fifty."

"Bloody hell, man!"

"As you know, I'd never done coke before. I didn't even know that it was coke, so that's what I've been trying to find out."

"That's worth a lot of money."

"Yeah, fifty times eighty Euros, so four thousand."

"Fuck me!" It sounded like Steve believed his story.

"Indeed. But keep it to yourself, yeah?"

"Yes, of course. So how are you going to shift it?"

"That's what I don't really know. Do you know how I should?"

"Well, fifty bags isn't a lot to get rid of. You can easily off-load it at clubs. It shouldn't take you more than a few weeks. I can give you some pointers of where to go."

This was the kind of advice Andy wanted to hear even though this obviously wasn't the truth of it.

"Yeah, I guess so. Is that what dealers usually do?"

"Proper dealers get regular customers. They get people's phone numbers and deliver it to them whenever they ask for it, but you probably wouldn't need that for the amount you've got."

This was the insight that Andy was looking for, but how would he get regular clients? Maybe he could discuss it with one or two people he sold to and gradually build up a list like that.

"Yeah, fair enough. I'll just do that then. Do you want to buy any more?"

"I will. I haven't got the money just yet, but when I get paid, I'll buy a couple of grams off you."

"Cool. Just let me know then and if you know anyone else, send them my way."

"Yeah, I know a couple of other teachers who do it. When we start back at school, I'll let them know."

Andy was pleased to hear this. He thought that he would be able to get started and feel his way with selling. The only issue was getting rid of the rest of it without Steve finding out. Would he have to tell him eventually or would he be able to sell to other people and keep that hidden? "Step by step," he told himself.

15.

Catarina got home after work, just another day where she went through the motions doing the accounts for her father's company. He ran an architecture company in the centre and his daughter had worked for him for the last three years. She still lived with her parents, but her older brother, Alfonso, had moved away to Madrid a year ago. Being the boss's daughter meant that she could take things easy at work and she rarely stayed until the office closed.

The Martinez family lived in a reasonably large flat in the Russafa district, just south of the centre. Señor Martinez had built up his business over the last twenty-two years and he was a driven man. With nearly thirty employees, he was very direct with them as he wanted to see his business continually grow, not just for him and his wife, Silvia, but to ensure that his two children would have something to inherit in the future. He was very proud of his achievements and, whereas he was not entirely ruthless in terms of his business practice, he didn't work in collaboration with any other companies in his sector.

Catarina was twenty years old. Each morning she would spend over an hour getting ready for work. She would spend half of that time applying her make-up and various creams to her skin and the other half choosing her outfit for the day, even though she would mostly be situated behind her desk, out of the way of the other staff.

Her relationship with her mother was hit and miss. For the most part they would not have too much to talk about, but Catarina would turn on the charm when she wanted something. She was an ardent follower of fashion and had an extended wardrobe full of dresses, skirts, blouses and shoes. When she came home, as on this occasion, she would often turn on her music and try on different combinations of outfits to think about how she would dazzle the men and how the women would look at her with envy.

As she stood in front of her full length mirror, turning this way and that to see if her clothes made her look irresistible, she thought about what it would be like to get her own place to live. It was not something she had the intention of doing for some time yet, but she longed for a time when she could have everything her way, holding parties for selected people who would similarly long for the next one. She would have a swimming pool where she and her friends would be accompanied by muscular, tanned men who adored her. Not so much her friends, but just Princess Catarina.

On the other hand, living with her parents meant she didn't have to pay for anything like food or bills. Silvia always cooked their meals and, although she had tried to teach Catarina how to cook when she was younger, she had little success with getting her to be interested in spending time preparing meals when she didn't have to do it.

Andy couldn't stop himself thinking about the bigger picture. Five hundred grams of cocaine would take a long time to sell. He pictured himself being known as a drugs lord, but this image made him shirk at the idea. Would he really turn into someone with greasy hair, a tacky suit and sat at his table that was covered in piles of cash? As he had only seen such people depicted in films, he didn't know if real life would be like that. It was unlikely, but he was still going to amass a lot of money. What would he do with it? He didn't want to have tens of thousands of Euros piled up under his mattress. If he became Valencia's drugs lord, people would end up knowing where he lived somehow. He had barely been out of the centre so far, so the city felt like it was a village to him. He could probably get away with depositing small amounts in his bank account every week. How much would not look suspicious? €200? He would need to think of something to tell Jesus that made it seem like he was doing some honest freelance work. Being a freelance cleaner would be easy enough. He wasn't going to give up his agency work just yet; he wanted to make sure that he had got his new actual freelance trade set up well, but if he made the full €40k over a year, he didn't think he would be able to slyly put all of that into his account.

He got a piece of paper to look at the sums. 40,000 divided by 12 was 3,333 or about €760 a week. If he put in, say, €300 of that each time, he'd still have more than half of it in cash. He thought about what he would spend his money on. As he'd grown up in a family that wasn't rich or poor, decently well-off but he still had to learn to manage his finances, Andy was not someone who wasn't used to throwing his money away. He knew he planned to buy a TV and a computer, maybe some better furniture and some more clothes, but he didn't think that would amount to a great deal. If he paid for everything in cash there would be a limit to how much he could spend at a time as he couldn't go into a shop with €500 in used notes, surely.

He was certainly out of his comfort zone, but hoped that it would be like starting any new job. He would learn things along the way, but the biggest fear for Andy was coming across unsavoury people who might beat him up and steal his money or cocaine. He had never been someone who had got into fights. He was more of a person that would flee from an aggressive situation. Would he have to learn how to man up? He had no desire to go down that road and didn't think he would be able to turn into a tough guy. It was just not in his blood.

He reeled himself back in and remembered what he was supposed to be focussing on for now – the fifty grams that apparently only existed. That shouldn't take long to get rid of. If he could shift that in a month, he'd be laughing. Four grand in his pocket seemed reasonable to keep mostly as cash. He could maybe put a thousand in his account and just get himself above his meagre means.

Andy made a tentative plan for the weekend; he would go out with ten grams on Friday and see if he could sell all that. He still felt nervous about making it known to any strangers that he was selling, but there was no other way around it. He'd have to bite the bullet and start speaking to people. It's not like he would be shouting from the rooftops or anything and hopefully it would be an easy enough way to get started.

Over the rest of the week, Andy set out again to wander the streets and find more clubs. He was getting to know the centre well now. "Maybe I should be a tour guide as well," he thought. "Show people where the good clubs are then sell them cocaine at the end of it." He wanted to venture further afield as well, but without knowing where anywhere was and the streets becoming more residential, he only found one other. It didn't help when it was daytime and places were closed. There were enough clubs in the centre to get started with and Steve was going to tell him about some more soon.

On Friday night, he didn't want to hear from his friends so that he could just get on with his mission and avoid questions. No-one texted him, so he made a plan of going to some of the ones he knew to hang around for a relatively short time, see if he could sell anything and if not, go on to the next place. Mosquito was the obvious place to start, so he got there at midnight. There weren't too many people there yet, about fifteen and this gave him the chance to scout out the clientele and try to gauge who might be interested. He saw a group of three guys who looked younger than him. Two with dark hair and one with long, blond hair. Maybe tourists, they may want a bit of extra fun if they were here for a short time. As he observed them, he became more nervous about going to talk to them. They may think he was gay and was trying to hit on one of them. How could he get close to them without looking dodgy? He casually walked in their general direction, but without looking at them. He wanted to see if he could hear what language they were speaking. He was only about three metres away when he stopped to pretend he was not taking any notice, but he couldn't hear them over the music. As he was doing this, he heard a voice come from over his shoulder. He turned and it was the blond one. "Hallo. Are you on holiday, too?" he asked Andy. Andy greeted him and said no, he was waiting for his friends to come.

"Okay. I thought that because you don't look Spanish, maybe you are a tourist." He could just make out that he had a German accent.

"No, I live here. Where are you from?"

"We are from Austria. I'm Tomas. Come and meet my friends."

Andy thought that this was a potential good sign. Getting to talk to three Austrian tourists already meant he may be able to turn the conversation towards drugs. Andy spoke to Tomas, Alex and Nils for a while, telling them about the nightlife scene here and asking what they were looking for. Andy was still reluctant to get to his point and the conversation was starting to die out as more people came in and attentions got diverted. The tourists were on the look out for girls, that was evident, and Andy wondered how he could get back to talking to them some more. Other than drugs, he couldn't think of anything to say when Tomas asked him if he wanted a drink. Andy agreed, which meant he should be able to stay with them for a bit longer. Tomas went to the bar and bought some beers and they all said "Proust." Everyone went back to looking around at the other people in there for a couple of minutes, when Tomas leaned in and asked Andy if he knew anyone who sold any drugs.

"Erm, yeah. I have some coke if you're interested."

"Really? That would be great."

THE EMPTY FLAT

"I have a few grams. They are €80 each." Tomas went back to his friends to pass on the news while Andy watched their body language to see if they looked likely to buy. Tomas came back and asked for two grams. Andy explained that they should go outside to do the sale and Tomas spoke to his friends, who surreptitiously handed him some money, then followed Andy out. The doorman paid no attention like last time and they walked a little way so that they were out of sight. Tomas wanted to taste it first and was satisfied, so he gave Andy the money and took two grams. He told Tomas to go back in by himself first as he thought that would look less suspicious. Andy pottered around for a short while, casually trying to spot any other potential buyers while smoking a cigarette; a perfect reason to go outside even though smoking was permitted indoors.

He put his cigarette out and went back in, behind a couple of women who'd just arrived. Andy went back over to the Austrians and they all looked happy to have done business with him.

"Well, that was easy enough," Andy thought. He felt like his first hurdle had been overcome and he felt more confident now.

As the night progressed and people started dancing, Andy was tempted to do a line himself, but reminded himself that he was 'working'. He could afford to buy his customers some beers, then he went to try to find some others. He noticed the two women who had been in front of him when he came in. They both looked Spanish and were well-dressed and attractive, but he wasn't there to try to pick anyone up. There were about thirty or so people in there now, so he liked how he was able to hide amongst the crowd more and not raise suspicion. Another half hour passed and he hadn't got anywhere yet. He wanted to be more proactive, but whenever he thought about it, the more reclusive he became. Time for another cigarette outside. A change of scenery might help.

There were six or seven people out there, all Spanish and chatting loudly. Their behaviour was too intimidating for him to go up to them and ask if they wanted to buy. This wasn't the way he should be going about it, but how would anyone else know that he had anything?

As he was stuck in this mental battle, those two women came outside. They were standing not too far from him and he noticed one of them look at him and give a little smile. She had her long hair tied back and he'd already worked out that she was the less attractive of the two in his opinion, but he smiled back. He stood there minding his own business, no longer looking at them, but looking for any signs from the other people around. The woman who smiled at him came over and asked for a light. Andy produced it and she spoke to him in Spanish, asking him where he was from. He told her England and she introduced herself as Ana. He went to shake her hand, but she laughed and said that people don't do that in Spain and she gave him the customary kiss on either cheek. Ana continued talking to him and Andy struggled to understand, but more or less got by. He wasn't interested in hanging out with her really, but he could tell she was as she told him that she liked his hair and touched it in a flirty way. Andy smiled with his mouth, but not with his eyes. He thought fuck it, he would just ask her.

"Quieres comprar cocaina?" he said quietly into her ear.

"La tienes?" She asked if he had it. He said he did and how much it was. Ana did the same thing as Tomas and beckoned Andy to walk off away from the door. They did the exchange and Ana wanted him to continue hanging round with her and her friend. He agreed to and they went inside, the women going to the toilet together, but Ana pointed out they would be back soon.

A few minutes later, after doing the deed, they came back. Both of them were trying to imperceptibly sniff the remaining coke that was stuck in their sinuses. Ana asked him if he had taken some, too.

He said he had, just in case they tried to coerce him in doing some, but explained it hadn't taken effect yet. By now, the club was fairly full and the atmosphere was improving. The women tried to get him to dance once they were getting high and Andy had to pretend that he was on the same level as them. He didn't really want to be in their company. Ana was flirting with him, but he fancied her friend more, which was annoying him. A bizarre love triangle, he thought. They kept saying things to him, but he couldn't understand them over the music. He kept up his charade for a few more minutes, but wanted to be rid of them, so he gestured that he was going to the toilet.

He used this tactic to go there, then disappear into the crowd and sneak his way out. He kept his head down and was out the door. When he was having a piss, he thought about what he'd achieved: three grams, €240. He was satisfied with that, but didn't want to go through it again, so he headed off home.

Having this much money in his pockets made him feel vulnerable. He kept an eye open for anyone who went past him when he was in a quiet area. He had no idea what he would do if someone tried to mug him, but nothing happened and he got back to his flat unscathed.

He shut the front door and breathed a sigh of extreme relief. He hadn't sold the full ten grams he went out with, but realised that it would be hard to even carry €800 in one go. This meant he'd have to rethink his tactics and it might slow down the whole practice, but he pulled out all the money from his pockets and dropped it on the table.

This brought him back to his senses and he calmed down. Two hundred and forty fucking Euros just for going out for a couple of hours. He tried to let it sink in, but it wasn't working just yet. He realised that he had been feeling pretty stressed all the time he was out, but he'd achieved something.

He got a glass of water, lit a fag and went onto the balcony. He was thrilled to see Precious outside, who meowed up to him. He made kiss noises to him or her – he would have to try and find out which one it was one day – but he didn't want to go back outside just now. Precious stayed around for a few minutes, then realising it wasn't getting much from Andy, sauntered off.

As tired as he was now, he couldn't stop thinking about exactly what had happened that night – how he'd managed to sell the drugs, what he felt he could have done better, and whether it was enough to just go about it the same way every time. He finally got to sleep after tossing and turning in bed for over an hour.

16.

As soon as he woke up, he thought "€240." It was about as much as he made in two weeks from his cleaning. This time he wasn't going to hold back on it and he would go and buy something more expensive that day. A television would be great. He missed watching the football, so, being something of an expert on knowing where the shops were, there was an electrical shop just over the ring road, so he went there and bought a moderately sized one for €150. It was reconditioned, but should do the job. He knew there was an aerial socket in his front room wall, so he lugged it back home and connected it. There were a decent number of channels for terrestrial TV, but a lot of them looked awful. Tacky shopping channels and low quality soap operas, but he would do some research and find where he could see the footy. He wasn't that fussed about watching much else, but it could be another useful background noise device for him and it made the place feel more like home.

He went back out and noticed that he was in a surprisingly chirpy mood. He knew the cause of it, but didn't feel that guilty about making some dirty money as everything had gone smoothly and in a friendly manner, so it all looked like he was going to carry on like this. Even if he only went out one night a week to sell a few grams, that would make him enough to live on. It was yet another sunny day, there hadn't been any other kind since he moved here and he went to get an iced coffee in television square.

He now wanted to work out if this was a plan he should stick to. Three grams sold a week would bring him around a thousand a month. With his rent so cheap at €160 and whatever the bills would be, he should be absolutely fine. Maybe €700 to spend on what he wanted and not having to work. It also got around the problem of having to deposit that much into his account. However,

Paul and the others would be starting back at school next week, so he would have all this time to himself, which he knew would get boring. What could he do with the time? There was no point in staying on with the agencies if he was making that much or probably more money and he hadn't got any work from the other he'd signed up to, but he would need a hobby of some kind. Or more friends.

Andy still wasn't that confident with his Spanish, but in reality, from living here it was improving more quickly than he realised. He would like to have more Spanish friends. The people were very sociable here, but he'd need to get talking to some people by chance to see if he could fit in with them. He knew things didn't happen that easily, but when left with so much time on his own, it was hard sometimes just to get round to doing some things if he didn't feel at ease doing them.

As he'd spent most of yesterday's money on a TV, he thought that maybe it would be a good idea to try and sell some more tonight. It might be good to get some more experience under his belt in case he lost the momentum by next weekend. He thought about just taking five grams with him and not making too much of an effort because of the uncomfortable feeling it gave him from watching everybody that went in. He wanted to try a different venue as well and not get too stuck on Mosquito. The clubs on Caballeros were too risky to try out as they were exposed, being on a main street, but he'd seen a few others hidden down dingy side streets. There was one called MX that he thought about trying out, so that was his plan.

Andy hung around by himself for the afternoon and got a text from Paul at half past six, asking if he wanted to meet them tonight. Would that get in the way of his plans? He could do with some company and it wouldn't be the end of the world if he didn't sell anything. He agreed to meet them.

He met both Paul and Steve at the usual place. Jessica wanted to have a quiet night in so she wouldn't be hungover before starting back at work and the two guys also weren't planning on having a big night. It was on Andy's mind all the time that the topic of his cocaine would come up, which he didn't want to happen unless Steve said he wanted to buy some. They talked about school and what Andy had been up to, but he avoided talking about last night and said he'd stayed in. Eventually, Paul couldn't keep it in any more and brought up the subject.

"So have you managed to sell any of your stuff yet?"

"Not yet," Andy replied. "I'll just take it easy and see what happens."

Steve didn't add to the conversation as he knew he was involved in it, which Paul wasn't a fan of.

"How are you planning to go about it?" Paul asked.

"I don't know. I'll probably just take a couple of packets out and see if anyone asks." As this was closer to the truth, he didn't feel bad about saying it.

"I just hope you're not going to get into any trouble. Be careful, yeah?"

"I will." That brought the topic to close quickly and they left it there. As they continued to sit around and observe the crowd in the square, Andy noticed something.

"There seem to be a lot of people here wearing glasses," he said. The others looked around and noticed the same thing.

"You're right," Paul said. "I hadn't noticed that before. I wonder what that's all about."

There were around twenty people in and outside Negrito with glasses on. They wondered if it was a group identity kind of thing. Did people with glasses subconsciously go there because they felt it was their crowd?

It was Paul's turn to get a round in and when he went to the bar, Steve wanted to delve back into the topic of the drugs.

"So did you actually sell anything?"

"Yeah, I sold three grams last night at Mosquito."

"How did it go?"

Andy proceeded to tell him how it happened and Steve congratulated him. Before they could talk any more about it Paul came back.

"There were three people at a table in there, all in glasses," Paul said.

"Ha, there's definitely something going on. Some kind of secret society," Steve said.

The other two stayed for one more drink and headed off, Andy saying he was going to do the same. It was getting towards one o'clock and Andy still wanted to go to MX. He made his way there to find it was a similar kind of club, but the music was more pop-based and less housey. It was a bit bigger than Mosquito and Andy was pleased to see there were more people already there this time.

He felt more secure about going in on his own with five grams in his pocket, but here, the doorman wanted to search him. "Oh, fuck," he thought and was about to make a quick exit, but didn't have time to make his decision. The doorman ran his hands over his body, but not searching for every detail. When he was satisfied that Andy wasn't carrying any weapons, he let him go in. Andy tried his best to keep a neutral expression and went inside.

His heart was pumping fast and he found it hard to calm down. What if he'd found the drugs? Would the guy have called the police? People were milling about the club and some were dancing, but Andy was stuck outside the bubble. He tried to look like nothing was going on inside his head, but was finding it hard to feel grounded. He tried to look at the other clubbers, but his eyes kept diverting towards the door. "Chill out," he told himself. "He didn't find anything." However, he felt out of his depth and had no desire to try to sell anything. He gave himself ten minutes to see if he could shake this fear, but couldn't properly settle, so he made his way out and went back home.

When he was back in the safe zone of his flat, he wanted to process this experience. He wasn't yet ready to be a drug dealer. Even though he hadn't got caught, the searching procedure had sent him into panic mode. He couldn't observe it as an outsider and see both sides of it. He put his hand on his chest. His heart felt normal, but he was still on edge. He took the bags out of his pocket and put them in a drawer. He wanted to be disconnected from them. "I'm not cut out for this," he said. Time for a cigarette.

17.

The next day, Andy didn't want to stay at home as he kept thinking about last night and wanted a change of scenery. He thought about texting Paul or Steve, but decided against it as he knew that he'd still have it in the back of his mind and be worried that either of them would bring it up again. He went back to television square with his self-study Spanish book to try and keep his mind occupied. It was another pleasant day with only a few light clouds drifting slowly by. He ordered an orange juice and opened his book. As he tried to make progress with learning verbs in the past tense, he found it difficult to concentrate and could only stick with it for about fifteen minutes. He gave up, closed the book and looked around. There were people walking their dogs, plenty of children running around the square and the usual leisurely strolls of all kinds of people criss-crossing each other's paths while engaged in conversation. He tried to take notice of what he saw and forced himself to mentally commentate on the clothes they wore or whether he found anyone attractive. After a while, he saw a woman to his right that he thought he recognised. He watched her as she crossed the square and realised that it was Ana. She was by herself and just seemed to be on her way somewhere. As she got directly in front of Andy, she stopped and looked for something in her handbag. She pulled out her phone and put it to her ear. Andy watched her for no other reason than he knew who she was and how her body language was. She stayed in the same spot while turning this way and that, not giving away too much about the type of conversation she was having. She turned towards Andy and he thought that she caught his eye, but she carried on talking and evidently hadn't. She spoke for a minute or two and put the phone back in her bag. From this, she looked over to the terrace where he was sat and at this point she did notice him. It didn't seem that she recognised him at first, but she spotted his blond hair and took a few seconds to register who it was. Then, he saw her give a smile and she came over to him.

"Hola, como estas?" she asked with a smile.

He replied that he was fine. She told him that she was due to meet a friend, who was now going to be late and asked if she could join him for a while. Andy didn't have any reason to say no, so he invited her to sit down.

As expected, their conversation soon turned to Friday night. She asked him where he went as he'd suddenly disappeared without saying goodbye. Andy just said he was tired and needed to go home. She noticed his book on the table and asked him how his Spanish was coming along.

"It's okay," he said. "I was looking at the past tense."

"My English is not very good," Ana said. "I study at school, but I not very good at speaking."

"It's good," he reassured her. "I can understand you."

She smiled at his words and Andy thought that she was about to start flirting with him again. Then she spotted a waiter and ordered a coffee. She would be staying with him for a while. Andy didn't really want her company for very long. He was starting to feel uncomfortable, especially as he'd walked out on her and the had issues of the language barrier, but she tried to speak to him in English and asked what his work was.

"I'm a cleaner." She didn't understand the word, so he told her in Spanish.

"Ah, bien. Cleaner. Where?"

He told her about the few places he worked in and the waiter brought her coffee to the table. She told him that she worked for a solicitor and they had a brief chat about that to pass the time. All of a sudden, she wanted to ask him about what she'd bought off him on Friday.

"The cocaina," she said, almost in a whisper "It was good. Do you have more?"

"Yes, but not now."

"No, no. In the future."

"Yes, that's no problem."

"What is your phone number?"

He thought it was fine to give her that as he sort of knew her and she seemed like she wouldn't be any trouble.

"Okay," she said. "I give you my number. Maybe we go for a drink one day?"

Andy wanted to keep her sweet so he smiled and nodded to her.

"Okay. I see my friend now. I write you when I need the ..."

She kissed him on both cheeks and jogged over the square to meet her friend, who didn't appear to be the other woman he'd seen her with on Friday. They walked off away from him and out of sight.

Andy felt that their interaction had gone quite well. She didn't come across too pushy and most importantly he had his first contact in his phone and hoped that she would become a regular customer. He felt more relaxed again as this was a far better way of conducting business. He wasn't sure how they would arrange the sales yet. Would they just meet up somewhere in public? At a club? Go to her flat? "Whatever," he thought. "Let's just take it as it comes." He looked down at his book and wondered if he should get back to his studying. He opened it to the chapter he was on, but wasn't really taking in what he was reading as he was now thinking that he was back on track with the drugs and thought of other possible contacts that would come about eventually.

Andy felt like he had a clearer head when he got back home. After his mind racing through so many conflicting scenarios, worries, hopes and expectations, he finally remembered that he still hadn't got round to finishing painting his flat. Now that he had some spare cash, he would go and get more paint tomorrow and try to get it done.

He brought back two large cans of light blue paint to do the main part of the living room. As he laid out everything he needed, he put his stereo on and was able to absorb himself in this activity for most of the day. This was exactly the kind of thing he needed and after three hours he got the sky effect on all four walls, went back to get some red paint for the lower section and finished it by early evening. His north facing window didn't help him to see how it really looked, but he stood back and admired what he'd achieved. It was a world away from the dirty walls he'd had for a month now and it helped to feel grounded again. He needed to do things that would take his mind off what he was struggling to deal with and the next day he would paint his bedroom. That too had textured walls which he also painted light blue. He left the ceiling white as that was in a good state and the pillars in the two corners at the head end of the bed were done in light brown. He was amazed at how much of a difference this made and it gave him a sense of well-being to be living somewhere that now felt like his own. He wasn't going to bother doing anything with the spare bedroom as he rarely went in there and didn't even have enough possessions to need to store anything in there.

It was now September and Andy had been in Spain for a mere six weeks. With everything that he'd gone through, it felt like about four months. He thought back to arriving in Bilbao and he could barely remember anything about it. When he looked back on Madrid, he knew he had made the right decision to leave there. He'd never felt settled and the memory of how busy it was didn't sit well with him. It was good to meet the Kiwi guys; a shame it didn't last, but Sean was the best person he'd known there. Andy smiled as he thought about how he'd given him a chance to do the cleaning for a few days and the advice he'd given him. Even though it had been a whirlwind of a time so far in Valencia, he was starting to feel like it was becoming a home for him. He just hoped that he'd get his head round things and start to feel more settled.

Thinking about Ana again, he wondered if he should pursue a relationship with her. He wasn't sure if he was attracted to her still, but she was definitely happy to see him again on Sunday. Maybe he should call her and go for a drink to get to know her better. Maybe a relationship with her would help him to integrate more with other Spanish people as he was bound to meet her friends. This was something he felt he lacked right now – proper friends. Paul was great, but Andy was hiding a big secret from him. Steve knew a bit more about what was going on, but he was still being kept in the dark to some extent. Andy wished that he didn't have to hold back the truth or even be in his current situation. It would be better to have a normal life, but then again, that would just mean working part time and earning just enough money to scrape by on. "Why does everything have to be so difficult?" he sighed.

He also wanted to avoid thinking about it all the next day and thought he really should check out the beach. He wasn't really a beach kind of guy, but that was one of things that drew him here and he hadn't even seen it yet. He wondered why no-one else he'd met had talked about it, either.

He found which bus would take him there and he got a few things together and headed off. It took about half an hour to get there and he was surprised to see that the neighbourhoods near the beach were pretty grim. He expected that there'd be expensive houses by the coast, but it resembled a council estate and he didn't notice anything that made it look worth checking out.

The beach itself was nothing very special except that it was very big. About four kilometres long, fifty metres wide and just flat, with no rocky areas or anything that stood out all the way along.

THE EMPTY FLAT

There were palm trees along the promenade, which added to the scarce ambience and a few little cafés and restaurants that didn't look like they would entice the tourists. There were no hotels, bars or clubs on the main road and he felt like the council were missing a huge opportunity for development. Just a great expanse of nothing. Hence, he didn't stay around for long as there was nothing to do, so he got the bus back.

On the journey, as the bus driver pulled over at the side of the road to pick up passengers, the driver got off the bus. Andy suspected he needed to check something, but he just went across the road and into a café. Andy was confused and guessed he needed to make a phone call. He watched the driver as he sat down at the counter and ordered a cup of coffee. No-one else on the bus seemed to be surprised at this, but Andy had never known this to happen before. After five minutes, the driver came back and they carried on their journey. Andy just sat there trying to figure this out, with a confused look on his face, but they made it back to the city without the driver deciding to visit his parents or anything.

After having three days break from making his business plans, Andy was inevitably drawn back into it. He'd got it in his head that he was starting to build up some regular contacts. Steve and Ana were two now and he was sure others would slowly start drifting towards him. He wasn't going to rush into anything yet. Just keep checking out the clubs, seeing which places searched people and which weren't bothered, but without taking any drugs with him. Andy felt that if he sold the odd gram here and there, it would help him and then, maybe after a month or two, the sales would pick up and he could make any more decisions as and when. He might ask Ana if she wanted to meet up this weekend; just for a coffee so they could talk instead of going out and getting drunk or high, and not being able to talk because of loud music.

Although he liked the idea of slowing things down like this, that huge package of cocaine in his home was still a burden that he had to deal with. Right now, he was keeping it hidden under things in his wardrobe, but if for some reason he got caught, that wouldn't take five minutes to find. He toyed with the idea of making something with a false base, but ideally he wouldn't keep it in something that was moveable as that would be easy to find or steal. The toilet cistern was a well-known place to store drugs, that much he was aware of, but the police would go there for certain. Also behind the bath panel was too obvious. As he looked around his flat, nothing seemed like a clever idea, but as he'd found it under a floorboard next door, surely that would be the best option. He still had no idea if the police had been round there, but there must have been something suspicious that meant the dealer who'd lived there had been found out. He remembered that where he'd found it didn't look very conspicuous, so maybe he should carefully select one in his flat as well.

Which room was he going to plump for? The spare room seemed like it would be another obvious place to look, but would it make any difference where it was? He just needed somewhere to keep the bulk of it and another place to keep his small bags that he would work on selling at any given time.

To Andy, it seemed like the kitchen would be the least suspicious for some reason. Then again, would those fucking cockroaches get to it and rip the cellophane open? That might lead to moisture getting in or mould. He didn't have any idea if coke went mouldy. He could do with getting a plastic box just big enough to fit it in that would squeeze under the floorboard.

When he finally deduced which board would look inconspicuous, one that was between the cooker and the bathroom, he very carefully prized it up then pushed it back down to see how it looked. It seemed to look the same, so he got it up

THE EMPTY FLAT 145

again and made measurements to go out and find a box that would do the job. Back to the cheapo shop.

After checking the measurements of boxes there, he couldn't find one that held 500 grams that was small enough, so went for two 250g containers that had sealable lids. This would also give him the option of storing half of it somewhere else if the need arose. He didn't know what that need would be, but better to keep his options open, he thought.

Back at home, he tested the boxes and they would both fit fine, so now was the task of meticulously scooping the cocaine into the two boxes without making a mess. He went through this process as though he was deactivating a bomb. Using a dessert spoon, he moved slowly from the cellophane to the boxes, gently pressing them down so that no dust would fly up. The concentration on his face was professional, rarely blinking whenever he took the next spoonful. The first box was full and he placed the lid on and sealed it. He looked happy with himself and moved it aside.

As he picked up the spoon again, he heard his doorbell ring. "What the fuck?" he thought. He instantly thought that the police were right on his tail. He looked at the table and started to panic. He didn't know what to do first. Who the hell was it? The only people who knew where he lived were Paul and Steve and they should be at work now. Ana? She didn't know, or did she? Who else could it be? He grabbed the full box and put it in the floor. He raced back to the living room and as carefully, but as quickly as he could, placed it beside the box as though he was putting a baby in its cot. He went back. The doorbell rang again. He looked at the spoon, which was the only piece of evidence left. Fuck it, he thought and threw it in the drawer of the sideboard. He opened the door and went downstairs, his heart almost beating its way out of his chest. At the last second, he tried to switch to calm mode and opened the door as normally as possible. It was Maria, the landlady.

"Buenos dias," he said, while at the same time thinking "Why the fuck are you here?"

She asked him if everything was okay with the flat. He replied that it was. She told him that she was just in the area and thought she would see if he needed anything. Andy said that he was fine. "Please go, please go," he thought, while trying not to look like he was hiding €40,000 worth of cocaine.

She asked if it was possible to see the flat. He had no choice but to say yes and let her in. She followed him up the stairs and his mind was racing with thoughts of whether he had hidden everything. It was then that he realised he hadn't put the floorboard back on. His eyes opened wider than if he'd just come up on coke. "Oh, fuck," he almost said out loud. They entered the flat and to his relief, Maria noticed the painting that he'd recently done. He looked at her as she looked around at the walls. She seemed intrigued more than impressed, but told him it was good. He was desperately trying to work out how he could get away from her for a moment and quietly put the floorboard back down. She moved towards the balcony and looked around the door frame. Andy used this distraction to make his move. With her back turned, he briskly walked backwards into the kitchen, softly stepping so she wouldn't have heard that he'd left the room. He grabbed the floorboard and pressed it down. At that moment, he heard Maria's footsteps getting louder. He stood back up just as she appeared round the corner. She inspected the kitchen and asked if everything was okay here. Andy nodded and said "Si," in as passive a way as Maria always seemed to be. She quickly looked through the bedroom door, noticed his paintwork there and was satisfied with her intrusion.

Without any more questions, Maria said "Vale, gracias" and walked back to the front door. Andy was having to stop himself from pushing her through it. He wanted her out of here five minutes ago. "Adios," she said as she went down the stairs. "Adios," Andy replied. He heard her close the metal door and he shut the front door. He put his hands up to his face and covered his eyes for a few seconds, not able to think of any words. Once the moment had passed, he sneakily looked out of the balcony window to see if she had gone and he saw her further up the street until she was out of sight.

18.

"How much longer am I going to get away with this?" Andy thought as he stared at the pavement beneath him. He couldn't believe he'd forgotten to put the floorboard back on, but at least he just about made it in time. He went back to the kitchen to see how it looked, but because he knew exactly which one it was, it was impossible to see it with innocent eyes. He looked around at various items in the room, not knowing what else he expected to see, then looked at the cooker. His thoughts became diverted as he remembered that he needed to sort out buying another gas bottle at some point. He still had no idea how much was left in it, but he would have to make a note of finding out how to order it. He'd seen lorries around the city with big bottles on the back, so they obviously got delivered. He could do with having the *Páginas Amarillas,* but was also unaware of where to get from from.

He took a deep breath and was glad Maria hadn't suspected anything. He wondered why she was always so passive about everything. He'd only met her three times, but she never showed any emotion at all. Maybe she'd had some bad tenants before; that would explain the filth he encountered when he moved in. He didn't know if she was married, had any kids or anything about her. He doubted that she would ever reveal anything about herself, but he wished she had phoned him before turning up. That was how landlords had to do things in England.

He didn't want to bother sorting out the gas today, but knew that there was a small *Telefonica* shop just down the road on the main street. He went along there to ask if they had any *Páginas Amarillas,* which they didn't and he was told they got delivered to the flats. Whatever, he'd have to do without for now and find a gas shop somewhere.

Andy had another stroll about town as it always helped to clear his mind. He thought about Ana and whether he should text her

THE EMPTY FLAT

to meet up at the weekend. She'd probably be at work now as it was half past four, so made a mental note to try later.

Right now he could do with some company. The others would still be at school, so that would have to wait, too. He didn't want to go home yet, so did his usual of going to a café for an hour or so, just watching people saunter by.

At eight o'clock, he texted Ana to ask if she wanted to go for a coffee on Saturday. He didn't hear back from her for half an hour when she said that she could meet. They arranged to go to the same place where they last met at midday. The arrangement didn't make Andy feel that excited, but he wondered if Ana was, as he was sure she was more interested in him.

"Should I play it cool and let her know that I just want to take things slowly?" he thought. He had to work out a few lines in Spanish to be able to explain himself clearly, but even in a foreign language it sounded too clinical and heartless, so he thought he might just see what happens on the day.

The next day, whenever he was in the kitchen, he tried to see if the floorboard looked less normal than usual. He guessed it looked fine even though he always knew exactly which one it was. Before too long, he decided to go out and get the gas sorted. He walked around the ring road and after about half an hour saw one of the lorries. He took down the phone number that was written on the side, but didn't feel confident to make phone calls in Spanish yet, so waited for the driver to come back and asked him how he should do it. It was as easy as phoning up, telling them his address and what type of gas and size bottle he wanted. He would have to give them his empty bottle, which was annoying as it meant he'd have to wait a day or two without being able to use the cooker.

This also made him think about the heating. It felt like it would be hot all through the year here, but would have to think about getting some kind of heating. He had no radiators or heater in the flat, but maybe when he was richer, this wouldn't be a problem. "I wonder when I will feel that I'm rich," he thought. "Maybe in a month or two?" It still seemed like an unrealistic outcome for him and being left alone with his thoughts so much, the time dragged on.

That evening, he had work at the office and was actually glad to go there as the day had been uneventful. He arrived at *Plaza de la Reina* at his usual time of seven o'clock. Usually, he saw no-one in the building, but just as he went through the main door, he saw a woman on her way out. He didn't pay much attention to her, but as she passed him, she seemed familiar. He looked over his shoulder but couldn't see her face any more. He turned his vision towards the inside of his head to examine the mental image that was still lingering in his short term memory. He could see her face; she was attractive, with make-up on and long brown hair. Dressed elegantly. He was sure he'd seen her somewhere before. He shrugged and carried on up the stairs thinking that he was bound to see some people more than once, given the amount of time he walked around the place.

While Andy was at work, he got a text from Steve, asking if he wanted to go out tonight. This made Andy smile as he was craving some human interactions now. The usual code of "Neg 10" was easily understood, then Andy received another text saying "Bring 2g". At this Andy beamed. Another easy sale. Perfect. He wondered if someone else who used it would be out, too.

After thinking about going out tonight, he remembered that he didn't want to be carrying around so much money and asked Steve if he could come to his place first. A simple "OK" was relayed back.

As expected, Andy went through the process of checking his flat carefully to make sure that nothing would look suspicious. He looked at the crucial floorboard three times until he was sure that it wouldn't be spotted and he kept five one gram bags in the middle

THE EMPTY FLAT

drawer in the living room sideboard. He then thought that he didn't even want Steve to know where he kept these, so as he knew he'd ordered two grams, he took those out as well as another two and put them in his jeans pocket.

Steve arrived shortly before ten o'clock. Andy welcomed him in and Steve's first remark was about his decoration work.

"Oh, this looks good, man."

"Thanks. It makes the place a bit brighter."

"Yeah, so much better than those dirty walls. So, how's things?"

"I'm fine, cheers. How are you?"

"Pretty good. School has started off alright. The students are settling into their new year, but no dramas to speak of."

"Good stuff. So I've got your two grams here," Andy said as he pulled them out of his pocket.

"Nice one," Steve replied as he took out the €160 from his wallet. "Have you managed sell much yet?"

"Just a few grams, nothing special, really."

"How much have you got left now?"

"About forty grams."

"Okay. I haven't spoken to anyone else about it yet. My mind's mainly on school at the moment."

"Sure, no worries. Just let me know when you do."

"How did you manage to sell them?"

"I just got lucky when I was out one night and some people asked if I knew where they could get some coke, so I told them I had it and they bought it."

"Were they locals?"

"One was, the others were some Austrian tourists."

"Well, that's a good start. You'll get rid of it in no time."

They headed off to meet the others, so still had ten minutes to talk. Andy told him that he was due to meet Ana tomorrow and that she'd bought a gram off him.

"Are you trying to get her as a regular contact or do you fancy her?"

"Hopefully as a regular contact. I'm not sure if I fancy her, to be honest. Just going to see how it goes."

"Yeah, fair enough. Just try and keep on good terms with her if you two don't get together, so that she keeps buying off you."

They arrived at Negrito and Paul and Jess were already there. They joined them at a table outside. They discussed how their first week back had been for them and Andy just told them about how he'd been painting the flat and that work was going alright. Paul seemed fine with that news and Andy interpreted his responses as not wanting to talk about the drugs.

They passed the time together for another half an hour or so as the usual crowds of revellers went this way and that. It was yet another warm evening, which always helped people to stay in good spirits. After a while, Jess went to the toilet and Steve got some drinks in. At this point, Andy started to feel a little tense. Even though Paul was his closest friend here, he was feeling somewhat distanced from him and couldn't think of anything to say at that time. Paul was also sat there without saying anything for a few seconds, until he thought of something.

"Still selling the stuff then?"

Andy didn't like the way he had been so direct and interrogative with his question, but told him the same thing he had told Steve. He wanted to keep this conversation to an absolute minimum. Paul just nodded and said nothing in return. Steve and came back with the drinks and Jess returned shortly after and this was a relief to Andy as he had felt the tension escalating in those few seconds.

The conversation turned back to usual things like some of the other teachers and students. Even though Andy was an outsider to all of this, he was glad to know the topic had definitely changed and he had escaped the brief interrogation.

As the evening went on, discussions turned to where they would go afterwards. Steve remembered that he wanted to introduce Andy to more places.

"I know. Let's go to MX. I reckon you'd like that," he said. "Have you been there yet?"

Andy remembered his panic attack from the time he went and wasn't sure if he wanted to mention anything.

"Er, no," he managed to say as this was hopefully the easiest way to stop any conversation developing from it.

"Yeah, it's cool," said Jess. "One of my favourites. I haven't been there for months now."

So it was a done deal with Andy feeling that he shouldn't try to convince them otherwise. If he'd suggested anywhere else, he would have to explain why and that would open the can of worms.

They headed over to MX at about half past midnight. In the time leading up to this, Andy had been racking his brain, thinking of where he should hide the drugs. They hadn't been detected last time, but no way was he going to take any chances. He went to the toilets and switched the two bags from his pocket to his sock, stuffed firmly down the inside of his right one.

The place was already buzzing and there were more people both outside and inside than when Andy had been before. He was glad about this. He could get lost in the crowd more, at least he hoped he could.

This time the doorman didn't search any of them, except for a quick look in Jess's handbag. Andy was the only one to pay particular attention to this, making an analysis of why it was different. It must be that they looked like a harmless group, or that the doorman recognised the others from coming a number of times before, he thought.

When they got inside, Andy had to remind himself to switch back to being just another ordinary punter. Paul had noticed him seeming a bit odd before he made this switch. He was aware that Andy was probably carrying some cocaine, so was also monitoring his friend and how he reacted.

It was Andy's turn to get the drinks in and as Steve and Jess were busy soaking up the vibes of the club, Paul was still watching Andy while he was at the bar, having switched into monitoring mode instead of being an ordinary punter. Andy brought the drinks over and without realising it, he felt a little better than when he was here before. Steve leaned close to Andy to inform him of something.

"I'm just going to the loo," he said, obviously indicating what he was going to do there. Andy nodded casually. Jess and Paul went to dance and Andy wasn't sure whether to join them yet as Steve going to do the coke meant that he would have to go and do some some as well. He hung around on the fringe of the dance floor and pretended that he was starting to feel the groove, with his mind on waiting for Steve to come back.

"Hey, Andy," he said when he did. "I met someone in the toilets who wants to buy. I said I'd have a word with you first. Did you bring any more with you?"

"I've got two grams. Who is it?"

Steve looked around and found the guy loitering with intent, not far from them. He nodded to him to indicate that he could buy. "That's him." The guy was looking very nervous. A skinny young lad of maybe eighteen or nineteen, who appeared to have some problems on his mind. Andy asked if he was Spanish, to which Steve replied that he was.

Andy causally walked over to meet him. He made sure of what the lad wanted to buy and told him how much it was. The lad reached into his back pocket and started to get his money out.

Andy stopped him immediately and instructed him to meet him outside in a minute. Andy went out to wait at the point that he described, to the right and where the crowd of people ended. He suspected that he'd never bought coke before and didn't know how to go about it, so he would have to be careful with dealing with him. The lad came out, looked around and caught Andy's eye. He went over and Andy led him further away to a discrete spot in the road.

The lad got out his money and gave it to Andy, which he counted then handed over the bag. He asked if it was his first time doing it as he felt a bit concerned, even though Andy had only taken it one time himself and was hardly an expert to talk him through everything. The lad said no, but Andy doubted that. Anyway, the sale was done and they separately went back inside.

Steve gave him a wink and Andy did likewise. This was turning out to be easier after all. He no longer felt nervous about being there and he thought he'd celebrate by doing a line himself and not worry about selling his remaining bag.

He joined in with the dancing and the coke was already working for Steve. Paul remained observant despite appearing to be at one with the group. He'd seen Andy go to the toilets, so knew what he'd been doing, but he tried to leave him be.

The group of friends were having a good night as time went on, Andy feeling happy and lifted, but still in control. Steve went to do another line and was the liveliest of them all. Jess could naturally fit in as she loved dancing anyway and didn't need or want any cocaine. After more time had passed, Andy noticed the lad who he'd sold to, who was to his right. His character had changed considerably and was dancing vigorously, but also seemed to be annoying some of the other people around him. He was facing some women and grinning at them while waving his hands in their faces. Andy could see that they were intimidated by his behaviour and pushed him away. He tried again and one of them forcefully shoved him away, whereby he tripped over and fell onto a couple behind him. This got the attention of a number of people in their area of the dance floor. The lad got back to his feet and was visibly angry with them. A man who had witnessed this scene and was probably in his thirties, taller and far more built than the lad, grabbed him by the collar and marched him to the exit. About twenty people were watching as the makeshift bouncer had a quick word with the doorman, who promptly threw him out.

Andy was so focused on what had happened that adrenalin kicked in and overrode the effects of the coke. He felt responsible for the lad's actions, but at least he had been ejected. Steve put his arm round Andy's shoulder.

"It looks like he can't handle it. He's probably snorted the whole bag."

"You reckon?"

"Yeah. He was totally wired. Out of control. He's only a kid. Let's hope he learns from this."

Andy nodded, worried that the lad would be okay. He wanted to go outside to see if he could find him. As he stood there for a short time, he reckoned the lad would have gone away by now, so tried to get back to the dancing. Most of the crowd had returned to the reason why they were there, but Paul was looking at Andy with a hint of scorn. Seeing what that kid had been like made him sure that Andy had sold him the drugs. He'd seen friends of his in similar situations and get thrown out after losing control. He wanted to have a stern word with Andy, but also didn't want to create a scene while he was out with friends, so kept quiet. Andy had lost the effects of the coke now, but could see that Steve was still buzzing. He wanted to enjoy himself, so went back to the toilets and snorted some more.

THE EMPTY FLAT

When he came back, Paul told Steve and Jess that he was going home. He didn't speak to Andy, but just indicated with his hand that he was going. His face showed that he was unhappy with how things were going and he walked out. Andy picked up on this and turned to watch him leave, which he did without looking back. Andy felt that there was tension developing between them and this stayed on his mind, meaning that he couldn't get back into the atmosphere and only lasted another half an hour.

When he got home, Andy was still wide awake and the thoughts of everything that had gone on that night were going through his mind on repeat. He stayed up for a while, listening to music, but not really taking it in. He went to bed and lay awake for some time, wondering if he was going to lose Paul as a friend.

19.

Andy had hardly any sleep and finally got up at eleven. He straight away started thinking about everything again and was not feeling settled. Then he remembered that he was due to meet Ana in an hour's time, but really didn't feel in the mood for it. He tried his best to shake off his mood, but by half past eleven thought that he should text her to say he couldn't make it. This could disrupt things between them, though, and he didn't want to mess things up in case he lost her as a contact for selling to. He reluctantly decided to go ahead with meeting her and headed to television square.

She wasn't there by twelve, which left Andy stewing in his thoughts again, while trying to force himself to let them go. Ten minutes later, she arrived.

"Buenos dias," said Ana with a smile. She had her hair tied back and was wearing a light blue dress of knee length. She kissed Andy on both cheeks. Her presence brought a light to his shadowed soul and he was brought out of his reverie.

She ordered a coffee and asked him how he was. He tried to appear livelier than he actually felt. He could tell she was in a good mood so it was better if he tried to emulate that. He told her he was a bit tired but fine and proceeded to tell her that he'd been out the night before. She said she had stayed in as she was tired from work, but felt good today. Her animated demeanour was more than he was expecting.

Ana was interested to find out more about Andy and she asked him about his time in Spain. He was able to tell her the truth, as much as was safe to, and she showed great interest in what he had to say, in his broken Spanish.

She told him that she was planning to go out dancing tonight and would like him to join her and her friend. Andy wasn't sure if he'd be up for it, but felt it would be rude to decline, so he said he would.

They spent a good hour together and Andy definitely picked up the vibe that she was interested in him. She complimented him on his hair and his eyes and he returned the compliment, mainly because he thought it was the appropriate thing to do, although he didn't mean it as much as she wanted to believe it.

As their time together was coming to an end, she asked him if he could bring some more cocaine that they could all take together. It sounded like she meant it in a way that was for them to have a fun night where they would all be on the same wavelength rather than asking if she could buy some, but as he'd sold three grams last night, he wasn't bothered about letting Ana and her friend have some for free. After all, he wouldn't be losing any money. They arranged to meet up at ten at Sant Jaume, a small café on Caballeros.

Through the rest of the day, Andy wasn't feeling like he was about to start a relationship, but thought Ana was nice as a friend. He didn't want to seem offish with her later, so planned to keep things on a good level. He had a nap in the afternoon and felt more awake when it was time to go out.

He wondered if he should bother taking any more coke to sell or whether he should have a night off. As it would be a time spent with new people, it was probably better to lay off the dealing for this time. He put one gram in his pocket and made his way to the bar.

As before, he was the first of the three to arrive and the ladies kept him waiting for fifteen minutes. Andy wasn't very impressed with their tardiness as he tended to stick to the agreed times. It was how he had always been. As the minutes dragged on he became restless, but the two women turned up, again with Ana radiating her lively manner. They both sat down at his table just outside the bar on the small terrace.

"This is Catarina," Ana said, who gave him a kiss on each cheek. Even though she smiled as she introduced herself, she didn't seem as outgoing as her friend.

They went through the usual chit-chat of Ana telling Catarina about the things she'd learned abut Andy so far. He felt he knew her from somewhere and realised that she was the one who had been out with Ana when he first met her. Catarina began to open up and Andy remembered that he found her more attractive that night, and in a clearer state of mind, he noticed that his attention was drifting more towards her than Ana. She had her hair down and was wearing a skin tight white dress. He took the opportunity to pay attention to her body when the ladies' eyes were elsewhere. They had a couple of drinks before heading down to Fox Congo. Ana wanted to have the opportunity to dance with Andy, though he wasn't feeling the same. He wondered if he would be able to make Catarina's acquaintance more, but considering who he was there to be with, this might not be the best plan to take.

Ana was quick to pull Andy onto the dance floor and she looked into his eyes and smiled more than if she just wanted to be friends. Andy joined in the dancing, but felt out of place as they were clearly better at it and more enthusiastic. He gently moved, but felt like a dad dancing with his two daughters.

Ana was refusing to notice that he wasn't feeling the music that much and allowed him to do his own thing. She'd had many times when dancing with men to see that they weren't always that up for it. Every now and then, Andy glanced across to Catarina and coyly smiled at her as he still wanted to gauge if she was interested in him. She wasn't giving much away and of course already knew that Ana had him in her sights.

They stayed for about an hour before moving on to Mosquito. Ana remained the most active of the three, but Andy was starting to come out of his shell after having had a few drinks and getting used to her company.

When inside, the conversation naturally turned to taking some cocaine. He let the women go first and he looked around the crowd as he was now used to doing, wondering who might be interested in becoming his customers despite him not having any more drugs with him.

Ana and Catarina came back and he took his turn to snort a line and before too long, inhibitions were lowered and Andy felt he could get into the night more freely. Ana continued to flirt with him and he let his guard down more, even though he was constantly aware that he still wanted to spend more time with Catarina, whose eyes were now beginning to light up.

As the night continued, Andy was caught between a rock and a hard place. The cocaine was preventing him from knowing what he should do and he managed to maintain a boundary between him and Ana because of the tension that he felt with wanting to get closer to Catarina. She was more open, but not revealing whether she was willing to take the bait of his frequent smiles, partly because they didn't seem natural and partly because Ana was her close friend. They partied on until Mosquito closed, but because Andy had been out the night before as well, he was now flagging and was no longer interested in spending time with either of the women. He bade them a quick farewell and got out of there before Ana could complicate matters by suggesting they carried on their night in some fashion.

Andy had another night of interrupted and abbreviated sleep and felt even worse than the day before. He wasn't in the mood to think about his companions from last night and just wanted to vegetate in his flat. Every now and then he reflected back on it and wondered if he'd made any faux pas. He couldn't be sure due to his artificial mental state, but thought that he had got away with it.

Should he even follow it up and get in touch with Ana again? He decided not to, though expected that she would text him at some point, at which he would take it from there.

He trudged through his cleaning job at the jewellery shop late afternoon with his mind not active enough to weigh up any options about what he was going to do next. He knew that he didn't like the comedown of cocaine, but knew that he enjoyed it while he was on it. He had a chilled night at home, watching football highlights as he slumped in his office chair. "I really could do with getting a sofa," he thought.

On Monday, his batteries were mostly recharged though he still felt a bit devoid of energy. He'd made €240 from the drugs at the weekend, which was decent. It meant he didn't have to worry about what he spent it on, but was still looking forward to the time when he would be making abut ten times that. He thought that it was about time he deposited some of the cash in his bank account before it stared building up too much, but also wanted to see if he could buy a sofa from somewhere.

To his surprise, he saw one that had been thrown out only five minutes from his place. He inspected it; it was black and vinyl covered, quite bulky but a two seater which was all he needed. There was a tear in the right side of it, but nothing that seemed too important. He noted it for later and headed to the bank to deposit €100. As expected, he encountered no problem with putting in such an innocuous amount and his thoughts returned to how he could get the sofa to his flat. He was definitely going to need some help with carrying it. The first person he thought of was Paul. He wondered if this would be a good way to get back in touch with him. It was a fairly small favour to ask and it could help to break the ice if there was any that Paul was bearing. He texted him when he was at work at the office and he was relieved when Paul agreed to help him afterwards.

THE EMPTY FLAT

Andy got back home and waited for Paul to arrive. This was the first time that he'd seen Andy's place since he'd decorated it and he was impressed. The fact that Andy hadn't descended into a drug-filled world with rubbish all over the floor made him feel somewhat better. Andy told him about his night out on Saturday, focusing on his interactions with the women rather than mentioning the drugs.

"It's a dangerous game, though," Paul said. "If they are close friends, then it's not going to work if you try to hook up with Catarina. That would cause a rift between those two and basically you're the one who would lose out."

"Yeah, that's true," Andy noted. "I don't know. I do fancy Catarina a lot more than Ana, but yeah, I get your point. Ana wouldn't like that and Catarina wouldn't do that to her friend."

"You might as well cut your losses. So, shall we got and get the sofa?"

They went out and the sofa was still there. They managed to get it back without too much of a struggle and Andy opened the door leading to the staircase. It only had one ninety degree turn in it, about halfway up and they just about got it through the door. The sofa was tough to get up the first section and combined with the angle that it needed to pass through resulted in being a failed mission. They couldn't figure out any way to position it and had to take it back down. They stood in the street and the only other option was to get it through the balcony doors.

"We'll never be able to do that, even if we had a ladder," Andy said.

"Yeah, it's way too heavy to risk hauling it up a ladder."

They gave up and took it down the road to the side street where Andy had found some things before. There wasn't much there so they dumped it.

"Alright, it's disappointing, but thanks for your help anyway."

"That's okay, mate," said Paul. "I've get to get back though as Jess is making dinner. I'll see you soon."

As he headed off, Andy felt that the ice had been broken. Their unsuccessful struggle with the sofa had at least been a kind of bonding session between them. Most importantly for Andy, Paul hadn't brought up the dreaded topic of drug dealing, so hopefully he had put it to rest and they would regain their friendship.

20.

Over the week, Andy wanted a break from what he'd been dealing with recently. Right now he wasn't bothered if he didn't hear from Ana. He hadn't heard anything from her for a few days, so took that as meaning she got the message that he wasn't looking for anything from her. He had no desire to get in touch with her, either, so he was able to push it out of his mind. He just wanted to get back to buying a sofa and, after trying a few nearby furniture shops, found a more compact two seater that they would deliver for him and carry up the stairs. It was dark blue with fabric seats and a high back, which he especially wanted so he could lean back and rest his head. He was now feeling like it really was his home. With his dining table near the balcony doors and his sofa against the opposite wall facing his TV which was just in front of it and his stereo on the other table, he was close to having all that he wanted. Further down the line he would look into getting a computer. He'd never owned one before and had only really used them at university, but the internet was starting to gain traction and that could be good to keep him occupied instead of worrying about drugs and women all the time.

On Thursday, he got a text from Paul inviting him to their flat as they were having a small party with a few other friends round. This made Andy feel happy as surely it meant that they were back on track again and it would be good to meet some more people. Shortly after, Steve texted him to ask him to bring a few grams with him. They must be the people he had mentioned to him a while ago. He bought a six-pack of beer and took them round the following evening.

The three who lived there were preparing the food. Based on the tapas theme, there were many different small dishes to pick and choose from. Andy helped out with carrying plates to the dining table and soon after he arrived there was another guest. This was

Josh, who also taught at their school. He was twenty-eight and was quite tall with a modern-looking haircut. Andy guessed that he was popular with the women as he came across as confident and easy to get on with.

They got chatting and even though Josh was much more outgoing than Andy, they were getting on well and Andy felt he could let his guard down more than usual. About twenty minutes later, two more turned up. This was Sarah and Callum, who were partners. They worked at a different school but Steve had known them for a year or so. Another nice couple of people, although quieter than Josh. Andy didn't feel a connection with them so much, but they had a pleasant evening together, getting to know each other and catching up on what people had been doing over the summer.

While people were milling around the room, Josh had a quiet word with Andy.

"Steve tells me you've got some coke."

"That's right. Do you want to buy?"

"Sure. Not right now, but I'll have a gram later. We'll have to swap numbers as my dealer is unreliable and he's sometimes not around for weeks."

"Absolutely. I've got a few grams I need to get rid of."

Josh smiled at him and shook his hand. It seemed like they were going to become friends and he was probably someone who Andy would like to go clubbing with.

"I know a couple of other people I can hook you up with, too."

"Awesome. I could do with some regular contacts."

"I'll sort it out for you. You can do it through me first until you get to meet them."

"Thanks, Josh. I appreciate that."

Andy wondered if Sarah and Callum were already going to buy, but they seemed more conservative, so he guessed they wouldn't. A bit later, Steve also had a word with Andy.

"Have you spoken to Josh about your stuff?"

Andy told him what they'd discussed.

"Nice one. I've spoken to a couple of other people. Their dealer is hard to get hold of."

"That's what Josh said."

"Yeah, probably the same guy. I reckon you'll be able to shift the rest of your stash in just a few weeks."

Andy smiled at this idea, remembering that Steve still didn't know the full picture. If Andy managed to sell another forty grams quickly, he could probably keep going, but how was he going to do that without Steve finding out? With the amount of talking going on right now, it wasn't something he could process, but at least things were looking up.

"So where are we going to go tonight?" Josh asked.

"I fancy somewhere different," said Steve. "What do you reckon, Paul?"

"Er, we could try Radio City."

"Oh yeah," said Josh. "I haven't been there for a while."

"What sort of music do they play?" Andy asked.

"Different things, but they play more British and American stuff," Steve said. "Some indie and rock."

"Oh, sweet. I'm up for that."

"Do you like indie as well?" Josh asked.

"Yeah, it's my favourite."

"Cool. Me, too."

Sarah and Callum were interested as they weren't into house music, so they all agreed to go there. Radio City was more off the beaten track, to the south of Plaza del Tossal, on Calle de Santa Teresa. When they entered, they were in the bar area and there was another bigger section behind that. It was more underground, which straight away appealed to Andy. They played more of his kinds of music, including some Britpop, like Blur and Pulp and eighties bands like The Smiths.

"I didn't even know there was somewhere like this in Valencia," he said to Josh, who he had been spending most of his time with. He felt that he could be himself more as he could tell that Josh was very approachable and welcoming and his jovial nature made it easy to drop his inhibitions.

"Yeah, it's good, isn't it? I haven't been for a few months now."

Even though Andy seemed to have made up with Paul recently, he didn't speak to him that much. With more people in their group and loud music, it was easier to stay talking with one or two people than the whole group being able to have one conversation. Nevertheless, Andy wanted to be on his best behaviour and not do any coke tonight in case it rubbed Paul up the wrong way. Everyone seemed to enjoy the music, although Callum rarely joined in with the dancing, as he was clearly uncoordinated from the rare times he was roped in by Sarah. Josh and Andy went outside to apparently have a cigarette, but mainly to discuss Andy hooking up with more contacts.

"So I just found this stuff, so I don't have experience really of how dealing works." He explained the fabricated story to Josh that became more believable to Andy now that he had had to use it a few times.

"Pretty simple, really. You'll want to get to know your customers to make sure you trust them. You can go through me first, that is, if you trust me!"

"Mate, I do. I'm glad to have met you."

"Cheers. Yeah, I think we're going to get on well." They both smiled at each other. "So I can introduce you to the couple of people I know, so you know they're not going to fuck you about or tell the police, then just get their numbers and deliver it when they ask for it."

"Okay. So it's normal for me to go to the people then?"

"Yeah, much better. You don't want people queueing up outside your door. Way too risky. People will probably buy on the night and already be somewhere, or you can just arrange meeting points that you know are safe."

"Right, yeah, that's simple enough." This was valuable information for Andy seeing as he had hardly shifted anything yet. "So do you want some now?"

"Yeah, I'll have a gram. Shall we both take some tonight?"

"I don't really feel like it to be honest. I know Paul isn't a big fan of it and it's kind of come between us a bit, so I'd prefer just to drink tonight."

"No worries. I'll just have a line or two."

Radio City was open till 4am, but Sarah and Callum left first by about 2. The others stayed on for a while, Josh not seeming much different when he was on coke as he had been full of energy beforehand anyway. He and Andy continued getting on well, which the other two guys noticed.

The three housemates noticed them bonding and Paul wondered if anything else was going to happen between them. He thought they had fallen for each other, but Josh had no homosexual inclinations. Andy felt a close friendship developing and although he thought Josh was good-looking, he wasn't interested in anything else going on between them. They stayed till after three until everyone bar one was tired.

The next day, Andy got a text from Josh asking if he wanted to go for a coffee. Andy was surprised that Josh wasn't drained of energy, but seeing how he was, it kind of made sense. They went to television square at two.

"So what did you think of Radio City?" Josh asked.

"I like it. It's more of my kind of place." They discussed what music they were into and found that they had even more in common. They talked about bands like Pixies and The Stone Roses and what gigs they'd been to.

"Do you plan to live in Spain for long?" Andy asked.

"Maybe two or three years. I've just been here for one so far, but I want to check out some other countries as well."

"Like what?"

"I fancy trying South America. Maybe Argentina or Chile, not sure yet."

"Yeah, they're probably a bit similar to Spain."

"Yeah. How about you?"

"I really don't know. I've only been here a couple of months, so I guess I'll just see how it goes." He was thinking about whether Josh would be the one whom he let into his secret about the cocaine, but thought he should wait first. He really needed to know that he could fully trust him first.

"So you said that you found a fag packet full of coke. That was a bit weird, eh?"

"Totally. I was just looking through some junk and there it was." He already felt a bit uncomfortable with lying to him, but had to go along with it for the time being.

"It couldn't have been there for very long or the dealer would have retraced his steps."

"Who knows? I guess I was just in the right place at the right time."

"It sometimes happens."

"So are you seeing anyone right now?"

"No. I met someone called Ana, who I met because she wanted to buy some coke and we kept in touch. We met here last Saturday, actually, but I don't think she's the one for me. I can tell she likes me, but I wasn't feeling it. To be honest, I fancied her friend more."

Ooh, that's not good. What's her friend called?"

"Catarina. She's beautiful and really stylish. You're right though, I was talking to Paul about it and he said it wouldn't end well if I tried to get together with her."

"Plenty more fish and all that."

"Yeah. So what about you?"

"I was seeing someone till earlier this year, but we broke up in April. She was hard work, really. She came across as jealous all the time."

"You probably have a lot of women after you."

"Haha, not all the time, but yeah, I do get some attention, to be fair. She picked up on that, even when someone wasn't trying anything. We just kept arguing about shit like that and I couldn't handle it any more."

"So is there no-one on the radar at the moment?"

"No. Things just happen when they happen, you know. I'm fine with being single for a while. It's a relief to not have someone on my back all the time."

"I'm sure you'll find someone soon enough."

"Ha, cheers. You too."

"I hope you don't mind me saying, but I have a feeling we'll become good friends. I find you easy to talk to."

"Oh, thanks, Andy. Yeah, we're on the same wavelength."

"I've been getting to know Paul since I came here. He was really helpful and if it wasn't for him, god knows if I'd still be here. He let me stay at his place before Steve and Jess came back."

"Yeah, Paul's a good guy."

"But like I was saying, the coke thing came between us. It felt tense at one point. He told me he's seen mates go out of control and he's really against it."

"Yeah, I've heard that. It's fair enough if he's been through that, but don't let it worry you. You've just got a bit to shift, then you'll be in the clear, won't you?"

"Yeah." Andy was almost bursting to confess to Josh how much he'd got and how he'd found it. He knew he was going to tell him eventually. Josh was level-headed and Andy felt that he wouldn't get judged, but it was still such a huge thing to come clean about, even if he hadn't got into drug dealing in the usual way. "So, these friends of yours. If you think I can trust them, just give them my numbers. The sooner the better, you know. Let me have theirs as well so I know who's texting me."

The two new friends stayed at the café for nearly two hours before Josh needed to go back for a nap. As Andy walked back home, He felt good that he had made a new friend and not just a mate. He looked forward to hanging out with Josh a lot more.

21.

Because Josh told him that the best way to be dealing was to deliver to people, he thought it would be a good idea to get a bike. He was getting a bit fed up with walking all over the city and if he had contacts who lived further afield it would make sense to shorten the time it took to get it over to them. It would also be a good way to spend his cash, which was already starting to pile up at home. He'd seen two or three bike shops around and on Monday he went looking. He wouldn't need to get the cheapest one he could find, but there was also no need to get something really expensive. In the first shop he went to, they had a good selection of bikes and he liked the idea of getting a mountain bike as he felt it would be more comfortable than getting a racer. It didn't take him too long to decide and he got a blue Ridgeback for €220. He didn't need much else other than a couple of lights and a lock and he spent another €20 on those. As he rode it back home, he realised that he'd just got a cool new bike just for selling three grams of coke that he'd got for free. It was hard to believe that this really was the case. How easy was life going to be? This was insane. Maybe to get a computer and all the parts, he could just sell about five grams in a weekend and that would be paid for.

When he got back home, he hoped that he would be able to lock the bike up in the entrance to the flat. The only thing he could attach the chain to was the staircase and he just about managed to fit it behind it without blocking the doorway. That should be secure there, he thought, better than leaving it out in the street with the junkies going around, who would probably find a way to break the lock.

He wondered if having his bike there would reveal who the mystery person upstairs was. They might complain about it, but seeing as Andy had never had any complaints about his music being on and rarely even heard any sound from up there, he thought that he should be okay. He guessed that it was someone old, who probably didn't have very good hearing, which suited him fine. If he wanted to have parties, then that shouldn't be an issue, either.

It was at this point that he thought he really should have a party. He'd hardly had people round except for a fleeting visit. It really was time that he did this, especially now that he was making new friends. He thought about who he could invite, basically the same people who were at the party the other night, but that would be enough. He remembered Ana and Catarina. Maybe that wouldn't be such a good idea. He'd love to be able to invite the latter, but he knew that that could get him in trouble. He'd still had no word from Ana so she must have got the message by now, although he was at risk of losing her as a contact so should probably ask her out for a coffee soon.

Andy thought about what he would do to make a party. He could just buy the food instead of making it from scratch. What about the drugs, though? Could he really have a bunch of people there, all going to the toilet at some point and walking over the crucial floorboard? How would anyone find out though? It was just like all the others. He could put a new nail in it to make sure that, for whatever reason, it didn't lift up if someone caught their toe on it. "My God, I'm getting fucking paranoid about this," he said out loud. He needed to work through this dilemma that hung over his head. "Just have a party, see that nothing happens and then I'll be fine." He thought it best to host one soon so he could get over this hurdle. Maybe this weekend. People could just come round for a few hours then they could go out like on Friday. Easy. He puffed out his cheeks. He wished it was that easy.

That evening, he had work at the office and, as it was the usual nice day in Valencia, he decided to go out early to get a coffee from the café next to it and hang out in the square for a while. He got there half an hour before he had to start, grabbed un café solo and

THE EMPTY FLAT

ambled around the square. "I still haven't been to Finnegan's," he thought. "We should do that at some point." After only going to the Irish pubs in Madrid, he hadn't been to any here. He didn't even know if there were any others in the city.

He sipped his coffee and looked at the people going by as he sat on a bench. With all the traffic bustling round this main square it wasn't exactly peaceful, but was a change from his normal routine at least. He checked his watch and it was five to seven, so decided to pop over to the office and finish his drink there. He stood outside it on the street and a minute later noticed someone coming out of the building. It was the same woman he had seen before, but this time he realised that it was Catarina. He instinctively called out her name as she exited and she looked over to him.

"Andy?" she said.

"Si, soy Andy." She didn't appear that pleased to see him. He asked her if she worked here and she replied that she did. He told her that he was the cleaner and she looked into his eyes with a blank expression and a slight nod of the head. The only thing she said to him was that she had to go and she abruptly moved on. Andy stood there quite bemused as he watched he fade into the distance. "Why didn't she want to speak to me?" Maybe there had been an issue between her and Ana. Had they fallen out over him? He downed his last sip of coffee, threw the cup in the bin and went into the office. All the while he had a frown on his face as he tried to work out why Catarina had been so cold with him. Had he done something to offend her when they were out that time? He racked his brain, but couldn't think of anything. Was she annoyed with him because he had effectively broken things off with Ana? He guessed that this could be the case, but why would he be in the bad books? Maybe Ana had been besotted with Andy and she was angry with him for not getting in touch. That feeling might have been relayed to Catarina and the reason why she had been like that with him. As he went about his work, he thought about other possibilities, but nothing else made sense, so that must be it. He wasn't sure that he wanted to leave things like that. Ana wasn't exactly an integral part of his life, but he hadn't meant any harm. He thought about texting her that evening, but if she was angry with him, what should he say?

Should he say anything about that encounter with Catarina? Best not to in case he had got it wrong. He should probably just keep it simple and ask how she is. That would leave an open canvas for her and he would be able to tell if things were okay or not depending on her response. He waited until half past eight to give her time to get home and settle down.

Ana didn't reply while he was at work, so he headed back home, checking his phone every couple of minutes. Just before he got to his flat, he hear his phone beep. "¡Hola! Estoy bien. Y tu?"

That seemed fine to him. He inspected the short text message and concluded that the exclamation marks before and after "hi" was a good thing as it added some expression to it. She asked him how he was, so expected him to respond back. If she didn't want to chat to him, surely she would have left that part out. After doing his detective work for a minute, he texted her to say he was also fine and asked if she would like to go for a coffee one day. He opened the main door and saw that his bike was still there. He quickly looked it over, but saw no sign of interference, so he went upstairs. Ana texted back to say "Yes, maybe at the weekend." So things seemed fine between those two. He told her that he would text her on Friday to arrange something.

Going back to what had happened a couple of hours ago, this didn't correlate with what had happened with Catarina. Ana, he was certain, wasn't angry with him. She was up for meeting him again, so what was wrong with Catarina? Maybe she just had her own issues. She might have just had a bad day or had fallen out with one of her other friends or something. After Andy had seen that there wasn't any problem with Ana, he thought it wasn't worth worrying about.

He went back to thinking about the party for this weekend. Which day would be better? He should just ask the others and see what was good for them, but he would try and push for Friday so he could get it over with. Paul would be the best one to text first, just in case he took it badly if Andy first asked Steve.

"Hi. Thinking of party at mine Friday. A good day 4 u? Ask others."

"Hi. Cool. Sat better for us. Work do on Fri."

"OK. Sat is good. Maybe at 9?"

"OK, We'll bring drinks."

"Sure. I'll get food. See you then."

"Alright, well Saturday is fine," he thought. Only one day later. He asked Josh, who said he would be able to come. Josh asked if he could invite other friends. Andy wondered if he meant those who would turn out to be his customers, which didn't sit well with him. As Paul would be there, he didn't want the cocaine to be brought up at all, conversationally or literally. "Sorry, just a small party." "No problem." Even anyone just talking about it would set Andy on edge. He knew it would be constantly on his mind anyway just from them being in the same place as the consignment. With Steve and Josh coming, they were bound to ask him at some point, but they both knew to keep it secret from Paul. Andy could always quietly ask them to leave any sales until they went out, but then again, that would mean he'd have to carry all that money with him again; something he wanted to get out of the habit of doing as it didn't feel safe to have a big wad of notes in his wallet. Maybe they could just inconspicuously go to another room and quickly do the transaction. Andy knew he really needed to get used to doing this and act more maturely. He still felt out of his depth, even though he had sold to strangers in clubs a few times.

Over the week, he thought about what food he was going to buy and how he could try to orchestrate what would happen at the party. In one way he would like to let it go and let everyone just go about things in a normal way, but he also wanted to make sure his secret would be safe. He could set things up so that people would generally stay in the front room by putting the food in there and having music on. There was no way to get around people going to the toilet. He wished he had a door in the opening, but to build something he would need permission from Maria, and after the incident where she turned up uninvited, he didn't want to go there at all. He settled for a middle ground and nailed a wire between the kitchen walls that formed the doorway and bought a throw to hang over it from the cheapo shop to at least give some privacy. Every now and then, he tried to put himself in the shoes of his guests and walk through the kitchen to the bathroom, but he could never make himself a true outsider and kept looking down at the floor whenever he did it.

On Thursday evening, Andy got an unexpected text from someone called Charlie. It was one of Josh's friends that he'd got the number off and Charlie asked if he could deliver two grams to him that evening. "Okay, here we go," Andy thought. "This is the first of the new way of doing things." He got the address and went on his bike to deal in a more controlled way. Charlie lived a bit further out of the city, in an area called Benicalap, to the north. It took him half an hour to find his flat and Charlie let him in.

"Hey, man," Charlie said. "Thanks for coming over."

"No worries, thanks for your order."

They went in and Charlie's flatmate, Liam, was in the living room, slouched back into the sofa, smoking a spliff.

"So you're friends of Josh?" Andy asked.

"Yeah. He said you've got some good stuff."

"It is."

"Let's have a look."

Charlie didn't seem to want to make much chit-chat, rather just get the deal done, which was fine with Andy. He felt nervous about being in a stranger's flat while carrying drugs. Charlie looked like he was in his thirties, with closely cropped hair and an unshaven face. Liam, about the same age, maybe older, didn't say anything, but just sat there with eyes half closed while he toked on the joint. He didn't offer any to Andy, who didn't want it anyway and Charlie had a look at the bags, rubbed a bit on his gum, rolled it around with his lips and said "Yeah, good stuff." He reached into his pocket and pulled out his wallet. "Is €150 enough?"

"Erm, it's €80 a gram, so €160."

"Yeah, but a discount for buying in quantity, yeah?" Andy started to feel uncomfortable as this was the first time someone had tried to get a discount. He wasn't sure if this was normal, but didn't want to get into an argument. He had to think quickly so that he didn't appear that he was a novice, so just said "Alright, €150." Charlie handed over the money, looking lazily at Andy, but not saying anything else.

"Okay, thanks. I'll be off then."

Charlie gave him a thumbs up and a wink, evidently fine with him leaving straight away. Andy shut the door behind him and went back to his bike. On the ride back, he thought about the scenario he had just been in. Those guys looked like proper junkies. The place stank of weed and they seemed to be in their own little world. Andy guessed that this was just part and parcel of drug dealing. Not everyone was going to be as friendly and accommodating as Josh and Steve and in the end, it probably was best just to do a quick deal and walk away with the money. The discount thing was on his mind, though. He'd have to ask Josh if this was normal, but it did make sense to him. He supposed that he should give a discount if someone ordered a bulk quantity. Andy wasn't going to lose out either way as every Euro he made was profit and it was probably easier to keep his customers sweet. He just had to make sure that he wasn't going to be taken advantage of all the same. Andy thought it was odd that they were friends of Josh as they didn't seem to be anything like him.

By the time he got home, Andy had got his head around things better. The ride back gave him time to reflect on things and he concluded that he'd made an easy €150, so he couldn't really complain about anything. It was better to see the seedier side of things early on, so he could get an insight into it. He just hoped that he wouldn't have to deal to anyone who was aggressive.

By Friday, he'd got in his head how he was going to organise the party tomorrow. He bought a range of food: some small snacks and some things he could just throw in the oven. It wasn't too much to cater for five people and he got some extra drinks in in case people ran out. A twelve pack of beer should do the trick. He was wondering whether he should go out that night. It would likely be a case of going out on his own because of the others' plans, but that could give him a chance to make some more money, then maybe not bother with it on Saturday. He wasn't sure what to do yet. He knew he was due to text Ana that evening about meeting for a coffee tomorrow as well. Should he ask if she wanted to go out tonight? Maybe she'd want to buy a gram, but maybe she'd take his invitation the wrong way and think that he was now interested in her. What about the issue with Catarina that he still had no idea about? He could go along to the office early again this evening to 'accidentally' bump into her again. However, catching her off-guard for the second time in a week could make things worse. Man, why were things so complicated with people? Why couldn't everyone just say it like it really is and stop keeping secrets? Needless to say, he decided against this latter idea. He might be able to find out from Ana tomorrow what the deal was.

Andy hadn't made plans with the others as to where they were going after the party. He hoped they realised it was going to be like the one last weekend and that they didn't expect to have a long one at his place. He'd have to make a point of stating that fairly early on. Organising social events really wasn't Andy's forte and he was feeling rather anxious about the whole thing. Given that his intention was to use it to calm himself down, it was like everything was going in the opposite direction. The crux of it was that fucking floorboard and what it concealed. He was getting through his cigarettes at a rate of knots that afternoon. He had to put the final nail in the coffin and put another nail in the floorboard to make sure it was properly fixed down. Surely that would sort everything out. "Right," he said to himself sternly. "Just get a few bags ready for tonight and tomorrow, ten will be more than enough, then nail that fucking board down." He grabbed a nail leftover from ones he'd used to make his ledge to get into the empty flat and went with the hammer into the kitchen. Before he could carry out this simple procedure, he had to inspect the nail and the ones in surrounding floorboards. Would a new one look out of place and give the game away? "Fucking hell! Even this is too hard to work out!" He didn't want to chance it so went into the spare room to lift a board from in there, take one of its nails out and use that instead. He got one that looked just like the others and hammered it down. It looked totally normal and he tried scraping his foot over it to see if it moved. Nope. Could he lift it with his fingernails? Nope. Thank God for that. He stood up, looked at his successful work and sighed out loud. He put the hammer away and went into the front room. He thought again about the routine of the rest of his weekend. "Oh, for fuck's sake!" he shouted. "The fucking bags!" He'd forgotten to get those ten grams ready first and rubbed his hands vigorously over his face in anger. He grabbed a flathead screwdriver and carefully prised up the bane of his life right now and carefully took out the packet. "I fucking bet Maria turns up again now," he said, putting the packet on the kitchen worktop, then going to look out of his balcony to see if she was coming. There was no-one in sight, but he checked this way and that three times just to be sure. How many grams did he have bagged already? He pulled open the sideboard drawer and saw he had three. He went back to the kitchen, took the scales and weights out and went through the process of measuring seven more grams, all the time listening intently to any sounds that were coming from behind him. It was as quiet as usual and he could just about make out the background noise of the neighbourhood: a dog barking some way off, a car horn in the distance. Nothing to be concerned about. He'd measured out five of the seven he needed when he heard another noise. Not coming from outside, but from upstairs. He stopped what he was doing and kept completely still. There definitely was someone up there. Was it a door closing that he heard? What was that? Footsteps? He kept listening out, but didn't hear anything else. He just wanted to know who was there just for the sake of being able to cross it off his list of things he wanted to be at peace with. He went back to his task and measured out the last two grams. This whole process actually calmed him down. Andy could apply himself to it methodically and shut everything else out. It was strangely cathartic to him. He closed the plastic container again, put in in the floor and pressed it down, focusing on the new nail that was in place. Another check that it wouldn't lift without an effort. Good. It still looked as normal as the others. Right. He put his equipment away and took the bags to hide in the sideboard. One more cigarette then he just *had* to go outside and take his mind off it.

He went down to the ring road where there would be a lot of activity. He needed to be surrounded by the noise of the traffic and people to give him a distraction and he walked up to the Calle de Quart and along the street to the Gothic towers just for something to look at. The two huge stone towers with an archway between them were so imposing and even though he'd seen them before, he stood and admired their magnificence to help him take his mind of the impending party. He walked around them for a few minutes, took a deep breath and headed back the way he'd come.

It wasn't long before he was due to go to work at the office. He thought again about going early just to try to see Catarina from a distance. He wanted just to see her, though not confront her, but he knew that it would add to his unsteady state of mind, so avoided doing so and instead arrived five minutes late.

As he approached the building, he paid careful attention in case she left late. He paused at the door and looked in first, but couldn't see anyone. He entered and went into the office. It was empty, to his relief, but he was intrigued to find out which was her desk. There were no names on any desks, just computers and papers in trays. He'd never bothered to look at any of these before, but maybe just something would give her station away. Surely her name would be on a document. He didn't know what he was going to do, should he find where she worked, but he had a quick look at some files. He didn't see her name on any of them and had nothing else to go on, so gave up and got to work. He thoughts turned to Ana and he would text her a bit earlier than last time in case she was already getting ready to go out. Should he suggest somewhere different for them to meet? They could go to the place near Tossal, where they met with Catarina before or somewhere he hadn't been to at all. He could ask her to choose a place. Yes, that would be better. At least he wouldn't have to go through the process of racking his brain yet again.

He texted her at half past seven to see if she still wanted to meet. She replied soon after to say yes. Where would she like to go? She opted for Café Sant Jaume, where the three of them had been that one time, to which Andy agreed and they would meet there at two in the afternoon.

As this was later than the times they'd met before, it gave him the option to go out tonight and see if he could shift another few grams. However, with what he'd been going through that day, he wasn't really in the mood for it and would leave it till later to see how he felt then.

He finished work and went back home to eat. He couldn't stop thinking about the party or checking that floorboard again and again. That was that. He had to go out, but wouldn't make any effort to sell any drugs. Should he take a couple of grams just in case? Sometimes he got lucky so he decided to do that. He was getting tired of going to the same places and remembered that he wanted to check out Finnegan's. Maybe he'd meet some English speakers there and just have a quiet couple of drinks.

Andy arrived there at ten and the pub was already fairly busy. They were showing rugby on TV; something he wasn't interested in, but he got a pint and sat down at the bar. He could hear a few English voices around him, as well as other languages that he couldn't discern. He didn't really feel like talking to anyone, so just looked around, glancing up at the screen to see something he didn't understand. There was an international game going on, but he'd never known the rules of rugby and didn't know any players. After twenty minutes, he was already bored, so thought he'd try his luck outside. All the tables were taken, so he just lit a cigarette and finished his pint.

He was at a loose end. He didn't want to go home and stew in his own thoughts, but couldn't think of anywhere else to go, so just went back to the areas he knew best to see what was going on.

THE EMPTY FLAT

He walked along Caballeros and the night life had already begun to blossom. At least he could just look at the people and see what they were up to. It was too early to go to a club and he didn't fancy sitting on his own at a bar again, so he just walked up and down the street a couple of times, never quite slotting into the atmosphere that encircled him, so by half past eleven, he went back home and watched TV for an hour.

Andy slept surprisingly well, considering his anxiety of that day and got up at nine. The first thing he did when he came out of his bedroom was look at *that* floorboard. Yeah, it's normal, just forget about it. He made himself a coffee and put his chair by the balcony to connect himself to the outside world. As usual, there was not much going on in his street and he thought about what he was going to do before he met Ana and decided to take his bike and ride around the Turia park in the old river.

This turned out to be the perfect distraction for him and riding among the trees and people lifted his spirits again. He hadn't been there for a while and made a vow that he would do this more often. It relieved him of his thoughts and he was able to immerse himself in his surroundings for a good couple of hours.

He met Ana at Sant Jaume and to his surprise, she was actually pretty much on time, being only five minutes late. She greeted him with her usual smile and Andy noticed he was more pleased to see her than he thought he would be. He was in need of some company right now and picking up that things were fine between them was encouraging.

"Sorry I didn't send a message," she said. "I was busy the last two weeks. Lots of family things."

"Don't worry," he couldn't say the same thing about himself. "It's good to see you."

They chatted about what they'd been up to since they last met, with Andy trying to stick to the basic things like buying a bike.

He certainly didn't want to bring up the anxiety he'd been going through, so just recounted a few everyday things that he'd done.

"I went to Radio City with some friends. Do you know it?"

"Radio City? Ah, yes. It's not music that I like. I don't go there."

"Fair enough. I prefer that kind of music."

"Do you have plans for tonight?" she asked.

"Some friends are coming to my flat. We're having a small party then we'll go out after. I don't know where yet."

"OK, very good. Where do you live?"

He wondered if she wanted him to give her his address, but just opted to tell her that he lived in El Pilar.

"El Pilar. Yes, it's not so good area, no?"

"It's not great, but it's cheap. I haven't had any trouble there."

"Is very central, which is good."

Andy was considering whether it was worth inviting Ana to the party. He wasn't sure if she would want to go on her own and hang around with all Brits.

"What are you doing tonight?"

"I go out with Catarina. We probably go to Mosquito or MX. I don't know exactly."

This was his moment to see if he could dig up some information about Catarina.

"How is Catarina?"

"She is good." Andy nodded, but that didn't help him resolve the issue that he felt with her.

"I saw her at work. I clean in the office where she works."

"Yes? She didn't say me."

"Yeah, it was unusual. I don't think she wanted to talk to me. We just said hello, but she went away. I thought she was upset with me."

"She didn't say something to me. I don't think there is a problem. We talked a few days ago. I think she is okay."

So Andy was no wiser as to what the issue was. He was sure that her reaction was due to him. She'd changed from leaving the office looking normal to going into shock at his appearance. He may have over-interpreted it, but thought he shouldn't try and drag the conversation out about her.

Andy and Ana chatted some more about minor things. As she seemed to be in her normal mood and wasn't bothered that they hadn't met up for two weeks, he suspected that she didn't want to be more than friends, which was ideal for him. They agreed to text each other later to possibly meet up. If Andy was with his group of friends and anything flared up with Catarina, he wouldn't be on his own. He thought he would try to meet up with them both somehow.

"Do you want un gramo?" he said quietly as he leaned in.

"Maybe later," she smiled.

"Okay. So maybe I'll see you later. I'll text you."

"Okay. Have a good party!"

They parted company and for the first time in what seemed like ages, Andy felt like everything was fine again. It left him in a good mood for the rest of the day and he was able to get the food ready for the party and he was no longer worried about it.

22.

By eight, Andy had everything ready. The food was laid out in the living room, he had four grams of coke in his pocket and everything else was hidden away. He couldn't help but check the floorboard a couple of times, but was feeling calmer about it now. By nine, no-one had turned up yet, but by ten past he heard the bell ring. It was Josh.

"Hey, dude. How's things?" he asked in his usual cheery way.

"Good, thanks. How are you?"

"Yeah, I'm fine. What's been going on?"

"Oh, the normal stuff. I bought a bike. It will be handy for delivering the goods."

"Nice one. Have you had many orders?"

"Well, I delivered some to those friends of yours. Charlie and Liam."

"Oh, sweet. Did everything go well?"

"Yeah, I guess. I had to give them a discount of ten Euros, which I wasn't sure about, but it's okay."

"Yeah, that's normal. How much did they buy?"

"Just two grams. Do you think they should have had a discount?"

"Well, I guess it's usual if someone buys as much as five grams. Not sure about just two."

"That's what I thought. I suppose they'll expect to want that every time."

"It doesn't matter. It's all profit to you, isn't it?"

"True. I'm not going to beat myself up about it."

"That's the spirit. So when are the others coming?"

"Any time now. I said nine o'clock to everyone."

"Okay. Well, let me buy a gram off you now then."

They quickly sorted it out and Andy put fifty Euros away in his wardrobe.

"They didn't seem like the kind of friends I'd expect you to have, to be honest."Andy remarked.

"Why's that?"

"They just seemed like drop-outs to me. The place stank of weed and they seemed a bit rough."

"Ah, they're okay. Yeah, they like to get stoned, but they're no trouble."

The doorbell rang again and the other three arrived. Andy let them in and they made themselves at home. It was the first time that Jess had been there.

"I like how you've painted the walls," she said.

"Thanks. You should have seen it before. It was horrible."

"Ha, yeah. It's not in the best area, but it looks good. Well done."

Everyone cracked open a drink and helped themselves to food. Andy put his stereo on and the party got off to a good start. Jess was keen to have a look around the flat and Andy showed her, while being cagey about it. He gave her a quick tour, not lingering too long in any room, especially the kitchen.

"Have you met your neighbours?" she asked.

"I don't have many. Someone lives upstairs, I think, but I've never seen them. There's no-one next door."

"That's good, then. You don't have to worry about making noise."

They went back into the front to mingle with the others. Andy tried not to think about what he was hiding and there was enough conversation to distract him, none of which was about drugs. They had a chat about what to do later. Andy said he had been thinking of going to Finnegan's, but said he wasn't impressed with it last night.

"Yeah, it's okay," said Steve. "It's decent to go if you want a quiet chat, but we don't go there that much."

As Josh had bought some coke, he was up for going out dancing again. He suggested they went to Mosquito, which Steve liked the sound of. Paul wasn't that keen and Andy guessed it was because drugs were likely to be taken. Andy still felt that there was an unspoken issue between them over this, but of course didn't want to go there.

Every time someone went to the toilet, it put him on edge and he was always monitoring it out of the corner of his eye. Each time someone came back, he looked at them, but they were oblivious to everything; the only remarks being about the lack of a bathroom door, which Andy felt was actually a good cover for what lay at the foot of it.

Steve said he was going to get people a drink from the fridge and asked Andy to come and help him carry some. They went into the kitchen to do a sly transaction and it went as smoothly as it should have. Just as they finished the handover, Paul appeared there.

"Let me help you carry something," he said. Andy looked startled and wondered if he had deliberately followed them to check up on what they were doing. Steve handed him a couple of bottles of beer and Paul didn't make eye contact with Andy. It all looked normal, but Andy was still suspicious.

They went back to the living room and things carried on as normal. They stayed around there till half past eleven before deciding to go out.

"Do you want a hand with putting things away?" Paul asked.

"No, it's fine," Andy said. "I'll do it in the morning." He was still suspicious that his friend was trying to uncover something, but Paul didn't give any indication that he was.

They went over to Negrito as usual and had a couple of drinks there. Andy reflected on how his first party had gone and told himself that he shouldn't have been so worried. He was glad to have got it over with and could relax now. He texted Ana to say he was going to Mosquito and after a few minutes got a reply to say that she was going there, too.

The group arrived there at one, but there weren't that many people in yet. Andy looked around for Ana, but couldn't see her. Josh went straight away to do a line, soon followed by Steve. Andy felt like he definitely wanted to join in now as he'd got over his hurdle and didn't give a shit any more. In fact, fuck it, he thought. He was going to do two lines.

About half an hour later, Ana turned up with Catarina. The coke had started to have an effect on the guys and Andy knew that he wasn't worried about clashing with the latter. He gave her a kiss on each cheek. She gave him a reluctant smile, which he hadn't interpreted. He tried to talk to her about how she was and where they'd been before here. She gave him short answers, but straight away Ana interjected and the slightly tense moment was pushed away.

Andy introduced the women to his friends, with Josh eager to become the centre of their attention and make sure that he kept them talking. This helped ease the situation and before long, everyone got into dancing. The three flatmates kept each other company, while Josh was evidently stealing the show by entertaining the women. He was clearly fixated on Ana and the both of them shared smiles and comments in each other's ears. Catarina was slowly coming out of herself though she wasn't opening up too much to Andy, who she ended up being left with. Josh pushed his bag of coke into Ana's hand and she took Catarina with her to the toilets.

"Ana's nice!" Josh said to Andy. "Are you sure you don't fancy her?"

"No, mate. She's all yours." Josh patted him on the back and carried on dancing. Andy wasn't fussed by this as he was in the moment. The women came back and they carried on as before. All eyes were on Josh and Ana, who were getting on like a house on fire. Andy wanted to talk to Catarina, but couldn't think of anything to say except that the other two looked like they were happy together. She nodded in agreement. When the coke had kicked in for her, her smiles were emerging more and she gave Andy more eye contact now. He wanted to capitalise on this and smiled heartily to her. They danced for a few more minutes with Steve joining in with them. Andy had his back to Josh and Ana. He'd almost forgotten that they were there, when Steve looked at him and pointed to behind him. Andy looked round and saw that they were kissing with their arms round each other. Andy was surprised, but laughed at this sight and left them to it. Catarina was watching them and also seemed to happy. Maybe she had got over whatever had been bugging her and Andy asked if she wanted to go outside for some air. She agreed and they went out to have a cigarette.

"How are you feeling?" he asked her.

"I'm good." She indicated with her hands and eyes that she was high.

"I think Ana is happy, too."

She smiled at this without comment, but Andy wanted to get her talking some more. He was feeling really attracted to her right now and wanted to say so, while also trying to stop himself from blurting it out. He remembered that he still hadn't found out why she had been off with him before, but didn't want to go there now.

"Do you like Ana?" she said.

"I like her as a friend," he said, trying to point out that he was reassuring her by looking into her eyes with a smile. "I like you, too." He held her gaze. She looked at him, wondering what he meant and what he was going to do next. She took a drag on her cigarette and blew out the smoke. Andy moved closer to her face,

THE EMPTY FLAT

but she showed no reaction. He closed his eyes and moved in for a kiss, but only felt the gentle push of her hand on his chest.

"I don't know," she said. "Let's go in."

Even though he had been rejected, the cocaine didn't let him feel it and he just followed her back inside.

Josh and Ana were still dancing and grinning at each other like a couple of teenagers after having their first ever kiss. Steve's arms were carving out his territory on the dance floor, while Jess's natural energy was keeping Paul in the mood. Andy thought that he'd try again with Catarina later. He offered her some more coke. She said no, but would maybe have some later. They joined the others with dancing and Andy was still free to let himself go. There were more people in there now, so this naturally (or chemically) raised the game.

Josh and Ana seemed unaware that they were there with anyone else. Catarina wanted to join her friend, but didn't want to interrupt. She became more distant to Andy, to which he was oblivious and he moved over to dance with Steve. Eventually, Josh went to the toilet, which gave Catarina the chance to grab her friend. She straight away said something in her ear, which Andy noticed and he watched them. Ana nodded at whatever it was and carried on dancing wildly, not letting her grin disappear. Catarina looked over at Andy briefly, but didn't indicate that she wanted to get closer to him. Josh came back and handed Ana the bag of coke again and she went to do another line.

Josh came over to Andy to ask if he had any more on him. He said he did and handed him another bag.

"I'll give you the money next time," he shouted in Andy's ear.

"Don't worry about it, you have it," he shouted back. Josh gave him a hug and went back to where he had been dancing. Catarina wasn't there any more and Andy wondered if she'd left. Neither of the women appeared for a while, so Andy thought they must be chatting in the toilets. He waited intrepidly for them to return and smiled when he saw them re-emerge. They both got back to where they had left off, inadvertently cutting Catarina out of the immediate group.

Andy wanted to do another line and used the decision to offer it to Catarina again. She told him she had already taken some, which made him happy and he went off to do his business. He was not even thinking about selling any, he was having a great time with his friends and didn't want anything else. He racked up a big line and did the deed.

He came back out and went into Catarina's space. She seemed fine with him joining her and dropped her barrier some more. They shared eye contact every now and then as well as cheesy grins and after what seemed like ten minutes, although it could have been one or two, he, without thinking, went in for a kiss again. This time she responded positively. He put his hands on her waist and she put hers on his shoulders. The kiss was passionate and Andy got lost in the moment. The hands moved further round each other's bodies and it turned into a full-on snog. Behind him, Ana noticed and tapped Josh on the shoulder to point them out. His grin almost split his face in two as they both looked adoringly at their friends who were completely lost in their moment.

Andy and Catarina continued kissing and whatever barriers there had once between them were completely destroyed now. They stopped and looked into each other's eyes with big smiles, kissed some more, then went back to dancing and totally enjoying their time together.

Catarina then beckoned Andy for them to join the other two, which he was happy to do. The four of them looked like the happiest people that had ever lived, with hugs flowing freely and energy radiating from their bodies. By the time the club closed, they were eager to carry on the night. The other three, who had been forgotten about, came over to say they were going home, so after giving them a goodbye hug, the four lovebirds went on to MX.

On the way, Andy remembered, at the last minute, to hide the rest of his coke in his sock. He was so high that he didn't care about being searched and invited the bouncer to do so. The bouncer could tell he was off his head and said he couldn't go in. No matter how much he protested, he only convinced the man further. Josh managed to get Andy to give up and they went away.

"Mate, you've got to take control of yourself when you're at the door. Act casually."

"Sorry, guys. I'm just too happy right now."

"Where do we go now?" Ana asked them.

They thought about other clubs they could try, but Andy was a liability. Josh suggested they just went back to Andy's and continued their party there.

"Yeah, sure. Let's do it!" Andy loved the idea.

They headed back to his with he and Josh talked about all kinds of random bullshit and the women doing likewise. Everyone was hungry, but Andy assured them that he still had some food and drink there. They stumbled up the stairs and inside. Straight away, Josh recommended that they did another line of coke, which Andy searched for in his pockets, eventually remembering it was in his sock. Josh made four lines and they took it in turns to snort it. Andy showed them what food he had and asked what they wanted to drink. The women just wanted water so he got them a glass each and he and Josh had another beer.

"Get some music on, man," Josh demanded. Andy didn't have anything they could dance to, so he put on the radio and found something that was close enough to what would suit them. Ana and Catarina were talking amongst themselves on the sofa, while the guys stood and walked around, continuing to talk rubbish. It was half past four and everyone was still wired, but no-one really fancied dancing any more.

"Let me know how much I owe you for the coke," Josh said.

"Ah, don't worry about it. I've still got loads."

"Haven't you sold most of it now?"

"Nah, I've got tons left."

"What the fuck are you talking about?"

Andy dragged Josh into the kitchen. "Mate, I've got half a kilo here."

"You're talking shit, mate."

"Seriously. You see that floorboard over there?" he said pointing at it, but Josh didn't know which one he meant. "I've got a box full of the stuff."

"Bullshit. You're off your head."

Andy got down on his knees and tried to prise up the floorboard. He couldn't get it to budge so grabbed a knife from the drawer and lifted it up. Josh leant over the cooker and saw the plastic box with nearly half a kilo in it.

"Jesus Christ!" he said.

"Shhh! The girls will hear you."

"That's not real, is it?"

"It is, man."

"How the fuck did you get that?"

"I found it next door."

Josh was standing there wide-eyed with a look of shock on his face, still not believing what Andy was saying and showing him. Andy pulled him closer and began to speak quietly.

"Don't tell anyone, but I went over the balcony and into the flat. I searched around in there and found this under one of the floorboards."

"Really? Is that what we've been taking then?"

"It sure is. I have no idea why it was there, but I took it and it's mine now. That's what really happened."

This groundbreaking story made Josh come to his senses as his adrenalin took over the effects of the coke.

"Andy. You've got to be careful here. What if someone comes back for it?"

"That flat's been abandoned and cleared. Whoever had it is out of here now. Fuck, I shouldn't have told you this. I was going to, but some other time. Keep it secret, yeah?"

Josh didn't say anything at first, but just looked down at the box. "Cover it up," he instructed.

Andy did as he was told, unaware of how he'd betrayed himself, let alone Josh. Josh put his hands on Andy's shoulders and said "We've got to talk about this, but not now." Andy was still smiling, but was starting to realise that not everything was good right now.

"Alright. Let's go back to the other room," Josh said.

The women were still talking, but were less animated now. Josh didn't have anything to say. There was a definite look of concern on his face. Andy asked if anyone wanted anything else to eat, but no-one did.

"I think I'm going to go home," Josh said. The women looked at him, noticing that something was wrong.

"What is it?" asked Ana.

"Nothing, I'm just coming down. I'm tired."

"You can crash here," Andy said.

"No, it's alright. I want to go home."

This change in the atmosphere brought an end to proceedings. The women didn't want to stay, either, as they sensed something was not right. They put their shoes back on, picked up their handbags and the three of them went quietly out. Andy just stood there looking at the front door. His brain couldn't properly process what he'd done wrong, but after a minute, it slowly dawned on him.

Part 3

23.

Mentally alert, but physically tired, Andy wouldn't be able to sleep for some time. Daylight was starting to creep in outside and he went onto the balcony, where he could just make out the three who'd left as they were near the top of his road. His mind was racing with what had just occurred, regularly interrupted with random thoughts about his night out. His mouth was too dry to have a cigarette, so he just stared at the wall ahead of him and tried to focus. He noticed something out of the corner of his eye and Precious was strolling towards his building. This was perfect timing as he needed something to slow his thoughts down. He went down and stroked his furry friend, who lay on his or her side and let him stroke its tummy.

Precious got up and walked over to the gate where he put the food. There wasn't any there at that time, so Andy went upstairs to grab a tin, which he was now buying. When he came back down, he was sad to see that Precious had already left the scene. He put some food in the dish anyway and went back up.

He inspected the aftermath of the party and the recent gathering. There were crumbs on the table and floor, but not much food left. He cleared up what he could see and put the remaining food in the fridge. He came back to sit on the sofa. He thought back to what had gone on in the club. He knew he had been kissing Catarina, which he should feel happy about, but he was rather nonplussed at that moment. Josh, Ana, those two as well. He recounted his conversation with Josh in the kitchen. It dawned on him that he'd given the game away completely. Fuck. He couldn't control his mouth. Would he tell the women? He didn't think so, Josh was a good guy, but actually, did he know him that well? He wasn't happy when he left. Andy couldn't come to any conclusions right now, so put some music on and had a look to see if he could clean anything else up. After wasting time for another hour, he just wanted to go to bed, but knew he wouldn't be able to sleep yet.

He tossed and turned for a couple of hours, with the same thoughts going through his head in a random order, interspersed with pointless mental ramblings. He finally dropped off for an unsatisfactory night's sleep.

He woke up just before midday, knowing that he wouldn't be able to sleep any more. He felt shattered, but dragged himself out of bed to get a glass of water. As he started drinking it, memories of last night invaded his low-functioning mind. He sat on the sofa, just wanting to merge into it as he gazed up at the ceiling. He knew he'd gone overboard with the cocaine and the beers and he could only remember vagaries of the previous night, shrouded in a mental fog.

As he gradually woke up, things started falling into place more and he knew there had been some issue with Josh and that everyone left abruptly at some point. What happened there? He tried to delve into his translucent memory bank, but it took him some time until he remembered.

"Oh, fuck me!" he said out loud in a groggy voice. "I've told him!"

He rubbed his eyes and groaned. What did Josh say about it? He couldn't remember. He must have been pissed off because he left straight after. The women as well. Did they know about it? He looked out of the balcony doors, which he'd left open overnight, but the sunlight hurt his eyes and stopped him thinking. Where was his phone? He needed to know if anyone had texted him. He found it on his bedroom floor and checked it. No messages, no missed calls. He went into the kitchen. The floorboard was in place and looking as normal. Did he take it off and show Josh? He wasn't sure. He got some more water and crashed on the sofa again.

Over the next hour, gradually, details of the night came back to him in small pieces. He remembered that he'd kissed Catarina. That went well, didn't it? There was some sort of invisible weight on his mind that prevented himself from feeling any emotions except for worry. He needed to get in touch with Josh, but expected that he would be feeling as rough as he did, probably still sleeping. Maybe with Ana. It would have to wait, but not for too long. Maybe a shower would clear the cobwebs.

It did bring him a little closer to the normal world, but important details still eluded him. When should he text Josh? At three? It was worth a try. If he was asleep, he could text when he got up. In fact, fuck it, he could just text him now and wait.

He thought about what he was going to say. More than anything, he just wanted to know if Josh was okay with him. "Hi, u ok? Can we talk when u r awake?" That should do it. He dropped the phone on the sofa and put his head back. Before long, Andy dropped off again, to be awoken when he heard something. He opened his eyes and wondered what it was. Had he heard the doorbell? He got up and went to the balcony. No-one there. Oh, was it his phone? He quickly grabbed it and there was a message. It was Josh. He opened it as fast as he could to see "Hi. Feel like shit. Not today."

Andy gritted his teeth and sighed heavily. "What the hell am I going to do with the day?" he thought. He had work to go to, not something he wanted to bother with yet. He needed to get some energy. Coffee and food was what was needed. He remembered he had some leftovers from last night, so looked in the fridge, but it didn't look appealing. He needed something more substantial than that, so got dressed and slowly made his way out of the building.

He just wanted to go somewhere close by and went to a standard café near the Mercat Central. He ordered a large sandwich and a coffee and got to work on refuelling himself. After he'd finished the sandwich and digested it, life was slowly trickling back to his body. He thought about Josh and hoped that he would come back to life later and contact him. What about Catarina? Did he get her number? He looked for his phone, but realised he hadn't brought it with him. "Jesus Christ..." He wondered if he should bother going back to get it. He didn't want to expend any more energy than he had to, but if someone was trying to contact him, he wanted to know as soon as. He drained his cup and trudged back.

His phone was still on the sofa, but when he checked it, there had been no messages. He stuck it in his pocket and went back out, knowing he didn't have any destination in mind. Fortunately, the food was doing its job and he felt reasonably alive, so walked into the centre, just to be away from home for a while. He looked through his contacts and he did have Catarina's number. He didn't know whether it would be a good idea to text her. Maybe she regretted having kissed him. What would he say to her? Maybe Ana would be better, but then again, she might be with Josh or also recovering slowly, so he concluded that he should leave everyone in peace for today. He went up to Sant Jaume, had another coffee and smoked a couple of fags.

With nothing else that he could think of to do, he might as well get the keys and go to work. At least it'll make the day go away faster. He was finished by a quarter past five and was annoyed that he still had so long left. The caffeine was giving him the same effect as the cocaine last night; his mind was running faster than it should, while his body wanted it to fuck off and leave it alone. He knew he could watch the football highlights that evening, so just sat in front of the TV, eating whatever he could be bothered to make and not really taking in what he was watching.

Everyone else would be at work during the day on Monday, so Andy was faced with not getting in touch with anyone until the evening at the earliest. He was feeling more or less back to normal now, so decided to ride his bike around Turia for a while. It didn't give him the same level of therapy as the last time as he couldn't shake the frustration of not knowing if the others wanted to have anything more to do with him or not. He had no idea if he was now considered the bad guy. He didn't think he was, but could have said or done anything while he was off his head. It was eating away at his brain.

He stayed in the park for just over an hour before going back home. He was due to work at the office again later and could try and bump into Catarina again. Would that be a good idea? Probably not. He'd rather get in touch with Josh first. As he was locking his bike up to the stairs, he heard the door of the flat upstairs from him close and slow footsteps being made. He looked up, but couldn't see anyone yet. He waited at the bottom and eventually, a figure came into view. It was an old man, dressed in quite formal attire, trousers and a cardigan over a shirt. His face revealed itself to Andy, which was heavily wrinkled with thick grey eyebrows and a mostly bald head.

"Buenos dias," Andy said as they made eye contact.

"Buenos dias," said the old man with a gravelly voice.

Andy told him that he lived in the other flat and pointed towards the door. The man nodded and said nothing else as he slowly passed him by and went out the door.

"Finally," Andy thought. He hadn't learned much, but at least the man hadn't complained about anything.

He decided not to chance bumping into Catarina and planned to turn up at the office five minutes late again. Just before he left, he got a beep on his phone. He rushed to see what it was and it was from Josh.

"Hi. Can I come round?" It seemed friendly enough, but didn't give too much away.

"Hi. Going to work now. Will text when I finish. 8.15ish."

"OK."

Even though this was good news that he could find out what Josh was thinking, he had to go through all possible situations in his mind for the next hour or so. This was one downside of working on his own. If he had something on his mind, he was stuck with it. "Well, it's not too long to wait. I'll try and get the work done quickly," he thought.

He got to the office at four minutes past seven and did what was becoming his routine check that Catarina wasn't there. A crafty look through the door first, open it, listen for a moment, go in quietly and keep listening out. He was in luck, there was no-one present. He got down to work, giving the desks minimal wiping, vacuuming only if he saw anything on the floor and a quick mop of the kitchen area. He was done by 7.55. He texted Josh to say he could come over in ten minutes.

"OK."

Andy would have preferred to see some kind of friendly word, like 'cool' or 'nice one', but he would find out soon enough. He made haste to reach his flat and thought it might be good just to make it look tidy enough. He didn't know why. Josh probably wouldn't even pay attention, but best to be safe.

The doorbell rang at ten past eight and Andy let him in. Josh wasn't in his usual happy-go-lucky mood, but had a slight air of friendliness. At least, that's what Andy chose to interpret.

"How's it going?" Josh asked.

"Fine, you?"

"Yeah, can't complain."

Andy wanted him to get to the point straight away. Fortunately for him, so did Josh. He looked in Andy's eyes penetratingly.

"You weren't joking, were you?"

"What do you mean?"

"About having half a kilo, of course."

"No, I wasn't," Andy said with an air of disdain. Come on, Josh, show me your reaction.

"Talk me through how you got it."

Andy relayed the story to him in detail and didn't have to make anything up this time. Josh listened intently, never taking his eyes off Andy's.

"So you can see why I kept it a secret.," Andy finished.

"I just don't get it. Why was it still there?"

"I don't have an answer to that. The flat looks like it's been empty for ages. There's no furniture apart from a few basics and it looks totally abandoned."

"So a dealer must have lived there." Josh just wanted to deal with the facts to try to work it out.

"Most likely."

"And for some reason, that dealer had to leave. Either got caught by the police or had to do a runner and couldn't come back."

"That's all that I can think of."

"Or he's been killed by a rival."

"I suppose it's possible," said Andy. "I hadn't thought of that."

"To be honest, that would be the best thing for you. No-one to come back for it. Half a kilo is worth a lot of money."

"I know that!" Andy laughed. "€40,000."

"Jesus..." Josh finally took his eyes off Andy to take this in. "So the fag packet was a lie."

"Yeah. I didn't know what to tell anyone. I had to come up with something that no-one would shop me for."

"Yeah, makes sense. So you've got how much left?"

"Most of it. I've only sold about thirty grams or something. If that."

"That's a hell of a lot to shift. I know a few people, but it would still take ages."

Andy liked the sound of that comment. It meant that Josh was on his side and was thinking of ways that he could help Andy to sell it.

"I just figured that if I can get a good number of regular contacts, then making five hundred sales isn't really that much."

"True. A few months, maybe. You could have forty grand by the end of the year."

Andy raised his eyebrows in a way that said "I sure could!" Josh put his hand over his mouth in contemplation.

"So no-one else knows about this?" he asked.

"No. you didn't tell the girls, did you?"

"No, I didn't say anything. I just said I was tired."

"What else did you three talk about after you left?"

"I can't remember. Probably just bullshit."

"Have you been in touch with Ana since?"

"Only a bit. I'm going to meet her on Wednesday. Have you heard from Catarina?"

"Not yet. I needed to speak to you first. I had no idea what any of you thought about this."

Josh confirmed that they didn't know anything. His mind was still whirring. He looked at Andy, then at the walls, table, anything that didn't get in the way of his thoughts.

"I'm just worried that there might be some comeback," he offered.

"I don't see what there could be. The flat is closed off and if the dealer wanted to rescue to it, or was alive to do so, he would have got it by now."

"Yeah, I dunno, though. You never know the whole truth when you're an outsider."

"Well, nothing's happened yet. I've just sold a few bags, as you know, and everything's been fine so far. If I just continue like this and start to get to know people more, it should shift more quickly."

THE EMPTY FLAT

"Let's hope so. Well, listen. You probably didn't want to tell me about it, either..."

"I was going to, at some point, just not yet. Soon, though."

"Anyone else?"

"No. I mean, Steve and Paul know I've got fifty grams. They're not going to keep tabs on how much I've sold, but I know there will be a time when it seems suspicious that I'm still dealing a few months on. I thought I'd cross that bridge when I come to it."

"I won't tell anyone. I promise you."

"Thanks, mate."

"Forty fucking grand... What are you going to do when you've sold it all?"

"I have no idea. I don't really like doing it, to be honest. It's not my thing and I'm a total newbie to this. I just want to get rid of it and then decide at the time."

"Where are you stashing all the money?"

"I put bits in the bank, but buy stuff with cash, like the bike and that."

"Yeah, sensible. You've got that worked out. But spending that much in cash won't be easy. Nor will putting large sums into your account."

"I know. Don't you think I've thought about all this?"

Josh finally smiled for the first time that evening. "Fair enough," he said. "Can I just see it again?"

"Ha, sure." They went into the kitchen and Andy lifted the floorboard. He pulled out the container and showed it to Josh.

"A fucking gold mine," he said as he looked at it from every angle. He passed it back to Andy and watched as he put it back.

"Alright, listen," Josh said. "I still can't get my head around it properly yet, so I'm going to head off. Just promise me you'll be careful with it."

"Course I will."

Josh nodded, satisfied with Andy's response and they went back to the living room. Josh went towards the door and suddenly looked back at Andy. There was a look of disbelief on Josh's face as he shook his head and smiled.

"See you soon."

"See you, Josh."

The relief that came over Andy after the door closed was possibly the greatest he had ever felt in his life. Josh wasn't going to stop being his friend and he wasn't going to tell the police. "I'm going to be alright," he thought, smiling to himself.

24.

Now, Andy felt that the coast was clear to get in touch with Catarina. As much as he'd been dying to find out how she was and what she knew, after meeting Josh, it didn't seem so urgent. He'd wait until tomorrow and be really friendly with her. He sat on the sofa and his natural emotions came out from behind the curtain again. He'd snogged the woman he fancied and they'd had a good night out. Maybe they would end up going out together, as well as Josh and Ana. He also felt relieved that he didn't have to string Ana along any more. That would be so cool if the four of them paired up. Going out with his girlfriend, his best friend and *his* girlfriend would be ideal. They could all go out dancing and doing coke together like it was the most normal thing in the world. Things seemed like they were looking up. "Okay, I'd be a drug dealer, which isn't the best, but yeah, hopefully I can be done with it before the end of the year, or just a bit after, then I'll have nothing to worry about."

Andy slept well that night and remembered everything when he woke up again. He lay in bed, smiling to himself and imagined that he had his arm around Catarina in bed.

He felt invigorated that day and after having breakfast, he got straight on his bike to go back to Turia. It was sunnier than the last couple of days and the beauty of his surroundings was mirrored on his face as he smiled along his route. He was not usually one to smile at strangers, but felt compelled to do so as everything in his life was coming together. He wished Catarina could be here with him and he resolved to text her that evening to ask if they could meet soon. Even though they'd had a great time together on Saturday, he couldn't remember most of what they spoke about. He still didn't really know much about her and looked forward to being able to do so. He should invite her to come here with him at the weekend. They could have a lovely picnic together.

He spent a good few hours in the park, taking in the colours of the flowers more than he normally would and playing with some of the dogs that came near to him. Had he really found his place here? He felt like he'd got to know Valencia pretty well by now and living there seemed completely normal to him, like he'd been there for years. He lay back on the grass and recounted what he'd been through so far since July. "It's only been two months!" he thought, but couldn't quite believe it. He remembered meeting the Kiwis in Madrid and getting a short cleaning job from Sean. "Yeah, a top bloke," he thought. "I hope his pub is doing well." When he thought back to his time roaming those busy streets, looking for work that never came about, it was like another life.

Then coming over here and staying in the Home hostel. He'd barely noticed it since, but he'd met some good people there, notably Paul. Remembering that time stopped him in his tracks. "I owe him so much. If it wasn't for him, nothing would have worked out the same. I probably would have given up by now and gone back to England." He wanted to show his respect to Paul for what he did; letting him stay in his place for a while meant that he found his flat on Carrer del Bany. He tried to imagine how things might have turned out if he hadn't met Paul.

"I'd probably have figured out getting the agency work eventually, but where would I have lived? I didn't know anyone who lived here then. Man, I have no idea. I probably would have gone somewhere else, like Seville. It's so down to luck, sometimes. I think Paul and I are drifting apart a bit. I'll have to think of some way to repay him."

This brought Andy back down to Earth, but he didn't want to lose the good mood he was in. "I'm a fucking casual drug dealer! Who would have thought that?" He hadn't called his parents for a while and thought he'd better do that soon. He'd just say that he was getting on fine with his cleaning, working a few more hours than was true. That should be enough to placate them.

He got back on his bike to reimmerse himself in the park and rode around for another half an hour. There was still plenty of time before work. He would treat himself to a nice lunch at a small café here then glide around town, wanting to appreciate the city more than he had done so far.

As he walked through the streets of the old town, anyone who noticed him would think he'd just had the best news ever; maybe he'd just become a father or got engaged or something. This was the best day that he'd had in his two months here and he didn't want this feeling to end. He bought a Spanish newspaper and sat outside a café, reading as much as he could to try to learn some new vocabulary.

He actually felt pleased that the day was drifting by slowly. Usually he got fed up with passing the time, but Andy felt like a different person. Eventually, it was time to go to work and he thought it was safe to risk getting there slightly early in case he saw Catarina this time.

He got down to the square ten minutes early and just hung around near to the main door. He saw a man come out looking very businesslike, but no-one else. He pouted his lip, but shrugged it off and went inside. The office was as it always was and he did his job with more enthusiasm than usual. How long should he wait before texting Cati (as he already called her in his head)? He thought one hour would be fine, so sent her a message to ask how she was and that it was great to see her on Saturday. She replied fifteen minutes later to say she was well and it was good to see him, too. Would she like to go for a drink soon? She didn't know yet. She was doing things with her family. Maybe at the weekend. This was enough for Andy. She hadn't turned him down and as far as he could see, she was as up for meeting as he was.

As he was walking down his road and approaching his flat, a man was coming the other way. Nothing unusual there, but this man, with a shaved head and a rough-looking face, seemed to be looking closely at Andy. The man didn't say anything, but was walking a little slower than normal pace. Andy got to the door and put his key in just as the man was passing him. He tried to pay no attention to him, though just as he was entering, he glanced over to him and the man had evidently continued watching him as his head turned away at that moment. Andy furrowed his brow, but closed the door and went upstairs. "Just another junkie," he thought and he soon forgot about him.

Thursday was a quiet day for Andy. His mental state was less elevated as it arrived back at its normal level. He was still happy, but not buzzing like yesterday. It was cloudier and looked like the amazing summer might finally be coming to a close as he noticed it wasn't as hot. He just went about his business as usual and prepared ten bags of cocaine for potential sales at the weekend. He didn't hear from Catarina, Josh or anyone else, but looked forward to making some plans for tomorrow night.

When he got up on Friday, the weather was indeed markedly different. For the first time since he'd been in Spain he saw clouds that were actually grey. He went out to get some shopping as just before he returned home, he was almost in shock when he felt a few raindrops on his head. He looked up and the darker clouds signalled the onset of rain. As he was putting his shopping away, the heavens opened and brought about a downpour that lasted for several hours. He watched it through his balcony doors and it made him think that he really should look into getting some windows put into the frames. He measured them and would go to the hardware shop that he'd been at a few times before as he remembered that they also sold glass.

The rain hadn't abated by the time he went to work. It had been solid for about six hours and was so heavy that you couldn't see the ground for the water that was relentlessly bouncing off it. Another thing Andy had never considered buying was an umbrella and he had nothing waterproof, so had to resign himself to getting soaked and working in his wet clothes.

This torrential rain would probably mean that no-one wanted to go out tonight. It was still delivering by the time he finished work and when he got home, he noticed some water on the floor inside by the balcony, even though he'd closed the shutters. It looked like it was able to get under the doors as well, but didn't know what he could do about that. He should probably contact Maria, but short of replacing the doors, which he doubted she would do, he had to think of some other solution.

Despite the weather, he thought he'd see if Catarina wanted to go out tonight anyway. She replied by saying that she was having dinner with her family. He knew she still lived with them, so didn't they eat together every night? Maybe it was a special occasion, but he didn't think much of it as it was the kind of night to stay in and curl up on the sofa watching TV.

The rain finally exhausted itself by half past ten and Andy welcomed the return of the quiet outside. If it was dry tomorrow, he would go to the hardware shop.

By stark contrast, it was sunny again on Saturday, though cooler and Andy thought that yesterday's rain was a huge announcement by Mother Nature that summer was over and it was time to get prepared for the autumn. He went to the shop and ordered his two panes of glass and was told that they would be delivered and fitted on Monday. They only cost €20, to his surprise, much cheaper than expected, so that was an easy job to get done. On his way back, he got a text from Josh, saying that he, Ana and Catarina were going out that evening and Andy should join them. It seemed that his expectation that the four of them would be spending a lot of social time together was actually happening. Even though the plans had already been made, he texted Catarina anyway to say he was looking forward to seeing her at Gecko, the bar in the square opposite Negrito at eleven.

With the rest of the day to himself, Andy thought abut how Cati always dressed so fashionably. Now that he was making good money, should he make an effort and buy some better clothes? She would surely appreciate his efforts, even though personally, he didn't really care about clothes. He thought he'd just buy a new shirt for the occasion and build up gradually. After browsing a few shops, he bought a plain, light blue shirt that looked quite trendy and hoped she'd notice later.

When he got back to the flat, he had a quick look to see if Precious had any food in the bowl, but to his surprise the bowl was gone. "Why would anyone take that away?" he thought. It couldn't have been another animal, surely. Very weird. He looked in his sideboard and he had another saucer that he never used, so put some food on that and placed it back in the same spot.

The friends met up at Gecko at eleven. Andy was pleased to see that everyone else had got there before him. He shook hands with Josh, gave two kisses to Ana, and Catarina did the same to him. He wondered why she hadn't kissed him on the lips this time, but maybe that was just the Spanish way. He sat down and straight away, Catarina complimented him on his shirt, which made him forget about what had just passed. They talked about the usual things, including the change in weather. The women confirmed that it was normal to have a storm around this time and yes, it meant that it would get colder now, but would still be fairly warm, even into winter. The conversation switched between English and Spanish and Andy tried to find out as much about Catarina as he could. Being in a group meant they didn't have time to themselves so much, but he learned that she had a brother in Madrid and that her father owned the company where she worked and he cleaned. Andy was still unsure of why she had seemed shocked to see him that day. It probably wasn't important, but he wanted to get it cleared up, regardless.

Catarina didn't appear to be as forthcoming as Andy had hoped. Ana touched Josh's arm and hands every now and then, but Catarina wasn't acting in the same way with Andy. They still spoke enough, but he was noticing a different vibe between the two pairs at the table. Maybe it was because Josh was more extroverted than he was and this reflected in Ana's behaviour. She was also more like that than her friend so maybe they would end up as the lively couple and the quiet couple. It was better than nothing and would surely develop as they got to know each other better.

As expected, the conversation came round to cocaine and both Josh and Ana would buy a gram off him that evening. Andy thought it would be good to sell at mates' rates, so reduced his price to €60 for them. Catarina declined buying one as well, even though she clearly used it. She told him that she would share it with Ana. He thought it made sense to let her have it for free as it looked like they were now going out with each other.

They went onto Mosquito and got down to the usual business of snorting a line or two. Andy managed to sell a couple of grams to some teenagers outside. He offered them his phone number in case they wanted to become his customers. He was now going about things in a more confident manner, whereas he had maintained his boundaries more before. It all seemed to be a simple and safe thing to do. When his high was starting to reveal itself, he became more confident still and went back outside to ask a few people if they needed anything. Only one person did, but again, it was easy work and easy money.

The group of friends had another good night, but again, it was Josh and Ana who seemed to be in the spotlight. Andy was feeling that he and his girlfriend should be emulating them and, although Cati came out of her shell more, he still detected the ramparts were up to some degree. She was proving to be quite hard work, but what could he do about it? He made sure he wouldn't get as high as last weekend as he didn't want to lose control and mess things up like then.

As Mosquito came to a close, Andy thought that they would head over to MX, but Josh and Ana wanted to go back to his for some alone time. This was Andy's chance to suggest the same to Cati, but she told him she was tired and would go home. The others made tracks and Andy offered to walk Cati to get a taxi. The mood had been flattened somewhat when he knew that he wasn't getting as much as his friend. He thought about whether this was the time to ask about the office scene. The coke didn't allow him to moderate his thoughts and he asked her about it. At first, she claimed not to remember it, but when pressed again in more detail, she told him that she was feeling anxious that he had shown up at her place of work when she only knew him as a drug dealer. That made sense to Andy and it cleared his mind. Hopefully, she wouldn't feel the same if they met there now, of course, but it was now no longer an issue to him. She found a taxi and gave him a quick two kisses before leaving the scene.

Andy stood there for a short while, feeling deflated and thinking that Josh was going to get lucky. It hadn't yet occurred to him that being under the effects of cocaine usually prevented that from happening, but he marched on home, not so physically tired, but still mentally alert.

Lying in bed, Andy was thinking at a hundred miles an hour. "I want to give her a hug. Nice eyes. Ana is always happy. Josh and Ana having sex. Will I have sex with Catarina? What does she think when she looks at me?" He couldn't form any coherent thoughts and was tiring himself out by being unable to stop. Unsurprisingly, when he woke up, he was still exhausted. The thoughts returned straight away and it was doing his head in. "God, I need to talk to someone. Josh will be knackered. I reckon Paul is the most level-headed." After lunch, he texted Paul to see if they could meet up. Paul invited him over to his place and Andy went straight there.

"How are you doing?" Paul asked.

"I'm okay, well, not that good. I'm confused."

"What's up?"

"I don't know what's going on with Catarina. She's really hard to work out."

"What do you mean?"

"Well, we were out last night with Josh and Ana. We were getting on, but I can't read her mind. Sometimes she seems friendly enough, but other times it feels like she's pushing me away."

"It could just be the case that she wants to take things slowly."

"I guess you're right, but it's driving me mad not knowing."

"You need to just accept that not every woman is clear with what she wants. Just try to take it easy and give her space."

"Yeah, sure. The other thing is I see Josh and Ana and they're getting along really well. You can see the chemistry between them and it's frustrating."

"You can't compare yourselves to them. They're different people and even if it's going smoothly for them, it doesn't mean you're going to have the same experience with someone else."

"Hmm, I get what you're saying. I'll try to ease off a bit, but I don't know what to do next. Should I text her or wait for her to text me?"

"I reckon wait for her. That's how you can find out if she's interested. If she asks to meet you, then it's a good sign. If you don't hear from her at all, then, well, it's obvious."

"Yeah. I've got to not expect too much and try not to think about her."

"Indeed. It won't be easy, but do your best and hold off. Were you both on drugs?"

Andy became tense as Paul asked this question. He thought he was going to get lectured, but knew that Paul would know he was lying if he said no.

"Yeah, not much, though."

"If you don't mind saying, you've changed since you started doing coke."

"Have I?"

"Massively. When I first met you, you were a quiet guy, who had his head together. You worked hard at getting your life sorted out, but I've seen you out, of course, and you act totally differently."

Andy thought about this for a while, thinking about how he used to be. He realised that Paul's words were true. Even though he felt good when he was high, he knew that it was messing with his mind as well. He couldn't think straight and he was sometimes irresponsible.

"Yes, I see what you mean," he said. "Maybe I should take a break from the coke and it will help me to get my head clear."

"I would. Best would be to stop it all together. How much have you got left?"

Andy had no choice but to go back to lying to his good friend. "I've got about twenty grams."

"So try and stay off it and just sell the rest. Then you'll be free from it and can get back to normal."

Andy nodded, knowing full well that it wasn't going to be that easy. He was in it for the long haul. He just wished he could off-load the whole lot in one go, but that was never going to happen. He thanked Paul and said that he was going back home to think about things. Paul looked at him with concern and saw him out.

Usually, at times like this, Andy needed to get out and have a change of scenery, but this time there was too much on his mind and he didn't need any distractions. He made himself a cup of coffee and sat down on the sofa in silence to work out what he should do.

He reflected on what Paul said to him. It would be good to stop doing the coke, but if he was going to be hanging out with the other three, doing the odd line was surely going to happen. Should he stop going out with them altogether? That would mean losing Catarina completely, but he didn't know if he wanted to do that. As Paul had said, it would be sensible to let it go at its own pace and see what happens. He didn't even know if Catarina would want to meet him without the others, as they hadn't even done that yet. Should he invite her to go for a coffee? Paul said to wait for her to contact him. Fuck, this wasn't getting any easier. He wondered if Josh would give him any other advice. He could do with a second opinion, but maybe he was looking for something that would make him feel better about carrying on what he was doing and not worry about changing. He felt closer to Josh and thought that having a chat with him wouldn't hurt, even if he advised something else. Andy wasn't going to trouble him today, but would leave it till in the week when they were both of sound mind again.

Through the rest of the day, he couldn't stop thinking about everything again and again. He wasn't quite so worked up about it, but he still couldn't see a clear path to take. He was having the glass fitted on Monday at eleven and the man turned up on time. Andy let him in and the man got the glass ready. He put the first pane up to the window, but it didn't quite fit. There was a gap of about a centimetre lengthwise. Andy had done the measurements wrong.

He didn't want to pay again for more glass to be cut, so got the man to put it in anyway. It was the same for both panels. With the gap at the top, it should at least be enough to stop the rain coming in, but he was annoyed that he'd got something so simple wrong. The job was done in a few minutes and the man left.

He looked at his new stupid windows and let out a sigh. Did he mess up the measurements because of the drugs? How could he have got it wrong? He wasn't under the influence of anything when he'd measured it. He remembered he wanted to make something else to try to keep the rain from going against the doors and an awning would be a good idea. This also gave him something to take his mind off things for a while and he wanted to get this done perfectly.

"Right," he said vehemently to himself. "Let's go and find some wood."

He measured up the length he would need, then measured it again and wrote it on a piece of paper. He could make two arms for it with leftover pieces of wood he still had, so set off to find his missing piece. He didn't care how long it would take. The more time the better, so he would have something else to focus on. He decided to go down streets he hadn't really seen before, so went across the ring road at the bottom of his road and explored the neighbourhood. Before too long, he found a wooden board, which would be ideal. It wasn't too thick, but when he measured it, it was three centimetres shorter than what he wanted. He would still be able to make it fit, but he didn't want his task to be over so soon, so made a mental note of where it was and carried on going. He had to force himself to look at the buildings around him, in case his thoughts drifted off. That one could do with a new paint job... That balcony is a bit rusty... He wasn't finding anything else suitable as he went around ten or so streets, but kept going anyway. He was convinced that he would find what he wanted if he kept looking for long enough. There wasn't as much stuff left in the streets as there tended to be in his area. Maybe it wasn't the done thing here. He kept searching for another half an hour and found very little else, so just went back to the piece he'd found and took that back home.

He held it up above the balcony doors. It would fit and it didn't really matter that it was a bit short. It just about reached across the gap. He dug out the other pieces of wood he had and thought about how to attach them. The board wouldn't reach out that far if he just put two arms at the bottom, so he decided to make two for the top. Okay, it wouldn't be perfect after all, but it should do the job. How was he going to fix the arms to the wall? He couldn't nail them on, that would destroy the brickwork. He didn't know the solution for this, so went to the hardware shop to ask.

He didn't understand what the man said to him, but he brought over some wall plugs and screws. He demonstrated that he'd have to drill into the wall, push the plugs in then screw into those, but Andy didn't have a drill. The man showed him electric drills that they had, which seemed like too much of an expense just for this job. The man showed him a hand drill, which was only €8, so he opted for that, plus a drill bit to be used in brickwork and four L-shaped brackets.

Andy made sure he measured twice where he wanted the holes to be and double checked if everything would fit. Drilling the holes by hand was harder than he thought and it took him about half an hour. He got the wall plugs in and screwed the brackets to the arms. He screwed each of those to the wall and was thrilled to see he'd done a good job. He lifted the board, expecting that it wouldn't fit, but it actually did and screwed it onto the arms, which he then realised he probably should have done first, but after fiddling about and swearing at himself, he got the awning complete. "Not a bad job," he said. He looked at the gap at the top and thought he'd be able to fix another piece over it in time. He had a celebratory cigarette on the balcony and didn't let his fuck up with the windows bother him.

He looked across to the empty flat. He couldn't decide whether it had been a God send or a rod for his own back by going in there. "Have I made a mistake here?" he thought. He had to convince himself that he'd had it good by being able to sell about thirty grams so far. That was around €2400. He hadn't got into any trouble doing it, but then again, surely it was only a matter of time before something went wrong. All it would take is one bad customer to get aggressive or someone to be under cover and tell the police. No matter how much he told himself things would be fine, the idea of some kind of danger still lingered in his mind. He wanted to keep as low a profile as he could until he was getting steady sales without having to do much. Then he'd be in control.

He managed to calm himself down and went out for a walk. It was still cooler outside, so he set himself a new task: to buy a jacket and an umbrella. He got this job done quickly and acquired a denim jacket and a full-sized brolly, so went for his usual coffee to pass some more time. He didn't want to go to Sant Jaume or Plaza del Negrito as it would make him think of Catarina. He went to television square as at least it had more of an association with Ana and he could just watch the people going by. It didn't particularly help as he kept noticing women who might just be Catarina. Almost every woman of her age had dark, long, straight hair, sometimes tied back and he couldn't help inspecting each and every one of them. He tried looking at the men instead, but this provided very little stimulation to Andy and his eyes kept drifting back to the women.

He couldn't put up with this for much longer, so he went back home, re-admired his awning and thought about what to do. It was time to get a computer, he thought and counted how much money he had left. He had €1,320 in cash. Would it be too risky to

THE EMPTY FLAT

buy a computer with cash? He should probably go and out another couple of hundred in his bank account, so went out to do that and saw that he had €815 in there. That should be enough, he thought.

He went down to the computer shop near him and started looking. As he didn't know much about computers, he asked the assistant, a smartly dressed man in his thirties, who advised him. To buy a whole set of equipment that seemed enough for his needs, he would spend just over €500. That wouldn't leave much left in his bank account, so he asked if he could pay for part of it in cash, part on his card. That would be no problem, so he settled it there and did a couple of trips to carry his new purchase back.

Andy didn't really know what to do with it, but had a look around to see what there was. He soon found the games Solitaire and Minesweeper, which filled his time for an hour or so. He didn't have the internet yet, so would have to go and get a contract. He felt that once he knew his way around, it would help to take his mind off things and he wanted to see if he could get more games soon.

He had a go on Paint, which he'd used when he was at university. That should keep him occupied, too and he managed to fill his time trying out different things before he had to go to work.

While he was there and went through the same issue of not being sure whether he should try to bump into Catarina, he wondered if he should quit his cleaning work now and focus more on selling drugs. He was confident that he would be able to make enough to comfortably live off and it would take away the burden of going to the office three times a week. If things didn't work out with Cati he would be more anxious about going there and then trying to avoid her. Selling three grams a week would make him €240, so around a thousand a month, which would be fine. It was likely that this was due to go up, quickly, he hoped, so was it worth staying in this job? He decided to see how he felt over the coming week and make a decision by Friday.

The next day he got a contract for the internet and a home phone number and someone would come to set it up on Friday. His Windows 98 operating system was in Spanish, which was tricky to navigate, but he thought it would also be useful to improve his Spanish. It had Office installed, which he'd used more than anything else and he decided to make a spreadsheet to keep track of his sales and contacts. He set it to record weekly sales, although by now he had to guess how much he'd sold so far. It made him feel very official to manage what was effectively his own business, but in case anyone found out about it, he named his file "Freelance work".

That evening he wanted to get in touch with Josh and meet up for a drink to go over what he'd already discussed with Paul. Josh agreed to met him tomorrow night and would come round to Andy's.

On Wednesday, he had exhausted about all he could think of doing with his computer by early afternoon. There was a lot he still had to learn about, but things should get more interesting when he had the internet. At eight o'clock, Josh came round.

"Did you have a good night on Saturday?" Josh asked, winking.

"Yeah, it was good. Nothing happened after you left. Catarina got a taxi home."

"Oh well, maybe next time."

"How about you?"

"Yeah, pretty good. Ana came round to mine. We did a couple more lines and talked for hours."

"I guess you got laid as well."

"Not till the morning. Guys can't have sex when they're on coke. Didn't you know that?"

"Really? How come?"

"You can't get hard when you're on that."

"Seriously?"

"Yeah," Josh laughed. "One of the downsides of it. Maybe it was good Catarina didn't come back if that's what you hoped to do. It wouldn't have been good to find out then!"

"Man, that's bad. How long do you have to wait?"

"A couple of hours or so after taking it. It's worth keeping in mind if you plan to have sex."

"I'll keep that in mind. So things are going well with you two?"

"Yeah, man. We're getting on really well. We're in touch most days. She's the right kind of girl for me. Always up for fun and a chat."

"I wish it was the same for me and Catarina." Andy proceeded to tell Josh the same things he had told Paul. He got more or less the same advice back, which he was disappointed about, but asked if Ana had said anything about what Catarina felt.

"She didn't say that much, to be honest. She just said that Catarina doesn't jump into relationships quickly. She takes her time to get to know guys, so I wouldn't worry about it."

"I don't know how long I can put up with that, though."

"Mate, you'll just have to see what happens. I'm sure she'll warm to you soon. You'll notice when things start to feel different. When are you seeing her next?"

"Paul said I ought to wait for her to contact me first. The thing is I don't even know if she will. It's hard not to think about it."

"Yeah, that's a tough one. How long are you going to give it?"

"No idea. Maybe she expects me to always get in touch first, so what should I do if I don't hear anything by this weekend?"

"I'll have a word with Ana to see if I can find out anything for you."

"Thanks, that could be useful."

Andy showed Josh his computer, although Josh knew little more about it than Andy. He wasn't that interested in them so after a short while, Josh headed back home.

On Friday he got his dial-up internet connection. He went to some sites that he knew about, like the BBC and Sporting Life. He realised that this had been his first real connection with UK life since being here. He'd pretty much forgotten about his home country, apart from speaking to his parents. It seemed strange to be reading articles about things happening over there. At the same time, Andy didn't know much at all about what was going on in Spain. He'd been stuck in his own world for the last two months and it made him think: was it better to be disconnected from the outside world or up to date with the news? He'd not been an avid news reader when he was living in the UK, but it was hard to avoid a lot of things. It was too much effort to try to keep up with news in a foreign language, plus even if he read stories, the people or places would mean nothing to him. In the end, he wasn't that fussed about missing out on the news. A lot of the time his own life got too much for him, he knew that very well, so he probably would have a look at what was going on back home every now and then.

Without realising it, he found that having the internet did keep his mind occupied and the time passed more quickly when using it. He liked not having to think about Catarina all the time, but he still had to go and work in the office that evening and still wondered if she would contact him.

His shift passed in the same way as usual. No Catarina and nothing of interest. He was supposed to make a decision about leaving by today, but felt it was too risky to do so, in case for whatever reason the drug dealing came to a halt. Andy wanted a safety net, so he thought he would hang on for a while longer and re-evaluate things in a few weeks.

He had no plans to do anything that evening. He'd got no news from Josh, so he must not have spoken to Ana like he said he would. Nothing from Catarina, so he turned on his computer and went back on the internet. It was cheaper to use after 6pm so he could keep himself busy for a few hours.

By ten o'clock he was bored of that, so thought he might as well go out and try to sell some more. It was becoming easier for him over time, so he got five grams ready. It was too early to be visiting the clubs, so he entertained himself by walking around the centre and observing people. He had a quick drink at a couple of bars he'd never been to just for a change, all the time keeping his eye open for anyone who looked like they might want to buy, though he didn't know what signs he could look for. He wondered what Catarina was doing and whether he might bump into her. He hoped he wouldn't as that would feel pretty awkward. He couldn't really imagine being excited to see her if she did show up. Maybe he was already getting over her after having no contact for a week.

By one o'clock it was time to head down to Mosquito. He felt at home there and saw the odd face he'd seen there once or twice before. As he drank his beer inside, all the time watching out for buyers, he noticed he felt more confident about what he was there for. He went into the toilet to see if he could sell. There was one guy in there having a piss. Andy waited for him to finish then asked if he wanted coke. The guy gave a nervous look to him, then looked away, shaking his head. This small, uncomfortable interaction made him think that it probably made him look suspect by being there on his own. He should probably keep a low profile and wait until the place was busier. He definitely wasn't going to take any himself tonight, but just try and mingle and slip in the odd friendly question to people.

Within the hour, the place was filling up. He noticed someone he'd sold to before and waited until there was a good moment to approach him. The guy didn't remember him at first, but after a few moments he recognised Andy. He said he didn't need any, so Andy told him to let anyone else know he was here and they could buy some. The guy nodded.

"Let's have a look outside," he thought. As always, there was a small crowd there and Andy tried to be as non-confrontational as he could as he moved between people. He found a couple who were after some, so they walked away and went through the process. He asked if they wanted his number, but they declined. He said the same thing about telling other people in case they wanted some and he hung around some more.

He was not getting any other business so he went back inside to try to get into the dancing. It wasn't as much fun when sober, but he would hopefully not stand out by doing so. Some people near him were looking like they were already high, but he asked them anyway. They said they were fine and carried on dancing.

Then he saw someone else he recognised. It was the teenager from a few weeks ago, who had lost control and got thrown out. Andy was surprised to see him back here. Obviously the door staff weren't very strict. This could be an easy sale, but Andy was hesitant to ask him after remembering what a mess he had got into before. He remembered what Paul had said about him being totally different when on coke and instead chose to ignore the lad. He didn't want to see him get in the same state again, knowing it was partly Andy's fault. As he pondered this, someone tapped Andy on the shoulder and asked him if he had coke. He must have been a friend of one of the people he'd already sold to. Andy quickly inspected him to work out if he was undercover, but he seemed quite drunk, so should probably be safe. They agreed to go to the toilets separately, the guy going first.

When Andy got in there, there were three other men using the facilities. He gestured to the guy to wait a minute. One of the others gave a shifty look to them both on his way out, which Andy didn't like at all. He didn't want to do the deal there. He suspected that the guy who left would call the doorman. He shook his head at the guy and went back out, trying to keep a low profile and see where the guy was. He spotted him not far away and he was talking to his friends. It seemed he hadn't notified the doorman, but Andy wanted to be out just in case. He looked over his shoulder and his customer came out. With his eyes he signalled for the guy to follow him, which he did. They went outside and just as Andy was leading him away from the door, the guy threw up on the pavement. Some of it splashed on Andy's trainers and he closed his eyes in annoyance. Should he sell it now? This guy was a mess. He threw up again, but Andy managed to avoid it this time. There was no way he was going to sell it now. Maybe most drug dealers don't care about the state of their customers, but Andy couldn't lower himself to that. He decided to call it a night and went back, having only sold two grams.

He looked in dismay at the state of his trainers on the way back. He took barely any notice of anyone as he was in a bad mood. He didn't even have a washing machine to chuck them in, so would have to soak them in the kitchen sink. He wouldn't be wearing them again for a couple of days.

Andy wasn't that happy with tonight's business. He'd made more of an effort than he'd done before, but only made €160. "I guess that's just how it goes, sometimes," he thought, but wished things would start speeding up. This was becoming a drag. At this rate, he'd still be trying to shift it for another year. "Surely it's got to change," he thought as he switched his computer on.

As he was waiting for it to start up, he heard something outside. It sounded like a chain rattling. Was it the one on his bike? Had he not shut the front door properly? He gingerly opened his door and listened, but there was no-one there. He tried to ascertain where the sound had come from. He hadn't seen anything else locked up outside. He thought he'd leave it a minute before having a look. He put his ear to his balcony door, but couldn't hear anything. He carefully opened it and peered out through the gap. There was no-one there. He opened it some more and listened. No sound, so he thought it was safe to go out. Again, there was not a soul in the vicinity, but he could see someone walking up the road. It was too dark to make out, but he knew it was a man. He looked over the balcony to locate a chain and the only one he knew of was the one on the gate under the empty flat. Had Precious been there and accidentally knocked it, making the sound? He couldn't see any sign of it. He went back inside, closed the doors and passed the next hour lazily browsing the web.

25.

On Saturday, the weather had picked up again and he texted Josh to see if he wanted to go for a coffee. "Sure, 1pm?" Andy didn't have anything else to do before that, so had a walk around. He thought he might as well have a coffee before meeting Josh and went to Sant Jaume. He managed to get some shade under a canopy and looked around as he waited for his coffee to be brought out. To his surprise, he saw Catarina going past. She saw him and it took a second for her to decide if she wanted to meet him. She came over with a smile on her lips, but not in her eyes and greeted him.

"It's good to see you," he said.

"You, too," she replied.

It seemed obvious to ask her if she wanted to join him and she said "Vale." The waiter came out with his coffee and Catarina ordered one for herself. This interruption in their slightly tense chance meeting already threw Andy off track, but he asked her how she was. She said she was fine and reciprocated the question.

"I'm fine, thanks. I'm meeting Josh later, but thought I'd come out and enjoy the weather."

"Me, too. I'm going to meet a friend soon."

"Did you go out last night?"

"No, I stayed at home. You?"

The conversation was struggling to get anywhere, but he told her a bit about going out for a quiet drink. She guessed that he had probably been selling drugs, but didn't go into it.

"Do you plans for tonight?" he asked.

"I'll probably go out with Carla. That's who I'm going to see."

Andy wasn't getting the message that she was going to invite him to join her. She didn't elaborate on what they were going to do and instead asked him how his week was.

"It was fine. I've bought a new computer, so I'm getting used to that."

Catarina nodded with interest in her eyes at hearing this news. "Do you have a computer?" he asked her.

"No. I use it at work every day. I don't want to see a computer when I go home."

He smiled. That made sense. They chatted for a little while longer, Andy asking how Ana was and Catarina replying that she was fine. She didn't want to talk about her and Josh in case it brought up things between them. She finished her coffee before Andy did and said she had to go. She got her purse and opened it, but said that she didn't have any money with her and would he be okay to to pay for it? He said it was fine and dismissed it with a wave of his hand. She gave him a farewell kiss on both cheeks and went on her way.

This gave Andy something to think about. The first time he'd seen her for a week, nothing more than chit-chat and no desire from her to make any plans to meet up. It was clear to him that nothing else was going to happen with them. He finished his coffee, paid and went for a stroll before meeting Josh back here in half an hour.

Josh was already at the table when Andy returned. Wearing his shades, light green t-shirt and knee length, beige shorts, he looked as cool as he always did. He greeted Andy with a hug.

After going through the motions of asking how each other was, Andy informed him of how he'd just bumped into Catarina and his thoughts of how it went.

"Right," Josh said. "I've spoken to Ana and she thinks that you should give her some time. She tends to be a big cagey when getting to know a guy, but she doesn't mean anything bad by it. She might still be interested, but try not to put too much on it. She's been with a couple of guys before who messed her about, so she doesn't give out too quickly."

"I see. I suppose that's fair enough, but the thing is, if it continues like this I can see myself losing interest in her."

"I know what you mean, but I think she is worth sticking with. Ana speaks highly of her, so after some time you'll probably see that for yourself when she starts to let her guard down."

"Alright, so act like nothing is happening, stay in touch and just see how it goes."

"Exactly. Don't beat yourself up about it. Just get on with your life. I find that women tend to respond better to you when you don't make it too obvious."

"How do you mean?"

"If you show you're interested in her, it'll be obvious and she might make you wait longer, but if you act like you're not bothered, then she'll come running to you, wanting your attention."

"Really? Have you had that happen before?"

"A few times, yeah. A woman can have you in the palm of her hand if she thinks you're begging for it! Make *them* work for it instead. You'd be surprised."

"Hmm, I've never thought of it that way before. Okay, I'll bear it in mind. So how's it going with Ana?"

"Still good. She's proper girlfriend material. We just knew pretty much straight away that we liked each other. We're going out later and you're welcome to join us."

"Ah, I don't want to be the gooseberry, mate."

"Don't worry about that. We won't make you feel like a spare part."

"Okay. What are you doing then?"

"The usual. Mosquito and MX. I think a few of her friends are going to be out, too. I've put a word in for you. I think you can expect some sales and maybe some regular contacts."

"Oh, right. That sounds good. I could do with that finally coming about."

"I'll get you sorted, mate."

"Cheers, Josh. I'll make it up to you as well."

"Don't worry about that. Just buy me a drink, that's enough."

"You've got mates' rates anyway and you always will. I'll see if Steve and the others want to come, too."

That evening, Andy met Josh and Ana in the square and Steve came along, too. Each of them arranged buying a gram for €60 and Ana said that some of her friends would get some. Josh was on hand to give him some more advice.

"As people tend to stick with their normal dealers, you might want to reduce your price a little to try to win them over. I reckon selling at €75 would be enough."

"That's a good idea," Andy said. "Maybe then if the word gets around, more people will get in touch with me."

"It might be a risk, though, if other dealers find out you're undercutting them," Steve added.

"As long as you keep it like that just for friends of friends, you'll be alright, I reckon," Josh said. "Sell for €80 to strangers and that won't take everyone away from the dealers. It's a dog eat dog world anyway and they know there's more than one dealer around. It's just how it is. You sell what you can sell."

That was enough to convince Andy and it sounded like he had a good new strategy to start building up his list of buyers.

"I'm just going to pop back and drop this money off, so I'm not carrying around too much. How many grams do you think I should carry tonight?"

"Ten should do it, I reckon," Josh said.

"Cool. I'll be back in half an hour, then."

He met back with them at Negrito and Ana informed him that a couple of her friends were already out and looking to buy. She helped to organise a meeting place just off Caballeros. Andy met David and Carlos, who he was able to discuss what deal he could give them and for the new price. They exchanged phone numbers and said they'll see what they thought of the coke later on, but as they seemed friendly and no trouble, Andy was confident it would work out. They told him they knew other people who might be interested and would send them his way, depending on their analysis of the product at stake. David and Carlos were going elsewhere for a drink to meet their mates and would catch up with Andy at the club.

When Andy got back to his group, he said he needed to go back and drop off the money again.

"It's a pain, but it looks like I'm going to have a good day of business. I'll meet you at Mosquito." He wasn't that bothered about going back a second time as this could be the start of a new opening and he would try to organise things so that he could do all the sales around the same time, then not have to worry for the rest of the night. He'd already made €330 and could even double that tonight. He quickly weighed out another five grams and headed out for the third time.

He met the others at Mosquito and people were already getting started on their objective for the night. By two o'clock, he'd sold another four grams and got more phone numbers. As there was still potential for this new crowd to send more customers Andy's way, he thought he'd hold off on the coke again to be on the safe side. As he'd made so much money with very little effort, he was in a good mood anyway and he was happy to join in with the party while under the influence of alcohol only. Two more grams were sold. It seemed the whole world was into coke, but Andy wasn't feeling that comfortable about having €450 in his pockets. He wanted to go back home again, but at this time of night, he would have liked to have a chaperone for safety's sake. Josh was the obvious one to ask, but he could see that he was focused on his night. Andy tried not to think about it and to see if he could stay out and relax. By the time Mosquito finished, everyone around them was in their own world, but Andy was trying to keep a level head. He was still thinking about the money he was carrying and just had to go back home again to get rid of it.

On the way back, he was nervously looking all around him in case he got mugged. When he came to a turning, he would sneakily look round the corner to see if it was clear before heading down there. If he saw someone, he'd pretend he was hanging around as he watched to see where they were going. It took him an extra ten minutes to get back and was very relieved when he closed his front door behind him. He stashed the money in his wardrobe, €880 in one evening. He could barely get his head around it. He stayed in for a few minutes trying to process this and when he saw how easy it was going to get, he wanted to celebrate with his friends and hopefully new friends, so took a couple of lines himself and headed over to MX. Now with nothing to worry about, just one partly used bag in his pocket and €20 in cash, he calmly went back into the centre. With his guard down, he didn't notice that someone was watching him from the shadow of a tree in the park just up his street.

The cocaine hadn't yet kicked in by the time he arrived at MX. He wondered if the doorman would remember him from last time, but seeing there was a fair number of people on various drugs, Andy didn't stand out from the rest. Hugs bombarded him from his happy customers, which made his share kick in and he was soon at one with the rest of them. Josh was too far gone to remember to ask him how his sales had been. He was bouncing around in his usual fashion, with Ana being the main focus of his attention. Andy had hardly thought about Catarina and whether he would see her tonight. He could just let go and let the atmosphere take him over. They carried on till the early hours, when one by one the group slowly diminished and Andy left just after six. With not a care in the world, he made his way back, still smiling and thinking about what a good and successful night he'd had. There was barely anyone left in the streets and the daylight was beginning to make its way to Valencia.

26.

The mysterious figure, who had been lurking in the shadows, had moved on by now. With very little else going on in their world, they had been perusing the area, which they were familiar with. The neighbourhood of El Pilar was one that had also been home. They were a somewhat integral part of its seedy underworld. Known to the prostitutes, who, as the reader will remember, claimed the upper end of Carrer del Bany as theirs, had been visited several times over the years by this character, but not so much in the last couple of years. Andy was lucky not to have encountered them that night. If it had been known that he was carrying so much money, it wouldn't have lasted long in his possession. However, Andy had been seen coming to and going from his flat that night and it aroused the interests of whoever it was. No detectable sound had been made from the person's footsteps as Andy passed the park and advanced to his destination, yet footsteps had been made as this character was interested to know where he was going. They had first seen him when Andy made his second trip back. Whereas it was fortunate that Andy had had his wits about him on that journey, it wouldn't have helped a great deal as this person was well experienced in knowing how to make someone very quiet very quickly. Seeing Andy come back out after a few minutes and head back into the nightlife gave some clues as to why he had done so. Sure, it could have been that he'd forgotten to bring something out, his phone maybe, this could have been dismissed, but Andy returning shortly after, then going back into town after another few minutes was something of a pattern. These are not typical actions to be carrying out so late at night. It was something to go on.

The mystery person was not at liberty to follow Andy back into town as the ladies of the night were on duty and there were other members of the public who could be heard in the near distance. They stayed waiting, expecting, if not hoping that Andy would come back a third time. It was a necessary procedure to remain hidden. Only one other person had passed through the park during this period, someone who was down on their luck and in need of a fix. A scruffy man with shoes beyond repair and matted black hair had been fixated on finding something of use on the paths: a discarded cigarette, which still had a small amount of tobacco that could be salvaged and put towards the roll-up that he was collecting for. The figure in the shadows stood still, breathing softly as their eyes tracked the destitute man, who left the park after less than two minutes, unaware that his innocent endeavour had been meticulously tracked.

At the same time, the figure had been scanning the immediate vicinity with their hearing in case of any other footsteps that could signal the return of the wanted man.

Another hour had passed while Andy was out for the next three. Concluding that Andy wasn't going to be back for the same reasons as before, the character emanated from the shadows, yet revealing themselves to no-one. They walked down the road, knowing exactly which one was our faithful Andrew Harper's abode, looking to the left to see if the road was occupied; it wasn't. The black metal front door was examined: securely shut. The balcony doors were in a likewise fashion fully closed. The metal bars and wooden frames of the glass panels on the doors at ground level, underneath the balcony were ones which could be employed to gain access to said balcony, but it was easily possible that Andy could have come back down the road at any time, so a risk was not going to be taken.

The person had got enough information for now and could use it to formulate plans for the near future. Andy's movements would need to be investigated more thoroughly before any relevant actions were to be made, so the figure moved quietly into the night, raising no suspicions from anyone.

Andy rose the following lunchtime, not feeling quite as bad as he had done the last time he'd gone out on a bender. With no relationship issues to deal with, but with quick recollections of what he had been up to until the early hours, he went straight to his wardrobe to cast his eyes on his loot. He rummaged under the spare clothes to be greeted by so many bank notes that he couldn't pick them all up in one go. He couldn't quite remember how much he had made, so collected them all (the cash he'd had before last night was stashed in a small metal box) and went gleaming into the front room. It was dark as the balcony doors were closed. Even though he knew full well that no-one could see into his flat, he only opened the shutters to let the light in. He paid little attention to the blue sky and went to his table. He sorted the notes into twenties, tens and fives and made stacks of hundreds of Euros. He smiled all the time that he completed each one, the last one falling a little short. He carefully counted them and, as he said "eight hundred and eighty," he grinned, remembering that number from last night.

"Fucking yes!" he said to himself. He thought back to the various people he'd met. "I've got loads of new customers!" He went to get his phone to look through the contacts list to see which ones were new and how many he'd got. Six new names, four men and two women. He got some elastic bands and wrapped up the bundles of notes in packs of €200. One of them would accompany him to the bank tomorrow, the rest would have to join what he already had. "I'm going to need to buy a safe," he thought, only half-jokingly.

Andy wished he could go out and celebrate with his friends, but knew that today would not be the right time. Maybe he should organise another party soon. He thought about inviting Ana's friends from last night, but with the amount of cocaine that would inevitably be taken, that might not be a good idea. He imagined that his flat would either get trashed or it would cause too much of a noise that the police may turn up.

By now, he estimated that he'd sold the fifty grams that most people thought he had, but with his ongoing trade, people like Ana and Steve would surely pick up on the fact that he had a lot more. "I'm sure they won't care. They'll be happy if I can keep supplying them," he thought. "I suppose they'll just think that I'm buying it now to sell on." In his mind, everything was going well.

The idea of quitting the cleaning came back to him and it now seemed like the sensible time to do so. It would probably clear any interference of customers asking to buy in the evenings while he was at work. He wanted to keep everyone happy and think of him as being a reliable dealer. That's how he would make sure they would always come back to him.

The next day, he went over to the agency office to inform Belén that he wanted to leave. She told him he had to give two weeks' notice, which he was fine about. He went to the bank to deposit the €200 he'd planned to put in and remembered about maybe getting a safe. Would there be any point to that? It would keep the money safe inside it, but if someone broke in, they would find it more easily and just take the whole thing. He dropped this idea and decided to see if he could come up with any more clever hiding places. Nothing came to mind and he'd already thought long and hard about this, but it was necessary now, so he liked the idea of setting to work and finding solutions that he could take pride in.

While thinking about his security, another thing that he thought of was to get a spare key. If he got mugged and lost his keys, he'd be buggered as it was, so he went to get two done, just in case. Josh should be fine about looking after one for him and he'd ask Paul to have the other.

He went back home and as he was going up the stairs, he noticed the window outside his front door. The frame protruded inwards from the wall and had a slight lip on it, which could house a key easily. He tried it out and thought this could be a good idea if he happened to lose his while he was out. He got some gaffer tape and covered the key. As the top of the window frame was above eye level, that should be safe enough.

He looked around his flat to consider his options for places to hide his money. There were many small places that could be used for small amounts. There were also many that he thought were too obvious, such as under the mattresses in his room and the spare room. Everyone knows about doing that. False partitions in his bedside table or in the sideboard could be good, but again, lots of people knew about doing that. He'd seen it in TV programmes and films a number of times. The more he considered things such as hiding it in a cereal box or biscuit barrel were way too obvious and it was not as easy as he thought it might be. He continued to look round. Books, no, way too easy to look through and pick up. It needed to be something that was too big to carry away, but too difficult to get open. It would be great if he could hollow out an area in his dining table surface, but that would be beyond his abilities. What other large furniture could he do something with? He'd have the same issue with the sideboard. He went back into his bedroom and looked at the bed. At the foot of the bed was one large wooden panel from the floor to above the mattress. Again, hollowing out was not an option, but he thought that if he could get another panel the same size as this one that he could screw on, then finish the edge with a strip that covered the join, that could hold a lot of money. He grinned to himself at this idea. "No-one would spot that," he thought. As he was so used to going out and scavenging for materials, that was what came to mind first. However, now that he was well off, he could pay to have a nice piece of wood cut. He wrinkled his nose at the memory of getting his window measurements wrong, so made sure he paid close attention to it this time, writing them down and checking again. He measured the width of the existing board and headed over to the hardware shop, where they now recognised him.

He'd thought about the shade of wood that was used on the bed. He wanted to get it close enough to that so that it blended in nicely. The man in the shop told him to come back in an hour and he could also buy the trim to go around the edges.

"Time for a coffee," he thought and headed out. Compared to how Andy had been at the start of his Spanish adventure, now, at the start of October, he was much more confident. He walked around the streets with an air of knowing exactly who he was. He'd been through a lot of emotional turmoil in this short time to prepare himself better. Even though he was very satisfied with finding his latest solution, he still didn't like having so much cash at his disposal. He didn't want to risk putting more in the bank, despite no eyebrows or questions being raised whenever he went in there. However, it was not worth the risk to try depositing as much as €500 just one time. As he drank his coffee and pondered this dilemma, he thought that he could perhaps put in amounts that weren't always rounded off to the hundreds. €280, €330? They'd probably just think he earned different amounts in different weeks. As long as he kept it below €400, that shouldn't look suspicious, he reckoned. Of course, his bank account would always be on the increase, but people save money, right?

He went back to the shop and paid €36 for the board and the trim, just pocket money now.

He carried it back home, which turned out to be more of a struggle than he thought as he couldn't properly get his arms around it. He'd just reached the street parallel to his, Carrer de Guillem Sorolla, when he needed to rest his arms. He was at the crossroads, where he would normally walk on to the top of his street and say hi to the prostitutes, but just for the hell of it, he went down Guillem Sorolla and through the park.

Andy's arms were aching and and he was having to watch where he was walking as the small park had winding paths and trees and bushes that sometimes got in his way. As he navigated his path, the eyes of a middle-aged man noticed this sight from under the brim of a hat, saw what was in front of him then looked down at the ground until Andy had gone past him. The eyes then lifted and watched him as he exited the park and went between the two buildings on his street and out of view.

Andy put the board against the wall next to the balcony doors as his forearms felt like concrete. As excited as he'd been about getting it fixed on, he needed to have a break first. He opened the balcony doors and pulled a chair towards them. He let his arms hang down as though he had lost use of them to let the muscles relax as much as they could. He gazed absent-mindedly at the only things ahead of him that gave any kind of visual stimulation – the old painted sign of "Muebles, Carpinteria". It would have been handy if this business was still open. He'd be able to get more furniture and DIY sorted a lot quicker. They could use a pulley to go from their window to his. "Oh well," he thought. "I can't complain. I'm basically getting everything for free now!"

After a few minutes, he took the board to his bedroom. All the time he expected it to not quite fit. If it was a bit big he could cut some off, but if it was too small again... He put it against the footboard, absolutely flush. "Wow, I've finally got there," he said in amazement. He took out the roll of trim from his pocket and tested to see if it covered the depth of the two pieces. Maybe just one millimetre too wide, but that was totally fine. He'd have to cut pieces for the three edges that showed. He could glue them onto the footboard and that would make a frame that his new one would slot into. He planned to use four small screws, one near each corner to fix it on, which he could unscrew in a minute to get to his money. He'd been thinking of how he would actually store it as the space between the boards was next to nothing. He thought about getting lots of envelopes to put notes in, maybe up to five thick or whatever would work. As he had 130cm by 50cm to play with, he could fit quite a lot in there, but he didn't want them to fall out every time. Blu Tack was the obvious answer to fix them all like a display that no-one but him would ever see. He'd got a couple of envelopes, so did a test and put five twenty Euro notes in and stuck it on. He pressed the new board against it and it seemed good enough. When screwed on, it would sit nicely, so he dug out his screws and had a few short ones that should do the job. He wanted this to look the most professional of anything he'd done so far. It had to look like it was nothing out of the ordinary. He measured three centimetres in from each corner and drilled the holes with his hand drill. "I think I should buy an electric one now that I can," he thought as he tried to keep it steady. The holes were made well enough and he stuck the envelope on and screwed it to the bed. "Looking good." He took the plastic trim and measured it extremely carefully so the corners would join up and cut it. He'd forgotten to get some glue, but would go back out in a bit and get lots of envelopes, too. He strode back along his street with his new-found confidence to El Cheapo.

He was back five minutes later. The eyes under the hat were still monitoring him. The fact that Andy was in and out so often made the man wonder what was really going on. There was plenty that he didn't know about, but his constant to-ing and fro-ing in the daytime and night-time seemed odd.

Andy spent the next hour meticulously filling his envelopes each with five notes, sticking rows of them to the footboard until he'd got nineteen of them in their new home. He carefully slotted the board into place and screwed it on. He took the trim and glued half the length of each strip and fixed it to the original furniture. It needed securing so he used some sticky tape to wrap around the edges. He felt proud of his achievement. Whereas he'd doubted his work many times regarding the floorboard, this time he was certain that no-one would guess what he'd done. "Buried treasure," he said in a deep voice as he furrowed his brow with a look of deep satisfaction on his face.

Andy left the glue to dry and went back into the front room. He sat on the sofa and thought about the party that he had in mind. Maybe he should have a meal instead for Josh, Ana and Catarina. It would be nice to have something more civilised than another debauchery session. Maybe that would impress Catarina and win her over. He ruminated over her for a couple of minutes. Did he still have any interest in her? He thought about how she looked. She was beautiful. She dressed nicely, but there was that invisible barrier that she always had before her. He remembered Josh's advice to play it cool and act as if he didn't fancy her, then see how she reacted. He liked that idea. He felt that he was now the man in charge and could make the rules. He would still be going to her office that evening, which brought him back to reality as his confidence faltered somewhat at the prospect of bumping into her. "Just go ten minutes late again." He put on his computer and played Minesweeper for an hour, had something to eat and went out to work.

He got there fifteen minutes late, but still had to do his usual safety check. Empty corridors and an empty office. Now that he had given his notice in, the work felt more relaxed than ever. He had not a care in the world, feeling he was now in control of his own life. He planned to go and buy some more clothes tomorrow and start dressing better. "I might as well use up that money," he thought.

THE EMPTY FLAT

When he'd finished, he texted Josh to invite him and Ana to dinner on Friday. Josh liked the idea and would ask Ana. Half an hour later, Josh replied to say they would come.

Andy felt hesitant to text Catarina. There had been no contact since her met her at Sant Jaume, but he had nothing to lose. If she said no, then it could still happen for the three of them. Catarina didn't reply for over an hour. He was marvelling at his handiwork in his bedroom when his phone beeped. "Si, gracias." She said she would bring drinks, but Andy said she didn't need to as he would get everything. "Vale, gracias," she replied.

He felt in control again. He'd got it his way and felt smug about it. "That will be make or break time," he thought. "If she isn't impressed, she can move on." This time he wanted to make an effort with cooking and planned to try a few things for himself over the week to see what worked.

He peeled off the sticky tape carefully and looked at his creation. It looked perfect. He stood back by the door to see it in less detail and it looked hardly distinguishable from before. Even if the bed moved for whatever reason, the new board was going nowhere. He opened a beer and sat down to watch TV for the rest of the evening.

27.

Over the course of the week, Andy had plenty to put his mind to. The idea of the dinner party made him feel that he wanted to splash out his money and impress his guests with some more improvements to his flat. On the back wall of the living room was an old painting that Andy didn't care about. It was a faded print of a countryside scene and it added nothing to the décor. He went out to look for a replacement and he'd remembered seeing an arts stall in the Mercat Central. After browsing through the print racks, he went for a large Kandinsky print of Composition VIII, which was about the same size as that dull painting and he might be able to use the frame for it. However, he didn't care if he needed to get a new frame as he was happy to be free with spending his money.

As the market was near to his place, he took it back to see. It wasn't the same shape as what was there, so getting it framed would be his next plan.

He also needed to get some recipe ideas. He would struggle with using a recipe book in Spanish, so searched on the internet and found a couple of sites that he could use. He wasn't confident enough to try something too complicated, but might try something with fish or chicken.

He bought some more clothes during the week, including some more expensive jeans and trainers. He'd thought about getting some smart shoes, but even though he could dress more fashionably, it just wasn't really his thing. He preferred to stay in his comfort zone and not try to become someone who he wasn't.

On Wednesday, he got a request for two grams to be delivered. It was to one of his new contacts that he'd met through Ana and he went over on his bike. The transaction went as smoothly as he would have liked and he was getting used to his easy way of making money.

"As long as it's always like this," he thought, "I don't see the risk. No-one else will know what's going on and I can make all that money in less than a minute. This is ridiculous, but I can't complain!"

By Friday, Andy had chosen his recipe for tonight, Tuscan chicken, as when he'd cooked fish, he couldn't stand the smell that lingered in the flat for the next couple of hours. He'd bought a new tablecloth for the large table that he had his computer on and brought it into the middle of the room. He had also got a candelabra to hold three candles, which went in the centre of the table and he'd bought a set of cutlery so that everything matched. With his new Kandinsky print framed and on the wall, he was very content with how his place looked. The smell of the chicken cooking permeated the air in the flat to compliment the front room. He had beers and wine in the fridge to hopefully be to everyone's tastes and he wore one of his new shirts with jeans.

It went through his mind that classical music playing in the background would be ideal, but was that being too pretentious? Probably. The others would probably wonder what the hell was going on, so he chose to play a selection of his indie CDs, like Belle and Sebastian, Pavement and Blur.

As meals in Spain tended to happen later, he invited his friends to come round at nine. They all arrived together and were equally taken aback with how his room looked.

"Wow, dude," Josh exclaimed as his eyes jumped from one thing to another. "You've done a good job here!"

Ana pointed out how much she liked the candelabra and Catarina, who was normally difficult to get much out of, was actually visibly impressed. She looked around, nodding her head and saying it was "muy bonito" while Andy analysed her reactions to see if he was likely to win her over.

He opened a bottle of white wine and poured everyone a glass. With the atmosphere set and his guests being pleasantly surprised at what Andy had prepared for them, relations between everyone were more relaxed than they had been before, with Catarina playing a more active role in proceedings. She was opening up more to Andy finally, which reciprocated his mood and the chat was flowing quite freely.

When the food was ready, Josh helped him to bring it through.

"I think you may be winning Catarina over," Josh said. "But remember to keep her hanging. Don't show that you're even noticing."

"I've picked up on that. Yeah, we'll see how the meal goes, but I'm going to act like there's nothing going on."

They brought the food through and everyone served themselves. At this point, Andy was starting to get nervous in case it hadn't come out as well as he'd hoped. People started tucking in and even though Andy didn't think it was that special, everyone else paid their compliments. Catarina kept having sneaky glances at Andy. She knew he appeared different and she was trying to work him out. He definitely seemed more confident. This time he was acting more like she was just another person there, of no particular importance, which made her make more effort to get his attention. Andy played it cool whenever she spoke to him, but he could see in her facial expressions that she was clamouring for his responses.

Andy felt that he had her in the palm of his hand and that Josh's advice had been very good. He brought in the second bottle of wine and as he poured Catarina a glass, he looked deep into her eyes with a wry smile and she looked like she had been stunned. She knew that he had won her over, something that she wasn't used to experiencing. Andy was having a new effect on her and she was overwhelmed. It took her a few seconds to rejoin the social circle after Ana spoke to her and she snapped out of her reverie.

After they finished their meal, everyone was satisfied. Andy had some dessert, but it was a shop-bought cake as he didn't have any experience as a baker. Catarina offered to help him take the empty plates into the kitchen and under the table, Ana held Josh's hand to prevent him from interrupting them. He got the message, although he hadn't been planning to help at this time. They both knew that Catarina's feelings had changed and wanted to let their little duckling go free and swim after the majestic Andy Harper.

In the kitchen, there wasn't much space to move around, so inevitably the two made some physical contact. Andy was fully in control of this game of chess and he gave Cati minimal eye contact, whereas she was craving it. He passed her some forks to take with the dessert plates, while he took the cake out of its container. At this point their eyes met and held each other's gaze as they stood in close proximity. Now was the time to encroach in the queen's territory and Andy leant in for the kiss. Catarina closed her eyes and received it willingly. Even though Josh and Ana could be heard talking and rearranging the table to clear the space in other other room, the two in the kitchen could hear nothing as they kissed passionately. It lasted for less than a minute as Andy remembered that they should go back. He gave another smile to Catarina and beckoned her to take the plates. She couldn't take her eyes of him as she followed him for the short distance.

As he put the cake down on the table, Andy gave a cheeky smile to Josh, who knew exactly what that meant. Josh looked down to try to hide his smile and readjusted himself on his chair. Catarina passed the plates out and for a brief moment it appeared that she and Andy had been partners for some time, such was the harmony between their actions. Ana also knew that something had happened in the kitchen and she was dying to know the details. The mix of progress that had taken place and the anticipation from the audience caused a disruption in the conversation, but fortunately the cake came to the rescue and provided a justifiable reason not to talk too much.

Shortly after, post-meal cigarettes were indulged in and glasses of wine were emptied once again. Still, no details had passed from one pair to another and nobody wanted to leave the evening there. Talk moved to what to do later.

"Let's go out dancing," suggested Ana.

"Yeah, sure," replied Andy. "I want to have a night off the drugs though. How about Radio City?" The ladies seemed open to that, although not massively impressed.

"We can go somewhere else, too," he said. "Fox Congo, for example. I don't mind. Wherever you want to go."

In the light of what had taken place, Andy didn't want to be concerned with selling any coke, either. Right now he was the captain of the ship and wanted to keep a clear head to navigate through the night. True, the alcohol already consumed and what would be added to that would impede the course of the ship to some degree, but Andy was happy to leave it on auto-sailor and see where they ended up.

As they walked over to Negrito, it was still too early to know if Andy and Cati should be holding hands. An undercover kiss and then being cagey because of the other guests had kept the shackles on them. Even Andy, with his newly found confidence, didn't know what to do. They all walked alongside each other, with Andy feeling like he had to hold back again, merely because he wasn't experienced enough to know what to do when it came down to it. Catarina wanted to hold his hand, but was waiting for him to offer his to her which wasn't forthcoming and this unsettled her a little. When they got to Negrito, there was relief from both parties for their respective reasons and Josh immediately instructed Andy to go to the bar with him, leaving the women to open their dams.

"Spill the beans, then," Josh said.

"Ah, we had a kiss in the kitchen. That's it, as obviously you were with us for the rest of the time."

"I could definitely see that something was going on. You played a good game, mate. Keep her hanging and she came running."

"I know. Thanks for the tip. I didn't think it would actually turn out like that, though."

"Let's give them some time to talk. You know what women are like. Especially Spanish women!"

"Fair enough. The trouble is, I don't know what to do next. I can't keep her at arm's length again now I've kissed her."

"Just ease off gradually, let her feel comfortable with you and things will just happen naturally."

"Alright. I think I get you."

They waited to get served and went back out to join the women, who were still talking until they saw the men approaching.

They appeared to be in good spirits to Andy, who paid special attention to their mood as he came back. He sat down next to Catarina and smiled properly at her, which she did in return. The atmosphere was more relaxed now and whatever the women had spoken about, it looked like everyone was fine about everything.

Catarina went back to talking about how much she had liked the meal at his flat and that he had made everything look so nice. This comment brought them closer together and they talked more freely about each other, confirming that they wanted to meet up more often. Smiles punctuated their words and it was Cati who provoked the first physical contact since they'd kissed. She moved her hand towards his beneath the table and he stroked her fingers as they looked into each other's eyes. Across the table, Josh and Ana were pretending to be in their own conversation, but they couldn't stop themselves from watching the other two. They kept looking at each other like proud parents, but tried not to be noticed doing so.

By the time they all wanted to go on somewhere else, Andy wasn't bothered about which venue they went to. He was happy to go to Fox Congo as the women preferred that. It was not a place where he had tried dealing, so there would be a good chance that he wouldn't get asked by anyone, either. He thought he had made the right decision to stay off the coke tonight, especially in case Cati wanted to come back with him later. All four of them got dancing after a short time of being there and the two new lovebirds were able to let go and put their arms around each other, getting lost in their kisses. It was a relief for Andy to have something totally different to focus on while he was in a club.

They stayed out not too late, until just after two in the morning when Josh and Ana declared that they were leaving. Andy asked Cati if she wanted to stay at his and she said yes. He was amazed that things had changed so much in just one night, but he was over the moon to take her back to his. It didn't take them long to get into the bedroom.

28.

When Andy woke up, he was surprised to see Catarina next to him. However, it only took two seconds for him to remember why she was there. She was still asleep with her face turned towards his and she looked peaceful. He smiled at her and looked all over her face to get to know every feature she had. The sun was coming through the home-made curtain just enough to see her clearly and even though he was thirsty, he wanted to stay there until she woke up. He wanted to put his arm around her, but didn't want to disturb her, so he thought back to last night as he watched her breathing in comfort.

Catarina remained sleeping for another ten minutes or so until she moved her leg into Andy's and the resistance woke her up. She took a few moments for her eyes to focus on him and she saw his big smile. She smiled back at him and said "Buenos dias." He said the same and she snuggled into his embrace. He kissed her on her forehead and she let out a contented sound, putting her arm around his waist. They stayed like this for some minutes, not feeling the need to talk. Andy was so relaxed and pleased that the connection between them felt so strong. Eventually, they got up and had a coffee together in the front room, near to the balcony.

"I don't think I've told you yet," Andy said, "But I'm going to leave my cleaning jobs."

"Okay. Why is that?" Catarina asked.

"I don't need the money from that. I'm making enough from selling the cocaine."

She didn't reveal her feelings about that, just nodded to him. He wondered if that meant she wasn't that happy about being with someone whose only job was drug dealing.

"Are you okay with that? About me making money from the drugs?"

"It's okay," she said, once again keeping her cards close to her chest. As far as he knew, she didn't know how much he still had and he thought about what he was going to tell her. It would have to come out sooner or later, but now didn't feel like the right time to discuss it.

That topic came to a close and Andy asked her what she wanted to do that day. He didn't want her to leave after the coffee, but instead wanted to make sure that their connection remained. He invited her to go out for lunch and said he would pay. Catarina responded positively to this and said that she wanted to take a shower first. He got her a towel and she went to the bathroom.

Now that he was on his own for a few minutes, he grounded himself and thought about how he should tell her about the drugs. She'd known that he sold through all the time they had known each other and used it herself, so hopefully it wouldn't be an issue. Should he lie and say that he used the money to buy more cocaine in the usual way that dealing worked? Should he own up to the truth? He needed to gain her trust more first as he felt that he needed to know more about her. She'd opened up more to him last night, but was being cagey again today. It was quite normal that when they were drunk and out partying that things would be like that, but in his mind it was going tot take more time. It would probably be better to not talk about it at all and just see how it went.

Catarina finished her shower. She didn't have any clean clothes to change into, so just put on what she had worn the day before. Andy went into the bathroom and had a shower.

Catarina passed the time by looking around his flat. The front room was still laid out as it had been for the meal. She looked at the furniture he had and his new Kandinsky print. She listened to work out if he was still in the shower and could hear the water running. She went over to the sideboard and opened the top drawer. There was not much in there except for two grams of cocaine in a small paper bag. She inspected it before putting it back as she had found it. She opened the next drawer down, but there was nothing much of interest there. The water was still in full flow. The same for the third drawer. She didn't bother looking any further and Andy came out a couple of minutes later. He got dressed into some clean clothes and they headed out.

The weather was pleasant enough, but not too warm. It would be tolerable enough to sit in the sun, so they went to television square. Andy said she could have whatever she wanted and she opted for a chicken salad, another coffee and an orange juice. To find out more about her life, he asked her if she'd grown up in Valencia and what her childhood was like. She told him that she had and things had been fine growing up. She told him about her brother, Alfonso, and that their relationship was fine. They weren't that close, but were like friends.

"When do you think you will move out of your parents' flat?"

"I don't know. When I have more money. I may stay there for five more years."

"In England, people usually move out of their parents' as soon as they can. As long as they can afford it."

"People have more money in England than in Spain," she explained. "It is easier for you."

"Maybe, but the cost of living is more expensive in the UK."

"Do you have brothers or sisters?"

"No, I'm an only child. I think that is why I'm someone who is quieter. I used to think that I would like to have a brother, so I was alone at home a lot of the time."

Their food was brought out and they continued talking about related topics. It was helping Andy to feel like he was getting to know her better, but he was doing most of the talking. Catarina pointed out that she didn't like being in her dirty clothes and would go home after lunch. Andy understood this and asked when she would like to meet next. She wasn't sure if she wanted to go out again tonight, but said she would send him a message. That was good enough for him. When they'd finished, he picked up the bill. He noticed that she didn't thank him for that, but from his observations, people here didn't tend to say thank you as much as in Britain, so he shrugged it off.

Catarina was going in a different direction to Andy, so they said goodbye and had a short kiss. She smiled at him and departed. Andy wanted to process the development of this weekend, so had a stroll through the town. Now that things had gone to the next level with Cati and it looked like they would be in a relationship, he kind of wished that he hadn't used the technique of making her work for his attention. His feelings for her were different. Realistically, he didn't think she would have become his girlfriend, but right now he was feeling good about everything and wondered if he'd acted like a dick. Seeing as he got the result he was aiming for, maybe not.

He went back home and rearranged his flat to how it normally was. He thought about how his secret money panel had lasted the night, especially considering that the bed had been more active than it usually was. He firmly believed that he had got things sorted in this respect. The only issue with it was that he didn't want the amount of cash to keep building up. Even though he was splashing out on things freely and didn't mind that, he would prefer to be able to use it more wisely and put it towards something more substantial for his future, but used banknotes were not appropriate for that.

He remembered that Catarina had used his shower and he felt quite proud of that. He would have to get some toiletries especially for her, so that she felt more at home. He wished he could separate the bathroom completely from the kitchen and put a door in as well as block up the space above the dividing wall, which was about half a metre up to the ceiling.

Andy found it annoying to know that he could easily afford to get this work done, but that it wasn't his flat. He doubted that Maria would mind if he offered to do it, but it didn't seem right to be spending money on something that he might not even have use of in a year or so. Even though he liked how he had got the place so far, he could afford to get a nicer place, but it came back to the issue of having the cash, but not a job. It was handy living so close to the centre, but being away from the prostitutes and junkies would be far better.

Andy hadn't seen Paul and Steve for a while, so texted Paul to see if he wanted to do anything tonight. Paul said he and Steve were going out later, so Andy could join them.

"Cool. I've got good news. Tell u later," he replied.

The guys met at the usual place and straight away, Paul wanted to know what the good news was.

"I've got together with Catarina, finally!" Andy declared.

"Oh, right!" Paul said, with surprise. "I suppose it was going to happen eventually. How did it come about?"

"I had a meal at my place and invited her, along with Josh and Ana. Both you and Josh told me to back off a bit, which I did, and it did the trick. She was impressed with the meal and when she helped me clear things away in the kitchen, we kissed, which sealed the deal."

"Good job, man," said Steve. "Women are a tough breed to work out, but I'm glad it worked for you. Are you seeing her tonight as well, then?"

"No, this happened last night. She stayed over and had lunch today and we got a chance to get to know each other more."

"It sounds like everything is going right, then," Paul said. "I hope it continues like that."

"Thanks, guys. So how's things with you two?"

Paul and Steve reported that life was just ticking along as usual. School was fine with no major dramas happening. They didn't have a great deal to report, so Paul asked him how Andy's life was outside of his new relationship.

"Yeah, things are good. I'm quitting my cleaning after next week."

"Oh?" Paul seemed confused by this news. As Andy was still feeling more confident, he thought that he might tell the guys more details.

"As you know, I've had the stuff to sell and that's been bringing in money."

"I thought it was going to run out soon though." Steve said.

"Yeah, I've sold more than the fifty I'd told you about. I have to be honest with you about something." Paul's face changed as he was suspecting that Andy had gone into full-time dealing and had invested in another batch. "I didn't actually find fifty grams. I found five hundred."

"What the fuck?" Steve said.

"I'll tell you the story in a minute, but the reason I said that I had fifty was because I was worrying about things and didn't know if I should keep it a secret. I didn't know if the police would find out or something, but I've got my head around things better now."

He went on to reveal the truth about how he came across the drugs as the other two stared intently at him, listening carefully to every word. After he finished telling them, everyone leaned back in the chairs and Paul didn't know what to say.

"This is unbelievable," Steve said. "How the hell did that get left there?"

Andy went through the possibilities that he'd discussed with Josh, which made sense to them.

"And what are you going to do when all that runs out, then?" Paul asked, wondering if that would lead to it being his long-term work.

"I still don't know. I'm sure I won't carry on selling after I've got rid of this lot. I stand to make getting on for forty grand, probably a bit less because of discount rates and stuff, but the problem is having too much in cash."

"Yeah, you can't take a wheelbarrow full of it to the bank, eh?" Steve said.

"Exactly. I'm taking manageable amounts every week and buying what I can in cash, like the computer and some clothes and that, but god knows how much cash I'll still have left over. Have you guys got any ideas?"

"You could open a second bank account and put some more of it in there," Steve said. Paul was staying out of the conversation at this point, with a pensive look on his face. "Maybe a third as well."

"Would that be safe?" Andy asked. "I mean, don't the banks know what each other is doing and be able to track me?"

"Who knows what goes on behind the scenes, but as far as I know, they're in competition with each other, so I doubt they'd investigate every customer, unless something looked really suspicious."

"So if I had three accounts and put in about three hundred a week to each, I'd be alright?"

"Yeah, that should be fine."

"Okay. That sounds good, then. I'll get onto that in the week."

Paul was still looking at Andy, unsure that he liked what he was hearing. "Have you had any problems with people when you've been selling?"

"No, not really. One or two little things that have made me uncomfortable, but that's just the learning process. I've got quite a few regular contacts now and am shifting it a bit quicker. I'll probably have to go and supply a few tonight, but I'm not going to take any myself."

"What, never again?" Paul asked, hopefully.

"I mean tonight. I will still use it, but I'm not going crazy with it."

"How often do you take it?" Paul continued, wanting to find out as much as he could.

"Maybe just at the weekends, so once a week, like most people."

Paul nodded, glad at what he'd said, but still wanting to get to the truth. "Honestly?"

"Yeah, man. I promise. I haven't become an addict. I like it, but I only do it when I'm going out dancing. Don't worry. I remember what you said to me before, but even though I didn't tell you everything to begin with, now you do know the whole truth. This is going to be a short term thing and then when it's done with, I'll see where I am and take it from there."

Paul appeared to be satisfied with Andy's words, though he couldn't help wondering if there might be one little pertinent detail omitted. They finished the conversation around the subject there and had another drink.

Andy had three orders that evening and had to go off to supply the goods, bringing in €400. He was going to go back to Radio City with the guys, but wanted to drop off the cash at home again.

He went back his usual way and past the park on his road. As he went, without a care in the world, he didn't see that he had been noticed by the figure lurking in the shadows again. The man had planned, as long as Andy appeared and left again like he had done before, to follow him into town, to see where he ended up. He couldn't be sure that Andy was dealing, but if he came back in a few minutes, he would probably have collected some more merchandise, thereby meaning he was going to make some transactions.

Andy came back out after one minute, having put the four hundred in his wardrobe for now and went back to meet the guys. The man in the hat followed him inconspicuously to find that he turned up at Radio City. He watched as Andy went in, but couldn't see him any more, so hung around a few metres down the road. The only thing he could do now was wait to see if Andy came back out to supply anyone. He wasn't going to go inside as he wanted to remain completely unknown.

Inside, the guys had a drink and got on with their usual night of dancing. After an hour, Andy got a text to request two grams at another club. Even though he wanted to have something of an uninterrupted reunion with his friends, he'd told them that he might have to pop out at some point. He needed to go to the gay club, which was only a few minutes away, so left the building. He turned left to head up to Plaza del Tossal, then left again to the gay club, paying no attention to most of the people around him. When he got there, he looked at the crowd who were outside, fewer than ten people. Two guys spotted Andy, one of whom was on his contact list. They went through the usual process and Andy headed back. Just before he got back to Radio City, a man was walking in his direction, with his face pointing downwards and bumped into him. He didn't say anything and carried on walking. Andy looked at him. It was just someone who was very drunk and probably trying to get home. The man in the hat had left his vantage point about ten minutes before Andy had come out, thinking that he was just having a regular night with his friends. He gave up his wait and headed off, none the wiser about what Andy was involved in.

29.

On Sunday, Andy wanted to see Catarina as he thought about her as soon as he woke up. He was experiencing the butterflies in his stomach that often happens when a new relationship starts. Going out for lunch again would be a nice thing to do, maybe also going for a walk in the Turia Park. He texted her to ask this, making sure she had enough notice to get ready. He waited impatiently as he smoked a cigarette and had a coffee and she replied after seven minutes.

"I have lunch with my family today. Sorry."

His heart sank at this news, but he knew she often did things with her family. Of course, he wasn't in the same situation, being over here on his own. He tried to rationalise his thoughts rather than get upset with her, but it might not be until next weekend that would see her again. He couldn't stop himself thinking that this might be bad for them, seeing as they were at the beginning of being together. He was about to go into his last week of cleaning, finishing with the jewellery shop next Sunday. This meant he would go to the office three times and could arrange it so he would bump into her. Thinking about this, he thought that he shouldn't have to do that any more as things were different. Cati would just want to go home after a day's work, so she might not like being kept around. Just then, he got another text message.

"We can meet at lunch tomorrow if you want. 13.00?"

He wasn't expecting that, but it made him feel foolish for letting his brain run off on its own. So she wasn't being difficult after all. He was glad that he hadn't been ranting to someone else, especially as he'd got it all wrong. He texted back to say that would be nice.

As he ruminated on what had just gone on in his head, he was quite humbled. "I've got to learn from this. Why do I always think the worst? I need to just carry on with my day and not let it get to me."

He turned on his computer and updated his spreadsheet of his sales. Given that he hadn't made a note of them in the beginning, his estimates were that he'd now sold fifty six grams. Just over ten per cent. He'd used a few for himself, maybe only three grams. A tenth of the way through his business project. He thought that he may be able to finish it by the end of the year.

He went to his wardrobe and took out the cash he'd put in there from last night's sales. Another five hundred and sixty Euros. It still amazed him how much money he was able to make in one night, for just handing little bags over to people and the whole thing being done in a minute. He thought about the conversation regarding opening more bank accounts. He still wanted to be careful, so planned to just open one tomorrow, put three hundred in, then wait another week or so and open another. Andy wanted to see if any questions were asked of him first, just to be on the safe side.

For the rest of the day, he spent most of it on the internet, listening to music and trying to learn about how to make the best use of the computer.

The next morning, his task was to go to another bank before meeting Cati for lunch. He wasn't bothered which one to go with, so went to the nearest one that he could think of. It was a regional bank and he took his tenancy agreement with him. It went easily enough and he decided not to give out any information about why he wanted to bank with them, as long as they didn't ask. He only had to say that he worked freelance, or *lanza libre*, and that was fine for them. He deposited three hundred and would receive his bank card in the post in a week or so.

At one, he went over to the office to meet Catarina. She came down at five past and they went to a different café, which was just off the Plaza de la Reina. Cati appeared to be in a good mood and happy to see Andy. They got on well and had enough to talk about during their meal. Andy felt that things were getting more relaxed and that she was opening up to him more as he didn't need to keep prompting her to get her to speak. When it was time to pay, she picked up her handbag to look for her purse, but Andy told her not to worry as he would pay for it again. With all the money he'd made at the weekend, it was no problem for him at all. Cati didn't argue the case and let him pay.

She told him that she wanted to go shopping for some clothes and asked if he would he like to go with her. Even though the nature of the exercise was not really to his taste, it would be doing something different with her, something that couples do, so he accepted and off they went.

They went to a few shops in and around the square and had a look through, to what seemed to Andy, most of what they had on sale. She asked his opinion of some things, but he didn't really know what to say other than "Si, me gusta." She bought a skirt that he actually did like. It was tight, which he liked to see her dressed in and she wanted to find some shoes to match it. As she looked through the wide selection of shoes, she pointed out that the ones she liked the most were more than she could afford.

"It is a shame because they are perfect. Better than the others," she said.

By now, Andy had got tired of the whole thing and wanted it to be finished. He asked her how much money she had and looked at the price of the shoes. They were €35 more than she had, so partly out of wanting to make her happy, but mostly so the shopping trip would be done with, he gave her the extra amount and she bought them. She gave him a kiss and a big smile, which did manage to warm his cooling heart.

THE EMPTY FLAT

Catarina needed to be back at work soon, so they walked back to the square. They didn't make any plans to meet up next and she gave him another kiss before heading inside.

Even though Andy hadn't really enjoyed his time accompanying her on her expedition, he thought it was just something that boyfriends have to do. He hoped that he wouldn't get dragged in too many times, though.

He spent the rest of the day at home, apart from having to go back to the office to do the cleaning. He thought about buying an acoustic guitar to help him pass the time. He'd learned how to play one a little a few years ago and found some websites that showed the chords to some songs that he knew.

On Tuesday, he went out to have a look through a few music shops. As he left his flat, he just happened to glance up at the empty flat next to his and noticed that the balcony doors appeared to be open. There was a small gap between them. He thought back to the last time he'd been over there and was sure he'd managed to put the catch back on. He stood in the street thinking about it. It seemed odd that it could have come undone, but supposed that the wind might have made it happen. He made a mental note to take a look at it that night and rectify the issue.

He went off to the shops. Without knowing too much about guitars, he tried playing a few until he found one that felt comfortable to play and didn't cost too much and went for one that was €150. He got a soft case for it, a couple of plectrums and took it home.

He went on the internet and found that some songs by Belle and Sebastian looked easy enough to play, so had a go at them. *Judy and the Dream of Horses* was quite simple, based on the chords A, D and E, and after a few attempts, Andy got it down quite comfortably. He wasn't much of a singer, but trying to sing interfered with his concentration, so he stuck to playing only. After a couple of hours, his fingers were sore, so he had a break and went back to it later.

By ten o'clock, he decided to go over the balcony and get the doors closed again. He put his ledge back on and checked that the street was empty. Just as he got onto the other balcony, he heard footsteps. He didn't think he had time to get in without being spotted, so he crouched down and kept still. The steps were coming from behind him and were painfully quiet. His heartbeat got quicker as he wished the person would quickly clear off. Before the person had gone past him, he noticed that the footsteps stopped. "Oh, shit," he thought. Had they spotted him? Were they wondering what he was doing? There was no way he could get out of this, but had no other choice than to keep still in case they hadn't seen him. But why weren't they going? A few seconds later, he heard a noise – chk, chk. A pause. Chk, chk, chk. Then the footsteps started again and he saw the person as they went ahead of him. It was just a guy who had stopped to find his cigarette lighter and carried on his way. Andy breathed a huge sigh of relief and watched him go out of view. He checked the side of the street that he was facing, then slowly turned his head around to see the rest of it. It seemed to be clear, so he cautiously opened the doors and went inside. He hadn't brought his torch with him, but had his lighter in his pocket. He hadn't intended to go in, but it was almost a force of habit, plus he wanted to be out of sight for a while. He inspected the catch on the door. It was still on there, so he should be able to close it again. He was compelled to just have another check on the flat, in case anything looked different.

Naturally, the first thing he wanted to inspect was the crucial floorboard. It seemed to be as he had left it, pressed back into place. He scanned the bedroom, which looked the same as he remembered, so went back out. When he returned to the living room, he did another quick scan. As there wasn't much in there,

there wasn't much that could be different. Then he noticed the sideboard. One of the drawers was open. Had he left it like that? It was clearly open, rather than being as though he hadn't quite fully closed it. He tried to think back to when he'd been through the drawers. "I'm sure I'd made sure that I left everything as it was. I didn't want to leave any signs that I'd been in here." Maybe for some reason he had been absent-minded and missed it, so he pushed the drawer in and went back to the doors. He listened through them, but couldn't hear anything. He opened them slightly to get a look. Clear. A bit more to get his head out. It looked fine. He went out and crouched down, pulling the doors to and using his little finger to ease the catch back on. One last check of the street. Everything looked good, so he made his way back and took off the ledge.

Now that he was back home and could relax, he thought back to that drawer. It had been a number of weeks since he'd been there, so couldn't work out if he'd made a mistake and left it open. He supposed that it was possible and anyway, what did it matter? No-one else had been there. He'd never been aware of a landlord going there, but maybe they had when he'd been out. They might have opened the balcony doors and not put the catch back on. Yes, surely that was what happened. Andy put the ledge in the spare room and played his guitar some more.

He barely thought about the incident again and instead his mind was more focused on Catarina. He texted her the next day to ask if she waned to come to his that evening. He was pleased to know that she would, when he'd expected her to reject it. As he would be working after her, dinner wasn't really an option. She went home first and had dinner while Andy got a takeaway on his way home. He thought it would be good just to spend a quiet evening together; maybe watch some TV or listen to music. He didn't think he was able to impress her with his guitar playing yet, so he bought a bottle of wine and she came round just after nine.

Catarina brought a bag with her, which contained a change of clothes and her toiletries. That alone set the mood for the evening as Andy wasn't sure if she wanted to stay over, but evidently she did and he was relaxed in her company. They sat in front on the TV, watching some programmes that she liked, but that meant very little to Andy. He didn't mind as they still chatted about things as any couple would and the evening exceeded his expectations as it was the case that they were getting used to each other and enjoyed their company. Cati was fine with Andy putting his arm around her and kissing her.

After they'd finished the bottle of wine, they went to get ready for bed. Catarina went to the bathroom first to brush her teeth and so on and she waited in the bedroom for him to do likewise. Her eyes scanned the room to see what he had there. Little more than the basics. The bedside table was easy enough to look into quickly, but he hardly kept anything in there, other than a box of condoms and an eye mask.

He returned promptly and they had sex for the second time. It was as enjoyable as before, although as Andy was more at ease now, it didn't last too long; about fifteen minutes in fact, which he apologised for, but Catarina said it was fine and she needed to sleep anyway because of work tomorrow.

They woke up at eight and Andy made some coffee. She didn't eat first thing in the morning, like him, so they had a relaxed morning with her getting ready for work and she headed off after an hour.

Andy was happy with how things were going for them. The uncertainty and anxiety was no longer in his head and he felt good for the rest of the day, choosing to go for another bike ride around his favourite park.

He mainly just chilled for the rest of the week, not worrying about when he would see Cati next. It was bound to be either

Friday or Saturday. He had a text to make a delivery on Thursday night and as Friday moved towards the evening, another couple of orders came in. He'd arranged to meet his girlfriend on Saturday night, which he was actually quite relieved about as he would have to keep heading off to sell the drugs. Hopefully it wouldn't be an issue for her if he had to do so when he was with her, but he thought he'd just cross that bridge when he came to it.

Instead he met up with Josh, who, for the first time in ages, wasn't accompanied by Ana, so they had a chance to have a catch up and talk about whatever they wanted.

Josh was intrigued to know how they were getting on and Andy was happy to tell him what they'd been up to.

"That all seems pretty good, then," Josh said. "I'm glad it's working for you both."

"Thanks. How's Ana?"

"She's fine. Out with a couple of girl friends tonight, which is fine as we've been spending a lot of time together anyway. It's good to have a night off once in a while."

The guys carried on chatting about what other things they'd been doing over the last week or so until Andy had to head off to make a delivery. It wasn't too far away and would only take five minutes to get back. He met three of his contacts and sold them three grams. Just as they went their separate ways, Andy was stopped by someone else. An older man who spoke in Spanish asked him if he had any coke. Andy was caught off-guard a little as he didn't know this man and he looked a bit rough. His eyes were quite menacing and he wasn't making any effort to be friendly. The man said he'd noticed Andy selling to the people just now and there was no way of pretending that he hadn't. Andy was still reluctant to talk in case he was undercover, but the man was quite smelly, including his breath which indicated he didn't look after himself. His teeth were brown, which made Andy think that he was probably safe.

"How much do you want?"

"How much do you have?"

Andy thought that was a weird question. Surely he couldn't afford much.

"I only have one gram with me."

"Can you get more for me? It's for me and my friends."

"How much?"

"Ten grams."

"Ten?" This sounded suspicious. This guy was clearly a junkie and wouldn't have that much money.

"Si, diez."

Andy thought about what to do. He could go back and get ten grams, but wasn't sure if this man would have the money. It was the most uncomfortable situation he'd had to deal with so far.

"Do you have the money?"

"I have it at home. How long do you need to get it?"

"Maybe half an hour."

"What price for ten grams?"

As Andy had worked with discounts before, he some insight into this at least. H offered it for seven hundred. The man didn't look impressed as he dismissed it with an erratic wave of his hand and a sneer on his ugly mouth.

"Six fifty," he told Andy. Andy agreed to the price and told him to meet him here in half an hour. The man nodded and lit a cigarette as Andy walked on. He went back to meet Josh as he needed to discuss this with him. He described the man and Josh also thought that it seemed dodgy.

"But ten grams in one go would be good," Andy said.

"Let me come with you. You don't know if he'll try to steal it off you."

"Okay, thanks. That's a good idea."

The both went back to Andy's and got the ten grams. They discussed possible outcomes and how they would react if something untoward happened.

"I'm going to stay close to you," Josh said. "When we see him, we'll let him see that we're together, then I'll wait just a few steps back while you sell it. I'll watch him to see if he reaches for a weapon and if he does, I'll go "Pssst." Make sure that you don't look scared and I'll give him an evil look, too."

"Alright. Fuck, what if he does pull out a knife quickly, though"

"I'll rush at him and catch him off-guard."

"Maybe if you stand behind him when I go to him."

"Good one. He won't be able to know what I'm doing then."

They felt better that they'd got a plan worked out. They tried to psych each other up as they got closer to the destination. As they turned onto it, Andy's heart was racing at the anticipation of seeing the man again. He couldn't see him at first and they carried on walking until the man popped out of the shadows and looked at them both. Josh gave him his most evil stare and stepped to the side to walk around him. The man watched him, not taking his eyes off his until he heard Andy ask him to show him the money.

"Show me the coke," the man said. This was turning into a real stand-off and Andy was way out of his depth. Josh barely blinked as he watched the man's hands which were for now by his sides. Andy gave him a glimpse of the bags from his pocket. The man looked at them and back up to Andy's face. He then turned round to look at Josh, who was about three metres behind him. He turned back to Andy.

"Don't fuck with me," the man said in a deep, raspy voice and walked past Andy without buying anything. Andy tracked his movements as the man sauntered off, clearly angry with the guys' strategy.

Andy and Josh looked at each other. They didn't say anything until the man was out of sight.

"Shit," Andy said. "That was bad."

"He looked like he could kill both of us," Josh said. "It's probably best that it ended like that."

"I bet he didn't have the money. I mean look at him. How would have have six hundred and fifty Euros?"

"You don't know what these guys get up to. They spend their money on drugs and booze more than on food."

"I don't want to go through that again. If anyone like that asks me, I'll just say no and walk on."

"Yeah, take no chances."

"So I've got all this coke on me now."

"I'm not in the mood for doing it after that," said Josh.

"I don't mean that. Me, neither, but I don't want to be carrying this much around."

"Let's just go for a drink and calm down first before we decide what to do."

"Good idea." They needed to be around people and in a familiar spot so headed to Negrito.

"I really don't think we handled that well," said Andy after having some time to reflect on it. "Maybe if we hadn't gone for the menacing approach, it might have worked out."

"Yeah, I agree," said Josh. "It's hard to know what to do when you don't know what to expect."

"I just hope I don't come across him again. Do you think he'd attack me?"

Josh didn't want to answer in the affirmative to that question. It was the last thing that Andy needed to hear. "Just don't go on that street or the nearby area. If you see him, just keep your head down."

That didn't do much to placate Andy, but he thought it was good advice, nonetheless. The guys had a beer and managed to calm down to some degree. They didn't feel like going out anywhere else as they weren't in the mood. They called it a day just after midnight. Andy wanted to be doubly sure he was going to be safe, so took a longer route home and entered his street from the ring road end. He paid special attention to every sound, although he didn't see anyone and made it back home safely.

30.

Luis González was sat on his dirty mattress in a bare room in El Carmen, often considered the roughest district in the old town of Valencia. He was staying there temporarily after he'd been released from prison. Someone who could only be considered an acquaintance had let him stay in his run-down flat that wasn't fit to rent out, while he got himself together and moved on. Luis scratched his closely-cropped head, which he hadn't washed for three days and was immersed in his thoughts of prison life, that comprised most of his thoughts these days. He'd been behind bars for three years after being caught in possession of cocaine and heroin. He got off relatively lightly as he'd had more of it stashed away, but the police didn't uncover any when searching his flat.

Luis was now forty years old and had been involved in drugs, both using and dealing since he was fifteen. He'd been in prison twice before, once for violent behaviour for eight months when he was twenty-two and once for robbery of a small general store for twelve months when he was twenty-nine. Because of his rough lifestyle and experience of being banged up previously, his third term was one where he was more of a man to be feared. He'd often been in fights with other prisoners and along with a couple of similar characters, most of the inmates tended to stay clear of them.

Upon his release, Luis was in no position to start a fresh life. He had long severed ties with his family and hadn't been in touch with any relatives since his mid-twenties. He hardly knew anyone here now. Some of his accomplices and acquaintances had either died or been incarcerated as well. He was lucky that he remembered where Francisco lived and that he agreed to let him stay in his flat. Francisco had been one of his drug customers, although these days he only smoked pot. He hadn't been particularly pleased to see Luis at his door three weeks ago, but as he hadn't been the recipient of any violence from him, he agreed to let him stay.

THE EMPTY FLAT

As drug dealing was the only thing he knew how to do, he had no interest in doing any other kind of work. However, without any money to his name, he was having to keep his feelers out to try to get back in the game. Francisco gave him some weed every now and then, mainly just to keep him quiet and out of his way and he had no intention of helping him to get back into the world of drugs.

Andy woke up feeling pretty pissed off. The thoughts of what had taken place last night irritated him, but mostly he felt anxious that he would come across that man again. What if he had got the money and they could have done the transaction smoothly? He spent the early part of the day kicking himself over making such a mess of it. He was beginning to regret getting into drug dealing as it seemed like he was now sinking into the dark side of it and things could get a lot more dangerous than last night.

He thought about getting out of the city for a couple of weeks. He was going to do his last shift tomorrow, so would be free from any obligations. Maybe that junkie would have forgotten him after two weeks. He was due to meet Catarina tonight, so could discuss it with her, although he didn't want to tell her what he'd been through.

As he weighed up his options – maybe head back to Madrid, seeing as he knew the place and one or two people, maybe to Alicante, which was nearby, or Barcelona. He didn't like the idea of leaving his flat, considering how much he'd got there in cash and drugs. What if that guy had followed him home? No, surely he would have beaten him up before he got in. What if he saw him again tonight when he was with Catarina? He really didn't want to put her through any of this. Andy's mind was a confused mess and he couldn't work out what to do. He called Josh and asked him if they could meet again. Josh was with Ana, but agreed to meet him in an hour as he could tell Andy was getting really worked up.

They met at television square as it was away from where the incident took place last night and Andy needed to be in an open area.

"Man, I don't know what I should do. I'm feeling paranoid about seeing that guy. Do you think I should go away for a while?"

"Yeah, it's probably for the best. You need to get out of this environment and clear your head. Just go to Alicante for a couple of weeks. There's plenty of Brits there, although it's past the main holiday season. You could probably do with some home comforts, though. It might help you relax a bit."

"Yeah, good idea. What if I end up losing my customers, though?"

"Don't worry about that. Dealers often disappear sometimes. Just let them know when you'll be back. That won't be a problem."

Andy was beginning to feel better after this chat. He had no idea what he would do in Alicante, but as long as he was away from here, that was all that mattered.

"I'll still be worried about all the stuff I've got in my flat, though. What if he knows where I live and breaks in?"

"Mate, that's not going to happen. You met him far away from your place and he fucked off. We were out for another hour or something after that and we didn't see him again, right?"

"Yeah, I suppose so. I'm losing my mind right now."

"I can see that. That's why you need to go away."

"What am I going to tell Catarina though? It will seem weird if I just tell her I'm going to Alicante all of a sudden."

"Just say you need a holiday. Simple."

"Alright. I'll just have a quiet night with her, do my last shift early tomorrow, then head off."

"Good. You've got a plan together. You'll be alright once you're there."

THE EMPTY FLAT

Andy needed some time to himself to get his head around things. He wished he could go away right now, but Catarina might be worried about him, and that bloody cleaning shift, which he didn't need to do, was a stupid barrier that he could do without.

He had a look on the internet to find out some things about Alicante. There were plenty of places to stay and loads of British pubs and restaurants that he could go to, so it was becoming more appealing to him. He planned to leave around lunchtime tomorrow.

He wondered if it would be better to invite Catarina round tonight, just in case that guy showed up. Or they could go to a different area and pretend it was just to have a change of scenery. He called her and told her his thoughts. Catarina said that she preferred to go out, which was his least preferred option, but she agreed to go somewhere different.

They agreed to go to Bar Mendi, which was nearer to her home. It was off the beaten track, but that was perfect for Andy as it was unlikely that the junkie would go around that way looking for drugs. He had a few hours to come up with a story as to why he was going away so suddenly.

They met at half past nine, after she had eaten with her family. He wanted to get straight to the point so he could get the conversation out of the way.

"I just feel like too much has been going on for me recently and I need a break," he explained.

"What is the problem?" she enquired.

""Not especially, I need a change of scenery. To be honest, I want a break from selling, you know... and I need a holiday."

"How long will you go for?"

"I think for two weeks."

"Vale. I can see if your flat is okay. Do you have another key?"

Andy thought about this for a while. On one hand, he would like someone to check up that everything was okay, but because of his secret, he didn't like the idea of her going there in case she found anything.

"No, it's fine. Josh is going to do that for me. I have given him the key." This wasn't so difficult a lie to make up and he thought he might ask him in the morning. He knew he could trust him and that he wouldn't take any of the drugs. In fact, to get around that, he could give him a couple of grams for free.

So Andy had got things settled with Cati. She didn't suspect anything and she had no reason to go to his place. He changed the subject to ask her about this area of town and what good places there were. Being away from the centre made him more relaxed. The thought of that man popped into his head every now and then when he forgot where he was, but the evening went fine. He got a couple of texts asking to deliver some coke, but he just replied with "Estoy en vacaciones por dos semanas." He told her that he was going to work early the next day, which was not strictly true, but it gave him an excuse not to invite her back as he needed his own space for a while, as well as to pack some things for his holiday.

He paid for the drinks and asked Catarina to call a taxi for him as he wasn't sure how to get back in the dark, as well as wanting to be extra sure that he wouldn't bump into anyone he didn't want to.

The taxi driver dropped him off on the ring road, which he was glad about. It felt much safer entering the street from this side. He saw a couple coming down from the top end, who didn't pose any threat and he got in long before they passed by. In the park, however, was a man in a hat, who was waiting to monitor his movements, but he had a dull night with nothing to stir him.

Andy couldn't sleep yet, so decided to pack his stuff for tomorrow. He wondered if he should text Josh now in case he slept in tomorrow. He'd probably still be up, so he did so and twenty minutes later got a reply to say that of course he would keep an eye on things for him. Josh would come over at eleven, which gave Andy a chance to go to work before that and head off as soon as he'd seen his best friend.

Whilst packing his things, he put a book in and some CDs. He wondered if it was worth taking any cocaine with him. Two weeks without any business seemed like a long time, even though he still had plenty of money at his disposal. As Alicante was a holiday destination, he could probably find some buyers easily, especially if they were English speakers. He'd still got the ten bags from last night and even though they were bags like any other, they felt tainted to Andy and he would like to get rid of them. He put them in one of his socks.

He went to work to do his final shift at nine thirty and was glad to have finally finished his cleaning. Now he was free to do his own thing, although he wasn't quite in the mood for relishing that yet. He posted the keys through the shop letterbox and went back home.

Josh came over right on time and was desperate to know how Andy was.

"I'm alright. Glad to be going away, of course, but I'm not fully relaxed yet."

"I totally get you. It's still in your mind, but you'll be fine once you're on the train."

"Sure. Thanks for checking on the flat for me."

"No worries. How often do you want me to come over?"

"I don't know. Whatever suits you. Can you make it twice a week?"

"Yes, mate. I'll text you each time I come to let you know. I'll come on Wednesday first."

"Cheers. That means a lot. Hopefully I won't be thinking about it too much."

"You'll be fine. Give me a hug."

The hug was just what Andy needed right now. It gave him a sense of security and he knew he could trust him. The one thing that Josh didn't know about was the secret money stash, but there was no reason why he would uncover it. After taking some out to use in Alicante, there was only €400 left in it, but he knew it would be safe.

Andy got the train at twenty past twelve and felt relieved when he sat down and was on his way.

The journey was two hours long and Andy wanted to switch off as much as he could. He just watched the landscape go by, hoping that he could watch the sea peacefully. Unfortunately, the train went inland, so it left him with his own thoughts. As soon as he started thinking about that unpleasant encounter, he got his book out. It was Dostoevsky's *Crime and Punishment,* which he'd been meaning to get into for a while, but it had been gathering dust for a couple of months. He managed to stay focused for most of the time and got into Alicante train station after reading forty-six pages.

He was quite surprised at how the town looked. It was more developed than Valencia, with the buildings in a much better state in general. It was obvious that this place was bringing in more money and it gave him a good first impression. He'd picked up a map from the train station, which wasn't too far from the beach. He already knew that was the area where he wanted to find a hotel. He'd got a short list from looking on the internet and went looking for them.

He went to one on Calle San Fernando, which, although it didn't have a beach view, was only about five minutes walk away from the harbour. He had a look and was pleased to be able to talk to the receptionist in English. The room was fine, cheap enough and good enough for a couple of weeks, so he thought it was not worth bothering to see any more. He went out and headed for the sea front, which had so many boats moored. Even though it was past the main holiday season, there were still a good many people around. He walked along the road until he entered an area that was more picturesque. "Why don't they do this with Valencia?" he thought. "Seeing how this place attracts the tourists and Valencia's coast is dreary compared to this, they are missing a huge opportunity."

Despite the big difference in the feel of the two places, he felt more inspired to be here. He knew he was safe and anonymous and he was starting to be glad he'd made this decision. The promenade, with its multitude of palm trees and open space, brought a sense of calm to him. He was glad there weren't so many tourists around and he didn't want the hustle and bustle of a holiday destination, so this suited him perfectly right now.

He went to a café and had some lunch with a small beer and watched the world go by. He wasn't even thinking back to his life in Valencia at this time, but was just happy to soak it all in. The temperature was only around 22ºC, but it was sunny enough to create the right environment for him.

Afterwards, he went for a leisurely stroll to see what the town offered. There were cafés and hotels everywhere and lots of shops that would attract tourists. He wasn't looking to buy anything in particular, but they would bring some distraction to him.

After spending so much of his time walking around in Madrid and Valencia, it was almost second nature to him to walk as many streets as he could and he didn't notice that he was following his usual routine; he was enjoying it too much.

He went past the fountain in the Plaça de la Porta del Mar and it brought him to the beach. He'd only been to the beach once since he'd been in the country, where he hadn't been impressed, but again, with the development, Alicante's was much nicer. He leaned over the rail between the promenade and the sand and gazed out to sea. This was the perfect antidote to the last couple of days and he knew he would be taking it easy with his book and some beers on this very beach. He wished he'd waited and checked into a hotel nearer to here. "Maybe tomorrow," he thought. He walked along the promenade for half an hour until he came to where the development ended and walked back with no plan to arrive at any destination.

Halfway along, Andy took off his trainers and socks and walked on the sand. It was at a perfect temperature to walk on and he noticed the few people who shared the space with him: people sitting in groups, a few walking around, some in the sea, nobody noticing him. Ideal. He sat down for a while just to look around at nothing specific. There was something calming about being around people, but not having anyone come up to him and not wanting to go to talk to anyone. It was like looking at a painting and noticing details which were enough to keep his mind occupied, but not to make him feel stressed.

Andy stayed there for over an hour, occasionally reading a few pages of his book, but it was too intense to accompany his situation, so he thought he might try to find something that was a nice relaxing read.

Despite being relatively rich and not having to worry about eating out or staying in a hotel, Andy had got used to this now. It was as though things were just like this. He wasn't throwing his money around, but he didn't need to think about what he was spending it on. Right now, he had over three thousand Euros to his name and he was used to making up to a thousand a week. He spent the rest of the day switched off from his normal life and was able to let the time pass over him like the gentle breeze that came in from the Mediterranean Sea.

As his hotel was a few streets away from the coast, it was peaceful there and he had a good night's sleep. He wondered whether it would be better to stay there longer or find somewhere nearer to the beach. He also wanted to find another book to read, so he had his objectives for the day and headed out to have some breakfast.

Because of being in a totally new town to him, there was always something that he noticed and kept his mind off what he wanted to leave behind. He walked around the shops, seeing quite a few that sold British things like baked beans, English newspapers and so on. He'd heard about these kinds of resorts before, but this was his first time as an adult to be in one. In a way he kind of liked it. As Josh said, it was good to have some links to home and they helped him feel grounded. By now, his Spanish was quite good, yet far from fluent, but it was always easier to revert back to his native language.

He found a shop that sold books in English and they had plenty of trashy holidays reads. They weren't really his style, but he picked out one that sounded less girly. There were a couple of Stephen King novels, none of which he'd read before, but upon reading the blurbs, the horror element was not what he was looking to connect with at this time. He needed something peaceful and easy-going that would help him unwind further. Then he noticed one whose title stood out to him: *Neither Here, Nor There: Travels in Europe*, by Bill Bryson. Right away the title resonated with him as that was the state he was in now, but being about travels in Europe was what he was doing anyway. He had a quick read of the first page and it sounded enjoyable, so he bought it as well as the holiday read.

Andy was unconsciously compelled to discover more of Alicante, so he wandered around for a couple of hours, hoping to find some bars that looked like they might be worth checking out later. He thought it made sense to go to an English restaurant just for the familiarity of the food and there were plenty to choose from. He was at the tail-end of the holiday season and many places would be closed at the end of October, so he'd got lucky by deciding to come out straight away. Today was the twenty-first so he had at least ten days before the options slimmed down.

After having some lunch on the way to the beach, he made his way there to start reading *Neither Here, Nor There*.

It proved to be the right choice as Bryson's writing was humorous and he'd done a lot more of what Andy had started, so he was intrigued to find out some more about different cultures and their quirks. He passed a pleasant few hours outside and got about a quarter of the way through the book. When he felt he'd read enough for today, he went to get a beer.

Now that he'd had time to re-organise his mind and it was bobbing on the waves that he saw before him, he looked inside himself to take stock of what he was going through. It was no surprise to know that Friday night was the first thing he needed to address. Three days later and being completely away from it helped him to get over it. "It was just one of those things," he thought. "I've got to expect that every now and then I'm going to run into someone dodgy, but he'll probably forget me. He'll probably be off his head the next time I see him." However, the very idea of *the next time* stopped him in his tracks. He had no idea or any way of knowing if he would see him again. Andy thought about himself and knew that he stood out from the Spanish because of his blond hair. He couldn't make it grow any faster and he didn't want to shave it off. "Maybe I should dye it, so I blend in more." This sounded like an easy fix and he might just give it a go.

Now that he had what he could call a resolution, his mind turned to Catarina. "God, I haven't thought about her since Sunday morning." He remembered the night out on Saturday, which was very low-key, but also fine. He knew that he had things on his mind that prevented him from properly being there with her, but it had felt a bit different. Was it that he was getting used to her being his girlfriend? It hadn't felt as exciting as when they finally hit it off. "Is that normal?" He wasn't quite sure what to make of it. Not seeing her for two weeks might end up being an issue as well, especially as he ran away so soon. Would she think he needed to get away from her? He'd have to text her later and be all nice to show her that he still liked her.

"Do I still like her?" He was confused that this question went through his mind. "Yeah, of course I do," he told himself. "Don't I?" He rested his chin on his hand and tried to work out how he felt about her. He thought about the things they'd done: lunch, shopping, meal, dancing – all nice things. "I do pay for her a lot. She's never paid for me. Hmm... then again, I'm basically getting free money. Isn't it right that I should be spending it on those close to me?" He thought back to the meal and that he'd bought everything, which ended up being a great evening. Andy just wasn't used to being in that position. Maybe he just needed more time to get used to it. This made money as the next topic to focus on.

"So it looks like I'm financially stable. I know it's been making me happy to know I've got plenty coming in regularly and that's because of what I'm doing. I've still got loads of cocaine to shift, so that will keep me going for a while. The sales are mostly going well and I've just got to expect that there'll be a few hiccups along the way. I need to be stronger and be able to deal with them. Fuck that guy. I'll probably never see him again, but if I do, I'll just avoid him. I'll focus on getting more good contacts. That shouldn't be a problem. Maybe I should stop spending it so much and try to save it. What am I going to do once it's over with? Am I going to stay in Valencia? I've good friends there and my girlfriend, so it's probably foolish to jump ship once I've sold it all. Living here might be nice, but what would I do? There's probably plenty of temp work with the holiday seasons, but do I want to work as a waiter or a barman? I don't think so. I'm not going to go back to cleaning. That'd be like going back to square one. Man, I don't know what else I could do. I suppose it is an option to buy more coke and keep doing that, but I can imagine that it's too dangerous a life to get into. I'm bound to get caught before too long and there's no way I want to go to prison. No, fuck that. Save the money and use the time to figure out what I'm going to do next. There's no rush."

Andy stopped thinking for a while and realised that he was doing well with getting his head around things. Even though he had no definite plans for the future, he was more settled with what was going on now and he believed he could make it work. He ordered another beer and lit a cigarette.

31.

That evening, he texted Catarina to tell her that he was feeling good and was glad he was on holiday. He asked her how she was and she told him she was fine. Work was normal, but everything was okay. He thought about Josh, but didn't text him as he was going to hear from him on Wednesday. He didn't really want to know anything about Valencia as he still needed to distance himself from that. He went out to an English pub not far from the beach and had a quiet night to himself, reading his book some more.

As he walked back to his hotel, the quietness of the street that it was on took away the holiday feeling. It was uninspiring and he decided he wanted to be based somewhere that would always give him something to look at. The next morning, he checked out and found another one near to the Plaça de la Porta del Mar. It was another two-star hotel, again adequate for what he needed and cheap enough. The weather was cloudier, but he still spent the day much like he had done yesterday, reading and drinking a couple of beers.

By Wednesday, Andy was over halfway through his book and although he was still enjoying it, the novelty of being there and going about his business in this way was starting to lose its appeal. He thought that he might just stay till Sunday or Monday and head back early.

That night, he got a text from Josh, who reported that everything was fine at his flat and he smiled at this news. "I've got nothing to worry about," he thought. "Everything will be back to normal when I return."

Thursday was sunnier again and he ploughed on through his book. It should be good to see what the weekend had to offer here. He had those ten grams with him and he was in the mood for shifting what he could again, maybe even finding a good club and taking some himself.

He went to a different English pub that night and thought he might see if there was anyone worth talking to as he hadn't had a proper conversation all week.

As he expected, the pub wasn't full, but there were a few groups in there. Andy thought staying at the bar would be a good move to see if he could get chatting to different people who came to get drinks. There was a group of lads sitting at a table to the side of him. They seemed quite outgoing types and they might be good to try to sell to. He drank his lager and before too long, one of them came over to get a round in. Andy looked across and said 'hi' and the guy, probably in his mid-twenties said "Alright, mate."

"You guys having a late holiday?"

"Yeah, it's our mate's birthday and we're here for a long weekend. What about you?"

"I've just come down for the week. I live in Valencia."

"Oh, right. What do you do there?"

He wasn't going to tell him the truth as it was a bit too soon to reveal his trade, so Andy just told him he was a cleaner still. "I take it you're all going to be partying then?"

"Totally. We're going to get wrecked."

"Any idea where you're going to go?"

"No, mate. Do you know any clubs?"

"I don't, but I'm up for finding something as well."

"Come and join us, then."

Andy had played his cards right and went over to join the group. They said their names, but he couldn't remember most of them. There were six of them and they were from Leeds. It wasn't the kind of group that Andy usually got involved with, but they seemed friendly enough and he tried to pretend he was like them. The conversation was full of rowdy chatter about pulling Spanish women and so forth. Andy did his best to play along with it, but he would prefer to do a sale and leave them to it.

As they hung out, a woman came into the pub with a bunch of flyers. They were for an eighties club, which she explained was near to there and it was open tomorrow and Saturday night. The guys seemed fairly interested and pocketed the flyers.

Andy wanted to get to the point and asked if the guys were interested in buying any coke.

"Yeah, man," said Darren, whose birthday it was tomorrow. "Do you know anyone?"

"I've got some. I sell a bit."

The guys' ears pricked up at this and they were definitely interested.

"Alright," Andy said. "It's best to sort it out tonight, so we're not doing it outside the club. I don't know what they're like here, so tell me how much you want and I'll go back to my hotel and get it."

"We all want some, don't we, lads?" said Antony, who he'd met at the bar.

"So I've got ten grams with me."

"Shall we get a gram each?" Darren asked the group. They agreed to and And told them it was €80 each. They seemed satisfied with that and talked about if they had enough cash on them. A couple needed to grab some more, but their hotel was only a couple of minutes away. They arranged the deal and Andy went to pick up six bags. As he walked, he felt that he'd handled this one very well. He thought he'd got his way in easily and humoured them enough to stay on their side. He knew he wanted to keep a gram for himself, but brought the nine he had left, just in case they decided they wanted more or if he met anyone else.

He was back at the pub ten minutes later and everyone had their money. They made a plan to finish their drinks and go onto another pub so that they could do the transaction outside.

They found a quiet spot and Andy dealt with each one separately so he could check the money was right. They didn't want any extra, so he pocketed €480. He said he might see them tomorrow at the club that they now knew about and he took the money back to the hotel with the three grams left, which was an easy way to leave their company.

In his hotel room, he was pleased with himself and it gave him the idea that coming over to here some weekends would be a good way to shift more, except that the holiday season would be over very soon. He'd have to wait till next year, by which he should have already sold the lot.

Back in Valencia, the man in the hat had been coming over to the park a couple of times during the week. He'd been past Andy's flat late at night and this was the first time seen that there were no lights on and no sound coming from there. This prevented him from finding anything else out about what Andy did, but he wondered how he could get in while he had the chance. He hadn't been there when Josh came over, so was oblivious to it being looked after. He also noticed that the balcony doors of the empty flat were closed, which he hadn't done when he'd managed to get in last week. This aroused his suspicions. There were two reasons for this: either the landlord had been round and closed them again or someone else had done it for some other reason. He could tell that it was easy to climb across from one balcony to another. Was that the reason why the cocaine was no longer under the floorboard? He knew this from coming over in the middle of the night and using a ladder to get up to the balcony.

On Friday, Andy finished reading his book mid-afternoon and was thinking about what to do that night. He was as in the dark as the guys from Leeds about clubs, but expected that there would be a few to check out as there seemed to be enough tourists around to warrant them being open. The locals probably had their own territory, meaning they would be more similar to ones in Valencia, but given how easy it was to sell to the lads, he was sure he could find some more to get rid of the other three.

The area around the beach started to liven up once it was dark. The pubs were more full of life than last night and it was easy to pinpoint who the tourists were from the volume of their drunken voices. Andy walked around without going in anywhere just to check out the lay of the land. He found the eighties club, although it was too early for that to be open yet. He saw another couple of places with posters that were designed to appeal to tourists. They also seemed quite poppy. Andy wasn't sure if that was what he wanted, but it might be alright just to go to somewhere different. He had a beer in one pub, watching the punters, but as the night went on, it felt too rowdy for him to interrupt a group, so he decided to play it by ear and see how things were by midnight or so.

He passed by one of the clubs he'd already seen and saw that people were congregating around the doorway. It was one of the tourist places and he thought he might as well give it a go. He'd put the remaining bags in his sock in case the doormen searched people. This was the case, but Andy played it cool and showed that he was fine with them searching him. The man gave him a quick running over with his hands and it was evident that it was only to see if people were carrying weapons. He got the all clear and went inside. The music was at full volume, with Abba's *Mama Mia* entertaining the punters. There were about forty people in there and the atmosphere seemed happy and friendly. He got a drink and did the usual of looking around to see who might be looking for some coke. He needed to latch onto a small group as he only had a small amount left and went to dance and see who he could make eye contact with. It was less threatening to do this with women as people would be checking each other out anyway. There was a group of five women who were probably in their mid-thirties. Andy guessed that more mature people were probably not going to be drug users and they might turn him in. A bit further away he saw some more women about his age and he moseyed on over to dance near to them. There were four of them and they seemed to be having the time of their life. He clocked one who he thought was attractive. A brunette with nice eyes and a cute smile had noticed him and she looked interested. It would be useful if someone fancied him so that he could get talking to her and after a couple more songs and a few instances of eye contact, he moved closer and said hello.

"How are you doing? Are you here on holiday?" he asked.

"Yeah," she said in a welcoming way. "What's your name?"

"I'm Andy."

"I'm Emily."

They went through some chit-chat of where they were from and what they did and a connection was being made. He didn't want to jump in too soon with asking if they wanted any coke, but would give it a few more songs. He asked her if she wanted a drink, which she did and he beckoned her over to the bar. She asked for a gin and tonic and Andy got another beer. They talked some more as she knew he lived in Spain and she wanted to know what it was like. Emily seemed to be happy in his company and the conversation was going freely, so he asked if she and her friends wanted any coke.

"Ooh, have you got some?" she asked.

"Yeah, I've got a few grams, three, in fact."

"Have you taken any?"

"Not yet, but I will in a bit."

"Maybe. Let me speak to the others."

She went back to her friends while he waited at the bar to observe their reactions. He noticed some nodding of heads and they looked over to him as they discussed it. Emily came back and said they'd like it, asking how much it was. He told them eighty a gram and she went back to report this to her group. She called him over to them and they said they'd buy all three. Perfect, he thought as he smiled to them. There was a table free at one side, which was fairly secluded, so they went to sit down. The women looked through their purses under the table and assembled the money between them. They subtly passed it to Andy and he had a quick check of the amount. He passed the bags over and they stayed there for a few minutes in order to not look suspicious for sitting down for only a minute. Two of the women went off to the toilets and Andy chatted with Emily and Sarah in the meantime. There was very little in the way of security and only one man was wandering around, who didn't appear to be taking much in. There was no aggression happening on the dance floor, so he was being quite passive. The two women came back and Emily and Sarah took their turn. Andy thought he should do his as well. He might have a fun night hanging around with this lot, especially after about half an hour.

More people came in and the partying carried on. Andy and the women went dancing again and as expected, the mood between them was exacerbated somewhat. Emily was fixing her eyes on Andy with a big grin and some other guys were trying to get her friend's attention. They were the usual lads who were trying to show off their masculinity, taking their hands and spinning them around. The women didn't look too taken with them, but in their heightened state were going along with it. One of them, the biggest guy, who was quite muscular, made a move on Emily and effectively pulled her away from Andy. She tried to make it clear that she wasn't interested, but he wasn't having any of it. Andy didn't know what to do as he wasn't her boyfriend, so felt he wasn't really in a position to intervene, plus the guy could probably knock him out with one punch. Andy carried on dancing, keeping his eye on whether Emily was okay with Mr Muscles. She looked back to Andy a couple of times and seemed to be indicating that she wasn't, but still, Andy didn't want to be the recipient of any aggression. The guy would have been aware that they weren't together because of Andy's passivity, but eventually Emily shook her head at him and walked back to Andy. The guy gave Andy an evil look, but instead of leaving the arena, stayed around as his friends were still there.

Andy thought it would be best if they moved away, so they went over to the bar. He tried to pick out the security guy, but couldn't see him. Mr Muscles didn't follow them and had his back to them now. Andy apologised for not getting involved, but explained why and Emily understood.

"Just pretend that you're my boyfriend," she said.

Andy got the idea, but wasn't sure what he should do. She smiled at him and leaned in for a kiss. He wasn't expecting this, but kissed her, partly out of politeness, partly because he thought it was better for her if he played the game.

"Let's go and dance some more," she said, evidently pleased with what she'd achieved. Andy submitted, with his instincts forcing him to see where that guy was. He was still in the same area, but had either seen them kissing or his testosterone levels had come back down to a relatively normal level and he stayed away from them. Before too long, that group of lads headed off after seeing they weren't getting anywhere with the women and homed in on another group.

Emily took Andy's hands as they danced. He was feeling like he'd got himself into something he shouldn't really be doing, but he thought Emily was very nice. With his cocaine-fuelled thoughts racing through his head, he concluded that it was only one night and he was here to let go and have a good time. Catarina would never find out, anyway. They both went to the toilets to do another line.

The club closed at three and they stayed there for the whole night, with Emily snogging Andy's face off at every opportunity. He was actually rather enjoying it now and had forgotten that he wasn't supposed to be doing this. As they were sitting at a table, the music changed and *The Power of Love* by Frankie Goes To Hollywood came on to signal that is was the end of the night. Emily dragged him onto the dance floor for some smooching until it finished and people were told to leave.

Emily looked into his eyes and asked "Shall we got back to your hotel?"

"Er, I think not," he replied. He wanted to, but even though he wouldn't be able to perform, he wanted to try to be a good boy, at least to some degree.

"Oh, come on," she insisted. "Let's have some fun."

"Sorry, I can't. I've got to get up early tomorrow."

"What for?"

He didn't have an actual reason to get up early, so thought of something quickly. "My train is at ten and I need to get back."

Emily looked disappointed. She didn't believe him as they'd already talked about what they were doing over this weekend. He'd said he was going back on Sunday, so she knew that there was some other reason.

"Have you got a girlfriend?" she asked.

He might as well be honest, seeing as she brought it up. "Yeah, sorry. I shouldn't have kissed you, but it just happened. I do like you. I think you're beautiful, but I shouldn't have."

"Alright. Well, never mind. It was nice to spend the evening with you. All the best."

"Thanks, you too. Sorry."

They went their separate ways and Andy got back to his hotel. He tried to analyse what he'd done, but his mind was still acting erratically. He accepted that he'd been unfaithful and wasn't going to tell Catarina. Emily was really nice, but these things happen when people were on holiday. At least he'd sold his ten grams and had a good night otherwise. It would be nice if Emily was here with him. No, forget that. She was really beautiful, though.

After finally getting to sleep around five and drifting in and out of consciousness, he got up at eleven. It was raining a little, which didn't help him to feel any better about what he'd done last night. He went out anyway to have a couple of coffees, but didn't feel like he wanted to eat as his mouth was too dry. It was noticeably quieter on the streets. Probably most people were nursing hangovers and mistakes they'd made last night. Andy wondered what he was going to do for the day. He didn't really have much reason to stay around now that he'd sold all his stuff. He just wanted to try to get his head together and work through cheating on Catarina to make himself feel better. As he mulled over things, he remembered that he'd planned to dye his hair. If he did it here, he'd have to stay checked into the hotel, or he could just head off and do it at home. He checked his watch. It was twenty to twelve. He looked up at the sky and thought the day wasn't going to be very exciting, so he headed back and checked out.

On his way to the train station, he reflected on how the week had been for him. He'd had some peaceful times and although last night was fun on the surface, the guilt was fuelled by the rain dripping on him and he arrived at the station in a grumpy mood. There was a train leaving in less than half an hour, so that was a small piece of relief. The journey back was uneventful and he got back home just after three.

Josh had only been around once during the week and was probably due to go again today, but he hadn't heard from him. Andy had forgotten to let him know he was coming back today, so texted him. Josh said he was already on his way, so would come anyway for a chat. Andy thought that sounded good, rather than stewing in his own juices for the rest of the day.

Josh turned up fifteen minutes later and asked how his week had been.

"Yeah, it was helpful. I think the change of scenery did me good. It's good to get away and have some space."

"Nice one. Alicante is nice. I've been there once for a weekend. How come you came back so soon?"

"Well, I thought I'd got what I needed from it, plus I couldn't think of anything else to do."

"Yeah, that makes sense."

"So how's everything been here?"

"Not much has changed! I just came round here that one time and everything was fine. I've been hanging out with Ana, of course and school is good."

Andy wondered if he should tell Josh about last night. On the one hand, he didn't want to go through it again in his own mind, but it was always good to talk about it with a friend and Josh was someone he could depend on.

"I managed to sell ten grams while I was there. It's really easy to sell to the tourists. Let me give you a gram for looking after my place."

"Mate. I only came once and that was for about two minutes."

"That's not the point. I still appreciate it. I haven't got any bags ready, actually, but I can measure you out one."

"Don't worry about it. Just give me one later. You don't have to though."

"No, I will do. What are you up to tonight?"

"We're doing the usual. Negrito then clubs. Do you and Catarina want to join us?"

"Maybe. I haven't got in touch with her yet."

"You didn't even tell her you were coming back early?"

"I didn't decide until today." He thought again about telling Josh, but he couldn't bring himself to do it. It was probably better if he left it a few days to see how he felt then. "I'll get in touch with the other guys as well and see if they want to come."

"Steve's already told me he's up for it. Paul's not sure yet."

"Okay. That's a plan, then."

They chatted some more about this and that, but neither one wanted to bring up the subject of the tense moment last weekend. It was better if they both managed to forget about about it and move on. Josh headed off and they arranged to met at ten that night.

Andy had a quick look around his flat, just to check that everything was how it should be. He took the secret board off his bed and put six hundred of what he'd made over the week in. It didn't feel that much of a relief to be back home. It was nice having a break and he'd enjoyed how different Alicante was, but the thoughts of Catarina were clouding his mind.

He went to sit on the sofa and decide what to do. His only other plan was to dye his hair, but that would also need to be explained to her and he didn't know if he should talk to her first about it or just do it and say he felt like having a change.

He held his phone with the messenger open to text Catarina. Should he wait a bit before seeing her so that he could have a clearer mind? His mental picture of Emily was still clear in his head and he imagined her smiling and looking into his eyes. He put the phone down and decided to go out for a walk.

The weather was miserable here, too, although it wasn't raining any more. Andy went to a chemist and bought some black hair dye. He was intrigued to know if people would think he was Spanish after he'd done it. He didn't want to go back just yet, but reacclimatise himself with the city. Unsurprisingly, nothing had changed, so after aimlessly walking for an hour, he went back.

He put his new purchase on his small dining table and thought about which order to do things in. Hair dye or Catarina? Fuck it, he would just do what he wanted and dye his hair. He'd still be the same person. She was always wearing different outfits, so what's the problem? He got to work and half an hour later, his hair was black.

He looked in the mirror and thought it made a significant difference. He stepped back to try to see if he would recognise himself. Being both the subject and the object naturally interfered with his judgement, but he was pleased with the look and hoped that it would disguise him enough from that man and help him relax when he was out tonight.

Andy felt more confident again for doing this, so he thought it was time to text Catarina.

"Hi. I'm home. Alicante was good, but one week was enough. How are you?"

She replied more quickly than usual. "Welcome home. I'm good. Do you have plans?"

"Going out with Josh, Steve and Ana later. Do you want to come?"

"Ana told me. Yes, I come out. Negrito at 10?"

"Great. Yes, see you later."

After all he'd been thinking about, the conversation seemed to go normally and it helped him to get back into the flow of his normal life. He would have to leave his new hair as a surprise to her, but he hoped she would like it and most of all that he wouldn't have to give a reason as to why he did it. It might be worth telling Josh though, in case he asked. He texted him to explain.

"Got you, mate. No worries. C U later," he replied.

He hadn't been home for too long before he got some more orders in for tonight. Two people texted him and between them wanted four grams, which he'd had to deliver before meeting his friends. They wanted them brought to their homes, which Andy was pleased about as he didn't yet like the idea of selling on the streets. He arranged to drop them off before ten and went on his bike, getting the money back to his shortly before meeting his group. He took another five grams with him as he expected they would want some and maybe another order would come in later. He left the flat at ten to ten.

On the way up his road, he passed the park. A certain someone was waiting there as usual, scrutinising the people who went past. He'd seen four or five since he'd got there about half an hour ago and when Andy passed, it didn't register that it was him. The giveaway clue was his natural blond hair, but it looked like some other local went by and the man in the hat couldn't see Andy's face in the darkness and dismissed him as not the man he was looking for.

Andy arrived undisturbed at Negrito and only Steve was there so far.

"Whoa. That took me by surprise," Steve said.

"Did you think I was Spanish?" Andy was eager to find out.

"I guess so. When did you dye it?"

"This afternoon. I wanted to see if I blended in with the locals more."

"Why's that?"

"To be honest, it's because I've been selling the stuff and I didn't want to stand out."

"Fair enough. Less easy to identify you."

"Exactly. Do you think it works?"

"I can imagine it would. Have you had any hassle from anyone then?"

"No, but I thought it was better to be on the safe side."

They caught up and Andy told Steve about his week away. During the conversation, Josh and Ana arrived, along with

Catarina. The latter's jaw dropped when she worked out who was at the table.

"What is this?" she asked in Spanish.

Andy smiled at her, but her expression was still one of shock.

"I thought I should become more Spanish because I live here," he said.

"But I preferred your blond hair," she said, clearly not impressed.

She sat down next to him with a look of disapproval, like a mother whose teenage son had done something without her permission.

"You don't like it?"

"No," she said, defiantly. She turned to Ana and said "What do you think?"

"I think it looks good," she replied, which added to Catarina's displeasure.

Josh had pretended he didn't know anything about what Andy had done and just smiled at him. He said he would get the drinks and asked people what they wanted. He made sure he took Ana with him so that Catarina and Andy could have a personal chat, despite Steve being in the mix.

Catarina didn't say much else, but Andy tried to get her to relax about it. He told her it was the same as wearing different clothes, but Catarina was adamant that she preferred his natural colour. Steve chose to sit back and pretend he wasn't there. The other two came back with the drinks and joined them.

They talked about Andy's holiday and he had to be careful to omit the real reason why he went as well as what had happened last night. Due to his lack of skills with lying, he'd gone through his script a few times earlier that evening. However, having a topic of conversation to go straight into helped Catarina slowly get used to her new-look boyfriend. Her face returned almost to normal, giving Andy the chance to ask her how her week had been.

"A normal week," she said. "I was working and spending time with my family."

As she hadn't said much, Andy wondered if that was all there was to say or whether she was still giving him the cold shoulder. As usual, Josh was on hand to guide the conversation back to normal topics and the tension gradually eased away. Andy still noticed an element of hostility in that Catarina wasn't being as tactile as usual, but he didn't want to push it and gave her time to get used to his hair. He hoped that giving her some cocaine would help to bring her round later, but he would choose the right moment to offer it to her. Andy didn't want to do any more tonight as he hadn't fully recovered from last night's and was a bit tired, but he would see how the night went.

They stayed at Negrito for a couple of hours and Andy didn't get any more orders, which suited him anyway. He gave Josh the gram he's promised him and Steve bought one for €60 before they headed to Mosquito.

Ana had managed to help bring Catarina back in from the cold by involving her in the conversation, which Andy had noticed her deliberately doing. He quietly thanked her and pressed a small bag into her hand just before they arrived.

When inside, Ana urged her to go to the toilets with her. As they were in private, they discussed the hair issue and Ana tried to convince her to accept it. Catarina reluctantly agreed to and they snorted a line each. When they came back out, she took a look at Andy and it didn't seem so bad after all. Steve and Josh joined in with going to another level, but Andy held off as he was already feeling too tired to be out much longer.

By the time the drugs kicked in, the tables turned and Catarina was more lively than Andy was, although he knew he had to make an effort to keep up appearances and did his best to match his behaviour to his surroundings.

He was aware of the need to make sure Catarina kept enjoying herself and she gradually came round to kissing him, which was a big relief to him as well as to the others.

By two o'clock, Andy was struggling to keep going and wanted to go home, but he feared that his departure would look like he was deserting her, so he stuck it out until it closed.

"I'm sorry, but I need to go home," he told everyone once they had got outside.

"No worries, mate," said Josh, keeping his support going for his wounded compatriot.

Andy looked at Catarina and he realised that he hadn't asked if she wanted to come back to his. He quickly added this question before it was too late.

"I want to dance more," she said.

"You can stay out, but I'm falling asleep."

All of the others wanted to continue their night, so Andy gave her a big hug, hoping that would satisfy her for now. She didn't seem too upset and was enthusiastic to go onto MX.

"I think I got through that in the end," Andy thought as he made his way home. "I didn't expect changing my hair colour to be such an issue, though."

He made it back home without anyone being there to notice him. The park had emptied over an hour earlier.

32.

On Sunday afternoon, Andy texted Catarina to ask how the rest of her night had been. He thought it would be good if they could meet up for a coffee so he could check to see if she was still in a mood with him for dying his hair. She told him it was good at MX and they'd stayed out until six in the morning. She didn't want to meet because she was really tired, but they could meet up during the week.

This gave him some peace and he thought it might be good to invite her for dinner mid-week and have her stay over. He waited until the next day before suggesting this and happily, she agreed. They would have dinner on Wednesday.

Andy didn't need to get out the big table just for the two of them, so he set up the small, round table, incorporating the candelabra and he thought it looked very romantic and would hopefully win her heart back. She came round at eight and they enjoyed his meal of fish with rice and vegetables. Catarina was in a better mood and she commented that she was okay with his hair now. Things between them seemed to be back to normal and they had light-hearted conversations and she was more tactile again. He'd bought a bottle of wine, which they got through fairly quickly and she asked if he had any more. He said he didn't, but he could go out and get another one if she wanted. She said that she would wait here while he did that.

Andy went into his bedroom to get some money from his wardrobe, while Catarina paid attention to what he was doing. There was a shop five minutes away, so he said he wouldn't be long.

Once she heard the downstairs door close, she waited for a minute in case he came back for some reason. When she was certain that he wasn't going to, she went into the bedroom. She looked at the wardrobe and listened for any noise coming from the front. It was quiet, so she opened the doors. At the bottom were his t-shirts and underwear. She lifted each section until she found where he kept the money that he had quick access to. She found a stack of bank notes and inspected them. There was €180 in tens and twenties. She listened again. Silence. She thought about how much would be safe to take without going too far and raising suspicions. Twenty Euros was probably for the best. She put the rest back as she had found them and put the t-shirts back on top. She closed the doors and went back to the living room, where she deposited the note in her purse. To make it look like she hadn't been doing anything, she sat on the sofa and switched on the TV. Andy came back five minutes later with the new bottle of wine. Catarina didn't care which one he bought, but smiled at him for going out to get it. He opened it and poured them both a glass before he joined her on the sofa and they snuggled up together, watching some vacuous Spanish soap opera, but not really paying attention to it.

Catarina joked with him that she liked his new hair colour and she ruffled it with her fingers. He was happy that she had come round and before too long, they went to the bedroom. While Andy had been outside, the thought of what he'd done with Emily crossed his mind, but he didn't feel too guilty about it now. It was just a thing of the past and he didn't want to worry about it any more.

This was the first time they'd had sex for a couple of weeks or so and Catarina was showing that she was enjoying it. For Andy, it was the best sex they'd had so far and he was feeling a stronger connection between them. Afterwards, he held her in his arms as they lay down and it crossed his mind that he might actually be falling in love with her. He didn't want to say it yet, but hopefully things would get even better before too long, so maybe at the weekend it would be the right time to let her know.

Catarina stayed over and when she had to get up for work, she told Andy to stay in bed and she would get herself ready and leave for work. She came back into the bedroom to give him a goodbye kiss and left.

Andy lay there half-asleep, feeling very contented. "She's really good," he thought. "Just gets a bit moody sometimes, but she gets over it. Yeah, I've got myself a good woman."

Catarina made her way to work, pleased with herself that she'd accomplished her task of obtaining twenty Euros and looked forward to the next time she could stay over.

Andy waited until Friday afternoon to deposit some more money into his two bank accounts, so that it would look like he'd just received it at the end of his working week. He put €250 into each one, which gave him a total of €2670 saved. He thought this was a decent amount and was happy to wait for more orders to come in over the coming weekend. He went to have a coffee in television square as it was dry and there was some sun at times. He smiled to himself as he thought of his girlfriend and wondered what they should do next. As they often went out with other friends, maybe it would be good to have another night for just the two of them. A meal was always a romantic gesture, but he preferred to go to a restaurant this time.

He watched the people go by as always when he noticed someone who he thought he recognised. Walking fairly slowly was that man who he'd had a run in with. He seemed to be looking around the floor, probably to find discarded cigarette butts to scavenge tobacco from. Andy was put on full alert from seeing him and didn't know what to do with himself. The man wasn't looking up at people, but he could do at any time. Andy didn't have his sunglasses with him, which frustrated him, but at least he wasn't blond any more, so if the man noticed him, he hopefully wouldn't recognise him. Andy put his elbow on the table and tried to obscure his face with his hand as naturally as he could, while peering through his fingers. The man went past him and it seemed he was going to be safe. He continued watching him anyway when the man came over to the terraces and started looking in ash trays on empty tables. He picked out a couple of cigarette butts and it looked like he was going to make his way along towards him. Andy's heart was beating hard. He needed to get away. He hadn't paid for his coffee yet, but it could be a good way to escape by going in and paying at the counter. The man asked a couple at a table if they had a cigarette, to which they shook their heads and tried to ignore him. This was Andy's cue. Black hair or not, his face was still the same and it was not worth taking the risk. He calmly got up and went inside the café. Having his back to the man was an ideal situation, but he was afraid of turning round and standing face to face with him. What else could he do to waste time? Look at his phone. Perfect. He took it out of his pocket and acted like he was reading a message that required a lot of concentration. Every second felt like a minute, but once he thought that it had been enough time, he slowly turned his head to see if the man was still out there. He couldn't see him, so he went towards the door. His eyes scanned the scene, but the man seemed to have left. Which way should he go? As the man had gone to Andy's right, he probably carried on in that direction. He was aware that he might be looking suspicious to the other people around him, so he looked at his phone again, then looked out as if he was waiting for someone to arrive. He stood there for another half a minute or so, then slowly left the café and went left. He had the feeling that the man's eyes were burrowing into the back of his head and Andy was very tense. He got to the corner of the square and could have gone into the street to the left, but didn't want to be restricted, so he turned right to go along the edge of the square. There were a few people around, all of whom Andy looked at. He passed by the flower boxes along the square's edge when he saw something he didn't want to see. The man was sitting on the floor with his back to one of the boxes and looking through his tobacco to roll a cigarette. Andy was about two metres from him and almost froze in horror. Once the shock had left him, he made his way in the opposite direction to the man down Calle de Navellos, where one of his banks was. He just marched on down the street like he was late getting back to work from his lunch, all the way to the end, where he came out at the ring road by the Turia Park.

Finally, Andy was able to take stock of the situation now that he knew he was safe. "Jesus Christ," he thought. "I can't believe I've seen him again after just one week of being back. Fuck, how often is this going to happen?" He lit a cigarette and tried to calm down. Even though he knew he looked different now, it wasn't helping him to feel that he was blending in. He thought about jumping in at the deep end and letting the man see him, just so he could find out if his disguise worked, but the thought of that filled him with dread. He walked west along the ring road, not knowing what his plan of action should be. "Should I grow a beard as well? That will come out blond and look weird. I don't think I want to go through that with Cati, either. Am I supposed wear a fake nose and glasses?"

He eventually made it back home and went straight to the sofa. He put his head in his hands and was thoroughly annoyed that he had to keep going through this shit.

During the afternoon, Andy kept trying to work out what he could do to resolve this. Right now, he hated being a drug dealer, even though most of the time it was fine. The bad experiences that he suffered were too much for him to handle and he knew he wasn't cut out for this. It also annoyed him that he couldn't talk to most of his friends or even his girlfriend about his problems. Only Josh was there for him. He thought it was likely that Catarina would dump him if he explained how difficult it was. She wouldn't want to be with someone who was putting himself at risk of being beaten up. Paul didn't want to hear about these things and Steve wasn't someone who he was as close to as Josh. There was nothing else for it but to ask to meet Josh that evening.

They met at a café that was out of the general area that Andy was used to. Josh didn't appear to be in his normal good mood today. He looked at Andy, who was visibly stressed.

"What's happened this time?"

"I saw that man again today." He continued to describe what had happened to him.

"This is doing you in, Andy. No offence, but you keep telling me things like this and I'm worried you're going to crack."

Andy looked dejected. He relied on Josh to be the man who would give him instructions as to how he could easily rise above it, but he was acting differently.

"One minute you're feeling good, then the next minute something happens and you come crashing down. You're way out of your depth with this."

"I know. This is totally not the kind of person I am," Andy said. "I just feel that I'm living in fear all the time. It only takes one little thing like seeing him and I've lost it again."

"So what are you going to do about it?"

Andy was surprised at this question. Josh had never asked him to sort it out by himself before.

"I really don't know. I can't talk to Catarina about this because I don't want to drag her into it. You're the only friend I can talk to."

Josh looked at him with a serious face, not saying anything. He didn't have a magic answer to give to Andy. They both sat there looking at each other blankly for a few moments.

"The obvious thing would be to say that you need to get away," Josh finally said. "But, of course, you've just done that. Then you come back and things have flared up again."

Andy listened and waited for him to continue, wishing that he would give him some advice.

"Listen. We're friends," Josh said. "I am here for you, but..."

"I know. I shouldn't be depending on you for everything. I'm sorry."

"You don't have to be sorry, but it does feel like I'm the one who has to clean up after you. As you said, you've got no-one else to talk to about stuff like this, which means it always comes to me."

"It's not fair, I know that," Andy said. "I wish I could say that I won't call on you again, but I just don't know where this is going. I wish I could just sell the whole lot in one go and be done with it."

"How much have you got left?"

"Still more than four hundred grams."

"Shit, that's still loads. I don't have any answer, though. I don't know anyone who would buy a bulk load. How much are you selling each week?"

"Ten grams at the most."

"So that would take at least forty weeks to get rid of."

"Unless I get more clients, but I'm worried about that in case I end up dealing with others who might be a risk to me."

Josh looked away, trying to think of something that Andy could do. He shook his head and said "No. I can't think of anything else."

Andy nodded in resignation. "Yeah, sorry. I've got to sort this out on my own. I won't keep coming to you about this shit."

Josh, in a way, wanted that to be the case, but on the other hand, didn't want to let Andy down.

"If anything serious happens, tell me, but yeah, try to sort things out. Be sensible and be safe."

"I will, thanks."

They left the café and Andy walked back home. He wasn't in the mood to meet Catarina now and just wanted to curl up on his sofa and not think about anything. When he got back, he texted her to say he didn't want to do anything that night, maybe tomorrow. She replied with "OK".

33.

On Saturday morning, Andy woke up with a face like thunder. He lay there staring at the ceiling, thinking about his conversation with Josh and said to himself "I've got to take control of this fucking situation." How he was going to do that was something that still eluded him, but he forced himself to have conviction and figure something out.

He got up and made some coffee, stronger than usual, and as he waited for it to brew, he noticed a cockroach on his kitchen floor. This one had avoided the traps he was still having to use. He looked at it menacingly, grabbed a glass and covered it at the first attempt. He went to find a sheet of paper and slid it under the glass. He didn't care for its attempts to crawl up the side of the glass and he took it to the bathroom and threw it in the toilet, immediately flushing it. He was not going to take any prisoners any more. The cockroach swam frantically around the water and was not being pushed down. The flush ended and it was still at the surface. "Fucking hell," he said out loud. "Is this what I'm going to be faced with? Die, you little bastard." The cockroach wouldn't die. It tried to get out, so Andy grabbed the toilet brush and pushed it down. He was determined to win this battle and squashed it against the bottom of the bowl, twisting the brush until it was no more. He looked at his achievement, swished the remaining bits off the brush and went back to the kitchen.

He poured his coffee and went to the front room. He opened the balcony shutters and looked out to see how the weather was. It was drizzling. He scowled at the clouds and thought "Bad weather isn't going to stop me." He didn't intend to be scared of anyone any more and wasn't interested in thinking how he was going to make this happen. He opened the doors and lit a cigarette, something he didn't usually do this soon after getting up. He wanted to feel like he was in charge. In charge of something. Somehow. He narrowed his eyes, took a drag and acted like he was the boss, the boss of his own life.

As he looked out at the abandoned furniture building and sipped his coffee, he told himself that he was going to face that man whenever he saw him next and stand his ground. The man needed to know that Andy was not someone to be messed with, but Andy also had to admit to himself that neither was the man. "I won't say anything to him," he thought, "but I have to give the impression that I'm not scared." He could feel his confidence depleting already, so screwed up his face and forced his determination back.

Andy finished his cigarette and went back inside to think about it some more. He imagined what the likely scenario would be if he came across the man. A dark side street, Andy on his own. Suddenly the man appears in front of him and says "Oye!" From the times he'd seen fights in the street back in England, the typical reaction was to put your fists up and look like you were prepared to punch the assailant. Usually what turned out was not a controlled boxing match, but a flailing of arms and the two people involved making a stupid mess of things. How should he respond more effectively? Punch him straight in the face? Kick out at him? He practised doing these things and pretended to charge at him and punch him. The guy could dodge it and make a move on Andy. He imagined what would happen if he kicked out at him. The guy could grab his leg and throw him to the ground. Then he would be in serious trouble. Then, all of a sudden, a realisation came to him: self-defence classes! Obviously! Why didn't I think of that before? His eyes lit up at the idea and he knew he had found the answer. He rubbed his hands with glee and grinned from ear to ear. "Right. That's today's objective!" he said to himself.

With his vigour renewed, Andy got dressed and went out. He needed to find somewhere that did classes. He didn't know where to go, except gyms, but he wasn't going to stop until he found something out. As he still didn't have a *Páginas Amarillas* in his flat, he would go to a café and ask to look at one. He went in the nearest one he came to and asked if they had one, which they did. He ordered a black coffee and took it to a table. He didn't know what self-defence was in Spanish, so he asked the waiter "Como se llaman las clases de defensa?" "Autodefensa," he answered. Simple. He looked through the book and found a few listings. He asked the waiter for a piece of paper and a pen and he wrote down the addresses of all the ones he saw. There were a couple that were fairly near to the centre and using the map in the book, he was able to find out more or less where they were from the post codes. He really hoped he would be able to get on a course straight away or at least not wait too long, so he'd ask at all of them first.

He finished his coffee and went to the nearest one, which was just over the ring road, not too far from where Paul and Steve lived. It was a sports club that did boxing and it was open. He went in and spoke to a guy who was in the entrance area. He asked if they did the classes, to which he said they did. Was it possible to join one? The guy said he'd get someone to talk to him about it.

Another man came out, who looked like he knew how to look after himself. He told Paul that they did courses, but the next one didn't start for another month. That was too long to wait, so he went onto the next place. Here, they had just started a course two weeks ago, so it was too late for Andy to join in. Andy explained that he needed it now and was happy to pay for the weeks they had already done. The man thought about it. He explained that Andy would be behind on the basics, so it was not a good time to join them, but the next course would start in January. Andy pleaded again and offered to pay extra if the man could give him some private classes to get up to speed with the course. This time, the man seemed more interested and said Andy could pay fifty Euros for two hours before Tuesday, when the next class would be and

THE EMPTY FLAT

Andy was more than happy to accept that. The classes would be once a week until just before Christmas. They agreed that he could come in on Monday at eleven and then again at five when the man had some free time. Andy showed that he was really grateful for this and would go back and get the money to pay him today.

He went back feeling very satisfied with this result. The sooner he could get started, the more confident he would feel and by Tuesday, he would effectively have had three classes under his belt.

Andy wanted to text Josh and tell him what he was going to be doing, but wasn't sure if he should say anything yet. Would Josh prefer it if he kept things to himself? Would he be happy for Andy that he was taking action by himself? He decided not to text him just yet, there was no rush. He would just bring it up when he next saw him and that decided that wasn't going to be at a time when he needed to get Josh's perspective.

He switched his thoughts to Catarina and instead texted her to ask if she wanted to go out for dinner tonight. She said yes as she liked being treated by Andy. He didn't even think at this moment about paying for the meal. He had enough money and was getting used to that being the situation. They would go to a Mexican restaurant at nine then have drinks afterwards. He didn't feel like he should be doing drugs tonight as after signing up for the self-defence course, it made him want to be more focused on bringing about a positive change and if he left himself in a vulnerable position tonight, it would undo his positive mood before he even started.

Andy actually hoped he wouldn't have to deliver any goods to anyone that night, either. If he got any texts, he might just say he was out of town. It wouldn't be polite to head off and leave Catarina on her own while he made a transaction, so he wouldn't even take any coke with him later.

Throughout the rest of the day, he felt more in control of his life again. He met Cati at the restaurant and they had a good meal, although she wasn't keen on the spicy food as much as he was. They went to a bar just off Caballeros, nearer to television square to be away from the action. Cati was in good spirits and the colour of his hair wasn't even raised in conversation this time.

He told her he didn't want to take any drugs that night and she was fine with that. This led him onto telling her about the self-defence classes. She was surprised to hear this and asked him why. He said it would be safer to be prepared when selling drugs because he never knew what might happen. She agreed that it was a good idea.

They went over to Fox Congo for a couple of hours and her displays of affection towards him made it easier to get through the cheesy Latino music that he still didn't like. He received two texts asking for some drugs, but he stuck by what he'd decided and they carried on their night without interruptions. They went back to his flat afterwards and had good sex again.

In the morning, Andy was feeling a bit hungover, as was Catarina and they stayed in bed for a while after waking up. She was waiting for a time when he would be out of the room for some time, thinking that just making a coffee wouldn't be safe enough as he could easily pop back in to talk to her. She wanted him to have a shower as they were sweaty after dancing and making love, which Andy thought was a reasonable suggestion.

Andy wasn't giving the sign that he was going to have a shower yet, so Catarina took the initiative and went for one herself. Andy offered to join her as he thought it might be a sexy thing to do. She declined, saying she just wanted to get clean, which disappointed him somewhat, but he didn't let it bother him. She gave him a kiss on the nose and went to the bathroom.

While she was in there, Andy wondered how much money he had in the wardrobe in case they decided to go out for breakfast. He had €140 plus another ten in his wallet. He went into the kitchen and started making some coffee. Catarina finished her shower and saw what he was doing. She asked if she could borrow one of his t-shirts, which he was fine about, but because that's where he kept his money, he preferred to find one for her. She got the idea that that was why he did it instead of letting her look for herself, but of course raised no objection. They had a coffee in the front room and after they finished it, he went for a shower. This was always going to be the perfect time for Catarina to carry out her mission and she waited until she heard the water splashing around, then went into the bedroom.

She checked how much money he had again and concluded that it was only safe to take another twenty. Considering that he made all his money in cash, but knew that he put some of it in the bank, she wondered why he only had a small amount in the flat. Did he keep some of it somewhere else, too? When she got the chance, she would do a more intricate search. Kitchen cupboards were a good bet, maybe in his books.

It took her less than a minute to go through the process and she was back in the front room long before he finished showering. He went into the bedroom to put some clean clothes on, including a new t-shirt and while he was there, thought he might as well grab a bit more money as he fancied going out. He took thirty Euros, but because he'd already counted how much was there, didn't pay attention to it this time. Catarina waited patiently, but also a little cautiously as she knew he was getting dressed. She took special notice of his demeanour as he came back into the front room and he seemed fine.

"Shall we go out, then?" he asked.

"Okay, let's go."

They had lunch at a café near to the Mercat Central and Andy paid for it again. It crossed his mind that she never offered to pay for anything and it was starting to make him uncomfortable. However, he didn't want to raise it as an issue as they were getting on well at the moment. He'd already perceived that she could fly off the handle at small things, so he just reminded himself that he was making easy money and much more than her, so he left it. She was eager to go home afterwards, so gave him a hug and went on her way. It wasn't really the kind of day to stay outside as it was getting cooler, so he just went back and thought about his self-defence classes tomorrow and spent a lazy day messing about on the internet.

Andy was in a good mood the next morning and couldn't wait to have his first lesson. He arrived five minutes early and went with Jaime into the studio where the classes were held. Jaime only spoke a little English, but they managed to get by. Jaime went through some introductory talks about what he should look out for, what he shouldn't do and how he could empower himself in front of a potential attacker. Andy learned about keeping eye contact and saying things that might put the person off-guard. They went onto some basic moves to defend himself and to interrupt a sudden attack, which he was told was likely to happen. Always go for the head or below the waist, Jaime said. That would inflict more damage and also affect the other person's balance, giving Andy time to follow up with another move. They went through a number of attack scenarios where Jaime would attack Andy in different ways and he was starting to get the hang of it. The first hour flew by and Jaime said he had made good progress.

When he left, Andy was already feeling like he could handle himself better. It took up most of his thoughts for the rest of the afternoon before he returned at five. Andy wanted to make sure that the actions would become cemented in his long-term memory.

In their second lesson, they repeated some of the things from the morning and explored some further techniques. They managed to get Andy up to scratch and ready to join the rest of the group tomorrow.

Leaving the studio again in a good mood, he really wanted to text Josh, but managed to stop himself. He thought that he might even be proud of him, but it was still connected with the life issues he was going through, so held off and reported his good day to Catarina instead. When she saw she'd got a text from Andy, she was apprehensive in case he'd noticed that some of his money was gone. She was relieved to know he was happy and that she had got away with it for a second time. She put her phone down and smiled to herself smugly. She'd been thinking of all the places where he might keep more money and looked forward to staying over again. She asked him if he wanted to do something during the week. He hadn't thought about it, but maybe they could have another night in one day.

"Wednesday?" she asked.

"Sure," he replied. He didn't really feel like cooking again, but thought he might as well just get on with it.

On Tuesday evening, Andy went to the studio for his first lesson with the rest of the group. There were six people in total: three women and three men. Their ages ranged from around twenty to fifty and they seemed to get on well. Having a common purpose was always a good way for people to gel and Jaime explained how Andy had got to join them and they welcomed him. They paired up, Andy being with a man in his forties called Raul. They recapped the techniques they'd already learned and Andy felt at home with them, being at the same level. Jaime gave them a couple more techniques to practise, including how to get the assailant to the floor and once again, the hour flew by and everyone was satisfied with what they'd learned.

A short while after he'd got back home, Andy was surprised to see he'd got a text from Josh. He asked him how he was and Andy thought this was heart-warming. He wasn't deserting him after all, which had gone through his head a couple of times since they'd last met. Andy thought this was fine to inform him of what he'd been doing and Josh said he was really happy for him and it was a great idea.

As he was on his own and had time to reflect on things yet again, Andy was in a good place; learning how to defend himself and feeling more confident, re-igniting his friendship with Josh and having an established relationship with Catarina.

He prepared a simple pasta meal for them on Wednesday and they had another quiet night in. He didn't need to go out to buy anything else, but she expected that this might be the case and focused her attention on looking through some other places while he was out of the room. Andy only went to the toilet one time, giving her a brief moment to flick through his books, which only amounted to four, and found nothing. She knew that she had to keep him on her side and giving him good sex was a sure fire way of keeping him satisfied.

As he hadn't sold anything since they were last out, he didn't have much cash in his wardrobe, but there was a couple of hundred in the secret place. Catarina had no idea that it was there, of course, and she only got a quick chance to look under the t-shirts when Andy brushed his teeth. There was only €50 there, so she had to leave it.

In the morning, she left him to stay in bed again while she got ready. She silently looked through things in the kitchen cupboard. Nothing in any of the boxes, either, which annoyed her. She knew he still had drugs in the flat, but he hadn't disclosed anything to her yet about the big stash. Even though Andy thought that they were getting closer, he didn't want to let anyone else know if he could help it. The fact that he had it in his mind that she was a bit of a freeloader made him reluctant to be totally upfront with her.

She went to work having had no success with pilfering, but had no intention of stopping there. There was bound to be more money that would appear over the weeks, so she told herself to stay patient and the time would come.

That day, Andy thought a lot about what he learned so far from his course and went over the techniques many times. He thought again that he would like to see the man, just to put things into action, but he was still at an early stage and needed to have more confidence first.

He was ready to get back to selling his coke and would deliver all the orders that he got, as he didn't want his contacts to give up on him. On Thursday, he had another text from Josh's friends, Charlie and Liam, who he'd felt uncomfortable with the first time. Even though he didn't expect to have any altercations with them, Andy thought it would at least be a little test of his reserve. Charlie had bartered his own deal before, getting two grams for €150 and Andy was fine with this being the case again. He texted Charlie to say that's how much it would be and he went over.

Their flat stank of weed again and the guys were in a similar state as before. Josh didn't talk about them much at all, so they obviously weren't close friends. There was very little chat between these two and Andy, which the latter was happy about. They did the sale without any further attempt to reduce the price and Andy went home.

On the ride back, he almost felt disappointed that he didn't get the chance to be more assertive, but laughed it off, thinking that he didn't really want to turn into a hard man, only if it was absolutely necessary.

Andy didn't want to have a weekend with just Catarina as he wanted to reconnect with his friends. He hadn't seen Paul for a few weeks now and of course, he wanted to make sure things were fine with Josh. He texted them both and between them, they organised a night out on Friday at the usual place.

It was like a big reunion as Paul, Steve and Jess came out, along with Josh, Ana and Catarina. This was the first time Paul and Jess had seen the new Spanish version of Andy and they teased him a little at first. Jess gave particular attention to him as she was more outgoing, which Catarina noticed and wasn't happy about. There was a certain amount of jealousy as it looked like Jess was trying to crack onto him, even though it was innocent and on a platonic level. Catarina instructed Ana to go with her to the toilets.

The rest of the group carried on catching up as normal, paying no attention to the other two abruptly leaving the scene. They were gone for nearly ten minutes before they returned with Catarina delivering a stony face, but not directing it at Andy so much. He didn't even notice that she had something on her mind and this lack of attention got her more agitated. The conversations carried on and during them, Andy got a text asking for three grams. He let Catarina know, to which she just nodded and said to the others that he'd be back shortly. With him not even noticing that Catarina wasn't happy, then just walking off, left her effectively steaming, which Ana noticed. She had a quiet word with her friend, but Catarina wasn't forthcoming with what she was thinking. Ana left it and ten minutes later, Andy came back. He'd had a routine sale and seen no-one untoward so was in a good mood. Catarina's expression hadn't changed and this time, Andy noticed it and asked her is she was alright. She just said she was, but he could tell she was holding back something. The atmosphere around the table was still happy, with laughter and light-hearted talk going on and Andy didn't want anything to get in the way of it, so he chose to ignore whatever the issue was and joined in with his friends.

Eventually, the unhappy party asked Andy how much he'd sold. He told her, which she noted, knowing how much money that was. This lifted her spirits somewhat and she gradually broke her wall back down. It would be in her interests to be on good terms with him so she could stay at his tonight. She thought he would probably sell more later, so this could be her chance to step up her game.

They all went onto Mosquito and Andy saw a couple of guys who he'd sold to twice before, before they got in. They got his attention and bought two grams off him, which Catarina noticed. Josh and Steve also bought some, meaning Andy's pockets were full again, to his dissatisfaction, but he couldn't be bothered to go back home now, so stuffed some in his wallet, more in his front two jeans pockets and the rest in his sock. Everyone except Paul and Jess got in on the action and had the usual night of fervent dancing. They ended the night at three instead of going on and Andy took Catarina back.

Their journey was full of pointless conversation and they were unaware of how loud they were talking. However, on Calle del Bany, it was so empty that it didn't matter. As they walked past the park, someone heard them speaking in English. The man in the hat had waited patiently, knowing that Andy was more likely to show up later at the weekends. Hearing them speak English got his attention, but he didn't recognise this couple. As they passed the park, the man silently moved over to watch where they went. He was confused that they went in through the only accessible doorway in this stretch of the road, but looking again at the English-speaking man, he guessed it was the same one from his height and his gait. They went inside. The man in the hat knew that the blond guy was now a dark-haired guy. It was useful to know.

With almost €500 left among his person, Andy wanted to put it away somewhere out of Catarina's view. She got a glass of water and sat on the sofa, leaving him to do what she also wanted him to do. He didn't count it, but got all the notes together and put it in its usual place. In the other room, Catarina's mind was racing with how much she could get away with. He went back in to join her in drinking water. They were both still feeling the effects of the cocaine, so found it hard to keep their thoughts inside their heads.

"How much money did you make tonight?" she asked.

"I don't know. I didn't count it," he said. That was exactly what she wanted to hear. "I sold three when we were at Negrito, then two more, that's €400. Two to Josh and Steve, so another €120." Before saying the final total, he realised that he didn't want to talk about such things with her, but it was too late now.

"Very good," she said. "Well done."

Andy wanted to change the subject, which she had no problem with and they talked about various unimportant things that happened during the night out. Despite neither of them being particularly interested in what they were talking about, they were unable to stop themselves and stayed up for another hour. Eventually, they decided to crash and had the usual unsettled night's sleep.

They got up around midday, both feeling the worse for wear. They went through the typical routine of coffee and showers. Catarina almost wished she didn't have to get up and do her job as she was exhausted, but she staggered to the bedroom because it was too good an opportunity to miss. Her handbag was still in there, so she could perform the task like a professional. She listened out to hear the water splashing and opened the door. The pile of money was huge. She didn't have time to count it, so took what she judged to be about ten percent of it, snatching €60 and quickly covering her tracks. Paul finished his shower sooner than she expected and he came into the bedroom naked. She had just put her handbag back down, but was clearly surprised to see him appear suddenly, her eyes wide as he walked through the doorway. This struck a bell in his head and he asked her what was wrong.

"Nothing," she said. "You just surprised me."

He glanced around the room as he had a feeling that something suspicious was going on. His wardrobe was closed, she was standing at the side of the bed near the window. She smiled at him and walked out of the room. Andy just stood there, thinking about what was going on. He remembered that he had told her how much money he'd made, although he couldn't remember the amount at that moment. He went through it in his head and, along with the €150 that he'd got from Charlie and Liam, that would be €670, minus a bit that he spent on drinks. He tried to work out how much he'd spent, but could only guess at about €50. "So, say €620, as there was nothing else in there before that," he thought. He closed the bedroom door and got the money out. He counted out €570. That was way off. He did the calculations again. There was no way he'd spent €100 on drinks. €50 was an overestimate. He checked his wallet and jeans pockets in case he'd missed anything, but there was nothing in there. He looked down at Catarina's handbag. He wanted to check her purse, but she could come back in at any moment. He remembered that she hadn't had a shower yet, so would act as if nothing was wrong and wait till she got in there.

He got dressed and pretended that he was happy. He smiled at her and sat down next to her, putting his arm around her. She appeared to be anxious, but was trying not to show it.

"Ah, it feels so much better to have a shower," he said, dropping a big hint. "Are you going to have one?"

"Yes, in a minute," she said. "I'm tired."

Andy had no choice but to let her do it in her own time.

Catarina was thinking about what she should do. She had no idea if Andy had caught her in the act, but he seemed to be acting normally now. However, given that she had a certain side to her that meant she knew how to act when she wanted her own way, if it was his technique, she was well-practised in employing this method.

She stayed sitting down to see if he said anything else. Andy was waiting for her to go for a shower, but they were both in a stalemate situation. After a couple of minutes of them not talking, he got up and put some music on. He went to look out the window and although it wasn't a great day, it was decent enough to go outside.

"Maybe we should go for a walk," he said, with his back to her, anticipating her response.

"I don't want to," she said.

"What do you want to do then?"

"Nothing. I might go home."

They were constantly trying to gauge each other's reactions in detail. Neither of them wanted to move any of their pieces and they studied the board carefully.

"Do you want some more coffee?" he asked.

"Okay, thanks," she said, meaning that she would at least be here for a bit longer.

Catarina thought that Andy didn't suspect anything as he did seem normal and she felt that her impenetrable barrier might be giving it away for her. He went into the kitchen and she decided it would be best if she had a shower. He prepared the coffee, giving her a quick smile as she passed by him.

The shower was turned on, but Andy wanted to wait a moment until he was sure she was going to stay in there. The coffee pot was set on the hob and he went into the bedroom.

He listened out carefully to make sure she was not coming and found her purse quickly. He opened it and saw there was €60 in there, in used notes. "Well, that adds up perfectly," he thought.

"Why would she have this much money in her purse after a night out?"

Even though he knew it was often impossible to work out why women did certain things, she would have had to go out with at least €80 or €90 to have this much left. Why would anyone do that? She didn't have to buy coke off Andy, so she had no need for extra money.

He put the purse back in her bag and went back to the kitchen. Then he had a brainwave.

As he'd already counted the money in his wardrobe, he thought of a way to bring this to her attention that didn't sound confrontational. She got out of the shower and passed him while he was pouring the coffee. They didn't make eye contact and she went into the bedroom. She was dying to find out if he'd looked in her bag. She had make-up in there, so had an excuse to be rummaging around in it. She opened her purse and saw the money was still there. She took out her make-up and went back to the bathroom.

Andy took the cups into the front room and waited for her. When she came back she saw the cups either side of a pile of money. She looked at it with some anxiety, then glanced up at Andy, who was looking at her.

"I'm a bit confused," he said. "I was counting my money and there's some missing." Catarina didn't say anything.

"I know how much I should have, but it's €60 less than it should be."

She desperately tried to think of a response. "Is it in your wallet?"

"No."

"Is it in your pockets?"

"No."

"You probably spent it last night."

"No, I didn't."

"Why are you looking at me like that?"

"I'm not looking at you like anything," he said. "Did you take my money?"

"No!" she shouted. "Why do you say that?"

"Because my money has gone somewhere and you're the only other person here."

"I didn't take it. I can't believe you think I did."

"Can you show me what you have in your purse?"

"Fuck off! Andy, why are you like this?"

"Okay. I'll be honest with you. I looked in your purse when you were in the shower and there is €60 in there."

"That is my money! You bastard!"

"I will ask you again. Did you take my money?"

"No!"

"I don't believe you. All the time we have been together, I've been paying for everything. I've bought you meals, drinks and you never say thank you for anything. Now I am €60 short and you have €60 in your purse."

Catarina knew she was stuck in a corner, but she was angry. Not only because he accused her of theft, but because he accused her of freeloading.

"I can't believe you say this," she said and grabbed her handbag. "I'm going home."

Because she didn't deny it this time, he was certain that she had taken it. She went towards the front door and said, "I don't want to see you again."

"Same here," he said, with no emotion. She didn't look back at him and went out. A few seconds later, he heard the downstairs door slam shut. Andy stood still, giving her time to go away. He didn't want to see her. He looked back at the table. The two coffee cups were steaming. He picked them up and emptied them down the sink. He went back and got the money, unscrewed the panel and put all but €70 in there and screwed the panel back on.

"Now it all makes sense," he thought. "She was just with me to take my money." He went to the sofa and lit a cigarette.

34.

Catarina stormed home, pissed off with Andy more than herself. Being manipulative, she didn't consider that she had done anything wrong. She didn't look at anybody, but stewed in her own devious mind. She was irritated that she'd only got €100 in cash. She'd hoped that she would eventually get over a thousand. When she got home, she didn't say hello to her parents and went straight to her room. She threw her handbag on her bed and sat down on her chair by her dressing table. She looked at herself in the mirror. A furious face looked back at her. Her plans had been thwarted and she'd been caught, which irritated her more than knowing that she'd betrayed him. She remembered that she still had one of his t-shirts that he'd lent her. She took it out of her wardrobe, got a pair of scissors and angrily cut it into pieces. She look at them scattered on the floor and thought "That's what I think of him." She heard a knock on her door. Her mother calmly asked her if she was okay. Catarina replied that she was, but nothing else. Her mother asked if she could come in. Catarina said no. She heard the footsteps fade away.

Andy was pissed off that he hadn't cottoned onto her earlier. He thought back to all the times he'd paid for things. That time when she wanted the shoes but didn't have enough should have been a red flag. He realised that it was all part of her game. "Keep him sweet and he won't suspect a thing," he thought. "Bitch."

He didn't know what he was going to do for the rest of the day. He wasn't going to be able to get this out of his mind, no matter how much he tried to distract himself. He found some sort of consolation in knowing that he'd worked it out quite early on.

He tried playing games on his computer, but couldn't properly focus and he was getting angry every time he made a mistake. He didn't know if it would be the right time to talk to a friends. Even though things seemed fine again with Josh, hearing this news might piss him off and it would just be more baggage to dump on him.

He could try Paul, but he didn't want to unload all his shit on anyone else. Andy wanted to remove every trace of Catarina from his flat now. He looked in the bathroom and took out the shampoo and shower gel that she used and dumped them in the spare room. There was nothing of hers in the bedroom, but he smelt the pillow and sheets and he could pick up the smell of her perfume. He took these off and changed the sheets. There was nothing else he could find, but he wondered if there were any other signs that she'd been snooping. He looked around the kitchen and front room, but couldn't see anything. He checked under the floorboard, but his stash was still there, so she hadn't discovered that. He heard his phone bleep in the front room. "That better not be her," he thought. "Or is she apologising?"

When he picked up the phone, it was a message from Josh.

"You split up with Cat?" he asked.

"Yes. How do you know?"

"She told Ana. What did you do?"

"Me? She stole money off me."

"She was angry at you. Did you fight?"

"No!"

"Can we meet? There is confusion about this."

"OK"

Andy hadn't been expecting Josh to offer to talk, so that was a surprise. They met up along with Ana at Café Sant Jaume at four.

"So what happened?" Josh asked.

"I'd made some good money last night and I knew how much it should come to. I was counting my money and it was sixty Euros down. I'd checked everywhere, but there was nothing else."

"You could have dropped it somewhere."

"No, mate. I'm very careful with my money. You know that."

"Accidents can happen, you know."

"Well, listen. I'd been in the shower and I went back into the bedroom and she was standing there, looking shocked at me appearing. I keep some cash in my wardrobe."

The other two listened carefully to make sure they didn't misunderstand anything.

"She looked suspicious then wouldn't take a shower for a while. Usually, she wants to get clean as soon as possible. Then, I had a look in her handbag and saw €60 in there."

"Well, that's possible, isn't it?"

"It's possible, but who takes that much money out for a night out?" This would be what she had left after buying drinks."

Josh turned to Ana. "Do you know if she takes a lot of money out with her?"

"I don't ask," she shrugged.

"Now, I've been paying for pretty much everything when we've been out and I can see that she has played me like a kipper. She's been using me and stealing my money when she's stayed at mine. When I asked her about it, she got angry and stormed out."

"That's no surprise when someone accuses you of that, whether they're guilty or not."

"But me being sixty Euros short and her being sixty up at the same time? It's pretty obvious."

"Ana," Josh said. "Be honest with us. Is Catarina like that?"

"No, she's a good woman. I know her well. She's my closest friend. We talk about everything."

"Maybe not *everything*," Andy suggested.

"Has she taken advantage of anyone else?" Josh asked. "Like any previous boyfriends?"

"I don't think so. I never saw that."

"So what did she say to you?" Andy asked. "About what happened today."

"She was upset. Very upset. She said you told her she was a thief, but she didn't take your money. She said you shouted at her and…"

"I didn't shout at any time," Andy interjected. "I was completely calm."

"She said you spoke to her like she was a piece of shit."

"I just asked if she'd taken my money and I explained I was missing some."

"This is what she tell me."

"I'm sorry, Ana, but she was lying to you. I could see in her face that she knew I had found out the truth. She was nervous when she saw the money on the table."

Ana looked at Josh, hoping that he would support her friend. He was pretty sure that Andy wasn't aggressive. He knew a little about how Catarina was and he could imagine that she was blowing things out of proportion.

"I think I believe Andy more than Catarina," he said. "I understand that she's your best friend and that you want to support her, but with Andy paying for meals and everything, then having the exact money in her purse that he was missing, the morning after a night out, makes me think that she is the guilty one here."

Ana could see his point, but she didn't want to imagine her friend was like this. "We don't know exactly what is true, Josh. We weren't there."

"Look," said Andy. "I'm not lying at all here. I have no reason to lie. Things were going well between us and I was happy, but then all this happened and I know she was leading me on."

"Okay," said Josh. "Well, there's nothing else we can say about it. All I know is that she has a different version of events, but my gut feeling is that she took your money. Sorry, Ana."

Ana just shrugged her shoulders and looked disappointed with his verdict.

"Thanks for coming to talk to me about this, though," said Andy. "I did want to ask you, but didn't want to put it on your shoulders."

"That's fine. Obviously we needed to know your side of the story as well."

Ana had nothing else to add to the conversation. She wanted to talk to Catarina again, but would need to give her time to calm down first. They said their farewells and left the café.

Andy spent much of the next few days mulling over things and constantly berating himself for being sucked in. Whereas he didn't want to see Catarina ever again, he thought about going over to her office just to see her from a distance so he could glower at her. He managed to restrain himself, however, but couldn't get her out of his mind.

He went to his self-defence class on Tuesday, which he needed to give himself some focus. He set his mind to his tasks and his partner this time was Julia, a woman in her thirties, who became quite frightened of his manoeuvres as he found it difficult to hold back. Jaime had to tell him not be be so forceful while they were practising and Andy apologised after he realised he was treating her like she was his ex-girlfriend. Jaime switched him to work with Raul again, which took the edge off and Andy returned to a calmer way of proceeding through the exercises. He said sorry again to Julia at the end, which she seemed to accept and everyone left.

That night, Andy was wondering if Ana had spoken to Catarina again yet. He expected that his ex would still lie to her and that Ana would not want to hang around with him any more. How was this going to affect his social life from now on? He didn't imagine that Catarina would be invited out if he was meeting his friends, but he was also worried that he would be the one left out and he would have to start all over again.

With him being left to his own devices, Andy got himself worked up, imagining that Paul and Steve would also not want anything to do with him. Paul was bound to think that the drug dealing was the root of all the problems, considering that he had expressed his dislike of the whole affair before. Should he start making friends with his contacts? He barely knew them and it probably wouldn't be a wise move to become a hanger-on to those that he sold to.

Should he move to Alicante? This seemed like a good idea as he'd thought of that while he was there. He remembered that he liked the place and that he could probably sell the cocaine more quickly there. However, how would he find somewhere to live without a job? He didn't know anyone there at all, although that was the same situation when he came to Spain. He thought about getting a bar job in one of the British pubs, but work would be seasonal and he might not have much work over the winter.

He stood on his balcony, smoking a cigarette on Thursday evening, unaware that he was being watched by the man in the hat who was lurking behind the street corner by the park.

His phone bleeped and he went back inside to find that Josh had texted him, saying that he had an update and could they meet at Sant Jaume tomorrow at seven.

That night and all through Friday, Andy wondered what the update would be about. Josh had not given him any clues as to what it was and he feared that Catarina had been believed by Ana and that Josh now thought that Andy had lost the money while they were out and just wanted to tell him that their friendship was over.

He kept watching the clock in the early evening, just needing to get this meeting over with. He arrived early at the café as he was losing his mind watching each minute drag by.

Josh and Ana came along only a couple of minutes late to find Andy already making progress with his beer. Josh shook his hand

and didn't look too upset with him and Ana gave him a kiss on both cheeks.

"How's it going?" Josh asked. Andy didn't want to bother with any small talk and just get straight to the point.

"I'm okay, thanks. You?"

"Yeah, I'm fine."

"So what's the news?"

Josh turned to Ana as she was the one who had first hand information.

"I have spoken to Catarina. I saw her yesterday." Andy nodded and wanted her to get on with it. "I asked her again if she took your money and she said yes." Andy's eyebrows raised at this. "We had a long talk and in the beginning, she said that she didn't, but we talked in detail about last weekend and about what you told us. In the end, she said that yes, she took your money when you were in the shower." Andy didn't want to interrupt, but see if she had anything else to add. "She knows she was wrong, so she gave me the money." She reached into her purse and took it out. "Here," she said as she passed it to him.

"Wow, I wasn't expecting that," Andy said. "I thought that you would believe her and that you were going to tell me that you didn't want to see me any more."

"No, mate," said Josh. "Ana and I talked about it some more over the week and Ana admitted that it sounded more likely that you were telling the truth, didn't you?" She nodded as she looked at Andy.

"So what does that mean for you and her?" he asked her.

"I don't know yet. I am not happy with her, but she said sorry to me. I am going to wait to see how I feel."

Andy understood that and it sounded fair enough. "Well, what can I say? Thanks so much for doing that. Let me buy you both a drink."

He ordered a couple of beers and looked at them both. He knew that they trusted him from the look on their faces. He demanded that he give them both a big hug.

After it had sunk in, Andy breathed a big sigh of relief. "I feel so much better for hearing that. Honestly, my week has been hell. I've been thinking about it over and over and I even thought about ditching everything and moving to Alicante!" The other two laughed.

"So what are your plans for the weekend?" Josh asked.

"Pfff, no idea. After this, I feel like I need to let go. Shall we party tonight?"

"I don't see why not," Josh said. "We're going to eat first. Do you want to join us?"

"That sounds like a great idea." now that Andy had been brought back to reality, his attention turned back to getting some grams ready for later. He told them he would pop back to his and meet them at nine.

He strode back as though he was a different person. His smile barely left his face all the way back. He looked at the people going about their business, noticing women who he found attractive, but his fixed smile drew some suspicious looks from one or two people. He walked past the Mercat Central and nodded to a man in a hat, who didn't return the gesture, but who looked round as Andy passed him and turned to follow him as far as the top of his street.

35.

As Andy walked down his road, the man waited at the top of the street, but the prostitutes were around, so he needed somewhere else to hide. He knew Andy's route by now, so it wasn't difficult to find a wall to wait next to. He had no idea if Andy would be coming back out, but it was always worth a try.

Andy pulled out the package and got his scales set up. Weighing out ten grams strangely felt a lot more satisfying now. He put it down to knowing that Catarina wouldn't be coming back so he didn't need to worry any more. It was his place and it was about time he started taking things easy.

He left the package in his sideboard, but still hidden to some degree under some spare papers he had. Thinking about the issue of carrying so much money around was still something he wanted to improve, so he made a mental note to buy some cargo trousers in the week, so he could easily stash the cash in the side pockets.

He got his first order of the evening while he was waiting to go back out. It was to deliver four grams to a contact's flat. "A perfect start to the evening," he thought to himself. He got his bike lights and headed off.

The man in the hat wasn't having such a fruitful time, so he thought he'd go and walk down Calle del Bany and see if Andy was at home. He'd just missed him by about two minutes and for all he knew, he wasn't home as the balcony doors were shut. However, having the insights into the world of drug dealing, there was a good chance that he would be back soon, unless he was going out for the night afterwards. He switched his vantage point to the bottom of the street. Andy came back twenty minutes later and went straight past the man without noticing him. There were still plenty of people and cars around, so he didn't stand out. The man hadn't seen Andy on his bike before, so this was a further insight into his activities. He could, of course, have just gone to the shops, but he had no bag on his person or panniers on his bike. He watched Andy go back inside.

When needing to scope out someone who one has a special interest in, one has to learn to be patient. The man had little else to do, but hopefully a lot to gain. So far, he was quite sure that Andy sold cocaine as the coming and going, especially at weekends, was a dead giveaway. He knew that Andy must have a reasonable amount as the clues he'd picked up were that Andy dealt quite frequently. However, Andy flitted about quickly and of course, the man never knew exactly when he would be operating, so it was hard to find a good time to approach him again.

Andy just had half an hour or so to wait before meeting Josh and Ana for their meal. The man stood his ground and saw him come back out and go up the road. With Andy being in a good mood, it affected the speed that he walked. This meant the man had to up his tempo to see where he was going, which, in his physical state was not an easy feat, nor did it look natural to observers. He didn't give a shit about anyone else, though, and due to his appearance, it was unlikely that a stranger would accost him and instruct him to slow down.

The man struggled to keep up with Andy, but managed it, only to find that he went to a restaurant. It was unlikely that he would be there to sell drugs, of course, so he gave up his pursuit and went to sit down on a concrete platform on Caballeros to recover for a while.

There was a good chance that Andy and co. would be in there for a couple of hours, so this wasn't worth hanging around for. The man would just trawl the streets again looking for anything that could be of use to him that someone had dropped on the floor.

Blissfully unaware that he was being tracked once again, Andy had a pleasant time with his friends. They didn't talk about Catarina at all and life was back to normal. When discussing where to go later, Josh gave Andy free reign to choose their venue and he went for Radio City. Another order came in while they were in the restaurant and Andy nipped off once they had finished everything to sell another two grams, while Josh and Ana went to Negrito to wait for him. He felt good about getting back into his routine. Despite knowing a lot more about how he could effectively defend himself now, he didn't really think about needing to as he didn't spot anyone that indicated any danger to him. The thoughts of Catarina didn't enter his mind, either and he was soon back with his friends.

They went over to Radio City and Andy handed Josh and Ana a gram each as thanks for helping him out with resolving the situation with Catarina. They went inside, took a couple of lines each and got into the music. They stood out as the most lively customers and a guy in his thirties approached Josh to ask if he had anything. He passed him onto Andy and they stepped outside to do the deal. Andy took his phone number and all this was observed by the man in the hat, who had been loitering around there, knowing that Andy had been there not too long ago. This was more evidence that he had a constant supply of the goods and he watched them go back inside. They stayed there until three, having had a great night and subsequently moved onto MX. The man in the hat had been walking up and down the street, just to keep himself vaguely occupied and kept a watch on the door. He was relieved to see the three leave and followed them to MX. Knowing that this club stayed open till very late, he decided to stay around for a while to watch what else went on. He saw Andy come out a couple of times and do some more transactions, which led to him exhausting his current supply and when he no longer saw him come out other than to have a cigarette, the man headed off and thought about what he was going to do now that he had enough information.

THE EMPTY FLAT

They stayed out till half past six and Andy, still buzzing but physically tired got back home in peace, the man in the hat having retired two hours previously.

When he finally emerged from his sweaty pit, Andy thought back to his night out, which was successful from both a friendship and a business perspective. He thought about how much he'd sold yesterday, which was eleven grams, plus the three that he, Josh and Ana had used. After downing a cup of coffee, he turned on his computer to update his spreadsheet. He was thrilled to see that he had finally sold over one hundred grams. From a mixture of regular prices, discounts and mates' rates, he'd made just over €7,400. He looked through the figures over and over, feeling very satisfied which how far he'd got. It was somehow worth going through the hardship that he'd experienced and put it down to being a learning curve.

"I think I'm over that hurdle now," he thought. With him making far more than enough to live on comfortably, he didn't mind if it took a few more months to sell the rest.

On Monday, he went to the shops to buy a couple of pairs of cargo trousers. He smiled as he thought of them being his work clothes and now he wouldn't have to worry so much about carrying lots of cash.

Tuesday was his fifth class of self-defence and he made sure he would apologise again to Julia, explaining that he hadn't been in a great place the last time. The session went well and there were no issues, only satisfaction at being even readier to handle himself if anything arose.

The rest of the week, Andy felt good about himself, going out to eat lunch a number of times and look around the shops to see what else he would like to buy. He bought a couple of things for the kitchen: a food blender and large wok to try to broaden his recipe knowledge to encompass paella and some Chinese dishes.

The man in the hat hadn't been around for a few days and was just biding his time for now, waiting for the right moment to take action.

Andy wanted to catch up with Paul as their meet-ups were less frequent these days. They went out for a drink on Friday night and Andy told him about what had happened with Catarina. He could talk about it quite openly now and it didn't make him upset to discuss her actions.

"So you're back on the market?" Paul asked.

"I haven't really been thinking about it, to be honest. It just feels good to be free at the moment."

"Fair enough. Although, I'm getting the idea that Jess kind of likes you."

"Oh, really?" Andy hadn't thought of her in that way before, but he thought she was a nice person. "What has she said?"

"Well, nothing direct, but every now and then she mentions you and her eyes lighten up."

"That is interesting. Hmm, she is quite attractive, very, in fact. That might be worth pursuing. Maybe we should go out for a drink and see what happens."

"I reckon she'd like that."

"What about you? Any romance in the air?"

"No, nothing. I haven't had any connections with anyone since I've been back."

"I've never seen you talking to anyone outside our group when we've been out, to be fair."

"Yeah, once or twice, but nothing more than small talk."

"How do you feel about that?"

"I don't know. On the one hand, it's frustrating, but I'm also getting used to it. I don't go out expecting that I'm going to meet anyone, so going home alone is not really a big deal."

"Hmm, okay."

That seemed to be the end of that particular topic and they sat quietly for a few moments, looking around at the other people.

"Can I tell you something?" Paul asked.

"Of course," Andy replied.

"I'm not sure how I should say this, but it's been eating me up for a few weeks."

"Go on," Andy was very curious to find out where this was leading.

"I think I might be interested in guys." Andy raised his eyebrows involuntarily, which Paul expected. He was interested to see what Andy's first reaction would be, but he didn't appear to be disgusted by the idea.

"Guys? Okay, there's nothing wrong with that."

"You don't think that's weird?" Paul asked, clearly at odds with what he was experiencing.

"Of course it isn't! Plenty of people are gay or bi or whatever. Some people don't find out for ages. I've heard of people being married then realising they're gay in their fifties or something."

"I don't know if I'm gay. I've been with women before and I've enjoyed that, but these days, I'm not really paying attention to them. Does that make me bi?"

"I don't know. It's not for me to say. It's for you to work out."

"Yeah, I know, but I'm really confused."

"Is there anyone, any guy, that you've got your eye on?" Andy realised as soon as he said this that Paul might say he fancied him.

"Not especially. I mean, it's that I've seen a few guys when I've been out and they've caught my eye, but I've never spoken to any of them. I suppose it's like I'm trying to work out how I feel."

"Of course. I guess it's pretty difficult when you've only just noticed that you're interested in men."

"Exactly. I just need to go through it and maybe I'll know what I want soon enough."

"Yeah. Don't pressure yourself. Just go with the flow."

"Thanks for listening to me. You're the only person I've told about this."

"Mate, no worries at all. I won't tell anyone else. I promise."

"Thanks, man."

"What about the gay club?" Andy wondered.

"Yeah, I've been a few times before, but now I feel a bit nervous, you know."

"At least you'll know that the men there are definitely gay."

"Not necessarily. I mean, you've been there, plenty of straight people go there, too."

"True, but gay guys make it obvious if they're interested in you, don't they?"

"I suppose so, but that kind of scares me a bit. It'd be a bit overwhelming."

"Right. How else would you go about it, though? It's a bit risky trying to chat up some guy when you don't know if he's gay or not."

"Yeah, I don't want to do that, but because I haven't done it before, I just wouldn't know how to go about it."

"I'm sure they would take the lead. They're the experienced ones."

"Of course, but I'm still trying to work out if I am, you know, like that."

"Well, listen. If you want me to go with you one time, I'm happy to do that."

"Okay, thanks. I'll have a think about it."

"So what else are you up to this weekend?"

"Nothing really, just the usual stuff. You?"

"Not sure yet. I'm happy to have a quiet night tonight. I might get in touch with Josh about tomorrow."

"We could get a few people together again, including Jess."

"Oh, yeah, I forgot you told me about her!" Andy had a quick think about it. "Yeah, alright, let's see if we can do that."

They hung out for another hour or so. Paul felt he'd bonded again with Andy after opening up to him. They didn't discuss what the latest was with the drug dealing, which, to Andy, made him respect Paul more again. Andy did get a text asking for a drop-off, but Andy quietly replied to it, saying he could get it to the guy at midnight. After he and Paul had called it a night, Andy went over. The meeting point was not far from Fox Congo and it went ahead as normally as it could have, without anyone lurking in the vicinity. Andy went for a stroll down to television square and made a roundabout circuit to his place, unaware that he was doing himself a favour.

He wasn't bothered that he didn't sell much that night. His time with Paul was more than worth going out for and he had plenty to think about back at his.

36.

On Saturday, he felt quite amused about one thing Paul had told him. He really hadn't expected that Jess liked him more than as a friend. He tried to picture himself with her. She was fun and she had a lovely smile. He supposed that, because he was with Catarina for a while, he didn't really look at other women in that way. Apart from that night with Emily, of course. He kind of felt glad that he had cheated then. Catarina deserved it in the long run. But did he feel like jumping into another relationship so soon? He had no longing for Catarina, that was certain, but should he just have some time to himself for a while? He couldn't decide. It would be nice to see her this evening, though, just to see if he could pick up any signs from her.

As he went about his day, the thought of someone having an interest in him put a spring in his step. He tidied his flat diligently, even though it wasn't particularly dirty. He got rid of receipts that he didn't need off his big table and sorted a few things out in the spare room.

As it was now November, it was starting to get noticeably colder. He had no heating in the flat, so should go and get something. A gas bottle heater made the most sense as he was sure Maria wouldn't pay to have anything permanent fitted. This made him think that he hadn't received any energy bills yet. Don't they come every month in Spain? It was nice not having to pay them, but he didn't want to get a huge bill after six months. But then again, money wasn't exactly one of his worries any more.

In the afternoon, Andy got a text from Paul saying that Jess and Steve wanted to come out that evening. He had a cheeky grin at this and they arranged to meet at Negrito at ten, as tradition would have it. Josh and Ana would join them. "I wonder if we should do something different," he thought. "We always go to the same few places. There's got to be something else worth doing. I'll ask the others later."

He got out his scales and prepared twenty gram bags. He wasn't going to take them all out, even though he had his new work clothes, but he just felt like doing something useful.

He went out to see if he could find a heater. The hardware store that he'd been to a few times didn't sell any as they mostly sold tools and wood and so on, but he went to ask them if they knew of anywhere. They pointed him in the direction of a small heating business and he purchased a medium sized gas heater, which they could deliver for him later that afternoon. "Things are falling into place again," he thought. "Why can't life always be like this?"

That night, he met his friends inside the bar for a change. People asked Andy how he was after his break-up and he replied that he actually felt fine, which was true. "It's like just getting rid of an old piece of furniture that you've had enough of," he said. The others laughed, although Ana thought that was a strange thing to say, judging by her expression.

Andy didn't know if Jess knew that Paul had said anything and she wasn't really giving anything away. Andy glanced at her every now and then to see if she was looking at him, but if she did, he kept missing it. He paid more attention to how she looked and acted while they were at Negrito.

Andy brought up the subject of going somewhere different. They came up with a few suggestions, but nothing in particular was finding a consensus.

"We could go to the gay club," said Josh. Andy looked at Paul to see what his reaction was. He looked a bit apprehensive at his.

"No, I don't really fancy that," he said.

"Why not?" Jess said. "It's a bit of fun."

"I'm just not in the mood for it."

"You're not really into the gay scene, are you?" Josh said.

Paul was noticeably uneasy at this question, at least to Andy's eyes.

"No, I'm fine with that. Just not tonight."

Andy didn't say anything about this as he wanted the conversation to quickly move on. "Is there somewhere further out of the centre that's any good?"

"There's La Tortuga," Steve offered.

"What's that?"

"It's a place past Plaza de la Reina. It can be a bit cheesy, but they also have some decent music on."

They discussed it and agreed that they would try it out. Just then, Andy got a text asking for three grams and he quickly made his excuses to nip off and settle that. He was back before too long, having actually sold four and they headed off to check out La Tortuga. It cost five Euros to get in and Andy said he would pay for everyone as he was in the money again. Everyone knew what that meant and Paul didn't put up any objection as he was feeling closer to Andy now.

They went in and it was a bigger place compared to the venues they usually went to. It was well done out and looked quite polished. It didn't really look like Andy's kind of place, but he called everyone over to the bar and got a round in.

They found a table and sat down for a while as it wasn't very busy yet. The music was typical Latino stuff and only Ana and Jess were looking enthusiastic about it, but after another drink, people's inhibitions were starting to fade and they got up to dance. Josh, Ana and Steve went off to do some coke, but Andy wanted to keep his wits about him. They all danced together and he was paying attention to Jess again. She was having a great time, but not showing that she was singling Andy out for any special attention.

By one o'clock, the place was quite busy. The group were still dancing when Josh tapped Andy on the shoulder and leant in to tell him something.

"Bad news, mate. Catarina is here."

"Fuck off, really?"

He signalled with his eyes as to where she was and he looked over and spotted her. She was with another couple of women, who he hadn't seen before.

"Oh, Christ. That is not what I wanted to see."

Ana was aware that she was there, too, but didn't go over to say hello. Catarina hadn't spotted them yet and Andy turned away so she wouldn't see him.

Jess noticed that something was wrong and came over to ask. Andy told her who had turned up and she just said "Oh, forget about it. Ignore her and let's just have a good night." Andy's mood had dropped considerably and he wasn't in the mood to dance right now. Josh and Ana took him off the dance floor to have a word.

"Look, mate," Josh said. "Okay, she's here, but try not to let it bother you. If she sees you and the rest of us, she'll probably leave anyway. She knows she's not welcome, so come on. Let's dance."

They rejoined their group and Andy tried to forget about her. It wasn't easy, but as far as he knew, Catarina still hadn't clocked them.

"I'm going to do a couple of lines," Andy told Josh, who patted him on the back to confirm he thought it was a good idea. In the toilets, there were three youngish guys talking to each other and Andy noticed the topic was drugs. As he was new to this venue, he wanted to tread carefully, so just splashed some water on his face while he thought about it. The guys seemed like they were no trouble, so he asked if they needed cocaine. Their ears pricked up and said yes. How much? They had twenty Euros each. Andy told them to wait there and he went into a cubicle and did two lines.

He came back out and gave them the rest of the bag for sixty and they acted like kids who had been given sweets. They all piled into a cubicle, to which Andy shook his head, thinking "Yeah, don't make it obvious, lads."

He came back to the main room and Catarina was walking in his direction. "Oh God," he said to himself. This was the first time she'd seen him and she threw her head back in disgust and turned to go back to her friends. Andy joined his lot, peering through the crowd at Little Miss Manipulative, who was waving her arms around and appeared to be angry. Her friends looked over and tried to calm her down, but she was having none of it. Andy shook his head and looked away. A few seconds later, Catarina suddenly appeared in front of him and slapped him across the face, shouting obscenities at him. Andy just stood there in shock. His self-defence tactics hadn't kicked in like they should have done, but seconds later, she was grabbed by a security guard and dragged away. They all watched as she was shouting, doing herself no favours and was swiftly ejected from the premises.

Andy turned around and the rest of his friends were looking at him. Jess asked if he was okay and put her hand up to his reddened cheek to softly stroke it. He came out of his shock and went to get a beer.

Jess followed him and was clearly concerned. He told her he was okay now, but his face was stinging. She gave him a big hug and looked him in the eyes lovingly. As he was still not feeling very settled, he wasn't in the mood to make any move, so he got his beer and they went back.

Gradually, things returned to normal and his cocaine kicked in. He wanted it to take him to a happier place, so let it flow into his system and his smile returned.

THE EMPTY FLAT

Jess did her best to help things and took his hand to dance, while Paul watched with a sneaky grin. They were getting on just fine and he waited for the inevitable to happen.

As Andy had just been through that ordeal with Catarina, all his friends wanted to do their bit with helping him to enjoy the night, so they were making sure that he wouldn't be going into his own world and thinking about her. This took his attention away from Jess somewhat and she also didn't want to steal the show, either. The club was open till four and all but Paul stayed there until the end. They headed back toward the centre and talked about whether people wanted to hang out some more at one of their flats, but Steve wanted to go home and Ana didn't fancy it, so people went their separate ways. Andy thought of inviting Jess to his, but something was holding him back. It still affected him that Catarina had shown up and he realised he still needed more downtime. Jess wasn't made aware of this reason, but accepted that Andy was tired, as was she.

Sunday was the usual recovery day for all concerned and Andy was still ruminating over what had gone on last night and trying to work out his feelings. He guessed that even though she was wrong to do so, Catarina needed to get it out of her system by giving him a slap. He was bound to come across her again in the future, but hopefully they would just ignore each other and it would get easier with time.

Over the next few days, he thought about Jess some more and couldn't work out how he felt about her. Maybe it would be good to go for a coffee with her, but then again, would that be giving her the sign that he was trying to get them together? He didn't want to lead her on and thought that talking to Paul again might be good. He might have some news for Andy if Jess had said anything at home.

Paul and Andy met up on Wednesday. Andy told him that the incident didn't really bother him as it didn't affect his emotions.

"So, nothing happened between me and Jess, but I was just wondering if she'd anything to you."

"Well, obviously we talked about what went on that night, but she didn't say anything about her feelings for you, to be honest. Do you want to go out with her?"

"I've been weighing things up and I don't think this is the right time. I could just do with having a break, like I said before, so I might leave it for a while."

"I understand," said Paul.

"The only thing is that if I leave it too long, then feel that I do want to be with her, she might have got together with someone else."

"Do you want me to say anything to her?"

"What do you mean?"

"As in just telling her that you told me that you want to be single for a bit, but not making it obvious that it's relevant to her."

"I guess that could be good. Sure, thanks. So what about you, then? How have you been since what you told me last week?"

"It's basically the same, really. I'm still curious, but don't know what to do."

"Alright, well, let's make a plan. Let's go to the gay club this weekend and just see what happens. I'm sure that you'll get talking to someone, but if it seems too much for you, then you can just come back over to me."

"Hmm, yeah, I guess. I know I've got to start somewhere."

"I bet it won't be as difficult as you think. When do you want to go?"

"It can be either night."

"Okay, let's go on Friday so you're not putting it off too long. You've just got to jump in and see where it takes you."

Paul smiled, knowing that Andy was giving him the kick up the backside that he needed. "Okay, Friday it is. God, we'll have to go somewhere first so I can get some Dutch courage down me."

When he got back home, Paul was feeling both nervous and glad that Andy was being so supportive. It would make things a lot easier to have a friend there as back up, but he couldn't believe that he was going to take his first steps.

37.

They met up at Radio City on Friday, away from the crowds that still flocked to Plaza del Negrito. Paul needed to be able to get his head in gear and fortunately it was quiet at this bar. They got their first beer in.

"So, do you feel ready?" Andy asked.

"I want to, but it's daunting at the same time."

"I know what you mean, but essentially, it's just the case of talking to people. Gay or not, they're still just people."

"I know that, but it doesn't make it any easier. I'm crossing into unchartered territory here."

"Yeah, but it doesn't mean you're going to meet someone then automatically be in a relationship with him. Like I said before, if you're not getting a good vibe, just walk away and come back to me."

"Thanks, Andy. If I was trying to do this by myself, I'd probably never have the balls to get round to it."

"You don't know what's going to happen, who you're going to meet, or what you'll be talking about, so there's no point in worrying, right?"

"Yeah, sure."

"So, let's change the subject. Any update about Jess?"

"Not much, really. I told her I'd been out with you and I said that the thing with Catarina just made you want to have a bit of time to yourself. She didn't say anything about her feelings, but it looked like she understood. I'm sure she did, she's a good woman."

"Yeah, she is. Obviously, she has been on my mind a bit over the week, but I'll see how I feel over the next couple of weeks or so."

"Do you think you're growing to like her as more than a friend?"

"Possibly. I suppose if I'm thinking about her, then it means I do like her."

They guys stayed for another two beers before deciding it was time to take the plunge. They headed up the road towards Plaza del Tossal, with a couple of beady eyes fixed on Andy from behind.

Andy chose to have a night off dealing as he didn't want to have to leave Paul on his own. He replied to a couple of customers to say he was out of town. They arrived at the club around midnight and there were plenty of people in there. Their plan was to get a beer, hang around to see what was going on and maybe have a dance. Even though it was exactly the same as anyone would normally do, Paul needed to know what he was going to do to keep himself grounded. After a while they had a dance. Paul was fairly reluctant to make eye contact with anyone as the people who he noticed to be obviously gay from the way they dressed and their camp dance moves were too overwhelming for him. This was not the kind of person he would be looking to talk to, so he and Andy tried to act casually, as well as not look like they were partners.

One guy was giving Paul the eye. He looked like he was in his forties and had a goatee beard and short, bleached hair. Wearing a leather waistcoat, Paul wasn't taken by him and tried to ignore him. They carried on dancing and the man came over to Paul. He was dancing very close, which Paul didn't like. The man kept smiling at him and asking him how he was. Paul tried to be polite, but not engage in conversation. The man wasn't giving up and came even closer so that they were almost in contact. This annoyed Paul and he shook his head at the man, giving him a disapproving look and the man moved away.

"God, they can be so full on sometimes," he told Andy.

"Yeah, it's a bit weird, isn't it? I mean it's good that they can be open about being gay, but it's a bit much, isn't it?"

They alternated between dancing and standing at the side, Paul seeing a couple of other men looking at him. Andy had some as well, but as the pressure wasn't on him, he found it easy to show he wasn't interested. After about an hour of being there, Paul caught the attention of someone else. This man was dressed in a similar way to him, just casual clothes, and Paul found him quite attractive. The man smiled at him. He was with his friends, maybe a boyfriend, so Paul waited to see what he could figure out. "God, this is hard work," he said to Andy. "Why does it feel so difficult?"

"Because it's new to you. You've never been with a guy, so of course it's difficult."

"I don't know if I should talk to him or wait for him to come over."

"He might think that we're together, so I'm going to give you some space and maybe he'll come over then."

Paul agreed to this with some hesitation and Andy went over to another part of the club. Paul tried his best to act naturally, but his heart was beating more forcefully. He didn't know what to do with himself, so had to go and dance, just to try to relieve some of the tension. The guy he'd been watching also started dancing and made sure he could see Paul. It looked like he was doing the same, seeing what the score was from how Paul came across to him. The smiles went back and forth between them and the guy came over after what seemed like hours, but was only about two minutes.

Andy noticed this from where he was positioned. He could see that Paul was looking more relaxed and the two of them were chatting a bit. It all seemed very pleasant and they appeared to be getting on well. They left the dance floor and carried on talking at the side. Paul seemed comfortable so Andy went to get another beer.

When he went back to his spot, he saw the guys still talking and soon after, they went to dance together. Andy smiled. This was a good sign. He didn't feel like he needed to chaperone him any more, so stopped watching them. He wasn't really getting into the music himself, so decided to step outside for a while to have a smoke and see what was going on in the street. There were people milling about outside the club. There was no-one he knew, so he just smoked by himself. From a distance, the eyes were still fixated on Andy, wondering if he'd been called out to make a delivery, but after five minutes, Andy went back in.

He was surprised yet pleased to see that Paul was still in the man's company. From what he could tell, the guy seemed more easy-going than the butch guys there. He thought he should be able to leave them alone by now, but wanted to get a chance to tell Paul first. The others were still dancing, but after a couple more songs, they left the dance floor. Andy thought he'd just go over and say a quick goodbye as he was getting bored of being there. He walked over and Paul saw him coming.

"Hi, everything okay?" Andy asked.

"Yes, this is Damian." He introduced them both.

Damian had a friendly face, but Andy didn't want to interrupt them too much. "I'm going home if you're alright. Is that okay?"

"Yeah, it's fine. He's a nice guy."

"Good stuff. I'll leave you to it, then. Have a good night."

Andy walked off and thought he'd just have a look in Radio City again. He was glad that Paul had met someone already. They looked like they could be a good match and hopefully he'd hear some news tomorrow.

In Radio City, they were playing rock music. There was a decent sized crowd, nothing special, but Andy wasn't really enjoying this, either. He had one beer and hung around for about half an hour before getting bored of that.

At least it was a shorter walk for him to get home. There were just a couple of streets that led him to his, so he walked down Calle de Santa Teresa, past the Plaça de Joan de Vila·Rasa and onto Calle de Viana, a shortcut that led to the park on his street.

It was very quiet round here. The area was almost entirely residential. He crossed the junction with Calle de Balmes. Just at that point, he received a blow to the back of his head. It knocked him straight to the ground. A kick to his face came swiftly after that. Andy was knocked out. The assailant could see he was unconscious, but gave him a kick to his stomach anyway, before searching through Andy's pockets, taking his wallet and his keys, then leaving the scene.

Andy lay there for several minutes, breathing, but not coming back to consciousness. Some other people were coming back from their night out and went along the same route. It was a man and a woman, who were quite drunk and giggling between themselves. Then they noticed what they thought was dead body. The woman screamed at this sight and the man looked at it in shock. His adrenalin kicked in and brought him back to his senses. He had to check if the guy on the floor was alive. He could tell he was breathing, but there was blood on his face and on the ground. The woman watched from a few steps back and her partner told her to call an ambulance. She did so and they were told to wait with the man until they arrived. The ambulance came in less than ten minutes, along with a police car. They questioned the couple, who said they'd just seen him on their way back and hadn't seen anything occur. The police took their names down and the paramedics carefully got Andy onto a stretcher and into the ambulance. At this point, Andy regained consciousness. He could barely speak and was told to stay quiet while they drove him to hospital.

Meanwhile, Luis González had entered Andy's flat without needing to disturb anyone. He didn't need his hat to disguise himself right now, so put it on the table, revealing his closely cropped hair to nobody. His eyes scanned the front room. He only had one objective. He looked in the sideboard cupboards and threw out the few bits that were in there. Nothing of interest. He opened the drawers and did likewise. As the papers flew through the air, they revealed a package. Luis picked it up and it didn't take long for him to know that this what was he wanted. His work was already done, but drug dealers would have cash stored as well. He tore his way through everything in the front room, throwing everything onto the floor. No money. He went into the spare room and made carnage of that, cutting open the mattress, but not finding any sign that money had been stored in that. The kitchen was next. Everything came out of the cupboards and boxes were ripped apart. Nothing. Into the bedroom. He lifted the mattress and inspected it to see if there was a slit in it. He felt for any money, looked in the bedside table and went to the wardrobe. The clothes were pulled out and frisked. He went to the t-shirts at the bottom and found the cash. There was only €75 there. Luis looked angrily at this, but pocketed it anyway. He looked down at the floorboards as that was where he'd hidden his cocaine over three years ago. He couldn't see that any of them had been tampered with. He went back to the other rooms and it didn't take him long to uncover the one that Andy had been using. He used his knife to prise it up, but saw that it was also empty. The bathroom also produced no results, so he went back into the front room. The only other things of any value were the TV and computer. They were too big and cumbersome to bother trying to steal, so he went to the spare room and took Andy's hammer. He cracked the screens of the TV and the monitor, as well as smashing the keyboard. Luis knew very well that the only other person in the building was the old man upstairs and he was virtually deaf. He had another look through the flat in case he'd missed anything. Standing in the bedroom, it didn't occur to him that he was so close to Andy's secret stash. There was little else in there, so with the cocaine and the small amount of cash, he quietly left the building.

In the hospital, Andy need to have x-rays. He was starting to be able to speak and could tell them his name. He lay still as they x-rayed his skull. There was no break, but his head hurt severely. They asked him if he was in pain anywhere else, but it was only his stomach. His arms and legs were fine except for where his knees had hit the ground. They explained that they were going to keep him in overnight to check his stability.

Andy lay in the hospital bed, not knowing what had happened to him. He couldn't think clearly and his head was throbbing. He was given a sedative and fell asleep within minutes.

The next morning, he was seen by a doctor. Andy was not in a state to speak Spanish, but the doctor was almost fluent in English.

"How is your head?"

"It still hurts. The back of my head." Andy found it hard to talk as his lips were swollen from where he'd been kicked.

"Do you remember what happened?"

"No. I was walking home and that's the last I remember."

"Did you see anyone?"

"No. There was no-one there."

"We have taken x-rays and nothing is broken. It looks like you were hit on the back of the head, then in your face. Probably kicked in the stomach when you were on the ground. Some people found you unconscious."

"How long will I stay in hospital?"

"You can leave today if your head feels well enough. The bad news is that we couldn't find any keys or anything else in your clothes."

"Oh, fuck..." Andy closed his eyes in despair. "My phone. Do I have my phone?"

"No, you had no phone with you."

"Shit. Oh, my god. My friend has my spare key."

"Okay. Do you know his phone number?"

"No, I just have it in my phone."

"Do you have his address?"

"Yes."

"We will take you there later. Don't worry. You will stay here for some more time, just to recover, then we will take you to your friend's home."

"Okay, thanks."

Andy lay back and rued his situation. He'd been mugged, from behind as well. He'd learned all that self-defence for nothing. Why did the mugger have to take his keys and his phone? Fucking bastard. At least he'd be able to get back in. He wanted to leave hospital as soon as he could, but would wait and see what the doctor said.

By lunchtime, Andy felt reasonably okay and said he wanted to go. He could stand up and walk, although doing so made his head hurt. It settled somewhat once he was up and he was discharged. The receptionist called him a taxi and he went over to Josh's flat. He just hoped that he hadn't stayed at Ana's. He rang the bell and Josh answered.

"It's Andy. Please let me in."

"Of course," said Josh through the intercom.

Andy went upstairs and Josh was waiting at his door. His eyes widened as he saw Andy's face. "What the fuck?"

"I got mugged last night."

"Holy shit. Come in, man." They went in and sat down. Andy told him what he could, which was very little.

"So that's why I'm here. Have you still got my spare key?"

"Of course." He went to get it. "I'll call a taxi and come with you."

Josh did so straight away and they got back to Andy's. There was no sign of forced entry, which was a big relief and they went up and opened his door. As he opened it, Andy saw that everything was not alright at all. He saw the mess all over the floor and his broken monitor and keyboard. "Holy shit!" he said. Josh came in and stood aghast at the sight. Once Andy had realised what had happened, he went to the drawer where the cocaine was. "It's fucking gone. They taken the cocaine."

He went to his bedroom and saw the mess in there. The bed board was still in place, but he looked in the wardrobe to find his money was gone from there. "They've taken some of my money." He thought about whether he should ask Josh to wait outside while he checked behind the board, but it didn't really matter now. He told him his secret and unscrewed it. He still had his €300 in there.

"Well at least they haven't got everything," Josh said. "Have you got any idea who it was?"

"The only person I can think of was that guy who we both confronted. How would he know where I lived?"

"He must have seen you dealing and has been following you."

"Fuck." Andy tried to think if he had seen anyone else looking suspicious, but no-one came to mind.

"You'll have to report it to the police," Josh said.

"Report that my stash of cocaine has been stolen? I don't think so."

Josh realised that it probably wasn't a good idea after all. They went into the front room to try to get their heads around things.

"So someone has got my keys. They could come back at any time."

"You'll have to get the locks changed."

"Yeah. How am I going to do that, though? Should I tell my landlady? She might ask me to leave if she knows I've been broken into."

"I don't see why she'd say that. You wouldn't be able to change them without asking her first."

"I wonder if the man upstairs heard anything," Andy said. "You stay here and I'll and ask him."

He went upstairs and knocked on the door. There was no answer. He knocked more loudly. The door opened and the man looked at him. Andy told him that someone had broken in and asked if he heard anything. The man said no. Andy sighed and went back downstairs. "Nothing. I don't think he can hear very well."

"You'll have to phone your landlady. Have you got her number?"

"It's in my phone, which I haven't got. Hang on, I think she wrote it on the contract." He looked through the papers on his floor and found it. "Here it is." Josh lent Andy his phone and he called her. He explained what happened and she wanted to know if any damage had been done to her property. Andy said that it was only his stuff. Maria said that she would let him change the locks and pay for it once he had it done.

"Do you know of any locksmith?" Andy asked.

"There's one on Calle de Quart."

"Oh, yeah. I think I know it. I'm going to have to go now. Can you stay here?"

"Sure."

Andy headed over there, looking around him as he went in case he saw the man from before or anyone who looked dodgy. It seemed clear and he made his way to the locksmith. They arranged that it would get done that afternoon and would give a key to the old man upstairs for the outside door. Andy went back and he and Josh tidied up the flat while they waited.

"What if the mugger comes back, though? Even if the locks are changed, he might still be after me."

"Well, considering that he's taken your drugs, he must have known you were dealing. I'm sure he's happy with how much he got away with. How much did you have left?"

"Fucking most of it. I'd sold just over a hundred, maybe one twenty in total."

"That's shit, but you've still got your money, at least."

"Yeah, I know, but I'm going to be paranoid about this now. I can't stay here. What if he comes back?"

"You can come and stay at mine for a while. Don't worry about that. You can sleep on the sofa."

"Thanks. I'll do that. Fuck. I mean, yeah, I've got a few grand in the bank, but what am I going to do now?"

"Look for a job."

"Yeah, but he's bound to be around. I saw him that one other time."

"I don't think he's not going to follow you now that he's got the drugs."

Everything was a whirlwind and Andy had no idea what he was going to do. The locksmith came over and changed the locks and Andy was able to pay in cash. He took the new key up to the old man, then packed a bag to go over to Josh's place. Now that they were out of the crime scene, Andy could relax a bit. Josh told him not to think too much about what he was going to do yet and just give it a few days.

Andy could hardly sleep that night. He kept waking up thinking that the dangerous man was in front of him. On Sunday, Ana came over to see how Andy was. She was distraught at the news and at seeing how bruised and swollen Andy's face was. Josh lent Andy his phone and he called Paul. He, Steve and Jess came over to Josh's and he went through the story with them.

"The one thing I hadn't told you was that I found half a kilo in the empty flat next to me."

"Half a kilo?" said Paul and Jess simultaneously.

"Yeah, I went across and had a look around in there and found it under one of the floorboards."

"Holy shit," said Paul.

"That must mean that whoever had put it there knew you had found it," Jess offered.

"How would they know that? No-one ever saw me go in there."

"You didn't know that someone has been following you, either," Steve said.

"So you think that maybe someone saw me go over and then knew that I'd taken it?"

"They must have done."

As they thought about it, that sounded plausible.

"But how would they have known it was in that flat to begin with?" Andy asked.

"It must have been a drug dealer who'd lived there," said Josh. "He got caught, sent to prison, now he's got out and tried to get his drugs back."

"But how...?" Andy remembered that one time when he saw the balcony doors were open again. "Shit."

"What is it?"

"A few weeks ago, I noticed the balcony doors were open. I thought the wind might have done it, but maybe he climbed up and got in, looked for the drugs and saw they were gone, had been watching me selling drugs and put two and two together."

This conclusion made sense to the others. It all added up. Josh repeated that this meant that the man should now leave Andy alone.

"I can't expect it's going to be that easy. I'm going to be looking over my shoulder all the time from now on."

"Why don't you move somewhere else then?" asked Steve.

"I haven't got a job, have I? I'm going to have to do that first before I can get a tenancy agreement."

"Look. You're going to stay with me," said Josh, "Until you have decided what to do next. We'll all keep an eye out to see if there are any jobs, won't we, guys?"

They all decisively agreed that they would. Andy didn't go to his self-defence class that week as he didn't want to show them that he'd failed at the first attack and also he thought it might unnerve the others and affect their confidence.

After spending two more nights at Josh's, Andy felt that he needed to face it and go and stay at his. Josh offered to stay with him for the first night.

"No, I've got to do this on my own."

"Just one night. I'll be worried about you, otherwise."

"Okay," Andy sighed. "Actually, that probably would be better. Ease myself in."

They went back to Andy's by taxi and found that everything was as it should be. However, the flat just didn't quite feel like it was his any more. With the computer and TV damaged, it looked different, but just knowing that someone had been in there and that Andy couldn't report it to the police made him feel uneasy. They put some music on as the stereo had, for some reason, not been touched, and drank a beer.

Josh slept in the spare room. The mattress was usable once they put a sheet over it. Andy lay in his bed for over an hour, thinking about everything again and again. How long would it be before he felt that nothing else would happen?

Josh had to leave early to go to work. This was the first time Andy was back in his flat by himself. He went from room to room, knowing that some dangerous man, who he was sure he knew, had touched everything in there. He got his detergent out and scrubbed every surface and door he could find. He wiped the door handles, even the bath and toilet seat, just in case he'd made any contact with that. Once he'd cleaned everything, he inspected the flat again. It still felt like the man was there.

Not having anyone with him and not having a phone, he felt alone. He didn't want to look out of the window as he expected the man to be standing in the street, laughing at him. Andy didn't want to stay inside, nor did he want to go out. He didn't expect that it would take him over like this. He thought it was going to be easier after a few days away. He had to get a new phone. He found his contract and went to the front door. As he held his hand on the catch, he hesitated. He couldn't turn it and he breathed deeply. He started shaking and had to run for a chair before he collapsed. He rested his arms on the table and listened to his heavy breathing. He could feel his heart almost ripping through his chest. Andy couldn't do anything. He was in complete panic. He needed someone to be with him. He needed to phone someone. He knew he couldn't have either of these. He looked around the room just to look at something. Something that might help him. The stereo. The sofa. The candelabra. It was like they weren't really there and he was just imagining them. He put his hands flat on the table. Was this really here? He tried to force his hands through it. The table was there. He gripped the edges of it. "Table is here," he said to himself. "Table. Here." He held onto it for some minutes until he felt himself calming down again. His breathing relaxed and his heartbeat slowed down. There were tears rolling down his cheeks and he blinked to clear his eyes as he needed to keep hold of the table for a while. Eventually, he was able to loosen his grip and watch his hands as he let go of it. He stared at nothing as he observed his breath. It was almost normal again.

Once he knew where he was again, he couldn't leave the flat. He hadn't eaten today, but hunger was not something that registered in his system. He slowly and carefully got up off the chair. He exhaled and checked to see if he was stable. It seemed okay. He walked over to the sofa as that would be a safety net if he needed it. He could manage that. He sat on the arm and felt its surface. The sofa was really there. The big table was within his reach. "Good. I can feel it."

He looked out across the room. He didn't know if he was ever going to leave the flat again. He looked up at the ceiling and remembered the man upstairs. He never left it, or hardly ever. Was Andy going to be like that now? He looked at the front door. "Do I need to barricade it? How will I eat?" He was losing himself again. Sofa. Touch it. He thought the man was standing behind him in the hallway. He couldn't look around. He kept still, hoping that he wouldn't notice him. His eyes moved to his right, but he couldn't see past the doorway. He very slowly turned his head, but no man appeared. Was he behind him in the front room now? He turned his head back. The room was empty. He was gripping the sofa so tightly now, but didn't even realise. Finally, he said to himself "I'm alone. There's no-one here." He managed to stand up, but didn't know what he was going to do. There was no way he was going to the front door again. Nor the balcony. He chose to go the other way, to his bedroom, cautiously checking the rooms that he went past. He looked at the bed and that was what he needed. It would hold him safely. He carefully got onto it and lay down on his back in the middle. That was better. Not so much to look at. He looked at the textured ceiling and his eyes traced the contours. Andy stayed like this for about half an hour until he finally felt that had returned to normal consciousness. He thought he had woken up from a bad dream. Had it been a dream? He wished it had, but he knew it hadn't.

Eventually, he sat up and looked around the room. It looked normal. He got off the bed and stood up. He touched the wall and ran his hand along it as he walked to the door. Everything okay. He went back to the kitchen and it seemed better. The thought of going to the front room was ominous. Should he risk that yet? No. "Let's try to drink some water. I'm thirsty." He got a glass out of the cupboard and turned the tap. He watched the water flow like it was the first time he'd ever seen it. He put the glass to his lips and drank. It was so refreshing. It was exactly what he needed. He drank the whole glass and the coldness of it helped to ground him. He put the glass down and felt a lot better. He'd gone up another level to normality. This was good. The bathroom would be easier to conquer than the living room. He went through the doorway and looked at the toilet, the sink and the bath. He recognised them and it gave him some more security. He wondered if looking in the mirror would be a good idea. No, not yet. What if he didn't recognise himself? "Okay, stay calm. Back to the kitchen." He saw it was still as it should be. "I've got that down." Recheck the bedroom. "Yes, that's good." He walked around these three rooms a few times until he was certain of them. When he was sure of himself, he was able to go and look at the front room from the doorway. He inspected everything that was in there and took some steps in. He touched almost everything in there and it all felt right again. His panic attack was nearly gone. He sat on the sofa and looked around some more. "Okay, that's over," he thought.

38.

Andy managed to get through the rest of the day without being sucked into another panic attack. However, he had to keep the balcony doors and shutters closed and play music on his stereo constantly. This helped with stabilising his mood and he chose CDs that were more upbeat. He slept better that night and when he woke up, he was feeling more normal again.

"Got to get back into my routine," he thought and made a coffee. He took it into the front room and looked at the shutters. "Should I? It is daytime. Surely that's going to be safe." He put the cup on the small table and looked over again. "Come on, push yourself." He lifted the latch on the right one and forced himself to open it. The daylight came as a relief and he stood there to try and take in the positivity of it. So far, so good. He did the same on the left one and it was like he had achieved a momentous challenge. He stepped back as he didn't want to see what, or who, was outside. He sat at his table and waited until his coffee was cool enough to drink. "I'm doing well," he thought and after ten minutes, finished his cup. He went to the kitchen to wash it and ate two biscuits – his first food since he'd got back. Then, he thought about what he was going to try to do that day. Opening the front door still seemed like it was too much to ask. He went into the front room to look at it from a distance. "I might be able to do it today." He went to get dressed, but opening the wardrobe brought back the horrible feeling that the man had been in here and taken his money. "He only got a bit. He didn't know about the rest." He tried going to the front door and it was as though it was giving off some force field that kept pushing him back. Andy didn't fall back into panic mode, but couldn't quite get there. "I think I need to look out of the window first." He moved over to the doors and inched his way towards them. It was a cloudy day and he couldn't see much of the ground with his privacy shield going around the balcony frame. He didn't feel too bad for this, however, but thought his next step would be to open them and make contact with the fresh air. This was daunting, but he knew if he left it too long, he wouldn't make it, so he opened them and decisively pulled them open. His breathing intensified as he prepared to cross the threshold. He held onto both door edges and took one step over. He kept his head still and moved his eyes around. The street was clear, as far as he could see. He slowly turned his head to the right and looked up the street. There was one person in the distance walking away from him. He was sure it wasn't the man he feared and the person soon disappeared from view. He looked left, realising that he'd left himself exposed on this side. He saw the cars going past on the ring road, but no pedestrians here, either. He checked himself to work out how he was doing and he seemed alright. "Maybe I'll just stand here for a while first," he thought before attempting to open the front door. He wanted a cigarette, but would have to go back in to get one, which he didn't want to risk in case it broke his frame of mind. Andy stood for about five minutes, scanning the street, but seeing hardly anyone and he felt ready to go out. He closed the balcony doors and shutters, picked up his cigarettes, his phone contract and his tenancy agreement and went to the front door. This time he was able to open it without too much trouble and went down the stairs. As he got to the bottom, he was faced with the heavy, black, metal door. From inside it looked like a huge barrier, but he held his nerve and pulled it open. The daylight again was a relief and he stepped outside, checking left and right quickly. No-one there. He closed the door.

    The phone shop was down his road and this was easier to go to than into the centre. He started walking towards it when he saw someone enter the street from the other end. Without even taking in who it was, Andy immediately froze. It was an old woman carrying a shopping bag and she looked suspiciously at him as he stood there. He tried to make himself come to as she might get scared of him. He walked on, not knowing how to handle himself. He got to the phone shop, but instead of going inside, knew what he had to do. Instead, he went the other way quickly, as though he was pulling himself along on a lead.

He went into the bank and told them he'd had his card stolen. Luckily, Jesus was there who knew him and he was able to sort things out. Andy cancelled all of his standing orders. On his way back, he went into an internet café to arrange one last thing. Then, he went home and got some of his clothes and CDs and stuffed them into his suitcase. He put his keys into an envelope and wrote "Maria" on it and put them into his letterbox. Andy then went to the train station and headed to Alicante.

39.

As he slumped onto the chair, Andy gave his eyes a rub and yawned vocally. It was quite a nice day, mostly sunny with a few scattered clouds, but he hardly took any notice of it at this point. It was just after nine thirty in the morning and he waited at his table on the terrace of the first café he came across. He put his backpack on the chair next to him, eventually got his brain into first gear and began to notice that the world around him was still in operation.

After a couple of minutes, the waiter brought out his black coffee, to which Andy said "Gracias," forgetting that he should have said "Thanks."

"Andy?" replied the waiter. "It's me, George." George was an old schoolfriend, whom he'd barely seen since they were sixteen. "It's good to see you back here. What have you been up to?"

Andy stared pensively at his coffee. "Not much, just trying to stay out of trouble."

Notes

This story was inspired the very flat that I lived in when I was in Valencia from 2001 to 2002. As it is described in the story, the features are exactly those of where I lived, including the address. The surrounding area is also what was there at the time, although the building has now been demolished. One detail I omitted was towards the end of my stay there when a large crack appeared in the bedroom wall and I could see daylight through it. This inevitably led to the need to demolish the whole building.

I chose to use this setting for my story as there was something about living there that resonated with me. I believe it was because it was the first time I'd had a place to myself. The way that Andy decorated and furnished it was how I actually did it. The only parts that were different were those that pertain to the story of finding the drugs. I never went into the empty flat and don't believe I ever thought about doing so. My rent was €160 per month and I never did receive a bill for the electricity.

The Negrito was my local bar and some of the clubs mentioned are real, others (where the illegal activity takes place) are fictional.

I enjoyed living in Valencia even though I was in a similar situation to Andy in that I only worked part-time (teaching English) and lived hand to mouth as he did in the beginning of this story. Valencia is a friendly and beautiful city and this is why I chose it to be the setting for this story. They really should do something with the beach, though.

Milton Keynes UK
Ingram Content Group UK Ltd.
UKHW012131110624
443988UK00001B/94